D0209464

Dorothy
Parker
Drank Here

G. P. PUTNAM'S SONS
NEW YORK

Dorothy Parker Drank Here

ELLEN MEISTER

PUTNAM

G. P. PUTNAM'S SONS
Publishers Since 1838
Published by the Penguin Group
Penguin Group (USA) LLC
375 Hudson Street
New York, New York 10014

USA · Canada · UK · Ireland · Australia
New Zealand · India · South Africa · China

penguin.com
A Penguin Random House Company

Library of Congress Cataloging-in-Publication Data

Meister, Ellen.
Dorothy Parker drank here / Ellen Meister.
p.   cm.
ISBN 978-0-399-16687-7
1. Parker, Dorothy, 1893–1967—Fiction.   I. Title.
PS3613.E4355D67   2015   2014040672
813'.6—dc23

Printed in the United States of America
1   3   5   7   9   10   8   6   4   2

Book design by Gretchen Achilles

In loving memory of
Michael Palmer,
who still inspires me every day

Dorothy Parker Drank Here

"She is a combination of Little Nell and Lady Macbeth."

—ALEXANDER WOOLLCOTT

1967

D*eath was like a bowl of soup.*

At least that's how it felt to Dorothy Parker. One minute she was aware of a terrible pain radiating from the middle of her chest, and the next she was floating in a warm, brothy bath, where everything around her hovered at the same temperature as her body. She couldn't tell where she began and the world left off.

Then she saw it—the white light. For a moment, she felt the pull, but caught herself in time. No thank you. Eternal happiness was simply not what she was cut out for. She would stay right here, wherever that was, and let darkness overtake her.

"Mrs. Parker?"

As if awaking from a dream, she opened her eyes to discover she was in the dimly lit tavern of the Algonquin Hotel, alone except for a familiar silhouette at the bar . . . and that damned white light hovering overhead.

"Mr. Benchley?" she said, though she would have known that full-cheeked profile anywhere. As usual, his hair was well oiled and his mustache neatly trimmed.

"I've been waiting for you."

Dear, dear Mr. Benchley. She took a seat next to him, where a fresh gin and tonic—her drink—was on the bar before her.

"How I missed you," she said. He was the most loyal friend she had ever known.

He looked at her, his eyes as tender and pained as ever. "I missed you, too," he said.

"Am I dead?" she asked. Everything seemed so solid, so real.

"Afraid so."

"Afraid? I daresay it's about time. Cheers." She drank her cocktail and it felt exactly as it always did. How could this possibly be death? She had expected nothingness, a black eternal sleep. But perhaps this was the true heaven—sitting at a bar with her closest friend. She avoided looking into the light.

"Cheers," he said.

"Where's Gertrude?" she glanced around to see if his wife was lurking nearby.

He pointed upward.

"Yes, of course," Mrs. Parker said. "Where else would she be? Saint Gertrude Aquinas. Lecturing the angels, no doubt."

"She was a good woman, Dot. Better than I deserved."

She took a quick glance upward. "I'll take good care of him, Gertrude!"

"She's been waiting patiently for me," he said, placing a hand on her arm.

"You're not serious."

He stared at her, his expression fixed. "She's my wife."

"But think of it, Fred," she pleaded, using her nickname for him. "Eternity is a long time."

"That's why I didn't mind staying here until you arrived. I knew the years would seem like a moment."

She waited for him to say something else. But then, she had always felt like she was waiting for Mr. Benchley to say something else. Finally, she asked him for a cigarette.

"Sorry," he said, patting his chest, "I'm out."

"So it is hell."

He shrugged, a wistfulness passing over his face. "We had a lot of good times here."

"Strange," she said. "How did we wind up in the Algonquin?"

"Remember that book we signed for Percy?"

She did. When Percy Coates, the hotel manager, had asked them to sign the special guest book that was supposed to offer eternity, he'd been so earnest they'd laughed but humored him. "So it worked. I'll be damned. Where are the others?"

"Everyone from our group is gone," he said, nodding toward the white light.

"The little shits. They couldn't wait for me?"

"It's a powerful draw, Mrs. Parker."

"Did you get to see them?"

"Woollcott and Broun were here when I arrived. Then Ross showed up and later Mr. Sherwood. We had fun for a time, but they all wanted to go."

"Did they ask about me?"

He smiled as if he knew she would ask. "Of course. It wasn't a real party without you. We all thought you'd be here any day. Who knew you'd outlive us all?"

"But surely I'm not the last."

"There are other signatures in the book, and I suppose they'll pass through. But they weren't in our crowd."

"My damned luck. Always late to the party."

"Finish your drink," he said, "and we'll go together."

"Go?" She tsked. "Over my dead body."

"That's more or less the idea."

"Leave if you must," she said. "But I'm staying right here."

"Now, Mrs. Parker. Don't tell me you're rejecting eternal peace."

"What's in it for me?"

He looked up, his tight brow softening as if in a trance. When he looked back at her, his eyes were wet. "Love. Can't you sense it?"

She waved away his comment. "Where did love ever get me?"

"This is different. Your parents will be there."

"Never cared for them."

He took her hand. "Alan is there."

"Did you have a head injury? Why would I want to reunite with my husband?"

"You loved each other."

"He left me."

"He killed himself."

"Same thing."

Mr. Benchley massaged his forehead and thought. At last he nodded and looked back into her eyes. "He was in a lot of pain, Dot."

"Guess what," she said. "Me, too."

"You're angry."

"I'm awake, aren't I?"

He stood, finished the last sip of his drink, and put down his glass. "I've been here a long while. It's time for me to go."

She shrugged. "Go, then. What are you waiting for?"

"You sure you won't change your mind?"

"Good-bye, Mr. Benchley. Send my best to Gertrude."

He shook his head. "You'll be lonely."

She held up her drink. "That's what this is for."

Mr. Benchley kissed her on the forehead. "See you around, pal," he said.

Just then, she heard the high-pitched yip of a small dog and looked down to see a familiar poodle trotting toward her. "Cliché!" she cried, remembering he had been in her lap when she signed the book, and that when Percy wasn't looking she had pressed his paw onto the last page. If she was going to hang around for eternity, she had reasoned, she would want his company. How perfect that it had worked. She bent over to scoop him up.

"Look, Fred!" she cried, but it was too late. Mr. Benchley was gone.

4

2007

It was late—well past closing—and the Algonquin Hotel's Blue Bar tavern was shadowy and still. Angel Ruiz hesitated at the doorway, but only for a second. So what if there was a strange shimmer below the one dim light on the wall? And who cared if the Haitian guys in the kitchen had sworn they'd seen *le fantôme* sitting by the bar late at night? It was his first day on the job and he refused to be scared. Besides, the staff at these old hotels always believed the places were haunted.

He clicked on the soft neon bulb over the bar and unlocked the cabinet. The drunk in room 1207—some famous writer in hiding, they said—had ordered three martinis and the night kitchen manager had instructed Angel to mix and deliver them. "The old man," she had promised, "tips big."

Angel stopped and listened to the deserted quiet, feeling the silence deep inside his ears. He went back to work, gently placing what he needed on the bar.

After pouring the carefully measured gin and vermouth into the metal shaker, he held the lid tight and turned it over and back, over and back. He gave it one last shake, then filled the three fancy glasses he had placed on the tray.

The darkness played tricks on his eyes. Was that a swarm of gnats hovering near the bar or just floating dust particles? He blew them away and focused on his task.

Las aceitunas, he thought. Olives. He looked around and saw a mini refrigerator under the bar. He had to kneel to see inside and found a large round jar in the back, the green orbs floating in liquid like detached eyeballs.

Angel hated olives and hoped he wouldn't have to fish them out with his fingers. As he rose, he was thinking about finding a fork he could use to pluck the slimy orbs from their cold bath and how his grandfather used to pop them in his mouth like candy. Disgusting.

And then he saw something. The tiny swarm had grown. It was now a mass of swirling dust particles floating over one of the barstools. As he stared, transfixed, they took on a recognizable shape, joining together until they weren't separate specks but one solid image.

The jar fell from his hand and crashed, shattering the silence. It was her—the phantom. And right before his eyes, she became a real woman, with dark impish eyes and a small hat.

Angel jumped back, almost slipping on the wet floor. He grabbed on to the bar and froze, unable to do anything but blink at the space that had been empty only seconds ago.

"Just as well," she said, peering over the bar at the olives rolling across the floor. "He likes his martinis with a twist."

He rubbed his eyes. She couldn't be real, could she?

The apparition picked up one of the drinks he had just made and took a sip. "Not bad . . . Angel. You may have a future here."

"You . . . you know my name?" A chill danced down his spine.

She pointed a dainty finger at his name tag.

"What do you . . . want from me?" he asked.

She tipped back the martini and finished it. Then she picked up another. "You'll need to make more of these. Cheers."

Angel watched as she sipped the drink, closing her eyes in delight. "I hope you have cigarettes in that pocket," she said. "I'm positively desperate."

"Cigarettes?"

"If you tell me they're bad for my health, I may scream."

Angel pulled a pack of Marlboros from his jacket, placed it on the bar, and stood back. She looked down at the cigarettes as if she expected him to do something. Finally, she extracted one and put it between her lips.

"A light?" she said.

He swallowed hard and took a disposable lighter from his pocket, but his hands were so damp from fear he couldn't get it to ignite. He tried again and again.

"I have all the time in the world," she said. "Literally."

Finally, a short flame rose and he carefully leaned forward to light her cigarette. She took a long drag.

"Delightful," she said, exhaling. She took another puff and blew smoke rings. Angel stared as she continued smoking and drinking. What *was* she?

The ghost flicked ashes into the empty martini glass, then shot him a glance and sighed, as if bored by his awe. Still smoking with her right hand, she held her left hand toward him, palm down. He looked at it, wondering what she wanted him to do.

"Go ahead," she said.

"Miss?"

"You're wondering if I'm real," she said. "So touch me."

Her hand was small and feminine, with fingernails filed into points. Angel lightly poked it, hoping she was nothing but air, light, and dreams. But she was solid—flesh and blood.

"Now that we have that out of the way," she said, "my request.

You see that book over there, inside the case?" She pointed to the dim wall light, and Angel noticed that the shelf it illuminated held some kind of antique book inside a glass display box. "Please bring it here."

He did as he was told, stepping over the olives to approach the shelf and examine the case. It was a heavy piece, with a mahogany platform and frame. The glass panels afforded a clear view of the book inside, which was open to a page of old-fashioned signatures written with the thin ink of a fountain pen. He lifted the hinged top, removed the book, and carried it back to her, placing it carefully on the bar.

"This," she said, pointing over the open page, "is me."

Angel scanned the names. They were all men except for one.

"Dorothy Parker?" he said.

"I don't suppose you've heard of me?"

He shook his head.

"Lucky you," she said. "Now, when you deliver the drinks to Mr. Shriver you will bring him this as well."

"You want me to bring the book to him?"

"Am I not being clear?"

"No. I mean, yes. But why?"

"My dear," she said, "where this book goes, I go. And I need to have a little chat with Ted Shriver. We are old acquaintances."

"I'll get in trouble."

"Nonsense. You'll come back in an hour and return the book to the shelf. No one will ever know. But first, clean up this nasty spill; it's never a good idea to leave a mess behind. Trust me on that."

All things considered, a hotel wasn't a bad place to die. You didn't have to see anyone, didn't have to shave, and once you emptied out the minibar, you could call room service and have a tray of martinis delivered right to your door.

On this particular night, Ted Shriver had ordered three, and drank the first one quickly. Then he took a Vicodin and lay down in bed to quiet the pounding in his head. In a short while he would be in a loose haze, and could spend the rest of the night sipping the other two.

He didn't expect to fall asleep—it was such an elusive prize these days—but he drifted into a light slumber and dreamed a living dust cloud was traveling about his chamber. The weak and weary night-mare seemed straight out of Edgar Allan Poe. Minutes later, a female voice roused him.

"I haven't got all night."

What the hell? Ted Shriver lifted his head and squinted to see a woman seated in the gold chair in the corner of his room. And damn if she didn't look like Dorothy Parker, who he interviewed back in 1967. Only, this woman seemed as if she were plucked from an earlier era. How many Vicodin had he taken, anyway? He picked up the bottle to check the contents.

"You are not hallucinating," she said.

He lay back down. "The hell I'm not."

"We have to talk."

He sat up and swung his legs over the side of the bed. This was a brand-new symptom—one his doctor hadn't warned him about. "I need another drink," he said.

"Of course you do."

He ignored the vision and approached the room service cart, which was right next to the chair where she sat. He picked up another martini and addressed the hallucination, wondering if it would respond to everything he said. "Pardon me if I don't *offer* you one."

"Quite all right. I'm way ahead of you."

Figures, he thought. *I've invented a vision that drinks.* Ted considered how he might describe the vividness of the image. Not that he planned to tell anyone, but as a writer he was prone to translating his experiences into prose, searching for the perfect adjectives, verbs, and similes. He leaned over to stare at her up close. She looked as real as the nervous waiter who had wheeled in the cart. Only, if he squinted, he thought he could see a soft shimmer outlining her form.

"This is a hell of a goddamned brain tumor." He closed his eyes, rubbed them hard, and looked at her again.

"What are you doing?" she asked.

"Trying to turn you into Gina Lollobrigida."

"Really, Teddy. How tiresome."

"Teddy," he repeated, smiling, as if he'd won a point against the mass growing in his head. "It knows my name."

"Of course I do. We've met."

"But you wouldn't remember that."

"And why not? It wasn't every day a handsome young man came to interview me. You wore a cheap suit, but you were a dream to look at."

Ted closed his eyes, recalling the day he had gone to interview the famous Dorothy Parker, shortly before her death and long after her glory days as one of America's most famous and audacious wits. She was living alone at the Volney Hotel, drunk and bitter, but not as depressed as he had expected. He was on staff at the *Atlantic Monthly* then, the pages of his first novel, *Dobson's Night*, still tucked away in the bottom drawer of his desk.

"You flirted with me," he said. In the article he had described it as "playful banter."

"Of course. You were a lovely, if ill-mannered, young man."

"I would have fucked you if I thought you were serious."

"My dear, I *was* serious. But I was over seventy years old. Even your grandfather wouldn't have fucked me."

Ted laughed—something he hadn't done in over a year, and it felt luxuriant. But it was fleeting. He sank into the chair next to hers. "I'd make it up to you," he said, looking into his lap, "but that ship sailed when this brain tumor docked. Cheers." At any other point in his life, impotence would have struck him as the harshest sentence, albeit well deserved. But now, his energy level as flaccid as his libido, the loss registered somewhere between nostalgia and sentimentality, like the memory of a rowdy old drinking buddy.

He took another sip from his glass, focusing on the familiar burn in his gullet. It was like coming home. He finished the martini in a few gulps.

"Feeling better?" she asked.

"Not yet." He reached for the last drink.

"When you do, we'll have a pleasant little chat."

"A word of caution against getting your hopes up," he said. "I'm not a fun drunk."

"Don't flatter yourself, dear. You're not much better sober."

He shrugged. It was true enough, though there was a time when he could turn it on if he wanted to. "I impressed you back then, didn't I?"

"You brought me Chinese food," she said. "That amused me."

He remembered. "Chicken chow mein and egg foo yong," he said. "Old-school Chinese food."

"Old-school?"

"It's 2007, Dot. Everything we liked is out of style. Tell me, is there egg foo yong in heaven? Give me something to look forward to."

She ignored his question. "You look dreadful."

He couldn't argue. His gray hair was wild and overgrown, and the illness had ravaged his face. He ran his hand over his chin—the stubble was now practically a beard. One thing he knew for sure: he would not leave a pretty corpse.

"I'm dying," he said.

"So I've heard."

"What? No sympathy?"

"Everyone dies," she said, "but I understand you're leaving behind a few decent books. That makes you luckier than most."

Lucky? It wasn't the word he would use to describe himself. Lately, in fact, he was almost pathologically regretful, replaying seventy years of mistakes, trying to figure out which one had led him to this—dying alone and unlovable in a Manhattan hotel room. Cheating on his first wife, Marlena, right after the miscarriage was probably one of the shittier things he had done, but telling her about it was the part he regretted. That look on her face never left him. It was more than the hurt of betrayal. It was the realization that beneath his curmudgeonly exterior there was no heart of gold. He witnessed the light leaving her eyes as the delusion vaporized and she saw the truth: she hadn't fallen in love with a misunderstood artist after all. She had fallen in love with a beast.

With Audrey, he had meant to redeem himself. She was his one chance at . . . well, maybe not happiness, but as close as he could hope to get. Her vulnerability had touched the softest part of him, and he had convinced himself that he could save them both. Of course, he screwed that up even worse. And then the whole damned mess with the book just annihilated any chance of getting back on track.

"I'm not sure history will be that kind to me," he said.

"I beg to differ."

"Haven't you heard? I'm the lowest form of life. A *plagiarist*."

"I assumed that was just a rumor."

"What difference does it make? Everyone believes it."

"Not everyone."

"Even my fans have their doubts," he said, wondering why he was bothering to argue with a hallucination. Did he really need to remind himself of his own dark reality?

"And yet you don't defend yourself."

"Why should I?"

"One simple public statement, Teddy. How much trouble could that be?"

Ted shrugged. He had never defended himself and wasn't about to start. He wondered how hard it would be to fall back asleep now.

"You are a stubborn man," she said.

"I've been called worse."

She went quiet, staring straight at him as if she expected him to elaborate. He didn't.

"Well?" she finally asked.

He stood, frustrated that his hallucination could be so coy—a trait with which he had little patience. "If you have a question, spit it out."

"Fine," she said. "How did it happen? How did three paragraphs from another man's book wind up in yours?"

He went to the bed and sat. "Fuck you, Dorothy Parker."

She folded her hands in her lap. "I assumed you wanted to talk about it."

He lay back, his feet still on the floor. "It happened after you died, so there's no logic to the turn this conversation has taken. My brain tumor is an idiot."

"My dear, I've been hovering about the Algonquin for many years. People talk."

"So you're not a hallucination, is that what you're saying?"

"Correct."

Ted closed his eyes and imagined the tumor growing, taking over. He hoped it would be fast—no hospital nights, no helpless shitting himself, no needing to be fed like an infant.

"It was Audrey," he said without opening his eyes.

"Audrey?"

"The plagiarism."

"I thought you didn't want to talk about it."

"Habit. I've been keeping the secret a long time. But what's the point of having a hallucination if you can't confess all your sins, right? It's not like you can hold a press conference."

"Go on."

He opened one eye, looked at her, and closed it again. He had never uttered the words aloud, so it was hard to find the language. But it was a simple story, and all he had to do was begin. He took a shallow breath.

"I finished the manuscript for *Settlers Ridge* and let loose—blind drunk for a whole week. I don't remember much, but I know I cheated on my wife, probably numerous times. It was my second marriage, the one I was supposed to get right. And Audrey was hellfire—somebody you just didn't fuck with. Smart, too. She planted the paragraphs, pulling them from a book I'd used for research. Of course, I didn't reread the book when they sent me proofs, and I never bothered to look at it again. I didn't know about the plagiarism until the *New York Times* article."

"And you never published another book? Never set the record straight?"

"Damned right." He sat up and rubbed his face, then went to the window and gazed into the New York night. Manhattan never got truly dark.

"Why haven't you told anyone?" she asked.

"Because I was a piece of shit. Because Audrey would have been dragged through the mud and I'd done enough to hurt her."

"That's almost noble."

His shoulders dropped. "Please."

"She destroyed your career."

He glanced at her, and saw more intelligence in her eyes than he expected. For a moment, he felt exposed. "I had a good run."

"Do you have a cigarette?"

"That's it? You're not going to try to convince me to go public? To do a publicity junket and clear my name?"

"It's nothing to me," she said. "But I really would like a smoke."

He sat in the chair, trying to decide if he felt lighter now that he had unburdened himself to this figment of his imagination. "Quit five years ago," he said. "For my health. Feel free to laugh."

"Is this when you start getting maudlin?"

"This is when we talk about death. Tell me what it's like."

"Like this," she said, indicating the space they occupied with a wave of her hand. "Awful. Lonely."

"No call from a 'higher power' beckoning you to the great beyond?"

"It has no appeal for me," she said.

"And why not?"

"An eternity with 'loved ones'? No thank you."

"Loved ones," he repeated, the words as sharp as glass splinters. "I'd rather gnaw my own leg off."

"I've been counting on that," she said, and cleared her throat.

3

Norah Wolfe never dreamed her obsession with Ted Shriver would pay off in any discernible way, yet here she was at twenty-nine, outside her boss's office, with information that might save their television show, *Simon Janey Live*, from getting canceled.

She was only thirteen when she first discovered the reclusive author. Her mother had handed her a worn paperback edition of *Dobson's Night*, and the novel's voice seized her from the start. It was the yearning she related to. Shriver seemed to understand the specific human pain of wanting and pushing away at the same time. It left her with a gorgeous ache, and when she turned the last page of the book and closed the cover, Norah's connection to the writer felt absolute. It was a breathless, consuming rapture—the kind of feeling you experience only when you're on the cusp of adulthood, old enough for something intangible to touch you that deeply, young enough to believe no one had ever felt it in quite the same way.

A year later, her mother was dead. And that was it. The only parent she had ever known was felled by a simple case of bronchial pneumonia, because her multiple sclerosis had left her too weak to cough up the blockage. And though Norah had been just down the hall when it happened, she hadn't heard a thing. Sometimes she still dreamed she could hear her mother's voice calling out weakly in the night. It was always the same—the slow realization that the faint sound was a call for help, followed by a confused jumble of fear as she struggled to reach her mother's room in time to save her. But something always got in her way, and she would wake up mired in guilt she couldn't shake.

Norah's mother had always told her she was strong—very strong—and at the funeral she realized it really meant *Strong enough to carry on without me.*

And she believed it, though she considered it a choice. As she sat in the chapel, staring down at her bare knees, Norah knew that she could decide to be strong . . . or to crumble. She was considering the second option—thinking about how it would feel to collapse with melodramatic flourish—when her uncle handed her a letter. *For Norah on my death*, the envelope said, in her mother's shaky cursive. She stared at it for several seconds, confused. Then she understood what it was and tore into it, her heart beating with excitement that she held a living piece of her mother in her hands.

Norah read it through three times, but the message she had hoped to receive wasn't there. Her uncle asked if she was okay, and Norah nodded. Then she folded the letter, put it in her pocket, and stared at the casket. She made her decision. She would be strong, not weak. But the intersection of repressed grief, her mother's secret, and her laser focus on the one person who understood her heart locked in the obsession with Ted Shriver. Even as she grew and matured, Norah never gave up the dream of connecting with him.

And now she might get her wish and be a hero in the process. She knocked again on her boss's door.

"Don't just stand there, sugar," said Didi Dickson, a pen between her teeth. Rail thin with deep-set eyes, Didi almost always looked overworked, but today she appeared even more stressed than usual.

Clearly in the middle of something, she had three open file folders spread out before her. Her office smelled like apple and spice, thanks to a basket of potpourri she kept on the corner table.

"You look frazzled," Norah said.

"You don't know the half of it, bubbeleh." Didi was a forty-two-year-old black woman from Louisiana, but had been a hard-driving New Yorker since her early twenties, and loved mixing Big Apple patois with her Southern slang.

She was the segment producer of *Simon Janey Live*, a nightly TV interview program with more prestige than viewers. Of course, when there was a major guest, like Steve Jobs, J. K. Rowling, or Bill Clinton—all of whom had been on last year—ratings soared. But the network didn't give a damn about last year or last month. All that mattered was that viewership had been in steady decline and that a solid lineup wasn't going to do it. They needed a guest who would make headlines—someone no one else could get.

"I got calls into publicists for Will Smith, Dick Cheney, Angelina Jolie, Al Gore, and Barry Bonds," she continued. "But even if one of them comes through, it might not be enough."

Norah cleared her throat. "What if I told you I might be able to get Ted Shriver?"

"I'd ask for some of whatever it is you're smoking, 'cause I sure could use it."

"I'm serious."

Didi leaned back and folded her arms. "You jerking my tail?"

"I know where he is," Norah said. "I know how to get to him."

Didi, of course, had no idea her associate producer had been tracking him for years, learning his past three addresses and even the name of his personal physician. Norah's real coup came when she befriended the doctor's receptionist, a chatty F.I.T. student who told her about his medical condition. "Refused treatment" was the term the girl had used, and Norah understood why he had moved into the Algonquin Hotel. Ted Shriver had gone there to die.

Didi straightened her glasses. "Where is he?"

Norah pulled out a chair and sat. "I'll tell you," she said, "but I want you to let me approach him."

Her boss laughed. "Sugar, you got to be kidding."

Norah had expected this. A month before, she had screwed up when she tried to take advantage of a chance meeting with an A-list celebrity. It was Kip Elliott, a leading man and notorious bad boy whose longtime girlfriend was in the studio being interviewed by Simon. When Norah found herself alone on the elevator with him she thought she had nothing to lose, as she had no way of knowing that delicate negotiations to sign him for the show were already under way. "Who the fuck are you?" he had said when she asked if he might be interested in a Simon Janey interview. She tried to charm him with her fetching smile, which infuriated him even more.

Later, his publicist told Didi that Kip thought the lanky brunette on the elevator had been sent to ambush him, and could not be convinced otherwise.

Norah could have been fired immediately, but Didi had a soft spot for her and decided to give her another chance. The ensuing lecture, however, included a lot of talk about boundaries, and Norah promised she knew where hers were and would never cross them again.

She meant it, too. The problem was that when faced with opportunity, Norah couldn't always control her brazen impulses. It wasn't exactly ambition that drove her—though God knows she loved this job and would do anything to make it work—but an instinct that told her if she didn't fend for herself she'd be devoured. Losing her mother at a young age left her with a feral survival reflex.

"Let me redeem myself," Norah said.

"Not with Ted Shriver."

"I can do this. I'm sure of it."

"First off, he hasn't done an interview in thirty years. Just because some pretty little thing knocks on his door—"

"Hear me out," Norah said.

Didi shook her head and leaned forward for a life lesson. "I know people like this, Norah. It's a million to one. Our only chance is if someone *important* approaches him. No offense, sugar, but he'll regard you as a cockroach. It'll make the Kip Elliott incident look like tea with your granny."

Norah nodded. The thing she most admired about Didi was her honesty. People in TV could be so full of shit, but this woman said what she meant.

"Shriver is different," Norah said. "I can charm him."

"And what are you going to do if he says, 'Charm *this*'?" She made a hand gesture to illustrate her point.

"He won't come on to me. He's too sick."

Didi's eyes widened, and Norah saw it—a flicker of interest.

"Sick?"

"Dying."

Didi touched her keyboard's space bar to wake up the monitor. "How do you know?"

"It's not online. It's not anywhere. I have a source."

"Reliable?"

"Very."

Didi squinted, thinking, and Norah had a pretty good idea what was going through her mind. In 1981, just weeks after Ted Shriver's fourth novel was published, charges of plagiarism surfaced and were instantly confirmed. On a single page of the book, there were three paragraphs that had been lifted, almost verbatim, from a nonfiction book by a Vietnam vet. The scandal had been huge, and Ted never commented on it, never published another word. His fans assumed there was a good explanation—especially since no one could find another instance of plagiarism in any of his other work—and theories circulated for years. Meanwhile, his detractors continued to vilify him, and he was particularly loathed among veterans. If Ted Shriver was dying, this would be his last chance to set the record straight.

Didi bit her lip. "Still," she said.

"Let me show you something," Norah said, walking around to her boss's side of the desk. She arched her fingers over the keyboard. "May I?"

Didi backed up her chair. "Please."

This was the big moment. The showstopper. Norah quickly navigated to a website that had a side-by-side comparison of three women who looked very much alike, with curly dark hair, pretty round faces, and intense pale eyes. She maximized it and stood back. Didi looked from the screen to Norah, who could have been a perfect fourth in the lineup.

"What is this?" Didi asked. "The Norah Wolfe doppelgängers club?"

Norah pointed to the faces from left to right. "Ted Shriver's first wife, Ted Shriver's second wife, Ted Shriver's last girlfriend."

There was a long silence as Didi stared at the computer, thinking. Norah knew it was still fifty-fifty. She sat down so her boss could look from her face to the screen.

"Where is he staying?" Didi asked.

Norah took a deep breath. "The Algonquin," she said. "I don't know what name he's registered under."

"Or the room number?"

Norah shook her head.

"I'll have to send a bushwhacker to do reconnaissance," Didi said. "Might take a few days, so I'll have to book them a room."

Again, Norah understood her boss's reasoning. She needed more information—either a room number or Ted Shriver's registration name—in order to call him. She wanted to make the booking herself. It was a defeat, but Norah wasn't ready to give up.

"Me," she said. "Send *me*."

Didi squinted at her. "And what if you find yourself alone on the elevator with him?"

"I won't ask him to do the show, I promise. I won't even tell him where I work. I'll just get to know him a little bit, get some inside info, and let you take it from there." She leaned forward, hoping Didi understood her sincerity. Sure, she wanted the booking herself, but she wouldn't risk going rogue again.

At least that's what she hoped.

"I don't know," Didi said.

Norah pointed to the computer screen. "I'm your best shot—you can see that. He'll warm to me. Let me have a few days in the Algonquin. I know I can do this."

Didi looked at the screen and then stared up at the ceiling. "Ted Shriver," she said, and Norah knew she was picturing the media splash of landing him for the show. It would be historic.

The room was quiet for several moments as Norah stared at her boss. Finally, Didi looked at her and sighed, and Norah could swear she felt the molecules in the air rearrange.

Didi gave one small nod to indicate her assent, and Norah leaped from her seat. "I promise I won't screw this up."

"You'd better not, bubbeleh," Didi said, getting back to work. "We need this."

4

Ted finished his martini, set down the glass, and stared at his hallucination. "I wish you weren't a product of my brain damage," he said. "I could enjoy this more if it weren't so pathetic."

"Most people touch me."

"Touch you?"

"To see if I'm real."

He reached over and grabbed her breast. She looked down at his hand.

"Well?" she said.

"It feels like a real tit."

"How charming."

He released her. "Proves nothing."

"Perhaps this will. On the bottom shelf of that room service cart, hidden by the skirt, there is an old book of signatures, lying open."

"I doubt that," he said without looking up.

There was a gentle rapping on the door—quick and determined—but Ted didn't move. The knock came again.

"Are you going to answer that?" his visitor asked.

"No." His curiosity about who might be coming by at this late hour was nonexistent. There was simply no one—friend or foe—he wanted to see.

"Good. Now be a dear and fetch the book."

"Get it yourself."

"Please, Teddy."

The knock came yet again, this time a little harder, followed by an unfamiliar female voice. "Mr. Shriver?"

"Go away," he shouted. What was the point of living in a hotel if he had to face every idiot who wanted to talk to him?

"I have a bottle of gin."

That changed everything. Ted approached the closed door. "What brand?"

"Bombay Sapphire, I heard it was the—"

Ted pulled open the door and saw a young woman with a cascade of dark curls. She looked startled, staring at his face as if it were something miraculous. He'd seen that look before and he knew what it meant. She was one of them—the acolytes.

"How did you find out I was here?" he demanded.

The girl recovered her composure and smiled. She had pretty teeth and round, doll-like eyes, but he was unmoved by her efforts to charm him. "Sorry to bother you," she said. "I wouldn't have knocked so late but I heard voices. I thought maybe you were watching TV, but I see you have company."

Ted glanced over his shoulder at his hallucination and then back at the young woman. "You can see her?"

"How do you do?" Dorothy Parker said.

"Hope I'm not intruding," the stranger replied.

"And *hear* her?" Ted asked.

"She's right there. Can I come in?"

"No." He grabbed the bottle of gin from her hand, slammed the door, and whirled around to face the woman in the chair. He squinted again, to recapture the shimmer he had seen before. "If you're not a hallucination," he said, "what are you?" He uncapped the bottle and took a swig.

"I suppose you would call me a ghost, though that wouldn't be quite accurate."

"But I *touched* you."

"Yes, yes." She waved away the comment. "I can take on corporeal form as long as the book is open. It's all very dull. Retrieve it from beneath the cart and I'll clarify."

Ted stared at her. Was she just another nut, or worse, a fan? Had she sneaked into his room somehow? Maybe she had balled herself up on the bottom of the cart. Carefully, he lifted the skirt that covered the shelf and saw the book she had described. He pulled it out and balanced it on one hand as he examined the opened pages.

"What is this?" he said, scanning the signatures.

"It's a party," she said. "Or it *was*. Now it's just me. Would you be a dear and put it down?"

"Answer my question."

The woman smoothed her skirt and folded her hands neatly in her lap. "It started with Percy Coates, the manager of the Algonquin back when—"

"I know who he was," Ted said. He had read enough about the group of wits who met for lunch at the Algonquin throughout the 1920s to know who ran the place.

"Our dear Mr. Coates was obsessed with two things—writers and the afterlife. He loved his Ouija board and was forever trying to 'make contact.' Then he met Madame Lucescu, a horrid little woman who presented him with this book. He asked everyone in our group to sign it, promising it would give us the chance to hang around after we died, and we humored him. Woollcott said, 'If we're going to be at a party for the rest of eternity, the drinks had better be free.'"

"Are you saying all these people are haunting the Algonquin?"

"Just me, I'm afraid. The rest have crossed over into the white light."

He looked dismayed. "Come on. There's actually a *white light*?"

"Awful, isn't it? The thought of spending eternity there?"

He laid the open book upon the dresser and closed his eyes against the dull pressure in his skull. "It's all awful—life, death, and whatever the hell you're in."

"I manage to amuse myself. You might even—"

"But everyone you know is dead." He rubbed his forehead, where the pain was starting to blossom and spread.

"I know *you*."

"Barely. And I'll be dead soon."

"Yes, that's why I came. You see, Teddy—"

There was a knock on the door again, and at that same moment the blunt ache in his head became a sharp stab. He knew that it would continue to escalate until the pain was blinding.

"I want to talk to you about that book of signatures," she continued.

"Quiet," he said.

"Don't be rude, dear."

"I'll be as fucking rude as I like."

"Now, Ted," she said, and the noise of her voice reverberated in his skull.

Then the knocking came again and it was all too much. He grabbed his head in pain.

"Maybe you should lie down," Dorothy Parker said.

"Mr. Shriver?" came the voice outside the door.

Was this it? Was this the pain that would take him down and end the whole damned thing? The thought enraged him. Where was his peace? Where was his final rest? He threw the bottle of gin against the wall, and the explosion of noise shattered him. With the last bit of strength he had, Ted Shriver reached for the book and slammed it shut.

Dorothy Parker vanished.

"Are you okay?" asked the young woman outside his room. He grabbed the doorknob and pulled, and there she was, blinking and smiling. He handed her the book and closed the door in her face.

That was the last thing Ted remembered before blacking out. He awoke sometime later to the sound of a vacuum cleaner moving up the hallway. It was daylight, and he was facedown on the carpet, but not dead. Definitely not dead. The pain was mostly gone, but he took two Vicodin anyway. Then he crawled into bed and slept until the sun set again.

5

After Ted Shriver slammed the door in her face, Norah looked down at the book in her hands, her heart still racing. The meeting wasn't what she had hoped—there had been no meaningful connection, no spectacular moment she could hold on to for the rest of her life—but she had seen him, spoken to him, looked into tired eyes the same shade of blue as her own. And he had given her this strange book. What did it mean?

She ran her hand over the surface. It was a musty relic, bound in leather, with the words *Guest Book* stamped on the cover. She carefully opened it and saw that it was a collection of signatures from famous literary figures, most of whom had belonged to the group that made this hotel so famous.

Norah closed the book and held it to her chest as she leaned against the wall, disappointment rising like a fever as she played back her few moments of face time with Ted Shriver. She knew it was naive to have thought there would be an immediate connection, but still. She had assumed that fate would intervene and create some special bond. Maybe she had never admitted it to herself in exactly those terms, but now that she had actually seen him, Norah understood that deep inside she had believed that something about her would spark a flame.

She made the decision quickly. She would take it back to the room Didi had booked for her, study the signatures, and figure out Ted Shriver's connection to these people. Tomorrow she would go to see him again, and she'd be armed with a conversation starter. He would be resistant at first, but he would invite her in and they would talk and talk and talk. She would tell him about the scene in *Dobson's Night* that moved her the most, the one where the father and son are walking to the wedding. Most people said it was too long, but she knew it wasn't. If anything, she wished it was longer. She could have read the dialogue between those two forever. It was desperate and tender and beautiful and real. And of course, she would ask him The Question. The one unanswered mystery of that haunting story.

After that, she would call Didi and give her a full report, explaining all she had learned about Ted Shriver's remarkable heart. There would be a pause as Didi took it all in. Then she would say something like, *Sounds like you made a hell of a connection with him, sugar. Why don't you go ahead and make the pitch? If anyone can sign him for the show, it's you.*

Norah headed toward the elevator and pressed the button. When the doors opened, a stocky, dark-haired man in a hotel uniform got out and offered a tense smile. Then he saw what she held and stopped. She tried to move around him, but he blocked her. His name tag said *Angel.*

"Excuse me," he said. "This book—where did you get it?"

She held it against her body. "Someone gave it to me."

"Please, miss. It belongs to the hotel."

She looked at the cover again. Of course it belonged to the hotel—that made perfect sense. But why was it in Ted Shriver's room? She didn't want to let it go.

"I just need to spend a few hours with it," she said. "I'll give it back to you in the morning."

He looked over his shoulder and then back into her eyes. "I'll get fired, miss," he whispered, then shook his head. "Why did I make the delivery?"

Norah was torn. She didn't want to relinquish the book, not yet. But this poor man—he seemed serious.

"Will twenty dollars—"

"No, please. I must put it back. You understand?"

"But I can return it tomorrow. Surely no one will come looking for it tonight."

"It is my first day, miss. If someone notices, I lose the job."

His eyes looked so sad, so earnest. How could she possibly deny his request? And yet, this book could represent everything she had spent a lifetime thinking about.

Angel reached into his pocket and pulled out a wallet. He opened it to a picture and turned it to face her. "Ana Sofia," he said.

She glanced at the photo of a baby girl with shiny black hair and large dark eyes, her mouth in an O as if mimicking an adult's expression of surprise. She wore a pink-striped bib. It reminded Norah of her own baby picture—the one where she's in the high chair, looking into the camera, while a hand holding a spoon hovers to the left. Her mother's hand.

Norah swallowed against a hardness in her throat. "Your daughter?" she asked.

"Eight months old," he said.

At last, she held out the book. She meant to release it, but somehow she couldn't quite relax her grip.

"It will be downstairs," he said, "in the Blue Bar. You can see it when you wish."

"What was it doing in . . . the man's room?"

"I delivered it there," he said. "The . . . the lady. She asked me to."

"The small woman in a hat?"

His eyes went wide. "You seen her?"

Norah nodded.

"He talked to her?" Angel asked.

"I suppose," Norah said. "They seemed like old friends."

"She is nobody's friend, miss," he said, pulling at the book again. "Why did the lady want him to have this?"

"So she can talk to him."

"I don't understand."

"Me, too," he said, and gave one last tug, pulling the book from her hands. Then he disappeared into the stairwell with Norah's best hope at connecting with Ted Shriver.

B ack in her hotel room, she ignored the four voice-mail messages from Didi and tried to sleep, but everything conspired to keep her awake—the disappointing meeting with Ted Shriver, the missed opportunity of the puzzling guest book, the mysterious woman in a hat. Who was she and what was her connection to the book? Most of all, Norah wondered why Ted Shriver had given her the book . . . and why it seemed less like a gift and more like a curse—something he needed to get rid of.

Another hour passed and Norah realized her efforts to sleep were futile. She rose and got dressed. She simply had to go downstairs and look at that book again.

At four a.m., the only light in the deserted Blue Bar was a dim wall sconce illuminating a small shelf. Norah approached it to see that it shone on a glass case that held the strange book. She opened the lid, removed the heavy tome, and carried it to the nearest table, where she sat down to scan the names again. They were almost all famous writers, most of whom had been members of the Algonquin Round Table, the legendary group of wits who started their daily lunch just yards from where she sat. Norah knew all about them because her college roommate, an English major, had been obsessed with these people. Her enthusiasm was infectious and Norah read a good deal about them herself.

Norah paused to let it all sink in. She laid her hand upon the book and closed her eyes to picture them seated around her. She imagined Robert Benchley coming in from the rain and closing his umbrella. *I need to get out of this wet suit and into a dry martini,* he would remark as he lowered himself into a chair.

Norah opened her eyes to discover she wasn't alone. The small woman who had been in Ted Shriver's room was seated at the bar, smoking.

"I didn't hear you come in," Norah said. She left the book at the table and approached her.

"I've mastered the art of sneaking around," said the woman.

Norah took the barstool next to hers and introduced herself.

"Dorothy Parker," said the woman, extending a hand. "Charmed."

Norah opened her mouth and closed it. Did the woman just say her name was Dorothy Parker? Norah looked her up and down—taking in her wardrobe—and the light came on. She was a look-alike, hired by the hotel to act the part of the famous writer when she was in her prime. PR people could be so clever. Of course, that didn't explain what she was doing in the famous writer's room.

"How do you know Ted Shriver?" Norah asked, hoping she could get the actress to break character.

"He interviewed me for *Atlantic Monthly* in 1967."

So that's how it's going to be, Norah thought. But she could play along, especially since she seemed to remember reading the interview in a collection of Shriver's essays.

"It was right before you died, wasn't it?"

"He was one of my last visitors."

"And now you're a ghost, haunting the Algonquin?"

"That depends. Do you believe in ghosts?"

"No," Norah lied. The truth was, she never forgot the visitation she had had from her mother on the night she died. Norah was only fourteen, and had been asleep, when she felt someone hovering over her. She opened her eyes and saw her mother out of her wheelchair, standing tall and strong, and Norah bolted upright. In an instant she knew her mother had died and her spirit had come to say good-bye.

"You're not leaving, are you?" Norah pleaded.

Her mother tilted her head and smiled, as if to say it was all okay.

"No!" Norah said. "You can't go."

Her mother put her hand to her chest in apology, and Norah wanted nothing more than to grab on to her. She felt so young. Not like a teenager at all, but like a little girl desperate for her mother.

"Mommy, please."

At last the spirit spoke. *It's okay*, she said, and Norah knew it was meant to comfort her, but she wasn't ready.

"Don't go!" she cried, but it was too late. The spirit vanished, and the words *Be strong, love* floated in the air, and then disappeared along with her.

"Tell me, dear," said the woman, "what is *your* interest in Ted Shriver?"

Norah shrugged. She didn't want to reveal too much. "It's personal."

"He's a difficult man."

"I've noticed."

The look-alike nodded toward the table with the book. "You should return that to him."

"I don't want to get anyone fired."

"Ah, you must have spoken to the nervous fellow who gave me his cigarettes."

"Cigarettes?" Norah asked.

"Surely you spoke to him. Dark-haired chap—name tag says *Angel.*"

"How did you know?"

"It's his first day so he doesn't realize it, but the book goes missing all the time." She paused to take a drag of her cigarette and flick the ashes. This was a woman who looked as if she was never in a hurry. Norah thought it was quite an act.

"They all think it's carried off and replaced by ghosts," the woman continued. "But of course, ghosts are the only ones who *can't* carry the damned thing." She exhaled, and the smoke wafted into Norah's face.

She's taking this a little too far, Norah thought as she fanned the air around her face. She stood. "I should go to bed."

"I thought you wanted my help."

"No offense, but I'm not sure there's anything you can do for me."

"I can tell you how to get Ted Shriver to talk to you."

Norah paused, holding on to the back of the barstool. "And I suppose you'd want something in return?"

"Naturally."

"And what would that be?"

"I need you to steal that book."

6

The egg foo yong wasn't a problem. All it took was a few phone calls to track down a Chinese restaurant willing to make it on special order. The bigger challenge was ignoring the intrusive call-waiting beeps on her cell phone. She hadn't listened to a single one of Didi's messages, but clearly her boss was getting frantic. Norah just needed to put her off a short while longer. It was the day after her first encounter with Ted Shriver, and she was on her way to his room for the conversation she had been looking forward to her whole life. Once that was done, she'd give Didi exactly what she wanted.

For now, the smell of egg foo yong filled the Algonquin's small elevator, and her companion, who had asked to be called "Mrs. Parker," seemed bored by the whole thing.

"Can't you hold this?" Norah said, balancing the antique guest book, open to the page the real Dorothy Parker had signed, on her right hand. She held the brown paper bag from the Chinese restaurant in her left.

"I cannot."

"Then let me close it."

"You may close something else."

"My mouth?" Norah asked.

"Clever girl."

Norah exhaled, exasperated. "Hold the egg foo yong," she said, and thrust the bag at her companion, who seemed annoyed. They looked up at the lights as the elevator ascended.

"Why is the book so important, anyway?" Norah asked.

"I can't go anywhere without it."

"I don't understand."

"Join the club."

"You don't understand, either?" Norah said.

"Of course I do. I didn't say it was *my* club, did I?"

Norah shook her head. Was this woman really a hired look-alike or just some delusional fruitcake? God knows New York is filled with them, she thought.

"Why is it so important to deliver the book to Ted Shriver?" Norah asked. "You never told me what you wanted from him."

"I need him to sign it," Mrs. Parker said.

"Why?"

"Because it gets lonely."

"Lonely?"

"Shall I get you a dictionary?"

Norah knew Dorothy Parker's reputation for having an acid tongue, but this woman was getting on her nerves. "Explain it to me or I'll shut this book right now."

"Don't be tiresome."

Norah began to move the covers together.

"For heaven's sake," the woman said. "The simple truth is that I signed the book, I died, I'm still here. If he signs the book, I'll have someone to keep me company—someone who has no desire to head into the light."

Norah stared. This crazy little woman clearly believed what she was saying. And Norah was trapped on an elevator with her. Worse, if they approached Ted Shriver together, he might assume they were *both* deranged.

When the elevator doors opened on the third floor, she had a flash of inspiration.

"Here we are," Norah said, ushering the woman over the threshold.

"Wait a second," Mrs. Parker said as she looked around. "This isn't the right floor."

"No, it's not." Norah grabbed the egg foo yong and jumped back into the elevator just before the doors closed.

She wasn't smug enough to laugh, but she did feel pleased with herself. Now all she had to do was knock on Ted Shriver's door. She would tell him she was returning the book he had given her. He would want to send her away, but the egg foo yong would be the perfect enticement to gain entry.

When she reached his floor, however, she was again waylaid by Angel, who blocked her exit.

"Get out of my way," she said.

"You give me the book *now*, miss."

"No."

"You want me to tell the manager?"

"Move."

"I am being nice, miss. I tell them you stole it and you will have big problem."

"Fine," she said. "Call security." Norah knew she could deflect any trouble by telling them there was a crazy woman running around the hotel, harassing guests and claiming to be Dorothy Parker.

She tried to move past him, but he grabbed the open book with both hands.

"Don't you dare—" she began, but before she could even finish her sentence, a look of terror passed over Angel's face. It seemed that he was staring past her, but she knew there was no one on the elevator with her.

"What is it?" she said, but he didn't answer. He just released the book, fled into the stairwell. Norah glanced over her shoulder and saw nothing but a few floating dust particles.

This place, she thought, *is filled with nuts.*

But it didn't matter. She had everything she needed, and was about to see Ted Shriver.

Norah walked down the corridor, nervous and excited about this very real chance to connect. This, she knew, could be it. He could let her in. They could talk. She could ask him about *Dobson's Night* and he'd answer. It would be wonderful, and she'd carry the moment around with her for the rest of her life, feeling more whole than she ever had. And later, he would agree to do *Simon Janey Live*, and they would make history.

When Norah turned left onto the hallway that led to Ted Shriver's room, she saw something that sunk her spirit. Standing outside his door, with folded arms, was a human mountain in a tight black T-shirt. He was at least six and a half feet tall, with bulging biceps that shone like polished stone. Even his neck was enormous—a tree trunk growing out of hard-packed earth. His head was shaved and he wore a gold earring. He was heavily cologned.

"Who are you?" Norah asked.

"Who are *you*?" he said back, his voice thick with the ravages of steroids.

"I'm . . . uh . . . a friend of Mr. Shriver's."

"Mr. Shriver doesn't have no friends."

"I need to return this to him," Norah said, showing him the book. "He gave it to me."

The man ignored her.

"Please," she said, "just let me talk to him."

"Walk away, lady."

"Are you hungry?" she asked, holding up the Chinese food.

"Yeah." He grabbed the bag from her hand. "Now go."

"I need to see him."

He glared at her. "Last warning."

His tone chilled her, but Norah refused to give in to fear. "I'm not leaving until I talk to him," she said. Her pet theory was that bullies like this always backed down if you stood up to them.

She was wrong. He put his massive hand on her neck with just enough pressure to be taken seriously, and Norah dropped what she was carrying. She didn't think he really meant to hurt her, but she knew things could go very wrong very quickly. She needed to stay calm, to find the right words to soothe his savage breast. Norah looked into his eyes, trying to get a read on his anger, and witnessed the same change she had seen in Angel as his fury gave way to a sudden terror. Only, with this guy, it drained all the color from his face.

He released her and teetered, his eyes rolling back. She stepped away and it happened—he hit the floor like a felled oak. The thud sent shock waves under her feet.

"What the hell?" Norah said. Startled, she turned around to see that Mrs. Parker was standing right behind her. Where had she come from?

"You're quite welcome, dear," the woman said. She stooped to pick up the bag of Chinese food, stepped over the massive body, and knocked on Ted Shriver's door.

Norah couldn't speak. She held on to the wall, dizzy and confused. This . . . person, or whatever she was, had materialized out of nowhere.

"Pick that up, will you, dear?" the woman said, pointing to the book lying open on the floor.

Dazed, Norah did as she was told, still confused as she watched Ted Shriver open the door to his room.

"Egg foo yong," Mrs. Parker said, showing him the package.

He looked at the body on the floor. "Is it poisoned?"

"The poor dear just had a terrible fright."

"I think we're about to have another casualty," he said, nodding in Norah's direction.

Dorothy Parker looked at her. Norah meant to speak, to form some sort of question, but she couldn't. There was simply no way to access language.

"She looks ill," Mrs. Parker said. "Let's get her inside."

He grabbed the bag from her. "If she's sick, call a doctor."

"Come now, Teddy. She's the one who got the food."

"My humblest thanks, miss," he said to her.

"Have a heart. The brute had his hands on her neck."

Ted's eyes widened. "He *what?*"

"If I hadn't come along when I did . . ." she said.

Ted gave the unconscious giant a kick. "I said no rough stuff, Tiny." The beast groaned.

"You're fired," Ted said, then he opened the door and ushered the two women inside.

"Get her some water," Dorothy Parker said as Norah lowered herself into a chair, still holding on to the open Algonquin guest book.

"Now I'm a nursemaid?" He opened his minibar, found a bottle of Evian, and gave it to Norah.

Dorothy Parker frowned. "I said *water.*"

"It *is* water."

"Doesn't water still come up through the tap?" she asked.

"Capitalism marches on, Dot. What good is free water when you can pay a hotel three dollars a bottle?"

"And people are okay with this?"

"Of course. America's love affair with commerce never cools."

"If you tell me they're still reading Ayn Rand I may spit."

Norah barely listened to the conversation. She took a small sip of the water and didn't feel any better. "Can someone explain what's going on?" she said.

"I think you know what's going on," Dorothy Parker said.

"Are you really a ghost?"

"Something like that."

"But you seem so real, so . . ." She bit her lip, thinking.

"I believe the word you're looking for is *corporeal*," Mrs. Parker said.

"Yes," Norah said, thinking about the visit from her mother on the night she died. She had looked real, too, but not like this, not flesh and blood. Her mother had appeared as particles of the lingering light that she had once embodied. This woman, on the other hand, seemed like she belonged here.

"It's because of that . . . thing," Dorothy Parker said, pointing to the guest book. "Anyone who signs it gets to stay around."

"Anyone?" This piece of information took the wind out of Norah. She looked at the bottles of medicine on the night table, then at Ted Shriver, who was sitting at a small table, pulling the Chinese food containers out of the bag. "Did you hear that?" she asked him.

He stuck a plastic fork into the food, pulled out a bite, and shoved it in his mouth. "Mm. This is good," he said as he chewed.

Norah looked back at Dorothy Parker. "You're talking about *immortality*," she said.

"Don't get dramatic, dear. My sphere is rather limited. I can't go anywhere without that open book, and I'm unable to touch it or move it, so I'm at the mercy of living souls."

At last Norah understood what she had been saying on the elevator. "And you get lonely."

"The living tend to avoid friendships with the dead. And then, of course, they have the pesky habit of dying and heading into the light."

"You want Ted Shriver to sign that book so that when he dies . . ."

He laughed.

"What's so funny?" Norah said.

He shoved another forkful of the Chinese food in his mouth and took his time with it. "The only thing I'm signing," he said, "is a Do Not Resuscitate. Let me have that water bottle."

"Teddy, allow me to explain," Mrs. Parker said. "If you sign the book, you get to decide if you want to go toward the light. Otherwise, you have no choice."

"I'll take my chances," he said as Norah handed him the water.

"You really want to spend an eternity with loved ones? Hasn't your father crossed over? Your first wife?"

Norah imagined the pure bliss of crossing into the light to join her mother. It had never occurred to her that there were those whose souls were so damaged they would reject a chance to connect with that kind of love. And yet here she was, with two people who simply couldn't accept eternal peace.

Ted Shriver wiped his mouth and stood. He approached the dresser, where Norah had placed the book.

"Norah, dear, find him a pen," Mrs. Parker said.

"Don't bother," he said, and slammed the book shut. Instantly, Dorothy Parker vanished. He handed the book to Norah.

"What did you do that for?" she asked.

"So I wouldn't have to listen to her. Now, if you don't mind, I'd like to eat in peace."

Norah swallowed hard. He was throwing her out again, and she couldn't give up without a fight. But what could she say? If she tried to explain how much he meant to her, he'd push her out even faster. She coughed a couple of times and got herself together.

"I'm hungry," she said.

"Hungry?"

She pointed to the egg foo yong. "Can I have some of that? Please? I've been carrying it around and the smell is getting to me."

He hesitated, and she touched her throat, signaling her vulnerability. Ted sighed and gave her one of the containers of Chinese food. "And take the book with you, too," he said.

She sat down and opened the folds of the white cardboard box.

"I'm eating it here, if you don't mind." She picked up a plastic fork as if it weren't open for discussion. She was staying.

He remained standing, holding on to the back of his chair, and Norah acted as if she had no idea he was thinking about what he could say to throw her out.

At last, he grunted and sat down. "Don't think of this as an invitation," he said.

"I wouldn't dare." The first thing she wanted to ask him about was *Dobson's Night*. She would start by telling him how much the book meant to her. And then, if he seemed even a little receptive, she would get to her question about the ending.

"Because as soon as you're done—"

"I won't overstay my welcome."

He squinted at her. "You're not a reporter, are you?"

"No, nothing like that."

"What do you do?"

Norah used the side of her fork to cut off a bite of the egg foo yong. She had never tasted it before and was surprised by how much she liked it. "I work in television," she said, swallowing, "but I'm not—"

"What's your title?"

Norah pushed around her food, wondering if she should lie. She caught his eye and could tell he knew she was thinking of deceiving him. He would see right through it. "I'm an associate producer," she said, hoping to score points for honesty.

"For what show?" he asked.

"It's not relevant. I'm really not here in a professional capacity. I've been a fan almost all my life. In fact, there's something I've been wanting to ask you about *Dobson's Night*. The first time I read it—"

"For what *show*," he repeated.

"*Simon Janey Live*," she mumbled, hoping he hadn't heard of it.

He stood so fast his chair fell over. "Get out!" he said.

"What?"

"Get the hell out. And take that goddamned book with you."

"But—"

He reached for the phone. "One more word and I'm calling hotel security . . . or waking Tiny."

Norah picked up the book, tucked it under her arm, and looked into his angry blue eyes. Her pulse beat in a rhythm of desperation. If he knew the truth, would he soften? She tried to detect even a microscopic crack in the fortress of his fury, but he was impenetrable. And while she understood that his anger wasn't personal (he barely knew her, after all), a ripple of pain headed straight toward a spot in her psyche she didn't even like to acknowledge.

"Out," he repeated. "And forget you ever met me."

She walked out and closed the door behind her, knowing it was the one promise she could never make.

7

In her hotel room, Norah laid the antique guest book on the dresser, opened it, and stood back. Not that she had anything to say to Dorothy Parker, she just needed a distraction from her misery. But nothing happened. The tough-tongued wit refused to appear.

She sat on the bed and pushed at her cuticles, replaying Ted Shriver's anger. She wanted to believe his dismissal of her wasn't absolute, that he had left open one small window of opportunity. But of course he hadn't.

She lay down, refusing to cry. She would not wallow. She would not dwell on her failure to connect with him. It was just one more hard knot in her long string of disappointments. She could get over it just as she had gotten over everything else.

And why shouldn't she? She got over losing her mother. And then her uncle. And three months ago, when Eric moved out of their Brooklyn apartment because he wanted someone "with a human fucking heart," she got over that, too.

But what did she have left? Besides her job, nothing.

Simon Janey Live had been a career change for Norah, and everything about it felt right. At her uncle's suggestion, Norah had majored in business with a concentration in accounting. It was the practical thing to do, a way to guarantee that she would always have work. But she hated it from the start. So two years after college, when a friend got her an interview as a production assistant for a nightly TV interview show, she grabbed it. The salary was pitiful, but a year later she was promoted, and then promoted again. She had found a great home at *Simon Janey Live*. And she was well aware of how it had become a surrogate family for her. Didi was her mother figure. Simon was like her father, a looming but absent presence. Jack, Harve, Cynthia, Marco, Janelle, and Eli were like the siblings she'd never had. And of course, there was the show itself—that heart-stopping excitement of live television, and Simon's extraordinary ability to draw out guests. It was magic. These past five years were the happiest Norah had ever been.

She picked up her cell phone and stared at the staggering number of messages Didi had left for her. Twenty-three. And she had not played back a single one. Was it possible she had been fired for going AWOL?

No, she told herself. Absolutely not. Didi was too protective of her to do that. She checked the time. 10:07 p.m.—not too late to call back. She ran her fingers over the phone, wondering if she should listen to the messages.

Norah stacked the pillows behind her and sat up straighter. She pressed the speed dial for Didi's number, put it on speaker, and laid the phone on the bed next to her.

"Where have you been?" Didi said.

"Sorry. I was—"

"I thought you were deader than roadkill. Did you get my messages?"

"I didn't play them back."

"Lord have mercy."

She leaned forward, the tone of Didi's voice making her uncomfortable. "Something wrong?"

"Yes, something's *wrong*," Didi said. "The show was canceled."

"What?"

"You heard me."

"Canceled?"

"This can't be a big surprise," Didi said.

"I thought we had more time."

"Have you looked at the board lately? One B-list director, a chick-lit author, an economist, for heaven's sake."

"But all those calls. Didn't anyone come through?"

"Hillary Clinton's on the schedule for next month, but we won't make it that far."

"Can't you call in more favors?" Norah said, because she knew her boss had the phone number of every top publicist in Hollywood and Washington.

"What do you think I've been doing? Every name I pass by the network CEO, Kent, gets the same response: *Not enough*."

Norah covered her eyes and took a jagged breath, trying to will away the lump in her throat. "And I can't help," she said.

"No luck finding Ted Shriver?"

"I found him." She batted at some gnats hovering nearby. "And then I lost him."

"Oh, child," Didi said, and her disappointment seemed to take the oxygen right from the air.

"I wasn't going to say a word about the show," Norah said. "I was just trying to get him to warm up to me. Then he sniffed me out and all hell broke loose. I'm sorry."

Didi went quiet for a few excruciating moments. Norah's eyes burned and she reached for a tissue.

"Forget it, sugar," Didi finally said. "He wouldn't have said yes anyway."

"He could have saved us."

"What difference does that make?"

There was another long pause.

"What are you going to do?" Norah asked.

"My résumé is out and about. Yours should be, too. Something will come up."

Norah felt nauseous. How long would she be able to afford her rent without a job? A couple of months? Not even. Not with Eric gone. She was barely scraping by as it was.

"What about your documentary?" Norah asked. Her boss's pet project was an independent film about what happens to reality stars once the cameras are turned off. She had been working on it about a year.

"Out of money."

"I'm sorry. Wish I could help."

"If you ever meet a generous millionaire—"

"How is everyone else?" Norah asked.

"Terrible. Janelle just bought a house. And Harve's daughter—"

"I know."

Didi got a call-waiting beep and Norah told her to go ahead and take it. She needed to get off the phone anyway, as the fight to hold back tears was getting harder and harder.

"Just one more thing, bubbeleh," Didi said. "I'm going to rush through the expense account for the hotel, so if you want to stay another night or two, I'll look the other way. It's not much. But maybe it'll help you feel better."

Norah thanked her and choked out a good-bye before hanging up. She went into the bathroom and splashed cold water on her face. It did nothing to wash away the darkness she felt. She tried again and again.

"What the hell am I going to do?" she said to her reflection.

"You will twist Teddy's arm until he begs to do your silly show," came a voice from the other room.

Norah dropped her face towel and ran from the bathroom. There was Dorothy Parker, seated in the chair next to her dresser.

"You've been here the whole time?"

"I hover occasionally."

Norah took the chair opposite her. She eyed Dorothy Parker, try-ing to detect something, anything, that wasn't quite human. She leaned to the left and thought she saw a faint glow floating above the woman. She moved in for a closer view.

"You're staring, my dear."

"You're . . . shimmering. Is it a halo?"

"Hardly."

Norah sat back. She closed her eyes, remembering how vivid her mother had appeared in that final visit. If only she had stayed a short time longer . . . if only Norah could have one more conversation with her.

She looked at Dorothy Parker. "Can you . . . contact people on the other side?"

"I suppose you have a question for someone who's passed?"

Norah sat up straighter. "Yes."

"Sorry, dear. I haven't exactly crossed over. I'm simply right here, or I'm not."

Norah sighed. It was silly to think she might be able to get some kind of message from her mother. "And when the book is closed?" she asked.

"It's like sleeping, except I never wake up next to a man I regret taking to bed. On the other hand, I never wake up with a hangover. Speaking of which, do you have a drink?"

Norah opened the minibar and read off the selections to Dorothy Parker, who chose gin and tonic. She made the drink and handed it to her, hoping the network would pay the whole bill, including a few outrageous minibar charges.

"You heard my whole conversation with Didi?" she asked, taking a seat.

"Your boss, I take it?"

Norah nodded.

"It sounds like you have a bit of a problem on your hands, Miss Wolfe."

"Miss Wolfe?" It sounded so archaic Norah almost laughed.

"I'm sorry, Ms. Wolfe."

"Please, call me Norah. And may I call you—"

"We already covered that."

"Yes, but I thought—"

"'Mrs. Parker' will suffice."

"Mrs. Parker," Norah repeated, and discovered she liked the way it rang with the gentility of a more civilized era. "What did you mean about twisting Ted Shriver's arm? Do you really think there's any chance he would agree to do a live TV interview?"

"Perhaps."

"You didn't see how angry he was."

"I can imagine," Mrs. Parker said, sipping her drink. "He has a lot of bluster."

"The gin didn't work. The egg foo yong didn't work. I don't know what else to do."

"Information is power."

"What does that mean?"

"Well, if you knew the true reason for the plagiarism, you could threaten to expose it. I'm sure he would rather tell the story himself than let the media fill in the details."

"Except I *don't* know the story behind the plagiarism."

The inscrutable spirit picked up her drink, closed her eyes, and took a dainty sip. "But I do."

A tingle of electricity prickled Norah's flesh. "What is it?"

Dorothy Parker finished the last of her drink. "Make me another cocktail and I'll tell you everything you need to know."

8

Ted rolled over and ignored the knocking at his door, but it came again—the insistent pounding of a fist. He sighed and looked at his clock. It was the middle of the afternoon.

"Go away!"

"I will not," said a man's voice.

Ted opened an eye. It had been over ten years since they'd last spoken—and twenty-five since they'd seen each other in person—but he knew who it was: Peter Salzberg, his erstwhile publisher and close friend. Had a day gone by that he *hadn't* thought about giving Pete a call? Probably not. And yet he didn't want to see him. Not now, not ever.

"Open the door," Pete said.

Ted sat up, swung his legs around the side of the bed, and assessed his pain level. It was a pretty good day—not more than a four out of ten. Still, he reached for his Vicodin and swallowed two with a sip of water. He rose slowly and went toward the door.

"I can hear you moving around," said his friend.

Ted pressed his forehead against the cold door. Despite himself, a spume of regret filled his chest with heavy air. "Is that really you?"

"I know you miss me, you son of a bitch."

He closed his eyes and recalled the first time he heard that voice. One of his friends at the *Atlantic* had passed the manuscript for *Dobson's Night* on to a rising young editor at Litton Press. A week later Peter Salzberg called him at home and said, "This is why I went into publishing."

"What are you doing here?" Ted asked.

"Just open the door. You owe me that much."

Ted remembered the fight they'd had when the plagiarism allegation surfaced. At first, Pete had been so even, so understanding. He had put a hand on Ted's shoulder and asked him how it happened. Ted wouldn't answer. Pete pressed. This went on and on, and Pete moved from sympathetic to bewildered to furious to betrayed. Ted hadn't even apologized. He had just turned and walked out, and had never seen his friend again.

"I owe you a lot more than that," Ted said.

"Damn right."

Ted pictured himself dying in this room, his body found by a chambermaid. He imagined Pete in his office, getting the news by telephone. He would call a few friends. *What a wasted life*, they would say.

They would be right.

Ted grabbed the knob, hesitated for a second, and pulled open the door. There stood Pete—a little shorter, a lot grayer, and about twenty pounds stouter than the last time they had seen each other.

Ted frowned, avoiding his eyes. "You got old," he said.

"You don't look so hot yourself."

"How did you find me?"

"Wasn't easy. Then you called Gene Hoffman to hire a goon to stand outside your door, and he called Oscar Schwarz, and he called me."

Ted shook his head. "Jewish conspiracy," he said. "I should have known."

"Oscar is German. You going to invite me in?"

"Do I have a choice?"

"No." Pete entered and handed Ted a brown paper bag containing something heavier than Chinese food.

"This isn't egg foo yong," Ted said.

"It's cognac."

Ted pulled the teardrop bottle from the bag. "'Courvoisier XO Imperial,'" he read off the label. "They didn't have Hennessy?"

"Shut up and find two glasses."

Ted poured as Pete produced two cigars, and the men sat opposite each other, drinking and smoking in silence. They puffed. They sipped. The cognac was like a warm bath for his bloodstream. And he had almost forgotten how much he enjoyed cigars. After a while, the silence felt easy, natural. But Pete was waiting for him to start, and he went for the obvious.

"How's Aviva?"

Pete ran his hand over the back of his hair, a self-conscious gesture Ted recognized. "She sends regards."

"Regards?" Ted laughed. "I'd still play poker with you in a heartbeat."

His friend looked at him and shrugged. "Women don't forgive. Not really."

"And men?"

Pete studied his cigar for a long time. "You shouldn't have disappeared."

"You were furious."

"Of course I was furious." He flicked his ashes. "But it's more than twenty-five years. I've gotten over it."

Pete's reputation had been trampled by the plagiarism revelation.

Eventually, the publishing industry chewed the story to a pulp, and Ted emerged as the sole villain. Peter Salzberg's name was cleared, and he went on to become one of the most respected men in publishing.

"And now you want me to come clean?" Ted asked.

"I don't really give a damn anymore."

"So why are you here?"

Pete picked up the bottle and poured himself another glass. He refilled Ted's, too.

"Can't you guess?" Pete asked.

"I owe you a manuscript." At the time Ted went AWOL, he had been under contract to write another book for Litton Press.

"Don't be an idiot."

"What, then?"

"Ted, you've got an *operable* brain tumor."

"Gene Hoffman has a big goddamned mouth."

"You've got to do it, Teddy. Let them save your life."

"What for?"

"I don't know. So you can get laid? Write another book? Drink a case of Hennessy? Teach a class? Win the Pulitzer? See the sunrise over the damned Alps? Pick one. Pick ten. Because the alternative is what we fight."

"I'm done fighting."

"I don't think you are."

"You don't know shit."

"I know this. Refusing this operation is your last *fuck you* to the world for not believing in you."

Ted stared into his drink. "And we were having so much fun."

"Don't get cute."

The men sat in silence for several minutes and Ted wrestled with a knot of turmoil even the cognac couldn't unwind. Should he pull out the box or shouldn't he? He glanced over at Pete and imagined him at the liquor store, deciding which cognac to buy and choosing the expensive one. Because Ted was his friend. And because Ted was dying.

At last he stood and went to the closet. He pushed aside a green valise and dragged a large cardboard carton from the floor in the back. Bending to lift it made his head throb, but he did it anyway. He carried the box to Pete and dropped it at his feet.

"What is this?" Pete said. "A manuscript?"

Exhausted from the effort, Ted dropped into his chair. "No," he said, rubbing the bridge of his nose, as if it would relieve the pressure in his head. As if anything other than death or a surgeon's knife would relieve the pressure in his head. "It's three."

"*Three* manuscripts?"

"It's been over twenty-five years, Salz. I had to do *something*."

"Are you giving me permission to publish these?"

"Do whatever you want. It's my best work, especially *Louse*."

Pete made a face. "'Louse'?"

"The book is better than the title."

"Rotting garbage is better than that title. What's it about?"

"A man who's not as complicated as he likes to think he is."

Pete picked up the box and put it on his lap. He stared down at it like he was witnessing a miracle. "Three new books by Ted Shriver. Sweet fancy Moses."

"Three *posthumous* books by Ted Shriver," he corrected.

Pete picked up the title page on top and looked down. "'For Audrey,'" he read. "Are they all dedicated to women who hate you?"

"*Genuine Lies* is dedicated to a girl I haven't seen since 1978, so I have no idea if she hates me. Met her at a book party. She had this hand tremor she kept trying to hide from me. It broke my heart."

"What about the third book?"

"*Under the El*. Dedicated to a certain male friend I may have inadvertently screwed over."

Pete stared at him for a moment to make sure he wasn't misinterpreting what he'd heard. "I'm touched," he finally said.

"See if you like the book first."

Pete put the box on the floor, reached into his breast pocket, and pulled out a business card. He put it on the table between them.

"What's that?" Ted asked.

"Top neurosurgeon in New York."

Ted looked at the card. "They're all the 'top neurosurgeon in New York.'"

"What did yours tell you?"

"That if I had the operation right away, my odds of surviving were good. Close to seventy percent."

"Seventy? Jesus, Ted, what are you waiting for?"

"With a ten to twenty percent chance of cognitive impairment."

"That's pretty low."

"Not to me."

"Let me take you to see this guy. Let's hear what he has to say."

Ted stood. "Thanks for coming by, Salz."

"Are you throwing me out?"

"I have to lie down."

Pete picked up the carton. "It'll take me at least a couple of weeks to read all this."

"Take as long as you like."

"I'll have questions."

"If I'm alive, I'll answer them. If I'm dead, probably not."

Pete didn't laugh. "I'll read *Louse* right away. I'll come back on Friday so we can discuss it."

Ted opened the door. "Bring Hennessy."

9

Dorothy Parker seemed so confident they would be able to talk Ted into doing the show that Norah got swept along in the current. Now that they were on the elevator rising toward his floor, however, she felt an undertow of doubt. She didn't disagree with the notion that deep down a part of him wanted to clear his name. She simply recognized that tapping into such a buried desire would be an enormous challenge. He had been dug in for twenty-five years, and a single conversation about appearing on *Simon Janey Live* wouldn't change that. Dorothy Parker wanted to use the information to black-mail him into doing the show—threatening to leak the story to bottom-feeders if he didn't agree to the interview. But Norah thought that would only enrage him.

No, the way to use the information was through reason—to break past the unjustified loyalty he felt toward his ex-wife. How long would it take to convince him that Audrey had done a heinous thing and didn't deserve his protection? Weeks? Months? The TV show didn't have that long to survive. And for all she knew, neither did Ted.

Norah closed her eyes against a vision of Ted Shriver's funeral—of his coffin being lowered into the ground as her mother's had been. She recalled that feeling of wanting to stay at the cemetery so her mom wouldn't be all alone. "It's time to go" her uncle had said, and all she could think was *I can't leave her here. Who is going to stay with her?*

"Are you all right, dear?" Dorothy asked.

"Fine," she said, avoiding eye contact, but her companion stared at her, waiting for more. "I said I'm *fine*," Norah repeated.

"Yes, of course. Silly me."

"If I wanted to talk about it, I would talk about it."

"One of us is willing to drop the subject, but that doesn't seem to be you."

Norah pushed the already-lighted button for the twelfth floor. "Has anyone ever told you you're exasperating?"

"Part of my charm, dear."

The elevator stopped on seven and the doors opened.

"Going down?" asked a heavyset woman with overbleached hair, loose jowls, and an ill-advised plaid suit.

"Up," Norah said.

The woman's eyes fixed on the open book in Norah's hand. "What is that?" she asked.

Norah pushed the *Close Door* button.

The woman blocked it and stepped inside. Norah looked around and realized she was alone. Dorothy Parker had disappeared.

"What do you want?" she asked, backing up.

The woman squinted at her. "Where are you going with that book?"

"What's it to you?"

"Do you work for the hotel?"

"Say yes," a voice whispered in Norah's ear. It was Dorothy Parker.

"Yes," said Norah.

"Are you a lawyer?" the woman asked.

"Why? Does she want to sue the person who sold her that suit?"

"Is there something I can do for you?" Norah asked.

The woman folded her arms. "Don't you know who I am?"

"Of course. How could anyone forget that upholstery?"

"I'm afraid not," Norah said.

"Are you playing games with me?" the woman asked. "I know they talk about me in the office."

"I'm sure that's not true."

"Of course it's true! And I'm *glad*. You know why? Because the only thing worse than being talked about is *not* being talked about. Dorothy Parker said that. You can look it up."

"Oh please, Norah dear, find out where she lives so you can poison her food."

"I believe that was Oscar Wilde," Norah said.

"Who?"

"On second thought, use your bare hands and strangle her now."

"You never heard of Oscar Wilde?"

The woman bit her lip. "Oh, right. He's that gay guy with all those famous quotes."

"I'm thinking of one right now: Some cause happiness wherever they go; others whenever they go."

"I'm afraid I don't know what you want from me," Norah said.

"I'm Edie Coates." She put her hands on her hips for punctuation.

"Great-niece of Percy Coates. She's suing the hotel for the guest book."

"What floor do you want, Ms. Coates?"

"I want my book."

"It's not hers."

"It's not yours."

"Is too."

"Now, children."

"I have nothing more to say to you, Ms. Coates."

"Why don't you just give me the book and save yourself a lot of trouble?"

Norah put it behind her back. "I'll call security," she said.

The woman balled her fists. "It's my book!" Her face contorted like a child's when she's about to cry.

"It is not."

"It is too!" She tried to reach around Norah to grab it.

"Don't close the book!" Dorothy Parker said, but Norah didn't know what choice she had. The woman was after it, and Norah couldn't possibly get a grip on it otherwise. She slammed it shut and pressed her back against it, wedging it between her body and the rear wall of the elevator.

Norah tried to stand her ground as the crazed woman shoved her, but the book began to slide downward. The woman gave Norah one hard push and her bottom hit the floor.

Edie snatched the prized possession just as the elevator doors opened. She tried to make a run for it, but Norah grabbed her ankle and she went sprawling. The guest book fell open upon the carpeted hallway, emitting a cloud of dust. As the two of them watched, the particles rose and joined together, forming a fuzzy image resembling a small woman in an old-fashioned hat.

"What the hell?" cried Edie Coates, scrambling to her feet.

The image became more vivid until the particles were inseparable, and the form quite human. Edie stared, frozen in place, her eyes wide in terror.

"I thought I told you not to close the book," Dorothy Parker said to Norah. She turned to Edie. "And as for you, my dear, *boo.*"

Edie Coates shrieked and ran, ducking into the stairwell.

"Come along," Mrs. Parker said to Norah, who picked up the book and followed her.

"What on earth was that about?" Norah asked, dusting her hip as they walked down the hallway toward Ted Shriver's room.

"About six months ago, a small article about the guest book appeared in the *New Yorker*, along with speculation that it was priceless. This attracted far too much attention, and within days some awful vandal ripped out the last page, depriving me of my most precious companion, Cliché, a French poodle who kept me company in some of my darkest hours—both in life and in death. About that same time, this odd woman slithered into the hotel insisting she was the sole heir to Percy Coates's estate and that the book was rightfully hers. But of course, it belongs to the hotel. It has always belonged to the hotel. In fact, several other famous guests have signed it in the years since Percy died."

"Like who? Writers? Celebrities? Have you met any of them?"

"Yes, dear. I meet them after they perish."

"That must be fascinating."

"Not as much as you'd think. Besides, they usually leave me after a single conversation. That damned white light they all think is so appealing. Here's Teddy's room."

Mrs. Parker knocked but there was no response.

Norah pressed her ear up against the door. "I can hear him," she said.

"Teddy, dear," said Mrs. Parker as she knocked again, "open the door."

Silence.

"Don't be childish. I need to speak with you."

Norah listened again. "I hear his footsteps," she said.

"Ted, I'm here with that charming young woman."

They waited.

"There's something you need to know, Ted," Dorothy Parker said. "I told her about Audrey . . . about Audrey and your book."

Norah heard a glass break. "Uh-oh."

The door opened two inches, remaining latched, and Norah could see a sliver of Ted's face. "You did not," he said. "You wouldn't."

"I would. And I did."

"I could kill you!"

"A little late for that."

"What do you want from me?" he asked.

"We just want to talk," Norah said. "Let us in."

"Not a chance."

"Mr. Shriver," she continued, "I understand that you feel a sense of loyalty to your ex-wife, but when you think about—"

"You understand *nothing*."

"Then explain it to us."

"Go to hell."

"Whatever crime you think you're guilty of, you didn't deserve to have your reputation ruined forever. The very fact that Audrey never came forward to exonerate you proves that she's no good. You have to believe me. What she did was . . . monstrous."

"And who do you think *created* that monster?"

"Fine. You were a terrible person. You cheated on your wife. Shouldn't she have forgiven you by now?"

He didn't respond.

"Think about it," Norah said. "You've celebrated over twenty-five birthdays and New Years since then. When do you get to turn the page? Shouldn't there be a statute of limitations—"

"Never," he said, and slammed the door.

"Teddy," Mrs. Parker said, knocking. "Teddy! Let us in and we won't go to the media with this."

Norah put her hand on Dorothy Parker's arm. "Forget it," she said.

"Why?"

"Because I just realized there's only one thing that would get him to change his mind."

"And what's that?"

"Audrey," Norah said. "We have to find her."

10

When Edie Coates's brother died at age forty-nine, she wept in relief. If only she had known he wasn't nearly finished with her.

Gavin had bullied her their entire lives. Her parents explained that he was "just jealous," which never made any sense to her. What was he jealous of? He was her big brother, and better at everything— sports, schoolwork, making friends. And it wasn't as if their parents showed her any favoritism. He just seethed with resentment that she was alive and occupying space on earth, and no amount of cowering on her part made any difference. As long as there was no one around to see it, Edie Coates's brother hit her every time she came within reach.

And then there was the mockery. On most mornings, her clothing made him snort with derision. And no matter how carefully she measured her words, he found her conversation worthy of ridicule.

Mealtimes were a special problem, as Gavin had decided that average-sized Edie was overweight, and insisted on calling her Chubbo, which he later shortened to Chubs, a nickname he would never tire of. Everything she put on her plate was subject to his scrutiny and derision, and her parents were too genteel to intervene. The strongest thing her father ever said was "Mind your manners, Gavin." And of course, that only made him angrier.

Eventually, she stopped eating dinner with the family, preferring to take food up to her room to eat in private. This suited everyone well. Her brother was glad to be rid of her. Her parents were grateful for the mealtime peace. And Edie found exquisite solace in being able to indulge without judgment. Soon enough, his nickname for her was not an exaggeration.

They lived in an old house that had belonged to her father's uncle, Percy Coates, an eccentric hotelier who had an odd obsession with death. The house had been filled with such strange relics—including several ghoulish taxidermy specimens—that the neighborhood kids called them the Addams Family.

As adults, Edie and Gavin reached an uneasy truce. They were cordial to each other at family gatherings, but she tried to keep a safe distance, as the danger of ridicule was never far off.

When her mother got sick, Edie moved back into the house to take care of her. Gavin couldn't imagine that she had done it out of any sense of obligation and accused her of trying to steal the house out from under him. Then, when her mother died and bequeathed the house to Edie, he brought his fury down like a storm. He called again and again, screaming in rage, until she stopped answering the phone. Then he wrote letters, threatening to sue if she didn't sell the house and split the profits with him. She ignored him, and made modest changes to the home. Notably, she packed up all the preserved dead animals and brought them to a storage unit, where she arranged them facing the door as if ready to attack whomever entered. For good measure, she draped the largest of the beasts—an open-mouthed leopard—with the silk kimono her parents had always warned her not to touch. It was said to possess secret powers that would bring the dead back to life, and had been one of her great-uncle's favorite acquisitions. She didn't believe it would awaken the long-dead cat, but she got a charge out of the gesture.

She mailed the locker key to Gavin, along with a note saying she had only paid for three months' worth of storage, and he was free to do with it whatever he wished. A few weeks later, he left a message on her answering machine saying she had "no fucking right" to remove the animals from the house, and that his lawyer would hear about it. She hired her own counsel at that point, and he sent Gavin a cease and desist letter.

He paid her one visit after that, demanding the antique train sets in the basement.

"I'll leave you alone after that," he said. "I promise."

She wasn't inclined to trust him, but she was so eager for peace she risked letting him into the house. She made sure he went straight to the basement, as there was nothing down there of value except for the trains. As he rummaged around, she went into the kitchen to finish eating her lunch. Edie had made herself a big bowl of mushroom soup, her favorite, and didn't want it to get cold.

When she came out, he was standing in the living room, holding two bags filled with trains and related paraphernalia. She wiped a bit of soup from the corner of her mouth and glanced at him to see if he'd noticed, but he looked wary himself. She scanned the room to make sure he hadn't taken anything. It was so jam-packed with generations of collectibles it was hard to tell if something was missing.

"Did you take anything from here?" she asked.

"Who would want any of this old crap?"

"Good-bye, Gavin. Have a nice life."

"You have soup on your chin, Chubs. And the place smells like dog shit."

He stopped contacting her after that, as promised, and didn't attend any more family functions. By that point, he was living with his girlfriend, a woman named Carol Steiner who was ten years older than him. As far as Edie could tell, they were like a million other mildly unhappy childless couples who thought they were smarter and less lucky than most people they knew.

About five years later Edie got a call from Carol, telling her that Gavin had died unexpectedly that morning from a massive stroke. Edie attended the funeral, accepting condolences from cousins and old friends, eager for it all to be over so she could finally get on with her life, free of her horrible brother.

A few days later, a FedEx box arrived at her house. It contained the mysterious silk kimono she had left in the storage locker, along with a note from Carol saying, *Gavin wanted you to have this.*

Edie stared at the gift, wondering what to do. She could have thrown it right into the trash, which would have been the end of her problems. But she brought it upstairs and hung it in the closet of the old guest room, where it had been most of her life.

That night, Edie was awoken about three a.m. by a man's voice calling her despised nickname. She sat up in bed, terrified. It was Gavin. His voice was unmistakable. But she knew he was dead—she had seen the body. That could mean only one thing . . . he had returned as a ghost. *My God,* she thought. *The kimono!* What a fool she had been! The family lore was thick with ghost tales, and she should have known this was a possibility.

She buried herself under the covers and tried to ignore him, but he called over and over, "Chubs! Chubs! I'm back!"

He went on and on, nearly driving her mad. Finally, she pulled out the baseball bat she kept under her bed and approached the guest room. She would simply grab the kimono, put it outside in the trash.

But when she reached the room, there he was, standing in the doorway, looking as real as he did in life, only paler and more hideous, the kimono over his shoulders like a prizefighter's robe.

"What are you doing here!" she shouted.

"Put the bat away, you idiot. You can't kill a ghost."

"What do you want?"

"I'm here to protect the house."

"Protect it? From what?"

"From *you.*"

She tried to take a swing at him with the bat but he was too quick pulling it out of her hands. He held it over her head as if he were about to smash her skull, and she dropped to the floor, cowering.

"Don't hurt me!" she cried. "Please!"

"You think *I'm* mean," he said, "you should meet the other ghosts in this house."

She felt a bit of urine leak into her panties. "Other ghosts?"

"If you don't want me to unleash them, you will do what I say. Never sell a single item in this house, do you hear me?"

"But I need the money!" she said. "I spent so much on the lawyers."

"To hell with the money."

Edie thought about her dwindling bank account. This house had so many treasures that she knew she could live off them forever. What would she do without them? Except for one disastrous stint as assistant to her father's stockbroker, Edie had never held a paying job in her life. She simply didn't have the constitution for it. Even the cheap apartment she had lived in with a friend had been subsidized by her parents.

Now her brother had cut off her only means of income. And so, with the ghost of Gavin as her controlling roommate, she continued to spend down her inheritance. Every so often she tried to sneak off with a small treasure but was always caught. And there was no chance of getting rid of the dreaded kimono because he never took it off. With money running out, she ate little more than day-old bread and off-brand canned soup she purchased at the dollar store. Edie was poor and miserable, and this made Gavin feel very rich indeed.

1968

There were dozens of names in the Algonquin guest book, and eventually they would all die. When they did, she would be in the Blue Bar, waiting for them.

For now, she had Johnny B., the young bartender she had months ago convinced to stick around most nights after closing. He was humorless, but at least he no longer fainted at the sight of her. And he was pretty to look at.

Dorothy Parker sat at the bar, a fresh gin and tonic before her. As she took her first sip, something near the display case caught Johnny's attention.

"That's funny," he said, staring past her.

She turned and saw a cloud of glowing pink dust particles hovering above the guest book. Was this the sign she had been waiting for?

The particles traveled to the doorway and began to merge, taking on the shape of a sylphlike woman in a diaphanous gown.

Dorothy grinned.

"What is it?" Johnny asked.

"Pour a double bourbon."

"Why?"

"You'll see."

As they watched, the form became more real. And then, there she was—a lithe and glamorous star, draped in liquidy satin.

"Well," said Tallulah Bankhead, "that was quite a ride. And how perfect that it ends here, where it all began."

"Welcome to hell," said Dorothy Parker.

Tallulah approached and kissed her on the cheek. "Darling," she said in her famously throaty voice, "if this were hell, Louis B. Mayer would be tending bar. Give me a cigarette, and tell me who this divine creature is."

"Johnny," Dorothy Parker said, "say hello to Tallulah Bankhead."

"Charmed," said Tallulah.

"Miss Bankhead."

"Johnny sticks around after closing to make me drinks," Dorothy Parker explained. "And he only fainted the first four times I appeared. Now we're old friends, aren't we, dear?"

"Yes, Mrs. Parker."

"Fainter or not, I think he's perfectly lovely."

"Save your breath, Tallulah. He's not our type."

She paused for a moment as it sunk in. "I see. Pity."

"He's already made you a drink. Bourbon, right?"

"You are divine, Dot. And Johnny darling, don't put away that bottle. I plan to be tight as a tick before I make my final exit." She sat down with a dramatic sweep of silk.

"Exit?" said Dorothy Parker. "Please don't tell me you plan a hasty retreat."

"Daddy's been waiting a long time."

"Let him wait a little longer."

"I'm not sure how long I can resist, darling. It's an awfully powerful tug." She put a hand on her heart. "Oh! Mother is there, too. I can feel it. How glorious." She closed her eyes. "And my grandparents . . . everyone. They're all waiting for their Tallulah to come home and throw tantrums again. Isn't it grand?"

Dorothy frowned. She would have to distract her old friend. "Remember when you first walked into the Algonquin? You couldn't have been more than nineteen."

"Sixteen, darling. I was sixteen. Insult me if you like, but don't make me older than I am. I can take anything but that."

"Alexander Woollcott took one look at you and said, 'That girl is going to be trouble.'"

"That's one review he got right."

"You were his pet for a time."

"And I would have bit him on the ass if I had the chance."

Dorothy nodded. Aleck could be quite a pill. Still, he had a remarkable heart when it came to his friends. "He got us all to chip in and buy you a new dress."

Tallulah laughed. "Oh, yes! I came to New York with only one dress I would dare to be seen in, and hadn't a dime for food, let alone new clothes. Oh, Woollcott—he was a ghastly critic, but he could be generous." She picked up her glass. "To Aleck, then."

"To Aleck."

They tapped glasses and Tallulah sipped her drink. "Have you seen him here?"

"He was gone by the time I arrived. They all were, the louses. Only dear Mr. Benchley waited. But he left me pretty quickly, and I suppose you will, too. So much for being the life of the party."

"Now, Dot, don't get testy. It's nothing personal. We are summoned."

"Since when did you ever do what was expected of you?"

"Never, darling. Never. But this is different. I'm sure you understand—you must have your own white light beckoning."

"My white light can be damned."

Tallulah picked up the pack of cigarettes on the bar and extracted one. "Would you be a dear, Johnny?" she said, putting it to her lips. He lighted it for her and she took a long drag. "I admit, it's divine to have this little stopover. It's been ages since I've been able to enjoy a smoke, and even longer since a drink could offer me any sort of pleasure. Do you know what my last word was? Bourbon! Can you imagine? Couldn't get a breath of air and all I wanted was a belt of Wild Turkey."

"Not a bad parting line. I'm sure they'll quote it in your obituary."

"And one day they'll attribute it to you."

"My curse. Of course, if they immortalize you in a play, it'll stick, and everyone will know it was the great Tallulah Bankhead who said it." She was appealing to Tallulah's ego. Surely the actress would want to stay around for such a thing. She stole a glance at her friend's reaction as she took a cigarette from the pack. Johnny lighted it for her.

"I'm afraid my life was too scandalous for the stage," said Tallulah.

Dorothy Parker took a long drag of her cigarette. "Not anymore," she said. "I understand there are naked hippies singing and dancing at the Biltmore this year. I think they call it Hair."

"I've seen it, darling. Those messy young people think they invented sex. They should have seen us when we were young."

"We had our share, I suppose."

"Speak for yourself."

"Tallulah, you're not honestly saying you didn't have enough sex?"

"Enough? Heavens, there's no such thing as enough. In fact, I wouldn't mind finding some sweet young thing to fool around with one last time before I go."

"Yet another reason to stay. Maybe you'll get lucky."

Tallulah looked around. "It seems rather deserted, Dot."

"A temporary setback. Tomorrow night at eleven p.m. the place will be swimming in boys." She paused. "And girls."

"Ah, yes, girls. I suppose my reputation precedes me. But c'est la vie, darling. My tastes are eclectic, my desires uninhibited. I make no apologies."

"Nor should you."

"What about others like us? Can I expect to see any of the old gang?"

"Eventually. Everyone who signed the guest book makes a stop here. Percy got signatures from most of our crowd . . . and dozens of others, too."

"Do tell."

"Writers, mostly—but a few delicious actors and actresses. See for yourself."

"I suppose I will, after my drink."

Dorothy smiled. She could see that Tallulah was interested in the possibility of a rendezvous with another notable or two before her final curtain. "Johnny, dear," she said, "bring us that guest book. We'd like to find a suitable date for Tallulah. And pour her another bourbon. She might be sticking around for a while."

11

As Norah carried the guest book back to her room, she explained to Dorothy Parker that if they could find Audrey and convince her to let Ted off the hook for his infidelity, they might both have a chance of getting what they want.

"My dear, don't you think she would have come forward by now if she had any interest in clearing his name?"

"Maybe if she learns he's dying."

"She probably won't give a damn."

"So we'll find another way to convince her."

Dorothy Parker pursed her lips, and Norah wondered if she was formulating an argument against searching for Audrey Shriver. Not that it mattered. Norah's mind was made up.

"You're a relentless sort, aren't you?" Mrs. Parker said.

Norah smiled. Her new friend had her pegged. She slipped her key card into the door and opened it.

"I suppose we could start with the Manhattan phone book," Mrs. Parker said as she followed Norah into the room. "After all, if she has any sense at all, she still lives in New York."

"We don't need a phone book," Norah said. "It's the twenty-first century."

"Oh, yes. The *Internet*. I've been hearing about that for years." She took a seat.

"You know what it is?"

"From what I understand, it's like a massive party line, only with computers instead of telephones—the whole world available to any-one with one of those little machines." She removed her hat and placed it on the dresser.

"That's an elegant way of looking at it," Norah said.

"And what's the inelegant way of looking at it?"

"That it's mostly about porn."

"Pornography doesn't bother me," Mrs. Parker said. "There are other things far more obscene—war, politics, the desecration of the English language."

"Irregardless," Norah said, and waited a beat for a laugh. Nothing. "You know that was a joke, right?"

"My dear, explanation is the enemy of wit."

Norah furrowed her brow conspicuously. "What do you mean, exactly?"

Dorothy Parker parted her lips to respond and then closed them. She gave the younger woman a gracious nod.

Satisfied, Norah opened her laptop computer and pressed the space bar, bringing the screen to life. She typed *Audrey Shriver* into Google search.

"How long will this take?" Mrs. Parker asked.

Norah hit enter. "There's an Audrey Shriver in Oklahoma, but she's a twenty-two-year-old marathon runner. There's also an Audrey L. Shriver who died in Glendora, California, in 2002." She clicked on the obituary. "Not her, either. She was ninety-eight."

"Astounding."

"I'd be more impressed if we actually found her."

"Anything else?"

Norah found an Audrey Shriver on Classmates.com, but since it was her maiden name, she knew it was a false lead. "All dead ends," she said.

"Don't give up," Mrs. Parker said. "I've learned that dead ends aren't always what they seem."

"Did I say anything about giving up?" Norah searched images to see if she could uncover any other clues. She found the picture she had shown Didi and studied it a moment. It yielded nothing, but the story it told seemed so personal that Norah couldn't help being drawn in.

"What next?" Dorothy Parker asked.

"Still searching." Norah clicked on a scanned photo that seemed to have been taken at some kind of celebration. It showed two couples seated at a dinner table, wearing clothes that dated the snapshot by several decades. She read the caption aloud: "'Ted Shriver and his wife, Audrey, attend a Columbia University fund-raiser with Litton Press publisher Peter Salzberg and his wife, Aviva Kravette, 1979.'"

Norah studied the picture, taken a year after she was born. She imagined her mother in Audrey Shriver's place, looking young and healthy in that sleeveless dress, her head tilted toward Ted. It was a scenario she could never stop herself from playing out. What if her mother hadn't died? What if she had never been sick?

Dorothy Parker looked over Norah's shoulder. "Heavens, but she's attractive. Like a young Elizabeth Taylor."

Norah couldn't argue—Audrey was striking.

"No wonder Teddy fell in love with her," Mrs. Parker continued.

"You think he's that shallow?"

"He's a man, isn't he?"

"But he's Ted Shriver," she said.

"Ms. Wolfe," Dorothy Parker said, "I, too, would like to believe the old wives' tales about the way some men will instantly forsake a beautiful woman to flock around a brilliant one. It is but fair to say that, after getting out in the world, I have never seen this happen."

"I have to believe she's more than a pretty face. He's protected her all these years."

"One would hope. Can you find her maiden name?"

"Trying," Norah said, navigating to Ted Shriver's Wikipedia page, which she had already read several times. She hadn't recalled seeing anything about his ex-wives, but it was worth checking again. As before, the page focused on his books and the scandal surrounding *Settlers Ridge*. The only biographical information said that he was born in Yonkers in 1937 and that his last known address was in Wilton, Connecticut.

Norah tried another tactic. She typed *Ted Shriver* and *married Audrey* into a search. One click and there it was—a bio that provided actual details of his life.

"Listen to this," she said. "'In 1979 he married his second wife, Audrey Brill, a reporter for *Newsweek* magazine.'"

"Grand," said Mrs. Parker. "Two clues for the price of one."

Norah typed *Audrey Brill* into the search field, and spent several minutes following false leads until something caught her eye. "There's an Audrey Brill who works as a writer for a public relations firm on Forty-second Street. I think that could be her, don't you? Should we call?"

"I think," said Dorothy Parker as she reached for her hat, "that we should pay a visit."

There were practical considerations. First, Norah worried about Dorothy Parker's appearance. Would her dress attract too much attention? She studied her for a moment, and decided that on the streets of Manhattan she could pass for a stylish woman with an eye for vintage clothing.

The more important consideration was the guest book. Norah had to figure out a way to carry it in an open position, as it was the only way to leave the hotel with Dorothy Parker at her side. She looked around the room until she found a piece of cardboard in the desk drawer. She laid it across the open pages of the book, then tied it in place with shoelaces she had pulled from her sneakers. Norah put the open book in a tote bag and carried it as they walked through the Algonquin's glass doors onto West 44th Street.

"Give me a moment," Dorothy Parker said as she placed a hand on Norah's shoulder.

"What's the matter?"

"I've not seen the sun in all these many years."

"Are you okay?"

"It's just a little . . . jolting to be about among all this humanity."

Norah looked around. "What do you think?" she asked.

A stooped homeless man pushed a shopping cart past them, and the smell of fermenting urine hung in the air.

"That we've learned absolutely nothing," said Dorothy Parker.

Norah looked at her companion, who seemed genuinely grim. "It's all right," she said gently.

"It most certainly is not."

"Do you want to stay behind?"

Dorothy Parker straightened her posture and arranged her hat, a valiant soldier ready to face the wide world of a new century. "Which way?"

"East," Norah said, pointing toward Fifth Avenue.

The weather was mild for May, and Norah wondered if Dorothy Parker enjoyed feeling the late afternoon sun on her back. She glanced over, and could tell her companion's anxiety had eased. She seemed almost happy.

A young couple, sleeveless and heavily tattooed, were so deep in conversation as they walked by that they didn't notice the small woman in a hat staring at them.

"Circus performers?" she asked Norah, who laughed.

"It's the style now," she explained.

"And what happens next year, when it goes out of style?"

They walked on, and a large transvestite in a bright red wig came up from behind.

"Have you ever seen anything like that before?" Norah whispered.

Dorothy Parker sized up the cross-dresser, who wore a clingy low-cut wrap dress in a bold print, with no falsies and a bit of chest hair showing above the deep V-neck. His purse and shoes were pink patent leather. Clearly, this was a man more interested in getting attention than in passing as female.

"Love your ensemble, dear," Mrs. Parker said. "It's inspired."

"Yours, too, honey," he said. "Retro chic."

As they continued on, Dorothy Parker looked up at the skyscrapers and down at the passersby. She read the signs in the windows and marveled at all the brisk walkers talking into their cell phones.

They reached Fifth Avenue, where Best Buy, Staples, and Duane Reade met at the corner, and she stopped. "I recognize nothing," she said. "And yet . . ."

"It's still the same?"

"No. It's different. But I'm still helplessly beguiled. Isn't that the damnedest thing? This cruel and wonderful city has always owned my heart. It's like a daring lover who conquers each sunrise with a brand-new passion. And despite everything—the years, the crime, the dirt, the extra pounds"—she paused as a group of tourists eating souvlakis passed by—"it still feels exciting, like something is about to happen. That is New York's magic. I believe it will always be the most hopeful place on earth."

She stood quietly for a moment, taking it in, until a man on his phone jostled them as he rushed by.

"Could you fucking *move?*" he said.

Dorothy Parker put her hands to her heart. "You see?" she said to Norah. "It never disappoints."

They walked on until reaching the East Side address of Tyler & Lowell, the public relations firm that employed Audrey Brill. Norah explained to Dorothy Parker that they would be stopped at the security desk.

"People used to come and go as they pleased," Mrs. Parker said.

Norah nodded, thinking about how much the city had changed in even her lifetime. "That was before nine-eleven," she said. "Since then, the whole city has been much more cautious. I don't know if you're even aware—"

"They had the television on in the hotel that day. Some poor souls covered in ash stumbled into the lobby that afternoon."

"A dark day," Norah said.

Mrs. Parker looked grim. "Worst part is what happened afterward."

"What do you mean?"

"Terrorist propaganda," she said. "It's been embraced worldwide—anti-Americanism throughout the Middle East, anti-Zionism everywhere." She held up a flyer that had been handed to her on the street. *THE HOLOCAUST IS A LIE*, it said. She crumpled the page into a ball. "They got exactly what they were after."

"But you're still hopeful," Norah observed.

"Isn't that a kick in the head? Now then, let's go find Teddy's ex."

They entered the building and approached the security desk. Norah told the guard they were there to see Audrey Brill.

"Do you have an appointment?" he asked.

"Not exactly," Norah said, producing her business card. It was, she knew, her ace in the hole. No PR person would ever turn down a chance to talk to an associate producer from a major TV show. "But I think she'll want to meet with us."

A few minutes later, a young secretary came down and led the two women to the sleek reception area of Tyler & Lowell.

"Ms. Brill will be right with you," she said.

Norah and Dorothy settled into the firmly cushioned waiting room chairs, watching the hallway through the glass doors. A few minutes later a woman appeared at the far end of the corridor, walking briskly toward them. She wore a black sweater stretched over massive breast implants and had ultrablond, ultrastraightened, ultrafine hair. Even from a distance, Norah could tell her face had been stretched, pulled, and injected. She was completely transformed.

"I have to warn you," Norah whispered, "that some women go way overboard with plastic surgery."

The woman pushed open the glass door. "I'm Audrey Brill," she said, extending her hand.

"I'm Norah Wolfe and this is my friend, Mrs.—"

"Campbell," Dorothy Parker said, using her second husband's name. "Dorothy Campbell. Nice to meet you."

"What can I do for you?" Audrey asked, arranging her mouth into something resembling a smile. The rest of her waxy face remained corpselike.

"It's actually a personal matter," Norah said.

"We're here about your ex-husband," Mrs. Parker said.

"My ex-husband?"

"I wonder if you know how much he still cares about you."

Audrey's smile dissolved into a thin line. "If he cared about me so much he'd cough up the seventy thousand he owes me."

"Is there not some part of your heart that harbors a bit of tenderness toward him?" Mrs. Parker asked.

"Toward that pig? Do you know how many times he cheated on me?"

"I understand," Mrs. Parker said, "but I have some news that might soften your feelings."

She folded her arms. "Go on."

"I'm afraid he's very sick."

"How sick?"

"He has a brain tumor."

Audrey blinked. She appeared to be in shock, though it was hard to read her expression. "Did he send you?"

"He has no idea we're here," Norah said.

"I'm so very sorry," Dorothy Parker said, laying a hand on the woman's arm. "Ted is dying."

At last, an actual expression registered on the woman's face. She lowered herself into a chair, put her face in her hands, and wept.

"It must be difficult to hear that about someone you once loved," Mrs. Parker said.

"It's not that," Audrey said. She looked up, and rivers of black mascara streamed down her cheeks. "My ex-husband's name is *Phil*."

"What now?" Dorothy Parker said when she and Norah were back on the street. "It seems all roads to the real Audrey Shriver are dead ends."

"I have another idea," Norah said, recalling the photograph of Audrey and Ted seated with another couple. "I think there's someone who might know how we can find Audrey."

"And who's that?"

"Peter Salzberg, Ted's publisher."

"Inspired," said Mrs. Parker. "Which way do we go?"

A short while later, the two women were at another security desk—this one at the newly formed Apollo Publishing Group, which had acquired Litton Press a few years earlier. Norah used the same tactic as before—showing her business card to gain entry.

"I'll need cards for both of you," said the security guard.

"I'm afraid I lost my purse," Mrs. Parker said.

The guard frowned.

"Wait a minute," Norah said. "I think I have one of your cards . . . *Didi.*"

She rummaged through her wallet and found a copy of her boss's business card. It was worn and gray, and had some notes scribbled on the back, but it would do. The guard called upstairs, reading off the names on the cards, identifying them as Didi Dickson, segment producer of *Simon Janey Live*, and Norah Wolfe, associate producer.

"Congratulations," Norah whispered to Dorothy Parker. "You've just been promoted."

"Hold on," the guard said into the phone, and then addressed Norah. "His assistant wants to know what this is in reference to."

"Ted Shriver," Norah said, and held her breath.

The guard spoke quietly into the phone for a few minutes and hung up. "Elevator bank to the left," he said, handing passes to the two women. "Sixteenth floor."

12

Peter Salzberg turned the last page of the manuscript, took off his glasses, and rested his head in his hands. He was overcome. The stupidly titled *Louse* was one of the most affecting books he had ever read. Driven by a narrator whose piercing insights were so astute that Pete had to take frequent breaks to recover, it pulled him in and pulled him along, as he ached for the pristine moment of recognition when the protagonist would shine the brilliant light of understanding upon himself, penetrating his dark cloud of self-loathing. But of course, he wasn't capable of that, which was the whole point of the book. The result was the most profoundly human story he had read in a very long time.

He would publish it, of course, and it would sell. Ted's controversial history would be a publicity machine that needed no fuel. And once readers got their hands on the book, word of mouth would do the rest. But awards? Never. Not with that plagiarism charge hanging over every page.

He took out a pad to start making a list of possible titles. The first one he wrote was the simplest: *Bad Husband*. He looked at it and put down his pen. Was that it? Had he found the perfect title for this book? He was a big fan of simplicity, and this one seemed to hit all the right notes. It was intentionally judgmental. And the word *husband* would let readers know that a relationship was at the heart of the book.

He turned to his computer and did a quick search to see if there were any current or forthcoming novels with that title. There was no rule about reusing titles—they couldn't be copyrighted, after all—but Pete knew that a fresh title would stand a better chance of making a splash.

To his delight, *Bad Husband* had a good clean history. He turned over the manuscript, crossed out *Louse* and wrote in the new title. Yes, it felt right. He was confident his marketing people would agree.

Of course, the thrill of bringing a brilliant new book to the world was tempered with a choking sorrow. Because after reading these pages, he understood that Ted's depression was immovable. He would not be able to convince his old friend to have the surgery that might save his life.

"Mr. Salzberg?"

Pete looked up to see Christopher, his assistant, standing at his door.

"There are two women from *Simon Janey Live* here to see you."

"To see *me*? What do they want?"

"They said it has to do with Ted Shriver."

"What about him?"

Christopher shrugged. "That's all I know."

Pete looked down at the manuscript. They must have gotten wind of his acquisition, but how? He hadn't even told his wife, for God's sake. Had someone in his office leaked it? Had Ted?

"Take them to Katie," Pete said, referring to his publicity director.

"They said it has to be you."

That clinched it, then. It had to be about the manuscripts. Pete opened the cabinet next to his desk, placed the pages inside, and locked it. "Fine," he said. "Show them in."

A short while later, Christopher led the two women into Peter Salzberg's office and introduced them. The smaller one—a dark-eyed woman wearing a hat—looked familiar, though he couldn't place where he knew her from. The other one was lithe and pretty, with the neat features of a news anchor.

"Have a seat," he said after shaking their hands. "What can I do for you?"

"We're here about Ted Shriver," said the telegenic one.

"So I heard, Ms. . . ." He trailed off, studying the business cards on his desk.

"Norah is fine," she said.

"He is dying," said the other woman in a clipped, formal accent. "Were you aware of that?"

Peter Salzberg shifted in his seat. Maybe they didn't know about the manuscripts after all. He hoped that was true; his control of the information was essential.

"Unfortunately," he said. "How did you find out?"

"Long story," Norah said. "The point is, we thought you might be interested in seeing him reveal the truth about his alleged plagiarism . . . on national television."

"Ladies, that's a battle I stopped fighting twenty-five years ago. Ted Shriver has never revealed the story behind that incident and never will."

"He revealed it to me," said the one in a hat.

He glanced down at her business card and looked back up. "I'm sorry, Ms. . . . Dickson. Can you repeat that?"

"I said, *he revealed it to me.*"

Pete folded his arms. It didn't seem possible. "And how did that come about?"

"He was drunk and on painkillers. He thought I was a hallucination."

Pete Salzberg drew a deep breath. The woman's explanation actually sounded plausible.

"It's true," she continued, and there was something about her eyes that disarmed him—an abiding wisdom that went as deep as a crypt. He was inclined to trust her.

"I assume you're here to tell me the story."

"We're here," Norah said, "because despite knowing the truth, we can't convince him to reveal it himself. And of course, that's what we want—for him to talk about it on *Simon Janey Live*."

"If you think I can convince him you're—"

"We don't," Norah said. "We don't think you can convince him, but we know who can. His ex-wife Audrey."

"So why have you come to see *me*?"

"We think you can help us find her."

"I might," Pete said, "but I need to hear the story first."

The smaller woman folded her hands in her lap. "My dear Mr. Salzberg," she said, "you seem like an honorable man. And I want you to promise that once we tell you this story, you will lead us to Audrey Shriver."

"I'll do what I can," he said. "I promise."

The two women exchanged a look and the younger one began. "It was Audrey," she said. "She was in a fury over his infidelity, and she planted the plagiarized paragraphs in *Settlers Ridge*. I guess she knew he would never proofread the book before it went to press."

"Why on earth would he keep that a secret?"

"To protect her," said the other woman. "It's actually rather romantic when you think about it. No man in heaven or on earth ever loved me that much."

"And besides," Norah added, "he thinks he deserves the blame, even though he's innocent. He's punishing himself for hurting her."

Pete stood and went to his window. He needed a moment to take this in. After reading the book and understanding the depths of Ted's guilty conscience, the explanation seemed so obvious he felt like a fool for not having seen it. Of course, when the scandal first broke, he had suspected Audrey had something to do with it. But once the marriage fell apart he couldn't understand why Ted wouldn't expose her crime, so he assumed there was some other explanation—like intentional self-sabotage. But this. This made perfect sense.

"He still cares about her," Pete said, realizing that was why Ted had kept silent all these years. The son of a bitch was a romantic after all.

"That's our conclusion as well."

For a moment, he felt a flicker of hope. If Ted still had feelings for Audrey, there was a fraction of a chance he might agree to the surgery. But then he remembered Audrey's fury. It wasn't just hurt and it wasn't just bluster. It was the blackest, most bottomless kind of loathing.

He turned to face the women. "She hates him, you know."

"Naturally," said the petite woman.

"You don't understand," he said. "Her hatred is . . . volcanic."

"We figured as much," Norah said. "But if she learns he's dying . . ."

"It's a fool's errand."

"Let us worry about that," she said. "Tell us where we can find Audrey Shriver."

He shook his head. "I can't do that."

"But you said—"

"Audrey hasn't spoken to me since she and Ted split up. The truth is, I don't know where she is." He took his suit jacket from the back of his chair and put it on. "But I know someone who does."

"And who would that be?" said the other woman.

He pushed in his chair and headed toward the door. "Follow me."

They did as he said, trailing behind him as they went down the corridor toward the stairwell. "Where are we going?" Norah asked.

"One flight up," he said, opening the door.

As they followed him up the steps to the seventeenth floor, he explained that a woman who had started as his assistant rose through the ranks to become a senior editor. She was later recruited by another publisher but was courted back to the Apollo Group with the offer of her own imprint, which meant that there was now an entire lineup of best sellers published under her name.

"She's quite the powerhouse," he said as they arrived at her office. He knocked lightly on the open door and she looked up. "Got a minute?" he said.

She took off her reading glasses. "What's up?"

"Ladies," he said, "I'd like to introduce my wife, Aviva Kravette."

Aviva Kravette reached across her desk to shake their hands, and Norah was impressed with her vibrancy. She had to be in her midfifties—possibly older—but she wore her chestnut hair smooth and long. On closer inspection, her face showed some signs of age, but she had such a youthful energy about her that Norah could feel a direct line to the dewy ingenue in the old photograph.

"They're from *Simon Janey Live*," Pete explained.

"Oh?" Aviva sat up straighter.

"Don't get excited," he said. "They're not here to interview you . . . or me, for that matter. They want Audrey."

"Audrey?" She sounded confused.

"Shriver."

Aviva grabbed her reading glasses and put them back on. "For heaven's sake."

"Hear them out."

"It's about Ted Shriver," Norah said.

"Ted Shriver is a piece of shit."

"Yes, dear," said Mrs. Parker, "but he's a dying piece of shit."

"So I heard. And I'm sorry, I really am. But my sympathy only goes so far."

"There are two sides to every story," Norah said.

"Oh really? Let's examine that. On the one hand, you have a vulnerable, madly-in-love woman who gave up everything for her husband. On the other hand, you have a drunken, out-of-control womanizer who used any excuse to go on a bender and sleep with starstruck young women. Two sides. You're absolutely right."

Norah fought the urge to defend him, to blame his alcoholism, to explain how much he had punished himself since then. But Aviva was right. He had behaved deplorably. There was no excuse. But if only she had looked into his eyes and seen the pain there. "What about the plagiarism?" she said.

"What about it?"

"Have you ever considered how it happened?"

"Of course. He tied one on for a change and typed in the wrong paragraphs. He was probably proud of himself for finding the type-writer keys."

Pete shook his head. "It was Audrey."

"What are you talking about?"

"Don't you remember how angry she was?"

"And why wouldn't she be?"

"But her *rage*," he said. "She was like a wild animal." He turned to Norah and Mrs. Parker. "She threw his typewriter out the window. Almost got arrested."

Aviva rubbed her eyes, like she was trying to erase the memory. "I couldn't talk her down. Her fury was impenetrable. God, I was worried."

"And she wanted *revenge*."

"But she wouldn't do that. Audrey of all people—"

"That's the thing," Pete said. "To her, nothing could be worse than a plagiarism accusation, so she set him up. What better way to get even?"

"Hell hath no fury like a woman in love with a scoundrel," Dorothy Parker said.

"I admit she was angry enough to do *anything*," Aviva said, "but he would have defended himself."

Pete approached her desk. "Do you believe Ted was in love with Audrey?"

"I suppose. I don't think he was ever happier than when he was with her, which made it that much worse. Anyone who could cheat on someone they cared so much about—"

He put his hand on her shoulder, and Norah watched the look that passed between them. It was something more than love—they were letting each other in. Norah felt it in her throat like a heaviness of air. She had to look away.

"What would have happened to Audrey if people found out she had planted those paragraphs?" Pete asked.

"She could have lost *everything*—her whole career. But if you think Ted was trying to save her from that, you're giving him a lot of credit." Despite her words, Aviva's voice had lost its conviction, and Norah sensed that she was on the brink of changing her mind.

"Don't you see? The destroyed reputation is his penance. He gets to protect Audrey and bear punishment at the same time."

Aviva pursed her lips, a faraway look in her eyes. "Oh," she said, and the color drained from her face.

"What is it?" Pete said.

Aviva shook her head. "I don't know. I'm probably remembering it all wrong."

"Will you share it with us?" Norah asked.

"Not until I'm sure. Because if Audrey did this, she can't plead ignorance. She knew full well how serious a plagiarism accusation would be."

"Audrey was a journalist," Pete explained to their guests.

"We know," Norah said.

Aviva stood and walked to her bookshelf. "Not only that," she said, retrieving a thick volume that looked like a textbook. She dropped it on the table in front of the two women.

"*Ethics in Journalism*," Norah read off the cover. "By A. L. Hudson." She looked up, confused.

"Audrey Louise Hudson," Aviva explained. "She remarried in 1985 and divorced in 1996, but kept the name."

Dorothy Parker leaned in and placed her finger on the title. "Dear God. She literally wrote the book on plagiarism."

"And she teaches a course on it at Columbia," Aviva said.

"Columbia?" Norah said. "She's right here in Manhattan!"

"Don't get your hopes up," Aviva said. "I don't know what you expect from her. But if you're counting on Audrey Hudson to help you get to Ted Shriver, you're dead."

"That," said Dorothy Parker as she stood, "shouldn't be a problem."

13

Aviva Kravette canceled her afternoon meeting to accompany Norah and Dorothy Parker to Audrey Hudson's apartment uptown. Pete said he had to get back to work and stayed behind. "Besides," he had added, "she hates me almost as much as she hates Ted. Guilt by association."

As their taxi bumped its way up Third Avenue, Aviva explained that Audrey taught only one class at Columbia and that the rest of her income was from freelancing. "But most of that's dried up," she said. "Audrey was always contentious with her editors, but it just got worse and worse. Now almost no one will hire her."

Aviva had called first, so Audrey was expecting them and opened the door almost the very second the buzzer was pressed.

"I made coffee," she said, instead of hello.

She was bone thin in a pale blue sweater and black slacks she didn't fill out. Norah was struck by her nervousness; the woman seemed as brittle as a crisp chip. She was still pretty, but her soft curls were now salt and pepper, and her delicate complexion was etched with fine lines. One aspect of her personality was apparent to Norah instantly: vulnerability. You didn't need to peel away any layers to see it. It was all right on the outside, chafed raw by life.

Aviva kissed her hello and introduced them as Norah Wolfe and Didi Dickson.

The apartment was small and stuffed with too much furniture— all of it just a bit too homely to qualify as shabby chic. Two small windows faced another building and let in very little sunlight. Framed prints by Salvador Dalí and René Magritte decorated the walls.

"Nice place," Dorothy Parker said, and Norah cringed at the sarcasm.

Audrey didn't seem to pick up on it. "It's small, but I make do," she said with a shrug.

"Of course you do, dear. All you need is room to lay your hat and a few friends."

Audrey blinked, not sure how to react, and Norah could tell she was wondering if it was intended as an insult.

"She's just kidding." Norah smiled kindly. "You have a lot of books," she added, trying to sound impressed. There were, indeed, a surprising number of volumes lining the shelves on two long walls.

"I'm a big reader. Have a seat."

They did as she asked, and everyone accepted a cup of the bitter coffee she passed around. Audrey lowered herself into a faded blue easy chair.

"These ladies have some news for you, Audrey," Aviva said. "It's about Ted."

Audrey jumped from her seat, her eyes wild. "What?"

"Relax," Aviva said. "They come in peace."

"I thought this was about a job!"

"I never said that," Aviva insisted.

"What else would I assume! I haven't had an assignment in *months*. You said you were bringing some producers. I thought—"

"I'm sorry if I gave the wrong impression. It's just that they have bad news and I didn't want to tell you over the phone."

"Just a minute," Audrey said, and left the room. Norah could hear her in the kitchen running the tap, and then . . . nothing.

They waited in uncomfortable silence until Norah spoke. "What do you think she's doing in there?"

"If she were sticking her head in the oven, we would smell gas," Dorothy Parker said, "so I imagine she's slitting her wrists."

"She'll be fine," Aviva said. "Sometimes she just needs a few minutes to . . . regroup."

Sure enough, when Audrey came back into the room she was more collected. If she didn't know any better, Norah would have suspected there were psychopharmaceuticals involved. Valium, maybe. Or Thorazine.

"Okay," Audrey said, sitting. "I'm ready." She closed her eyes.

Aviva reached over and patted her knee. "This isn't a firing squad, honey."

"I still hate him, you know," she said quietly, as if it were a secret.

"Of course you do."

"He said he would never cheat on me. *Ever.* He promised."

"That should have been your cue," said Dorothy Parker. "The next time a man says, 'I promise,' run. It means he's agreeing to something he's never been able to accomplish before. And as we all know, men do not change."

Audrey sighed. "Just tell me whatever it is you came for, because—"

"Ted's dying," Mrs. Parker said.

"What?"

"Brain tumor. We don't know how much time he has."

Audrey opened her mouth, but no sound came out. Tears spilled from her eyes. She ran into the kitchen again.

"Come back!" Aviva said.

"Don't be so shocked, dear," Dorothy Parker called after her. "People die every day."

Aviva went after her friend, leaving Mrs. Parker and Norah alone in the living room.

"Be gentle," Norah whispered. "She's very fragile."

"A china cup is fragile," Dorothy Parker said, putting down her coffee. "This woman is a cracked teapot."

"A guilty conscience can do a lot of damage. She may have spent her whole life looking over her shoulder, wondering if she'd get caught. This visit could be her worst nightmare."

"Perhaps she's eager to confess and end her self-torture."

After several minutes, Aviva came back into the room with her broken friend. Audrey's face was ashen, her nose red and swollen from crying. She clutched a tissue.

They sat together on the sofa, opposite Norah and Dorothy Parker.

"There's something else you need to know," Norah said, leaning forward. "I think Ted still has feelings for you."

Audrey blew her nose. "Why are you telling me this?"

Norah sat back, troubled that Audrey didn't seem the least bit surprised. She had been hoping this revelation would change everything.

"I didn't think you knew," Norah said.

"Let me show you something," Audrey said, rising. She went into her bedroom and came out with a rectangular plastic container. "He still sends me a birthday card every year." She sat down with the box on her lap and pulled out a sample. "This is from 1992: 'Thinking of you. Happy Birthday.'" She put it back and took out a few more. "From 1987: 'Heard you got married. Happy Birthday.' From 2002: 'Hope you are well. Happy Birthday.' Here's a longer one, from 1999: 'Saw your article in the *Times*. Good job. Happy Birthday.' They're all like that—mundane, uninspired. Not what you would expect from one of America's most treasured literary figures."

"I guess he never really wanted to let go," Norah said.

Audrey's shoulders began to shake and she broke down in sobs.

"Oh, honey," Aviva said.

"I'm so very sorry," Norah said, and realized it felt like they were consoling a grieving widow, instead of confronting a woman who took revenge on her husband by ruining his life. There were, she knew, some people who had a kind of genius for helplessness, eliciting sympathy and concern wherever they went. Audrey was the type of lost soul who got help from people on the street. If she asked for directions, no doubt a stranger would lead her to her destination and ask, "You sure you'll be all right from here?" No one could resist feeling sorry for her.

Still, Norah was there on a mission, and she wasn't going to back down simply because this woman was about as stable as plutonium. She just had to approach the subject slowly and carefully so she wouldn't explode.

Norah cleared her throat. "I get the sense that maybe deep down you still love him, too, and—"

"No!" Audrey said. "I hate him. I hate him and I'm glad he's dying."

"I don't think you mean that," Norah said.

"Of course she does," said Mrs. Parker. "This is exactly what she's been waiting for."

"*Didi*," Norah said, trying to make eye contact. She simply had to find a way to convey that this was the wrong tactic. This broken creature had to believe they were on her side.

Dorothy Parker ignored her and leaned toward Audrey. "You believe he'll take your secret to the grave. Isn't that why you're glad he's dying?" she asked.

Audrey looked up. "Huh?"

"You see, dear, we know what you did."

The color left Audrey's face with alarming speed, and Norah was sure she would pass out. Aviva saw it, too, and made her friend put her head between her legs just as her eyes started to roll back.

"Breathe," she said.

After a few moments, Audrey slowly raised her head. She was sweating and trembling. "I want to be alone now," she said.

"That doesn't sound like a very good idea," Aviva said.

"Just *leave*."

"Let's talk about this."

Audrey stood and they all looked at her. "Excuse me," she said.

"What do you need?" Aviva asked.

Audrey ignored her and went into the bedroom. The door slammed shut.

"That woman buzzes around like a mosquito," Mrs. Parker said. "I'm tempted to swat her with a newspaper."

"You need to leave!" she shouted from the bedroom. "All of you."

Aviva stood. "Audrey, honey, come out and we'll discuss it."

"Get out!"

"We just want to help. It'll feel better to get it out in the open."

"I said, 'Get out!'"

"Please," Aviva said, "open the door. I'm worried about you."

Audrey didn't respond, but they heard her walking around inside the bedroom. There was shuffling and the sound of a drawer being pulled out. And then the door opened, and there she stood, still trembling, but focused. And in her hands, pointed right at Aviva, was a gun.

14

N ever, in a million years," Aviva said as the three women spilled out the front door of Audrey's apartment building and onto the street. "I mean, I knew she was unstable, but . . ."

"You sure you're okay?" Norah said, trying to convince herself that she was only concerned about Aviva. But in fact, she had been quite certain Audrey's anger was directed at all of them.

"I didn't even know she owned a gun."

"My dear," Dorothy Parker said, "people like that always own guns."

"This woman was my *friend*."

Norah stiffened her hand to see if it was still trembling. She took a long, slow breath to calm herself and to connect with the notion that Audrey had wanted only to frighten them. She coughed several times and regained her strength.

"If it makes you feel any better," Norah said, "I don't think she actually would have shot you."

"It doesn't."

Norah saw several yellow cabs waiting at the light and stepped off the curb to hail one. "You'll feel better when you get to your office," she said, waving toward the traffic.

"Better still," Dorothy Parker said, "let's get her a drink."

"I could use one," Aviva said, "but I have to get back to work."

A taxi stopped and Norah opened the door for Aviva.

"Work will be there when you return," Mrs. Parker said. "I can promise you that."

Norah held on to the cab door. "I think we've taken up enough of her time."

"In or out," said the driver.

Aviva scratched her cheek, indecisive, and then let out a breath. "Thanks anyway," she said to the driver. She shut the door and pointed across the street. "Hamilton's. They make an old-fashioned you could die for."

"That has me written all over it," said Mrs. Parker.

A short while later, they were seated at a dark booth with wooden bench seats. Dorothy Parker made quick work of her gin and tonic and was on her second while Norah and Aviva still nursed their first drinks.

"I can't believe she did that to me," Aviva said.

"I must admit," said Dorothy Parker, "there are people I've wanted to kill over the years, but I've never had the gumption to pull a gun. I wouldn't have guessed she had it in her."

Norah stared. "You're not actually *defending* her, are you?"

"Defending? No. But it's hard not to feel a touch of grudging respect."

"I feel like she stuck a knife in my back," Aviva said.

"An odd metaphor for a gun in your face," Mrs. Parker said.

Aviva looked at her. "I'm talking about the betrayal. She *lied* to me for more than twenty-five years. And I was always so good to her. I would have done *anything* for Audrey."

"She's very damaged," Norah said.

"It's pronounced *deranged*," said Mrs. Parker.

Aviva sipped her drink. "I introduced them, you know—Audrey and Ted. I was living downtown and Audrey was friends with my roommate. We got very close. She was always high-strung, but smart and perceptive. Challenging, even."

"And Pete was your boss?" Norah asked.

Aviva smiled. "An office romance. And Ted was a rising star. He was always kind of boorish, but he was so brilliant we all decided it was part of his charm. So I introduced him to my friend. I thought they made such a great match—you should have seen them together. He doted on her. And she was happier than I ever thought she could be. I felt like some kind of genius for bringing them together. Then when he cheated on her—God, I was furious. How could he do that to someone so fragile? He had to know it would break her. I wanted to wring his neck. And then the plagiarism thing happened and I thought it was just another casualty of his sloppy drinking. But now—"

"Are you inclined to forgive him?" Mrs. Parker asked.

"I don't know," Aviva said, and sighed. "It's complicated. I've been furious with him for so long."

"But he didn't deserve to have his career destroyed."

Aviva looked down. "That was unfair to him, unfair to all of us. He was so brilliant. God knows how many more books he could have written. His impact might have been substantial." She stopped to sip her drink. "Despite everything, I'm a huge fan of his work. I've never wavered on that. In my opinion, Ted Shriver has a place among America's greatest novelists."

"I read *Dobson's Night* at thirteen," said Norah. "Even then, I understood that he was a genius."

"All this time I thought he sabotaged his own career, and that enraged me as much as the cheating—that he would deprive us of the books that might have come next. I never dreamed Audrey was capable of such artifice."

"Hell hath no fury," Mrs. Parker said.

"I understand fury," Aviva said. "But she lied to me for so long. In fact . . ." She closed her eyes. "That vague memory is getting sharper. I think I tried to suppress it all these years."

Norah leaned forward. "Were you involved in the publication of *Settlers Ridge?*"

Aviva nodded. "I was Pete's assistant then. Nothing was electronic in those days, of course, and I was responsible for logging in the manuscripts. Somehow I got the wrong copy of that one. No wait, it was Audrey who told me I got the wrong manuscript. That's it—that's what happened!" She sat up straighter, closing her eyes to picture it. "I remember now. Audrey called and said that Ted had accidentally sent the wrong version and would I please throw it out, because she was going to send the final manuscript over by messenger." She opened her eyes. "That must have been when she planted the paragraphs."

"She played you, my dear," said Mrs. Parker.

"I never imagined—" Aviva said.

"I wish we could compare the two manuscripts," Norah said. "That would give us proof."

Aviva looked absently at her bracelet watch. "Maybe we can," she mumbled.

"What?"

She stared straight at Norah. "I saved a lot of manuscripts back then—especially if I thought the author might have historical significance one day. It wasn't even for the value. I just had this romantic notion that I was a part of literary history and had a . . . *duty.*"

"Wait," Norah said. "You *saved* both of those manuscripts?"

"I don't know," Aviva said. "I might have."

"My dear," Dorothy Parker said, "you could turn out to be the hero of this tale."

"Do you know where they would be?" Norah asked.

"We have a house in Connecticut. I put all those things in the attic. I haven't looked at any of it for years. It's so dark and dusty I never go up there. I can't even remember what we ditched and what we kept."

"When can you check?" Norah said.

"Pete and I are supposed to go there next month."

"We might not have that much time," Norah said.

"I don't think I can get up there any sooner," said Aviva. "I'm presenting an award tonight, and tomorrow I have a meeting I just can't postpone. Then I'm off to London for a week."

"We'll go," said Mrs. Parker.

Aviva looked at her. "What?"

"Norah and I. We can leave immediately."

"You want me to give you the keys to my house?"

"Why not?"

Aviva pursed her lips.

"Do we look like criminals?" Dorothy Parker said.

Norah's right knee shook in excitement. She imagined shining a flashlight into a dusty attic and coming across the treasure of a life-time. She put a hand on Aviva's arm. "Please," she said. "I promise we won't touch a thing except for those manuscripts in the attic. You can trust us. I . . . I've been a fan of Ted Shriver's almost all my life. I wouldn't do anything to—"

"Okay, okay," said Aviva. "What the hell."

"You'll give us your house key?" Norah asked. She was excited.

"Sure."

"And directions?"

"Of course."

Norah paused and swallowed. "Just one more thing," she said, and looked into Aviva's face, hoping to convey how trustworthy she was.

"Yes?" Aviva said.

Norah hunched her shoulders apologetically. "We don't have a car."

"You've got to be kidding."

"I live in Brooklyn. I take the subway."

Aviva shook her head, and Norah wondered if she had pushed too hard. But the woman opened her purse, put cash on the table and stood. "Let's go," she said.

"Where to?" Norah asked.

"I need to show you where my BMW is parked."

15

N orah pulled Aviva's luxurious BMW into an empty spot on Eleventh Avenue, across the street from the building where *Simon Janey Live* was shot. She wanted to get to Connecticut before dark, but this stop was important. Didi needed to know she was onto something. She needed to know there was still hope.

Norah opened her purse and rummaged through it for her ID badge, which was attached to a blue lanyard. She pulled it from the bottom of her bag and slipped it over her head.

"Wait here," she said to Dorothy Parker as she threw her purse onto the backseat. "I'll just be a few minutes."

"My dear, you should know by now that I am never in a hurry. Take your time."

"You want to listen to the radio?"

"Thank you, no. I'd rather just sit quietly and watch New Yorkers bustle about in their frenetic way. It's a music all its own."

Norah got out of the car and dashed across the street into the office building, where Mr. Mazzera, the stoic security guard she had known since she started working there, stood like a fixture listing slightly to the right, his arms folded, his gaze watchful.

"Hey, Mr. M.," Norah said, and he nodded, his eyes going right back to the sacred task of watching for threats. It was as if he were born to keep them safe.

Norah took the elevator up to the fourth floor and pushed through the glass door to the reception area of SJL Productions, where the walls were lined with poster-sized photos of Simon interviewing some of the most famous people on earth. There were politicians and generals, rock stars and movie stars, scientists and preachers. Over the years, *Simon Janey Live* had become an institution. Norah took a labored breath against the pressure of responsibility squeezing her lungs. There was too much at stake for her to fail.

"I thought you abandoned us," said Patti Garland, the husky-voiced receptionist.

Norah quickly turned, wondering how Patti could think such a thing. But the receptionist was smiling, and Norah realized it was meant in good humor. She gave Patti's shoulder a squeeze before passing into the hallway.

She went straight to Didi's office, which was empty. Norah lingered for just a moment to take in the homey scent of her boss's apple spice potpourri. It was hard to imagine a day when the memory of this sweet smell would dissipate into nostalgia. Her eyes watered.

"I think she's with Simon," said a voice behind her. It was Marco, Didi's young assistant, and Norah had to fight the urge to hug him and murmur that it was all going to be okay.

She walked down the hall toward Simon's office, but paused as she passed the door to the engineering booth. She pushed it open a crack and peered into the dark interior, where Eli and Cynthia—whom she considered friends as well as coworkers—sat in front of a single monitor, their faces glowing with reflected light. They wore headsets and stared straight ahead, their mouths open like children watching Saturday morning cartoons. Only, they were most likely cutting video for a promotional spot. She closed the door quietly and continued on.

The door to Simon's office was closed, but Norah could see into the room through the small window. He stood in front of his desk, talking to Didi, his neck bent forward and her head tilted back so they could see eye to eye. Simon was remarkably tall—almost six-foot-six—and was sometimes referred to as "hair handsome." Norah understood. At sixty-eight, a full head of hair compensated for features that fell well short of pretty.

Didi held still, listening to what Simon had to say. Norah felt certain they were discussing the dissolution of the show and what would happen to the staff. Maybe today was the day they would tell everyone to pack their things and go home. Maybe they were trying to find the right words. Simon put his hand on Didi's shoulder and she nodded gravely. Norah felt a sharp stab of grief that cut dangerously close to the wound left by her mother's death. She knocked lightly on the door.

They looked up at her, and Didi said something to Simon before he motioned her into the room.

"Everything okay?" Norah said as she entered.

"I think you know the answer to that, sugar," Didi said.

Simon rested on the corner of his desk and folded his arms. "I know you tried following a lead to Ted Shriver," he said.

Norah tried to suppress a smile, but she couldn't tamp down her pride. "That's what I came to talk to you about."

Didi's posture went erect. "You signed him?"

"No, no," Norah said, frustrated. She came to offer hopeful news she thought might excite them, but now it felt like she could do nothing but burst the bubble she had accidentally inflated. "I don't know. I think I have a good chance now. I'm on my way to Connecticut to find some hard proof about the plagiarism. I mean, proof that will exonerate him. And I think I can use it to convince him to go public . . . on the air."

The room was silent as Simon and Didi considered her news.

"Ted Shriver," Simon repeated, frowning.

Didi looked at him and nodded. "That would have done it," she said.

They continued looking grave, and Norah stood there awkwardly for a moment. What had she expected? Confetti? An embrace? Clearly, they weren't convinced she could pull it off. This surprised Norah; she thought they believed in her.

"I can do this," she said.

Didi put a hand on her arm. "Norah," she began, and her tone was so compassionate that Norah wanted to scream. She did not need placating.

"You don't understand," Norah said. "This is real. I'm following a trail that could save the show. It feels solid. It feels . . ." She couldn't think of a way to defend herself that didn't sound defensive and juvenile.

"What's in Connecticut?" Simon asked.

"I'm not sure," Norah said. "But if it can save the show—"

"Bubbeleh," Didi said, her voice a little stronger, "I'm not saying you shouldn't go. Just don't get your hopes up. Our baby is taking its dying breaths."

Norah shook her head. She didn't want to hear it. "The show may live," she said, and left.

16

Norah hoped that once she inched the car out of Manhattan the roads would open up and she would have no trouble reaching the house before nightfall, as Aviva had warned that groping around the dark attic would prove difficult. But the crawl of rush hour traffic was frustrating, and it was six thirty by the time they merged onto the Hutchinson River Parkway. Dorothy Parker lit a cigarette.

"Would you mind?" Norah said, coughing.

"I suppose you want me to open the window," Mrs. Parker said, studying the car door. "Is this the correct button?"

Norah took a quick glance and her irritation dissolved, as she realized Dorothy Parker probably had little experience with electronic car windows. "Never mind," she said, and pressed a button overhead, opening the sunroof—a small feat she thought was sure to impress.

Dorothy Parker looked up, shrugged, and went on smoking.

"I thought that would tickle you," Norah said.

"My dear, there have been open-roofed cars for as long as I can remember. I'd be more impressed if this damned thing had an ashtray."

"Isn't there *any* technology that knocks you for a loop?"

Dorothy Parker thought for a moment. "I suppose I found that computer net amusing."

"*Internet,*" Norah corrected. "And *amusing* is a tame adjective for technology that's revolutionized the world."

"I can't see how it would have changed my life very much."

"There must be *some* modern invention that would have made a difference in your life."

Mrs. Parker considered it. "I've heard people speak of *cash machines.* I should like to see one of those. God knows there were times I could have used one."

Norah laughed. "You know they don't actually print money, right?"

"I'm dead, my dear, not stupid. And speaking of cash, you might discern that your purse is a few dollars lighter."

"You took money from my wallet? Why?"

"A sad-looking fellow approached the car while you were in your office building."

"But you didn't need to help yourself to my hard-earned—"

"He was needy."

"I'll bet," Norah said, and maneuvered into the left lane, hoping to gain at least a few car lengths.

"Don't be a cynic, child."

Norah stole a quick glance at her passenger. "Did *you* just call *me* a cynic?"

Dorothy Parker took a drag of her cigarette and blew the smoke toward the open sunroof. "I know my reputation," she said. "And regardless of what they say about me, I was not a cynic."

"Not even about love?"

"Least of all, my dear. My romantic choices were driven by the stupidity of hope."

Norah shook her head and replayed the phrase *driven by the stupidity of hope.* The sentiment came perilously close to her attitude about this mission they were on. She considered that for a few moments before changing the subject back to technology.

"I can't believe there isn't a single advance that excites you."

"I've had many advances that excited me. Unfortunately, most of them left in the morning with barely a good-bye."

They were quiet for several minutes as Norah concentrated on driving and Dorothy Parker finished her cigarette. She released the butt through the open sunroof, and found the button to close it. Then she opened it again. She did this several times.

"What are you doing?" Norah asked.

"It occurs to me that mechanical things have become quieter."

"At last—something that impresses you!"

"Hardly," Mrs. Parker said. "If *people* changed, I'd be impressed. Gadgets merely mark the inevitable march of progress."

"I guess that's why your writing still resonates," Norah said. "You understood exactly what was timeless about the human soul."

"Oh, I'm useless on matters of the soul. My expertise began and ended with heartbreak. I had a lot of practice at it, you see."

"Me, too," Norah said, "but I can't write a poem to save my life."

"You don't look like a girl who's had her heart broken very often."

Norah pictured Eric's face the moment before he walked out the door. He looked so hurt, so disappointed, as if there was something he expected her to say. But what *could* she say?

"My boyfriend walked out on me just a couple of months ago. I think that qualifies."

Mrs. Parker looked at her and paused. "How did it make you feel?" she said.

"When he left? Shitty. Angry. I don't know. He said things that cut right through me."

"And what did you do?"

"Nothing. What *could* I do? Anyway, I don't play victim. I just pick up and move on."

Mrs. Parker was quiet for a moment and then said simply, "I see." The tone of her voice implied that she understood more than Norah was letting on—perhaps more than Norah herself understood.

"What do you see?" Norah asked.

"When this man left, you weren't heartbroken, you were insulted. There's a difference."

"I think you're splitting hairs."

"I think you've never been in love."

Norah tightened her grip on the steering wheel. "Of course I've been in love."

"Fine. What do I know?"

"Okay, maybe I wasn't in love with Eric. That doesn't mean I'm incapable of it." Her eyes burned as she remembered how his parting words had pierced her. But later, her hurt had turned to anger because she realized he had never understood her. It wasn't that she had *no* feelings but that she had too many.

Norah swallowed against a knot in her throat and did what she always did when pain threatened to overwhelm her—she drove forward. Only, this time she did so literally. The road opened up at last, and she gave the fierce engine a burst of gas and let the speedometer fly.

She was so focused on the road she almost didn't notice the light tapping on her shoulder. "What is it?" she said.

"Slow down."

"No," she said, and kept pressing forward. Now that the traffic was clear, she wanted to make good time.

"Slow down," Mrs. Parker repeated.

"There hasn't been a cop for miles," Norah said, "and we need the sunlight. I'm not slowing down until we get there."

"I understand," said Dorothy Parker, "but I think you just missed the turnoff."

The unplanned detour was only a few minutes, but by the time they arrived the sun was low in the sky, and Norah knew that darkness was imminent.

Aviva and Peter's house was set back from the road at the end of a long driveway. The simple exterior—pale gray clapboard with white trim—wasn't particularly inspiring, but once Norah put the key in the door and let them in, she understood the charm of this waterfront country home. It was an open floor plan straight to the back of the house, where large picture windows framed a vista of the dusky blue Long Island Sound stretching across the horizon.

"Lovely," said Dorothy Parker, walking directly toward the back. "Look, dear. There are chairs and a table facing the water. We should relax with a glass of wine out there before we begin."

"Not a chance," Norah said.

"Didn't Aviva say we were free to help ourselves? She mentioned a bottle of Bordeaux."

"We have less than an hour of sunlight left," Norah said. "We need to go straight up to that attic. If you want to relax on the deck, it'll have to wait."

"Very well," said Mrs. Parker. "We'll get right to work. But afterward, I want to see what modern technology has done with a simple gadget that never really needed improving: the corkscrew."

Norah found a lantern flashlight and gloves, per Aviva's instructions. She put the tote bag strap over her shoulder and carried everything upstairs to the quaintly decorated guest bedroom, which had access to the attic through a panel in the ceiling. She pulled on a rope to let down the ladder.

Norah knew the attic would be dusty, but it was worse than she had imagined. Everything was coated in a mossy gray layer. There was no charm to the scene—no rocking chairs or antique cribs or precious old steamer trunks. Most of the space was filled with cardboard boxes and oversized paintings—or what she guessed were paintings—wrapped in kraft paper. There was also an old headboard, a television, and several large trash bags. A square window in the far corner let in a dramatic slash of sunlight.

Norah hung the lantern flashlight from a hook in the ceiling and approached the cartons stacked against the far wall.

"We're looking for something marked 'Manuscripts seventy-nine to eighty-one,'" she said, and ran her gloved hand over a box to brush away the dust, which she could already feel in her throat. The neat block printing read TAXES/FINANCE 1990s. The next box read SCRAP FABRIC.

"I guess the dust doesn't bother you," she said to Dorothy Parker.

"Not a bit."

"Good. You start on that side of the room." Norah wiped another carton and the dust was so noxious to her lungs that she pulled her shirt over her nose and mouth as she continued working. She had only cleared six more boxes when she realized she had to leave the room for some fresh air.

"Be right back," she said, descending the ladder. She went into the kitchen to pull off the gloves and splash some water on her face, reminding herself that healthy people didn't choke to death from inhaling dust. She was strong enough to cough up whatever got in her lungs.

Norah cleared her throat and went back up the ladder, only to discover that Dorothy Parker had disappeared.

"Great," she muttered, angry that she had to do it all herself while Dorothy Parker became one with the dust. Norah cleared box after box, trying to ignore the coating in her throat. She dragged several across the floor so she could get to the ones in back. So far, she didn't even find anything related to publishing. They were all personal items—photo albums, trophies, vases, books, records, and old files.

The sun was getting lower in the sky, and she could barely read the labels as the lantern cast only a small pool of light. Soon, she'd have to find a flashlight to decipher the words. A couple of dry coughs turned into a full-blown fit that left her dizzy. She didn't want to go downstairs again and waste precious sunlight time, so she continued on, trying to keep her mouth shut tight and breathe only through her nose.

She quickly cleared four more boxes, but it was now too dark to read the writing; it was time to find that flashlight.

There was nothing in the cupboard where she had found the lantern and gloves, but she struck pay dirt under the kitchen sink—a heavy, black Maglite. She pushed the button to turn it on and nothing happened; the batteries were dead. She spent the next fifteen minutes looking for replacements, but came up empty. She wished she had thought to ask Aviva for her phone number.

Norah helped herself to a glass of cold water from the refrigerator dispenser, then went back up the ladder, hoping the dim light of her cell phone would be enough to help her read the labeled boxes. She cleared the dust off a carton, held her phone up to it, and was excited to discover that it said *LITTON PRESS/1976–1978*. At last—she was getting close!

Norah imagined confronting Ted with the smoking gun that exonerated him and convicted Audrey. He would be furious at being forced to tell the truth, but he would do it. Ted would feel it was his duty to go on live TV and explain that he had driven her to it. Norah could envision him sitting across from Simon Janey, holding on to the arms of the chair as the interviewer leaned forward and asked the questions America wanted to hear.

Norah's cell phone emitted a low-battery warning sound. Worse, the lantern hanging from the ceiling was getting dimmer. There wasn't much time.

She managed to clear the dust from three more boxes, but her cell phone went completely dead. She retrieved the lantern and brought it closer, hoping she had struck gold, because she knew this was her last chance. Unfortunately, the boxes were even older, dating back to 1974.

It was now too dark to search. She went back down the ladder to think, and to run through her options. She could keep looking through the house for more batteries or flashlights. Maybe there was even an extension cord that would enable her to run one of the bedroom lamps into the attic. If all else failed, she could get back in the car and try to find a local drugstore that was open late.

While scrounging around in the kitchen drawers she found a charger that was compatible with her cell phone, so at least there was that.

"I don't know if you can hear me," she shouted up into the dark attic, "but I'm running out to see if I can buy some batteries. If you have any sense at all, you'll keep looking while I'm gone. The sooner we find that box, the sooner we can leave."

17

Dust. Darkness. Clutter. It meant nothing to Dorothy Parker. All she had to do was relax into her formless state and let her particles settle where she wished. Finding the right carton had taken her almost no time at all.

Of course, she wasn't going to tell Norah that, as the ambitious young woman would want to pack up and head right back to the city. That bottle of wine and the deck overlooking the Long Island Sound presented a rare opportunity for Dorothy Parker, and she wasn't about to give it up.

And so she hovered in the attic, letting the clock run out. Meanwhile, she found something even better than the Bordeaux—a dusty bottle of aged Glenfarclas Scotch that had probably been long forgotten. No doubt it was quite valuable—a rare treat.

When she heard Norah leave to buy batteries or some such nonsense, she let her particles settle into corporeal form. Then she hid the carton that was labeled *LITTON PRESS/1979–1981* by simply pushing it to the other side of the attic, so that it was grouped with the boxes Norah had already looked at. She would wait until morning to tell Norah it was there. Meanwhile, she carried the Scotch and the tote bag out of the attic.

Dorothy Parker found a bar glass in the kitchen cabinet and ice cubes in the freezer. Perfect. She brought her glass and the bottle of Scotch out onto the deck, where she eased herself into a wooden Adirondack chair overlooking the Sound. She took a small sip of the drink. It was like nuts and honey and something she couldn't place. The last time she had tasted such exquisite Scotch was during Prohibition. She was in a terrible depression—over a man, of course—and had been thinking about a quick solution involving razor blades and a bathtub. Then Mr. Benchley showed up at her door with a bottle of Scotch—the real stuff. It was dearer than gold in those days, and he wanted her to have it. She had never known anyone so caring and loyal. Dear Mr. Benchley. She took another sip and realized what else it tasted like. Friendship.

She looked across the dark water, aware that the Gold Coast of Long Island was out there on the opposite side, invisible but stolid, the old estates crumbling or fortified, razed or rebuilt. After decades of eavesdropping on conversations at the Algonquin, she had learned that the nouveaux riche were still drawn there, taken in by the promise of buying their way into a place at the table of American royalty, a class that invented itself when the nation was so young it was possible for a man to build an empire on nothing but ruthless ambition and audacity.

She had amused herself at those great estates, spending drunken weekends at lavish parties. It was all such a blur, though she was pretty sure the wild affairs at the Swopes' estate had inspired Scott to write that Gatsby book. She didn't remember it the way he did, of course. Mostly she recalled avoiding the bacchanalia by sitting at the driveway with a drink while waiting for other guests to arrive. Then there were those awful dinners, where she was expected to entertain the luminaries. She was dutiful, of course—it was the rent she paid for her room and board. Once, she was seated between Albert Ritchie, governor of Maryland, and a boorish pal of Swope's—a newspaperman who couldn't hold his liquor. In the middle of dinner the reporter emitted a loud and ghastly belch. The table went quiet for a moment and she seized the opportunity by turning to the governor. "You will, I trust, grant him a pardon."

She probably wouldn't have remembered the incident if not for the way it had been quoted for the rest of the miserable weekend.

Still, she almost never turned down an invitation to those parties. After all, the food and drinks were free. But regret often bore down on her the moment she arrived. Woollcott was usually the ringleader, finding friends with obscene wealth who would entertain them for days at a time. One such horse's ass was a banker with a massive estate in Cold Spring Harbor. When she arrived, everyone was in such good cheer she wanted to spit. She could barely wait for a kindred spirit to arrive, and at last someone did. It was Mr. Benchley. "I knew it would be terrible," she said as he got out of the car, "but I didn't know it would be as bad as this. This isn't just plain terrible. This is fancy terrible. This is terrible with raisins in it."

God, how she missed him. He was one of the only true friends she'd ever had. She would go into the white light in a second if she thought she would get to be with him. But no, he was traveling in his own circle, and that didn't include her.

Dorothy Parker polished off the Scotch in her glass and poured another.

18

N orah pulled into the driveway, ready to get right back to work
and find that carton with Ted's manuscripts. She rushed into
the house with the flashlights and the extra batteries she had just
bought, and saw Mrs. Parker out on the deck, relaxing. Damn her.
Didn't she understand they still had work to do? Norah dropped her
package on the counter and went outside, armed with indignation.

When she got close, however, she saw that Dorothy Parker's eyes
were barely open and her face wet with tears.

"Are you okay?"

"Pardon?"

Norah glanced down and saw the half-empty bottle of Scotch on
the side table. "Seriously?" she said, picking it up. "You drank this
whole thing?"

Dorothy Parker tilted her head back to look at the bottle.
"Not yet."

"We're supposed to be looking for something."

Mrs. Parker held her hands toward the expanse of water. "Can't
we just appreciate what we have?"

"Thanks a lot for the *help*."

"You need to have more fun, dear. Pour yourself a tall one."

"Where did you get this, anyway?" Norah said, examining the bottle. "It looks expensive."

"I should think so, yes. Terribly expensive."

"You can't just take something like this. They might have been saving it."

"Save? One should *save* money perhaps, but not Scotch. Of course, I've never done either. But if I were rich, I'd spend all my money on expensive liquor and share it with my friends. Yes, that is precisely what I would do."

"I'm getting back to work."

Mrs. Parker stared at the horizon and sighed. "I would have made a darling millionaire."

Norah headed back toward the house and hesitated, wondering if she should close the Algonquin guest book. When she opened it again, Mrs. Parker would be sober and able to help her search the attic. She glanced back at her drunken accomplice, and saw her staring across the water, weeping. She decided to leave her alone with her memories, and went upstairs to search on her own.

It took several hours to examine all the other cartons, as Norah had to take frequent breaks to clear her throat. At last, she had to admit defeat. There simply was no box of manuscripts from 1981. The trip had been for nothing.

Tired, hungry, and dirty, she closed the attic door and went out onto the deck to check on Dorothy Parker, who was snoring softly. She wished she could sleep, too, but it didn't seem right. Despondent as she was, Norah wanted to return the car, as she had promised.

She went into the kitchen and made herself some coffee so she could stay awake for the drive home. It did nothing for her spirits, but she managed to tidy the house so that it looked as clean as it had when they arrived. She splashed some water in her face and went out on the deck again. Dorothy Parker was still asleep.

"Mrs. Parker," Norah said, shaking her shoulder. "Mrs. Parker?"

Norah knew that all she had to do was close the book and open it again, and Mrs. Parker would make a sober companion. But she decided she was in no mood for company, anyway. She would drive home in silence, a closed guest book on the seat beside her.

Shortly after she hit the road, Norah's bladder reminded her about that coffee she'd had before leaving, and so she found a gas station with a restroom. She needed to fill up the tank, anyway.

Afterward, she hesitated before pulling back onto the highway, wondering if conversation would help her stay awake and focused. But was she really in the mood to talk?

The driver behind Norah honked.

"Okay, okay," she said, and merged into traffic. She drove on in silence, but after a while, the steady *thump, thump* of tires on pavement became hypnotic, and she realized a distraction would probably do her some good. She opened the book on the passenger seat, and Mrs. Parker's form took shape right on top of it.

"Where are we going dear?" she asked.

"Back to the city."

"Thank goodness."

Norah glanced at her. "You seem recovered."

"Quite."

"You looked so melancholy out there. At first I thought it was just the Scotch, but then I realized you were probably reminiscing about the good old days."

"Hardly. To quote Franklin Pierce Adams, 'Nothing is more responsible for the good old days than a bad old memory.'"

"Sorry to hear that," Norah said. "I thought you might share some happy stories to cheer me up."

"Why do you need cheering up? Didn't you find the carton you were looking for?"

"Why would you assume that?"

"Because we're heading back."

"It wasn't there."

"It most certainly was," Mrs. Parker said.

"I looked everywhere."

"My dear, I saw it. I know precisely where it is. Now turn this automobile around."

Half an hour later they were back in the attic, and Dorothy Parker showed Norah where the carton was.

"How did I miss this?" Norah said, dragging it to the ladder.

"I'm sure I have no idea."

Norah carried the carton to the kitchen, going over it in her mind. She had carefully read the labels on every box. There just didn't seem to be any way she could have missed it.

She dropped the carton on the countertop and looked around for a pair of scissors to cut through the tape. Unable to find one, she pulled a long chef's knife from the block on the counter. She stared at the reflection of her eyes in the blade, wondering how she had missed seeing the carton when she had read the label on *every* box she pushed aside. There was only one way that particular carton could have wound up in that spot—Dorothy Parker put it there.

And she knew why.

"It was you!" she said to Dorothy Parker as she held up the knife. "You hid it from me so you could drink that Scotch."

"You don't have to get touchy about it," Mrs. Parker said.

"I think you're confusing me with Audrey Hudson," Norah said. "But that doesn't mean I'm not furious."

"If you hadn't closed the book, I would have told you."

Norah was in no mood to argue. She needed to see what was inside that carton. She carefully sliced through the tape that was holding it shut, and took a deep breath. "If you believe in prayer, now would be a good time."

"I believe a lot of things—that true love is impossible, that no person in the history of the world ever had a happy ending, that the only cure for a hangover is another hangover. But I do not believe in prayer."

"Suit yourself," Norah said, and closed her eyes for a moment to ask her mother—or whatever guiding spirit might be watching over her—to please make sure both versions of Ted's *Settlers Ridge* manuscript would be found inside this box.

She opened the top flaps of the carton, and there were indeed typed pages inside. But the manuscript on top was *Good-bye, Hollywood* by Marilyn McIntyre. Norah's heart beat faster. It *had* to be in here. It just had to.

She lifted the manuscript, which had been bound in a rubber band that had long ago disintegrated, and carefully set it aside. And there, underneath, she saw it—a title page typed in old-fashioned Courier font:

SETTLERS RIDGE
by Ted Shriver
Final Draft

A chill traveled down Norah's back. "God," she whispered.

Dorothy Parker looked over her shoulder. "Is that it?"

Norah gripped the manuscript like she was lifting a sacred relic. Beneath it was another copy with the same title page, but a handwritten note on a narrow slip of yellow paper was clipped to the top. It read: *Aviva, here's the final version of Ted's latest. Please discard previous.—Audrey.*

Norah looked straight up and whispered, "Thank you." Then she laid both manuscripts side by side. Each bore a stamp in the lower right-hand corner. The first manuscript was stamped *RECEIVED JAN 7 1981* and the one with Audrey's note was stamped *RECEIVED JAN 8 1981*.

Norah began turning over the pages, comparing the different versions. The one on the right, with the yellow note, was on the slick, chemically treated paper of an old-fashioned photocopy. Norah continued flipping pages, looking from left to right. This went on for several minutes until she reached a page in the photocopied version that appeared to be on typing paper.

"Look," Norah said. "She retyped a whole chapter."

And there it was—the page that contained the three paragraphs that were not in the original.

Norah sat down to take it all in. Here was absolute proof of Audrey's culpability, and she knew exactly how she would use it to reel Ted in. This could change everything.

19

I t's me," Pete said, knocking on the door to Ted's hotel room.

There was no answer. He put his ear to the door and held his breath. At last he heard the soft creak of the mattress and exhaled.

He knocked again. "Don't ignore me."

"I'm tired."

"So what? I've been tired since 1992."

"You're a pain in the ass, you know that?"

"Another thing we have in common. Open up. I brought Hennessy."

The door opened and Pete thought his friend did indeed look tired—even worse than he had on their last visit. And he feared that, with each passing day, the tumor grew and Ted's chance of surviving the surgery diminished.

"Jesus," he said, studying the blue-black crescents under his friend's eyes, "don't you sleep?"

"I'll sleep when I'm dead, which won't be long now."

Pete handed Ted the liquor store package and a box of cigars. "No excuse for the way this place smells," he said, walking into the room. "You stockpiling dirty dishes?"

"If it bothers you, leave."

Pete moved the grimy plates from the table onto the room service cart and wheeled it out the door of the room and into the hallway. He went to the window and opened it. "Wouldn't kill you to let them come in and clean once in a while," he said.

"If it wouldn't kill me, what's the point?"

Pete went into the bathroom, rinsed out two glasses and brought them back into the room. He opened the cognac right under his face so he could experience it—the sweet gas of fermentation quickly blossoming into the syrupy aroma he loved. He took a deep sniff and then poured the drinks.

"I have a new title for you," he said, handing Ted a drink.

"Duke? Emperor? Prince of Darkness?"

"For *Louse*, I mean."

Ted straightened in his seat. "You read it?"

"I did," Pete said. He couldn't resist withholding praise for at least a few beats, because he knew what was coming.

"What did you think?"

And there it was. Pete smiled. He never knew a writer—from the meekest neurotic to the most blustery curmudgeon—who didn't need his ego stroked.

"I wept from the magnitude of your genius."

"Fuck you."

"I'm not entirely kidding. Okay, maybe I didn't weep, but I could have. This book moved me. The cross-purposes of Alston and Macy were excruciating. His emotional paralysis was heartbreaking, but her arc felt so unexpected, so . . . hopeful. I honestly didn't know you had it in you. I loved these characters, Ted. I loved the imagery— that house, the town. Everything. It's your best yet."

"You'll probably be disappointed in the other two."

"'Thank you' would work, too."

Ted lifted his drink to toast. "Glad you liked it."

Pete touched his glass to Ted's. "Me, too."

"You said you had a new title?"

Pete swallowed a sip of cognac and let himself enjoy the warmth creating a path to his middle. He put down his glass. "What do you think of *Bad Husband*?"

Ted sipped his drink and considered it. "A little obvious."

"And *Louse* isn't?"

"I guess it works." He closed his eyes to think. "*Bad Husband*. I suppose that could grow on me."

"This one could go all the way, Ted—National Book Award, Pulitzer . . . who knows?"

"Not with my history. I'm a notorious plagiarist, remember?"

Pete took a deep breath. This was going to get rough. "That's what I wanted to talk to you about."

"Not this again. I told you, there's just—"

"Those women came to see me," Pete said. He held his drink in both hands and leaned forward until his friend looked him in the eye. "I know it was Audrey."

Ted put his glass down hard. "Bitches," he muttered.

"It was bound to come out."

"I'll write a letter to the *Times* denying it. My dying words."

"No you won't."

"Don't you get it? I don't give a shit about awards."

"I think you do. And besides, you can deny it all you want, it won't matter." He stopped and glanced at Ted, whose focus had wandered. He stared into the distance, his brow tight, like he was trying to figure something out. Pete assumed he was going through his options, looking for a way to suppress the truth.

"Ted," Pete said, waiting for eye contact. He didn't want to drop the bomb without his friend's full attention.

"Hm?"

"I'm sorry, pal, but we have proof. *Hard* proof." Peter Salzberg rose and laid a hand on his friend's shoulder. "We found the old manuscripts—the one you turned in and the one Audrey doctored."

Ted knocked Pete's hand away and stood. He went to the window and looked out. He pounded the wall with his fist.

"I know you're angry," Pete said, "but listen—"

"Burn them. You hear me? Burn those fucking manuscripts."

"I can't."

"Of course you can."

"I don't even have them."

"What?"

"Those women producers," Pete said, "from *Simon Janey*, they—"

"Goddamn it!" Ted pulled at his own hair and turned to face Pete. "You listen. Those little shits are blackmailing me to go on that fucking TV show. And for what? I'm supposed to explain how I drove her to it? You think anyone's going to accept that? She'll be torn to shreds. The vultures will pick at her bones."

"You think I give a damn if you go on the TV show?"

"What do you want, then?"

"You know damned well."

Ted threw his hands up.

"Like it or not," Pete said, "it's going to come out. And when it does, she's going to need you. If you won't have the surgery for yourself, have it for Audrey."

"Oh, please."

"I mean it, Ted."

"You think she's going to hate me one iota less when this comes out? You think *my* shoulder is the one she's going to cry on?"

"She might."

"You don't know shit."

"Don't you at least owe it to her to stick around . . . to try to mitigate some of the bad press?"

Ted turned back to the window and put his hand on the glass as if he were trying to hold on to something in the distance. "I'm not having the surgery."

"You're an idiot."

"What else is new?"

"What do you think you're proving? Haven't you punished yourself enough?"

Ted sat down again and picked up his cognac. He took a sip and closed his eyes. "I'm not like you, Pete. I don't have a wife and kid to live for. You have two grandchildren, for God's sake. What do I have on this earth? A glass of cognac? A book award? It's all meaningless."

Pete tried to imagine how much fight he would have in him if it wasn't for his family. He pictured Jacob, the baby, the way he had looked last week when he fell asleep in the car seat, his small red mouth open, a strand of clean saliva wetting his shirt. Babies. Even their spit made your heart ache with love.

It was true—without his family, Pete had nothing. Still, there had to be something Ted was willing to live for. "I'm not ready to give up on you," he said.

"Now who's the idiot?"

There was a sharp rap on the door and Ted held his head in his hands. "Just tell them to go away," he said to his friend.

"Who is it?" Pete called.

"Aviva!"

Ted grunted. "If she's here to castrate me," he said, "tell her it's a moot point."

Pete opened the door and kissed his wife on the cheek. "I thought you were on your way to London."

"Taxi's downstairs with the meter running—I have to be at JFK in an hour. Just couldn't leave yet." She turned to Ted. "God, you look terrible."

Pete glanced at his wife and could see she was truly unsettled by Ted's appearance. She swallowed hard.

"I tried making a deal with the devil," Ted replied, "but it didn't work out. You, on the other hand—"

"If you tell me I look great 'for my age,' I'll rip your heart from your chest."

Ted bowed his head. "It's good to see you, too, Aviva."

"What is it—twenty years?" she asked. "No wait, twenty-five."

"And you've been busy. I understand you now rule the world."

"A little corner of it."

"You publish a lot of crap."

"You always were a snob," she said, approaching him. She kissed him on both cheeks, European-style.

"You don't hate me anymore?" he asked.

She took his hands in hers and knelt in front of him, looking into his eyes. "Ted Shriver, you are probably the biggest horse's ass I have ever known. You cheated on a woman who would have done anything for you. Then you blew a brilliant career in order to punish yourself. And now you're letting yourself die because you think you'll earn points for martyrdom. For a genius, you are *astoundingly* stupid."

"You can put that on my tombstone."

"If it were up to me," she said, "I would."

"Why did you come?"

"Despite what you think of my taste in literature, I've always been in awe of your talent." He tried to pull away but she kept going. "No, listen. I mean it. I think it's obscene that you're letting the world believe you're a plagiarist. If you want to let yourself die because you think you deserve it, that's your business. But as an artist—"

"Okay, I get it. You're an emissary from the literary world. But what the hell do you need my blessing for? You've got your proof. If you're going to destroy Audrey, don't expect me to sign off on it."

Aviva dropped his hands and stood. "She destroyed *herself*, Ted."

"I thought you were her friend."

"That was before I knew what she did. And before I knew she had been lying to me for all these years."

Ted picked up his glass and downed the rest of his cognac. "Have you seen her lately?"

"Yesterday."

He put down his glass. "How is she?" he said softly.

Aviva folded her arms. "Not good."

"Sick?"

She shook her head and sighed. "Physically? No."

Ted nodded. They all knew Audrey had always teetered on the edge. "How bad?"

"She pulled a gun on me."

He stared at her, trying to determine if she was serious. "Is that a joke?"

"I wish."

Ted stood and paced the room. "When she gets scared, she just can't control herself. She's like a trapped animal—she'll do anything to escape."

"Are you *defending* her?"

"She's damaged."

"That's my point," Aviva said. "She was damaged before you met her. You didn't do this to her."

"I broke her."

"You were a piece of shit, I'll grant you that. And for a long time I believed you pushed her over the edge. But I see now that she was hanging by such a frayed thread that *anything* could have sent her spiraling."

"Someone needs to help her," he said.

Aviva stared at him, frustrated. She shook her head and sighed, and Pete thought she looked like she needed fortification. He offered her his cognac and she took a sip and turned back to Ted. "I don't know if that's possible," she said.

"Poor Audrey," he said.

"For twenty-five years 'poor Audrey' made you take the blame for something she did. Now it's her turn."

"She doesn't deserve it."

"Like hell she doesn't," Aviva said. "Listen, I have to go. I'm sorry." She gave Ted a hug and looked into his eyes one last time. "If I don't see you again—"

"I don't do sentimental."

"Okay, then. I'll see you around."

Pete gave her a kiss good-bye and opened the door for her, only to discover the petite woman producer standing outside holding a tote bag.

"What are you doing here?" he asked.

"I need to speak with Teddy," she said. "I heard voices, so I thought I'd wait."

"You could have knocked," he said. "I'm sure you're very busy."

"You'd be surprised."

Aviva apologized to her, explaining that she had a taxi waiting to take her to the airport.

"Have a relaxing trip, dear."

"Me?" Aviva said. "Never. I go in, I do my business, I leave."

"Like the Luftwaffe. Bon voyage."

Aviva waved and disappeared down the hallway.

"See you Tuesday!" Pete called, and then turned to the other woman. "You may as well come in."

"Delighted," she said, holding tight to the tote bag that was slung over her shoulder. Then she took a deep breath and stepped over the threshold.

20

"Can I offer you a cognac, Didi?" Pete asked.

Didi? Ted looked at Dorothy Parker to see her response to the strange nickname, but it didn't seem to register.

"I certainly hope so," she said.

Pete went into the bathroom to rinse out another glass and Ted leaned in toward her. "Why did he call you *Didi?*"

"Get rid of him and I'll explain."

"I'd rather get rid of *you*," he said, though he didn't exactly mean it. For the moment, at least, he was glad for the company.

"Sorry we have to use bathroom glasses," Pete said, coming back into the room. "Next time I'll bring snifters."

"Don't worry about her," Ted said. "She'd drink straight from the bottle if she had to."

"True," she said. "I've sipped whiskey out of everything from a gold flask to a stained teacup. I'll drink from anything but a slotted spoon."

Pete poured a glass of cognac and handed it to her. "Did you know that during Prohibition people in speakeasies hid their liquor by drinking it from teacups?"

Ted leaned back and smirked, curious to see how Dorothy Parker would handle Pete's misapprehension.

"You don't say," she muttered, her expression unchanged.

"It's true."

"Why, the poor things. How awful it must have been for them."

Pete pulled out the desk chair and sat, and Ted could tell he hadn't picked up on the sarcasm. And why would he? As far as Pete was concerned, she was just an ordinary woman.

"I imagine it was pretty exciting," Pete said.

"Like being tied to the railroad tracks," Mrs. Parker responded.

"I take it you don't romanticize the Prohibition era?"

"My dear Mr. Salzberg," Dorothy Parker said as she sipped her drink, "there is nothing romantic about living with the constant fear of having your skull cracked open by a billy club during a raid."

"Come on—it was postwar and pre-Depression. There's plenty of photographic evidence to suggest the revelers were having a grand old time."

"They were drunk, dear, there's a difference."

"What do you think, Ted?" Pete asked. "Are *drunk* and *happy* mutually exclusive?"

"*Life* and *happy* are mutually exclusive," he said, rubbing his head. At the moment, speaking took more energy than he could comfortably manage. Still, he hoped they would stay awhile. It wasn't that he was hungry for company, but sometimes he felt like the quiet would swallow him whole.

"There's my boy," Dorothy Parker said.

Pete shook his head. "I'm outnumbered by cynics."

She put down her drink. "The best thing I can say about Prohibition is that poisonous gin didn't always blind you. Sometimes it finished the job and killed you."

Pete laughed. "Isn't there anything about the Roaring Twenties you admire?"

"Admire? I admire a poem that leaves me speechless. I admire New York on a shiny blue and white autumn day. I admire the simple love of a dumb animal . . . especially if he dresses well and picks up the tab. But I most certainly do *not* admire a ten-year party filled with fools who were overly impressed with themselves."

"But the *writers*," Pete said.

"The worst of the lot."

"I have to disagree with you," Pete said. "A lot of brilliant authors came out of that era."

Dorothy Parker took a pack of cigarettes from her bag. She pulled one out, put it to her lips, and placed a lighter on the table in front of Pete. "Far outnumbered by ghastly ones, I assure you," she said.

Pete picked up her cue and lit the cigarette for her. "You have the most interesting friends," he said to Ted.

"She's not my friend."

"Nevertheless," Pete said, finishing his drink. "I'd better be going." He stood. "I'll be back tomorrow, Ted."

After Peter Salzberg left, Dorothy and Ted sat in silence for several minutes.

"I suppose you want me to explain why he called me Didi," she said.

Ted shrugged. "My curiosity has waned. You can leave now, if you want."

"I'll do nothing of the sort."

"I'm not signing that book. And I'm certainly not going on that talk show. So we have nothing to discuss."

"You know, Norah and I found your original manuscript, as well as the one Audrey altered."

Audrey. Her name was a storm and its aftermath. That was how he thought of her—like dark, angry clouds and hurricane winds. Like a home with its roof blown off. Like the frail kitten found shivering under a chair.

The worst part of it—the part he tried so hard to capture in the novel Pete had read—was his own black heart. Aviva found his boozy callousness despicable. She assumed that getting blind drink for days and cheating on Audrey again and again was selfish and irresponsible. But it was worse than that. His real crime wasn't indifference—it was cruelty. He had hurt Audrey intentionally. He wasn't aware of it at the time, but later, when he examined himself in the same harsh light he shone on his characters, he knew. Her pain had lit him up, made him feel alive. It excited him.

And for that, he had to be punished.

"So I heard," he said.

"You understand what this means," she said.

"Yes, you're going to finish the job I started and destroy Audrey completely." His head began to throb and he welcomed the pain.

"That is not our intent."

"No? Didn't you pay her a visit that nearly scared her to death?"

"I think you got that backward, my dear."

"Aviva told me. But what did you expect? You can't ambush someone who's that unglued and assume they're going to keep it together." Ted closed his eyes, picturing Audrey as that kitten trembling under a chair. Only, he was the storm that blew the roof off the house. And now these women were stomping through the wreckage without watching where they planted their feet.

"You don't understand her," he continued. "You don't even know how frightened she felt. She's been carrying the secret for a long time."

"You think I don't understand desperation?"

"Is that how she seemed? Desperate?"

"Indeed. She thought we had come to offer her work. Apparently, she is in need."

So Audrey was out of work and probably strapped. Ted finished the last drops of cognac in his glass and poured more. He wished

DOROTHY PARKER DRANK HERE

there was some way to get her to cash the post-alimony checks he had sent. She didn't need to be broke on top of everything else.

"Can't Aviva help her find work?"

"I suspect she has tried."

God. How he'd ruined her. And now everyone was trying to convince him to stick around for Audrey's sake, when the best thing he could do for her was vanish forever.

He imagined what it must have felt like for Audrey to open the door for these women, assuming they were there to offer her a job, only to discover they had come to tell her they knew the terrible secret she had been keeping.

Then another thought occurred to him and he looked around, confused. "How did you get in here? I thought you couldn't go anywhere without that guest book."

She held up the tote bag. "It's in here," she said. "I can't carry the book itself, but if it's inside something, I can bring it with me. In a manner of speaking, I've been liberated. I can now cross a threshold from room to room."

"And this is where you choose to be? Of all the places in the world?"

"Teddy dear, consider what this could mean for you. Audrey is going to fall to pieces once the story of her plagiarism comes out. And where will you be? Dead and gone—of no use to her or anyone else. And she will *never* stop blaming herself. But if you sign the book—"

"Stop," he said.

"If you sign the book, you can go see her."

He sighed. "This conversation is over."

"Think about it, Ted."

"Time for you to leave."

"What about Norah's television show?"

He rose, grabbed the tote bag, and headed toward the door.

"I've been thrown out of better places," she said, following him. "But I'll leave you with this to think about: Why abandon her now, when she needs you the most? Haven't you hurt her enough?"

"The best thing I can do for her," he said, "is drop dead." Then he opened the door, threw the tote bag into the hallway, and Dorothy Parker disappeared from his room in a cloud of dust. He watched for a moment as the particles hovered outside his room, but before they could take form again, he slammed the door.

21

Norah believed *Simon Janey Live* still had a chance. The discovery of those manuscripts could convince Ted to do the show so he could mitigate the damage to Audrey. Still, she knew she had to do the responsible thing. And so she had reached out to the five most influential television people she knew, sending off her current résumé.

Norah opened her laptop to check her e-mail. Two had written back, saying they didn't have any openings. One said she would keep her résumé "on file." Another simply ignored her. The last one—a network showrunner—told her he forwarded her e-mail to the executive producer of a new reality show about people who have overweight pets. Seriously? Chubby Chihuahuas? Dumpy dachshunds? She'd rather go back to accounting.

Norah tried making a list of other contacts she could reach out to, but her heart wasn't in it. She loved working on *Simon Janey Live*. And it wasn't just her coworkers. She believed in the show. She loved being in the studio and watching it live, that heart-pounding moment when Simon put his hand to his mouth just before letting out *the* question—the one nobody had dared ask. Sometimes it was the question you didn't even realize was important until you heard it. But there it was, on live television. And as the camera closed in on the guest, you could tell if they were trying to come up with a way around the answer. Then came the best moment of all—that tiny sigh. And you knew they were going to give it all up, right there on live TV.

There was a knock on the door and Norah opened it. Dorothy Parker had returned. As always, her expression was inscrutable.

"Any luck?" Norah asked.

"I was unceremoniously dismissed," Mrs. Parker said, walking past her.

"But you told him about the manuscripts?"

"Apparently, Peter Salzberg beat me to the punch."

"And?"

"He's intractable."

Norah paced the room, thinking. There had to be another way in. "Did you learn anything?" she said.

"That, my dear, is a question people asked me my whole damned life."

"You didn't get a single fresh insight?"

"I can tell you he seems quite convinced Audrey wants him dead."

Norah considered Audrey's unequivocal reaction when they brought up Ted's name. "He might be right," she said, sitting. Still, there was something about Ted's feelings for Audrey she couldn't quite understand. It was as if she were missing the center gear that made the whole machine run. "Did he talk about her? What did he say?"

"He's worried about her lack of employment."

"I wish he was worried about *mine*. I may be days away from being unemployed."

"My dear, this could be helpful information. Teddy longs for Audrey to get work. If you could facilitate that—"

"I don't have those kinds of connections, Mrs. Parker. I work for a

TV show that's about to be canceled." Norah knew Dorothy Parker was right—at this point, their best chance at getting Ted's cooperation would be to come up with a plan that would help Audrey. But what could they do for this pathetic woman?

"Perhaps you can entreat your boss to make a recommendation."

"First of all, it's kind of hard to get behind a recommendation for someone who pulled a gun on your associate producer. Besides, Audrey's not a TV writer. Her career is in print journalism."

Mrs. Parker lowered the tote bag onto the floor and took a seat. "Pity."

Norah stared down at the bag containing the guest book, and an idea hit her right in the throat. "My God," she whispered.

Dorothy Parker followed Norah's eyes to the tote bag. "What exactly are you thinking?"

"I know how we can help her." Norah smiled. It was perfect. She reached into the bag and pulled out the Algonquin guest book, which was still held open by the piece of cardboard tied in place. "This," she said, "is our answer."

"Norah, dear—"

"Listen, if we promise Ted that we can catapult Audrey's journalism career by giving her the lead of a lifetime, he'll agree to anything. I bet on it!"

"Someone already wrote a story about the guest book. It was not that long ago, and it certainly didn't change anyone's career."

Norah leaned forward. "That was just a story about a book of signatures. This would be a story about the book's power. It would be about *you*."

Dorothy Parker tightened her lips. "That, my dear, is simply not possible."

"Why not?"

"Even a benign article about the book had devastating consequences. That awful Edie Coates showed up, claiming ownership.

And someone had the nerve to tear the last page from the book, depriving me of my dearest companion."

Norah understood. Dorothy Parker had explained to her about losing her dear little poodle. After that, her loneliness became unbearable.

"But this could fix everything," Norah insisted. "We can tell Ted we'll give Audrey the story only under two conditions—he has to agree to go on *Simon Janey Live*, and he has to sign the book."

"Your little plan would leave me completely vulnerable. Anyone could claim possession of the book, and then where would I be?"

"I'll protect you," she said, holding tight to the open book in her lap. "I'll talk to the hotel management and make sure the book is kept someplace safe."

"That will never work."

"Of course it will."

"If you think I'm going to show up and do parlor tricks for Audrey Hudson or anyone else, you are very much mistaken."

Norah untied the shoelaces from the guest book and removed the cardboard. She stared down at the brittle pages, browning at the edges.

"Leave that alone," Mrs. Parker said.

"Don't you trust me?" Norah said.

"I trust no one."

Norah thought about all the people who could attest to the existence of the book's famous ghost—Angel the staff member, Tiny the bodyguard, Edie Coates the upholstered. Even Peter Salzberg and Aviva Kravette could be interviewed about the woman they had believed was Didi Dickson. And with a little more digging, who knew how many others could turn up? The truth was, she didn't need a cooperative spirit. In fact, the story might be even sexier without hard proof. The air of mystery would invite controversy and speculation. It could grow and grow until Audrey herself was a celebrity.

Norah didn't want to be unfair to Dorothy Parker, but what other choice did she have? This was her last chance to save *Simon Janey Live* . . . and to connect with Ted Shriver. She would do her best to protect the book and keep it out of the wrong hands. And if Dorothy Parker one day found herself in an untenable situation, perhaps it would be the motivation she needed to go into the white light. And that was where she belonged, wasn't it?

"My dear," Dorothy Parker said, "I believe we can find a better way of accomplishing your goals."

"I believe," Norah said, "that we've exhausted every other possibility."

"Then our journey has reached an unhappy end, because your proposal is simply not acceptable to me. I will not go along with it. Now, get me a drink."

Norah rose, went into the bathroom, and applied the plum-red lipstick that made her look formidable. She coughed and cleared her throat. "I'm sorry to have to tell you this," she called as she inspected her hair and fluffed her dark curls, "but I don't believe this journey is over."

"Whatever do you mean?" Mrs. Parker asked as Norah emerged.

"I mean," Norah said, "that I don't need your permission." Then she closed the book and Dorothy Parker vanished.

I know you can hear me," Norah said as she knocked on the door of Ted Shriver's room. "I wouldn't have come back if I didn't have something very important to tell you . . . about Audrey."

"What about her?" Ted said through the closed door.

"I have a lead for her—a story she'll be able to sell to almost any magazine or newspaper in the country." Norah moved closer and put her hand on the door, envisioning Ted right on the other side, just inches away. "She'll never be out of work again."

Ted opened the door a crack, leaving the latch in place. "Why would you do that?"

Norah stared through the small space at his tired eyes. They were bloodshot and pained. "To get you to agree to come on *Simon Janey Live*," she said. "That's the condition."

He went quiet for a moment. She waited, searching for hope in the silence. If he didn't tell her to fuck off, he might agree. That is, if he was actually listening.

"What's the story?" he finally said.

Norah swallowed, relieved. "Dorothy Parker," she said, holding up the Algonquin guest book. "That's the story. I'm going to tell Audrey the truth about this book."

"Why would anyone believe it?"

"Witnesses. Me, you, that frightened hotel employee, your monster bodyguard, Pete and Aviva. I'm sure there are others, too."

"People will think she's crazy."

"People already think she's crazy. The point is, some will buy it, some will be skeptical, and *everyone* will be talking about it. She'll wind up on talk shows. She'll get a book deal. It'll be huge."

He looked down, and Norah waited, listening to him breathe as he contemplated her offer.

"It's what she's always wanted," he finally said.

"So you agree? You'll do the talk show if I give her what she needs to write this story?"

"How do I know you won't pull the rug out from under her?"

He was looking right at her. Couldn't he sense her devotion to him?

"I wouldn't do that to you," she said, and felt sure he would understand how loaded those words were. Her affection was complicated but formidable. Surely he could feel that.

"TV people are the scum of the earth."

"Don't you trust me?" she said, and realized that her voice came out small, like a little girl's. Her eyes dampened but she wouldn't look away. She stared straight at him, willing him to trust her, to understand that there was a bond between them that she never would break.

"Why should I?"

She swallowed against a tense tangle of nerves in her throat, and knew she had to offer something real. "I know what it means to carry a secret around for someone you love . . . to protect someone who can't protect themselves. I've been doing it my whole life."

He blinked, and she felt something change. He knew she was telling the truth.

"Who is it?" he asked.

"What?"

"Who are you protecting?"

This time, Norah had to look away. She wiped her nose with the back of her hand, ashamed of herself for losing control.

"Look at me," he said.

She took a jagged breath and stared back at him. "My mother," she whispered. The confession took so much energy from her that she had to hold on to the doorframe to keep from collapsing.

"I'll do your stupid show," he said.

"You will?" Norah almost couldn't believe it. She told him about her mother and he had softened. It was almost too good to be true.

"I just told you, didn't I?"

She looked into his eyes so he would understand the depth of her gratitude. "Thank you," she said.

"Don't flatter yourself. I'm not doing it for *you*. Just get Audrey to agree to write the story, and we'll talk."

N orah's first thought had been to meet Audrey in a public place, which seemed a good deal safer than being alone in the apartment with her. But the conversation was going to require privacy, so after a lengthy phone call in which she explained to Audrey that she was, in fact, coming over to discuss a job with her, the high-strung journalist promised to behave professionally. And Norah decided to take her at her word.

She pressed the buzzer on Audrey's apartment door, holding the Algonquin guest book in one hand and a ten-week-old Cavalier King Charles spaniel puppy in the other. It was the cutest, softest, most alluring dog she could find, and a critical part of her strategy.

"I'm unarmed," Audrey said as she opened the door to her apartment. She put her hands up as if to prove she had no intention of reaching for a gun.

"That makes two of us," Norah said. "Put your hands down."

"You brought me a puppy?" she said, taking a step back.

"It's not for you."

"Good, I'm scared of dogs."

Norah glanced at the pup, which was about as scary as a scoop of warm mashed potatoes. "He's not going to hurt you," she said. "Can I come in?"

Audrey opened the door wider and Norah walked into the living room.

"What's his name?" Audrey asked.

Norah sat on the sofa. "I'm calling him Jim Beam."

"Funny name for a dog," Audrey said, sitting opposite her in a faded blue easy chair with rolled arms.

"I thought *Whiskey* was too precious."

"Why did you bring him?"

"I'll get to that soon," Norah said. "First, I want to tell about *this*." She placed the Algonquin guest book on the coffee table between them, then leaned back, getting comfortable with the puppy. He gave her hand a lick and she petted his silky head. He was easy to get attached to.

"What *is* this?" Audrey asked, reaching for the book.

"Tell me if you recognize any of the names."

Audrey skimmed through the pages. "I recognize almost all of them," she said. "Mostly twentieth-century American writers, heavily skewed toward the Algonquin Round Table era."

"Exactly," Norah said. "In the nineteen twenties, the book was owned by the manager of the Algonquin Hotel."

"I think I read an article about this."

"You did, but it didn't tell the whole story. That's why I'm here. This book holds a lot of secrets."

Audrey's eyes welled with tears. She reached for a tissue and blew her nose.

"Are you crying?" Norah asked.

"I'm just so grateful you're giving me a story."

Under different circumstances, Norah would have considered being forthright about her motivation, just to be sure there were no surprises down the road that might derail this fragile creature. But given Audrey's reaction the last time Ted's name came up, she knew it was best to keep him out of the conversation unless absolutely necessary.

"Wait until you hear what it's about," Norah said. "Because it's going to take a lot of guts to write this piece."

Audrey composed herself, then reached for a pen and stenographer's pad on the side table. She opened the cover. "I'm ready."

"Just listen for now," Norah said.

Audrey put down the pad and nodded. "Go on."

Norah took a moment and proceeded with the facts Dorothy Parker had given her. "During the Round Table era," she began, "the manager of the Algonquin Hotel was a man named Percy Coates. They say he worshipped writers and loved having them around the hotel. But he had another obsession: contacting the spirit world. In his efforts to make the connection, he reached out to people all over the globe who were reputed to be gifted mediums. Eventually, he found a Romanian woman named Madame Lucescu."

"How does this tie into the book?"

"She's the one who gave it to him. I understand he paid a small fortune for it, because it was said to possess special powers." Norah leaned in. "Madame Lucescu explained to Percy Coates that anyone who signed it would have the chance to stay in the physical world after they died."

"And?"

"And she wasn't lying."

"What do you mean?"

"I mean that as long as the book is open, anyone who signed it rematerializes after they die. Most of them cross right over into the light, but one in particular has stuck around . . . and you've met her."

There was a long pause as Audrey took that in, her brow creased in confusion. Then her eyes lit up as if she just heard the punch line to a long joke. She laughed so hard she doubled over. "That is rich!" she said.

"It's true," Norah said, trying to turn the conversation serious. "Every word of it."

Audrey looked irritated. "You must really think I'm some kind of idiot. I mean, I'm temperamental, but I'm not stupid."

"I'm going to prove it to you," Norah said.

Audrey closed the book and pushed it back to her. "I'm not going to make a fool of myself," she said.

"I know it's hard to believe, but—"

"It's *impossible* to believe. I don't even know why you came."

Norah sighed. "Do you remember that woman I was here with?"

"Your boss?"

"She wasn't really my boss." Norah opened the book and turned it back toward Audrey. "You see that name?" she said, pointing to the middle of the page.

"Dorothy Parker?"

"Didn't the woman I called 'Didi' look familiar?"

Audrey folded her arms and sat back. "Okay, so she looked a little like Dorothy Parker. That's meaningless."

"Give me a second," Norah said. She positioned the open guest book in the middle of the table. "Mrs. Parker," she said, talking into it, "I know you're mad at me, but I think I can make it up to you." She held up the puppy. "Can you see this? I bought him for you. Maxed out my credit card. He's yours to keep, but you have to appear right this minute or I'm taking him back."

Nothing happened.

"Please, Mrs. Parker," Norah said. "Look how cute he is. He needs someone to love him. He's lonely, just like you."

Audrey sighed, exasperated. "And they say *I'm* crazy."

"Hold on," Norah said. "I know I can get her to appear. She won't be able to resist this puppy for much longer."

Audrey shook her head. "I'm thirsty," she said, rising. "Can I get you something?"

Norah declined and Audrey went into the kitchen. The moment she was gone, a swirl of dust particles settled themselves upon the faded blue chair, and Dorothy Parker's form quickly emerged. She held her hands out toward the dog.

"Give him to me," she said.

"Forget it," Norah said. "Not unless you show yourself to Audrey."

"We've been over this, my dear."

Norah stroked the puppy's head and gave him a kiss. "He's so darling, isn't he? I've never seen a sweeter puppy." She spoke to the dog. "You're a little dumpling, aren't you? Oh, yes you are."

Dorothy Parker stamped her foot. "I want that dog *now*," she said through her teeth.

"I'm sorry, I can't hear you," Norah said. "Can you speak up?"

"I must have him," Mrs. Parker whispered.

"What's going on in here?" Audrey asked as she walked back into the room.

And just like that, Dorothy Parker vanished.

"Did you see her?" Norah asked.

"Sure. Little woman in a hat—the ghost of Dorothy Parker."

Norah stood, excited. "You did?"

"Absolutely. She came with Oscar Wilde, Charles Dickens, Mark Twain, and Santa Claus."

Disappointed, Norah sat down again. "Didn't you at least hear voices?"

"I heard *your* voice."

The puppy rolled over on Norah's lap. He wanted his belly scratched and she complied. His little hind leg twitched in ecstasy.

Audrey picked up the book again. "It's a pretty interesting relic, and certainly valuable. But I just don't see how there's a story here."

"Uh-huh," Norah said, not really listening. She knew Dorothy

Parker was so enamored with the puppy that it would be easy to coax her out again. The trick was distracting her, if just for a second. All she needed was for Audrey to catch a glimpse. She considered another tactic.

"I think Jim Beam is thirsty, too," Norah said. "Do you mind if I get him some water?"

"Help yourself," Audrey said, nodding toward the kitchen.

Norah placed the docile little pup on the table next to the book. "Keep an eye on him for me, okay?"

"Does he bite?"

"He's two pounds, Audrey. I think you can handle this." She went into the kitchen and started opening cabinets, intentionally making noise.

"What's going on?" Audrey called.

"I can't find a shallow bowl!" Norah said, and continued creating a racket.

Just as she had hoped, Audrey came into the kitchen . . . without the dog.

"These are all too deep," Norah explained, indicating the pile of bowls she had placed on the counter.

"Did you look in the oven?" Audrey asked.

"The oven?"

Audrey opened it, and showed Norah the piles of dishes she had stored in there. She pulled out a shallow china soup bowl. "Will this do?"

"Thanks," Norah said, inspecting the bowl. It was an old-fashioned pattern—probably something her grandmother had given her. Norah turned it over and saw the name Wedgwood printed on the bottom. She filled it with water from the tap and handed it to Audrey.

"You want *me* to give it to him?"

"I'll be out in a minute," Norah said quietly. "I'll just put these bowls away."

Audrey hesitated.

"Go on," Norah said. "He's harmless. Just make sure you step in very quietly so you don't startle him."

Finally, Audrey walked out, and Norah continued making noise in the kitchen, banging together metal mixing bowls. Her goal was to make it sound as if there were still two people in the kitchen. She strained to listen carefully over the clanging, and then she heard it—the distinct sound of fine china breaking. And then, a scream.

Norah ran into the living room, where she saw Audrey standing, her face white and her hands shaking. The broken bowl was at her feet. Jim Beam was on the shabby blue chair. Norah went to him and scooped him up. His poor little body was trembling. She petted him gently.

"Are you okay?" she said to Audrey.

"She was there. I saw her."

Norah smiled, satisfied. "Why don't you sit down," she said, leading Audrey back to the blue chair.

"She was right here," Audrey said, running her hand through the empty space over the seat. "She was petting the dog. Then she just . . . vanished."

"She does that."

Audrey lowered herself slowly into the chair, as if she were afraid she might sit on something. "Was it really her? It looked like her. It looked like Dorothy Parker, sitting right here in my living room. And then she turned to dust and vanished. Am I imagining things? Did I really see that?"

"Of course you did," Norah said. "Hold Jim Beam for a minute. I'll clean up the mess and then we can chat." She handed Audrey the dog, and got some paper towels from the kitchen.

"I'm sorry about your Wedgwood," Norah said as she cleaned and dried the floor.

Audrey remained expressionless, absently petting the tiny puppy.

"You seem shell-shocked," she continued. "Can I get you any-thing?"

"I've never seen a ghost before."

Norah threw the mess away and came back into the living room. She was going to take the dog back, but Audrey was still stroking him.

"So what do you think?" Norah said.

"Think?"

"About the book, about writing the story."

Audrey looked down at the pup. "He really is cute. *Awfully* cute."

"Focus," Norah said. "I need you to focus."

"I never knew dogs could be so sweet."

"Audrey," Norah said, "this is the opportunity of a lifetime for you."

"Opportunity," Audrey repeated.

"Listen to me," Norah said. "If you write this story, you'll be a star. It's going to get national attention. Your career will take off."

Audrey stared at her blankly. Norah took the puppy from her arms, and it seemed to break her reverie.

"Are you paying attention?" Norah asked. "This is what you've been waiting for. You're going to have work again—more than you can handle. I wouldn't be surprised if you got a book deal. But you have to concentrate now."

"Okay," Audrey said, and she did indeed look focused. Her de-meanor had transformed—she was back in the conversation.

"Do you understand how big this story is going to be?"

"It's going to change everything," Audrey said.

"Exactly."

"Was that really Dorothy Parker?" she asked.

"Hand to God."

"Are there others?"

Norah shook her head. "Apparently, there have been others, but they all crossed over to the afterlife. Doesn't make the story any less astounding, does it?"

"It's the story of a lifetime," Audrey said, "but it'll never work, not unless I have witnesses. *Reputable* witnesses."

"I can get you those," Norah said. "A few anyway."

"Like who?"

"There's a hotel employee who saw her. He'll be great—he even interacted with her."

"Will he talk to me?"

"Oh, I'm sure he will," Norah said, though she wasn't sure at all. In fact, she thought it might be damned hard to get Angel to open up. "And there was another man who saw her—a big tough bodyguard. He'll add some great color to the story."

"Who else?" Audrey asked. "This is going to be a tough sell. I saw her *myself* and I hardly believe it. I'll need some people who seem like they would never in a million years believe in ghosts."

"There's a woman named Edie Coates who says she's the great-niece of Percy Coates. She's suing for the book."

"That will add some spice to the article, but it's not enough. Who else?"

"Aviva and Pete saw her, but I led them to believe she was my boss."

"That doesn't get me where I need to be. If they had actually seen her materialize it would be different."

"I'm sure you can find others if you ask around at the hotel. She's been hanging around the Algonquin since 1967—there may even be some retired people you can interview."

"I'll investigate," Audrey said. "That's my job. But I need you to tell me every person you know of."

"That's it," said Norah.

Audrey squinted at her. "I feel like you're holding something back from me."

For a twisted wacko, Audrey was remarkably astute. But Norah didn't want to set her off by telling her about Ted.

"I'm not holding anything back," Norah lied.

"Are you sure there's no one else?"

"I'm sure."

"I've been a reporter for a long time," Audrey said, "and I've learned to read people. It may be my only true talent. And right now my bullshit detector is in the red zone." She folded her arms. "I can't take this story unless you're fully honest with me."

Norah sighed. She still felt like bringing up Ted's name was just too risky—it could push Audrey over the edge again. "There is someone else," she said, "but I don't think you'll want to talk to him."

"Why not?"

"I can't tell you."

"Yes, you can."

"Trust me, Audrey, this isn't something you even want to know."

Audrey stared at her, as if trying to glean the truth. Then she stood and paced the room while Norah held on to the puppy. She continued petting the velvety spot under his neck until he fell asleep in her arms. It was easy to get attached to the little guy. She wondered if there was any way she could make room for him in her life.

"Okay," Audrey finally said.

"Okay?"

"I'll take the story." She paused. "But I want the puppy."

"What? No. You don't even *like* dogs."

"I like this one."

"Audrey, it's a big responsibility. You have to feed him, walk him, take him to the vet. A dog is not a hobby." Even as she said it, Norah understood that she was trying to convince herself that she couldn't possibly have a dog at this point in her life.

"I understand all that."

"A few minutes ago you were afraid to let him in here."

"I know it sounds impulsive, but he did something to my heart." She walked over to Norah and took the sleeping puppy from her arms. She kissed his head and laid him to rest on her shoulder. "I've never taken care of anyone else in my life and I think I can do this. I think we'll be good for each other."

"You'll need a carrier and dog bowls. You'll need squeaky toys and wee-wee pads. You'll need puppy food—lots of it."

"There's a pet store one block away. They have all of that."

"Can you afford it?"

"I'll make it work."

Norah looked at her face and could see that the dog had a calming effect. Clearly, he was good for her. But was she good for *him*? Could she really give the pup a reasonable home? Norah had only known him for about an hour, but she already felt a sense of responsibility for this little creature.

"I don't know," Norah said.

Audrey sat down and shifted the sleeping puppy to her chest. Without opening his eyes, he stuck out his tiny pink tongue and licked her hand. "See?" she said. "We're bonding."

"What about the gun?" Norah said.

"What about it?"

"I don't want to give the puppy to someone with violent tendencies."

"It's not loaded," Audrey said. "I don't even have bullets. The gun is just for show. A friend gave it to me after I was robbed—he thought it would help me feel safe."

Norah didn't say anything. She was trying to figure out if Audrey was being honest.

"You don't believe me?" Audrey said. "Go see for yourself. It's in the night table under my copy of Strunk and White."

She went into Audrey's bedroom and found the pistol just where she had said. Norah had never held a gun before, and picked it up carefully. It was heavier than she expected. Norah examined it for several minutes, trying to figure out how to check for bullets. She found a button near the trigger, and assumed it was a release for the magazine, which she could see protruding from the bottom of the handle, but how could she know for sure?

Norah coughed against a scratch in her throat and reasoned it out. If it wasn't a trigger, what was the worst that could happen?

Holding the gun pointed away from her and as far from her body as she could, she pressed the button. The magazine fell out of the handle and hit the floor. Norah picked it up and inspected it. There were no bullets inside. She looked into the gun and there was nothing there, either.

So Audrey had been telling the truth—the gun wasn't loaded. Of course, that didn't prove anything—she could have ammunition hidden somewhere. Norah couldn't very well search the entire apartment, but she did take a look in the night table drawer on the other side of the bed. There were no bullets, but she found something else—a hardcover copy of *Dobson's Night*. She picked it up and read the opening paragraph she knew so well. She was about to put it back when she noticed a small bookmark sticking out. Norah turned to the page and saw that Audrey had tabbed the very scene that had stayed inside Norah's heart all these years. She imagined Audrey rereading it again and again, just as she had.

She returned the book to the drawer and went back into the living room, where she saw Audrey sitting on the floor playing with the dog. To Norah, she no longer looked like a dangerous explosive, but a broken woman who simply couldn't figure out how to put herself back together again. Norah didn't know if little Jim Beam would help, but he certainly couldn't hurt. And Audrey would be an attentive pet owner. In fact, Norah figured that the worst thing she would do was spoil the pup.

"Satisfied?" Audrey said.

"I have a leash and a baggie of puppy chow in my purse," Norah said, "but you'll need to go shopping right away."

"Of course," Audrey said.

"And you're going to have to find a way to take care of him and write the article at the same time. You think you can do that?"

"I do." She picked up the dog and stood to face Norah. She was actually smiling.

"And another thing," Norah said. "I can't leave the guest book with you. So if you want to inspect it again, you'll have to come see me."

"I understand."

"Do you have any more questions?"

"Just one." She looked down at the dog and then back at Norah. "The other person who saw Dorothy Parker . . ."

"Audrey—"

"It was Ted, wasn't it?"

Norah looked into her eyes, which already seemed so much more accessible. Not that all the crazy was gone, but there was enough humanity there for Norah to understand that she could handle the truth.

"Yes," she said quietly, and watched closely to see the reaction.

Audrey simply nodded, and Norah knew what would happen next. Audrey was going to visit Ted Shriver.

23

As a child, Norah never had a pet—her mother's illness made it impossible. It wasn't just that she was too sick to care for an animal but even a minor allergic reaction could be fatal. Multiple sclerosis was a cruel disease—devastating and unpredictable—and her mother did everything possible to minimize the risks. But Norah grew up knowing it might not be enough, and that her mother could be taken from her at any time.

She was only six when she learned this lesson. Her mother had been hospitalized for pneumonia, but her grandmother refused to tell Norah her mother was sick. "She needs to rest" was all she had said, and Norah was confused. Why did her mom need to go away to rest when she had a perfectly good bed at home?

The answer became clear over the next several days, as her grandmother had moved in and assumed her mother's duties, making breakfast, doing laundry, checking homework, supervising bedtime. Whenever Norah vexed her grandmother, which seemed to happen all the time, she was told, "If you want your mother to come home soon, you have to be a good girl."

Norah understood the message. It was her fault that her mother needed to go away to rest. When she knocked over her milk at breakfast, needed help tying her shoelaces, requested a glass of water at bedtime, couldn't find her gloves, asked too many questions, got knots in her hair, fell down and cried, dropped a slice of pizza on her lap, didn't shut off the television, left a wet towel on the floor, or did anything else that required attention, she was exhausting.

So she knew she should be quieter and more well behaved, but she just couldn't. In fact, the longer her mother was away, the worse she got. Years later, she would understand that she had been acting out, but at the time all she knew was that everything infuriated her and she didn't feel like she had to listen to her grandmother, her teacher, or anyone else. Worse, any punishments she received only fueled her fury. Send her to her room? Fine, she would pull out all the dresser drawers and upend the furniture. Make her miss recess? Perfect. She would spend the entire time scratching ugly black drawings all over her printing exercises.

Finally, her uncle Mickey came by to take her to see her mother.

She burst into tears the second she entered the hospital room, where her mother was sitting up in bed, her dark hair full and beautiful and familiar against the stark-white sheets. Norah knew she should say something, but she couldn't. The sobs had taken over.

Her mother moved to the side of her bed so Norah could crawl in next to her. Uncle Mickey sat in an orange side chair.

"It's okay," her mother said, stroking Norah's hair. "I missed you, too."

Her uncle said something she couldn't hear over her own crying. She couldn't make out her mother's reply, either. At last she took several jagged breaths to quiet the sobs. She stared up at her mother's pale face to see if she looked like she'd had enough rest. But how could she tell? Norah never understood what grown-ups meant when they said someone looked tired. Her mother looked like her mother, except that her lips were chapped with white flakes of skin that moved when she talked.

"Are you still tired?" Norah asked.

Her mother pulled a tissue from a box near the bed and wiped Norah's face. "Not today," she said.

"When can you come home?"

"As soon as they let me."

Her uncle Mickey told a few jokes that made her mother laugh, and then he gave Norah some change and told her to go to the soda machine and get her mother a Sprite. Norah hesitated, looking from her uncle to her mother, sure that it was a test. She had to prove she could do this on her own. Her uncle put more quarters in her hand and told her to get one for herself, too.

Norah took the coins and stood in the hallway, just outside the room, unsure of what she should do next. She had no idea where the soda machine was, and wondered if he had given instructions when she was sobbing. As she stood there, thinking, she overheard the conversation between her mother and Uncle Mickey.

"You think Mom's scaring the shit out of her?" her mother said.

"Mom could scare the shit out of Cujo," he said.

"I have to get out of here," she said, "before this place kills me."

The coins dropped out of Norah's hand. This place was going to kill her mother! She ran back into the room, crying, pleading, begging her mother to get out of bed and come home. She couldn't hear the response or anything her uncle said. She only knew she had to get her mother out of the hospital before it carried out its evil plan. She needed her mother. She wouldn't let her die!

Norah didn't remember much after that. She knew that her mother didn't come home that day, and that she had cried so hard and so long her face went numb. She wouldn't talk to anyone after that, certain that they had all left her mother at the hospital to die.

Of course, she eventually understood that the hospital was not trying to kill her mother, and that she had gone there to recover from pneumonia. But the fear took such deep root in Norah that even her logical adult mind couldn't dislodge it. It was as if the synapses leading to that dense knot of terror had been cauterized, leaving her phobic of hospitals for the rest of her life.

She was embarrassed by her fear, and covered it up by sending friends elaborate bouquets when they gave birth, and calling to say she couldn't wait to meet the baby. When Didi was hospitalized with appendicitis, Norah called to confess the truth and there were never any hard feelings. But when Eric needed stitches in his foot and she asked if his brother could take him to the emergency room, he thought it was inexcusably cold. Eventually, he said he forgave her, but she could tell that he never understood how someone so strong could be cowed by an irrational fear.

When Norah walked through the doorway of the Algonquin Hotel she scanned the room for any sight of Angel, who was probably on the lookout for her. She clutched the book to her chest, and for a moment, Norah had the vague sense that she had forgotten something. It disoriented her. What could she have left behind? Then she realized—the puppy. Of course. And suddenly she felt bereft and empty without him.

It was the way the boy felt in *Dobson's Night*, when he looked over his shoulder at his father standing on the church steps. The first time Norah read the book she had to put it down after that scene even though there were only a few pages left. She felt like she would never be able to contain herself again unless she got someone to understand how deeply the dialogue had touched her. The problem was, the only person she wanted to talk to about it was the author himself.

She had gone into the kitchen, where her mother was making

dinner. She was still able to stand for moments at a time, as long as her wheelchair was nearby, and she had risen to flip over the burgers she was cooking. The kitchen smelled like beef and fried onions.

Still holding the spatula, her mother lowered herself back into the chair and turned around to face Norah. "Done?" she asked.

"Almost."

"What do you think?" She wheeled herself toward the kitchen table, which was Norah's indication to sit down. Her mother didn't like having a full conversation with someone who was standing. But Norah just couldn't sit. Not yet.

"I . . . I can't even talk about it. I love it so much I want to *do* something, but I don't know what."

"I understand."

Did she? Norah wasn't sure her pragmatic mother was capable of grasping the magnitude of emotion roiling through her.

"I think I need to write him a letter."

"Honey, sit down."

"I have to finish reading it. I'm almost done."

"We need to talk."

Norah turned to walk out of the room, but there was something about the tone of her mother's voice that stopped her. "About what?"

"Please. I need you to sit."

Norah felt a chill. There was important news coming and she couldn't tell if it was good or bad. "Why?"

"It's about your father."

Her father? She grabbed the back of the chair to steady herself. It was the big mystery of her life, and she had been forbidden to ask questions about it. All Norah knew was that her mother had been single and alone, and wanted desperately to have a child. The way she told it, she faced almost insurmountable obstacles. Then she met a man who swept her off her feet, and she knew from the start she would have his child. *I don't ever want you to think he abandoned you,* her mother had said. *If he knew about you, he'd be here. But I didn't tell him. I couldn't.*

She never explained what she meant by that, and Norah was left to wonder *why* her mother couldn't tell him. But she was about to learn the truth, and it became the one secret Norah could never tell another soul.

I n the Algonquin lobby, Norah was waylaid by a man with a heavy accent. "Excuse me," he said, and Norah held the book tighter to her chest. But it wasn't Angel—it was a tourist who wanted to know where he could get a taxi to Saks Fifth Avenue. Norah directed him to the doorman, and then glanced around the lobby to see if she had a clear path to the elevator. Angel was not in view, but a loud, familiar voice caught her attention, and she turned to see Edie Coates having an intense conversation with the maître d' of the Lounge restaurant.

Norah put her head down and walked as fast as she could to the elevator. Just as the doors opened, she heard Edie's voice call out, "Hey! Wait a minute!"

Norah pushed the *Close Door* button as Edie headed toward her. "I want to talk to you!" she called.

Why were elevator doors so damned slow? Norah pushed the button again.

"Please! I need to speak with you," Edie called out. "About the book. About the—"

The elevator doors shut, and Norah couldn't be sure of the last word Edie had said. It sounded like *dog*, but it couldn't have been. How would Edie know about Jim Beam? No, Norah thought, she must have imagined it. Surely Edie had said, "about the ghost."

Yes, that was it. Norah needed to get her mind off that puppy.

24

Baseball was one of the few things Ted Shriver could still lose himself in, and this was a good game. The Yankees were playing the Mets at Shea, and were up by one. It was the bottom of the fifth, the tying run was on second, and Pettitte was pitching.

Someone knocked on his door. He ignored it.

Lo Duca—a hard guy to strike out—was at bat. Pettitte threw a fastball and the scrappy Met was all over it. He swung and hit a high fly to deep right field and it sailed over the fence.

The knocking came again.

"Goddamn it," Ted muttered, and kept his eyes on the screen as the runners rounded the bases and the Mets took the lead.

The person outside the door rapped about ten times in fast succession, and Ted couldn't help feeling like the intruder had somehow ruined Pettitte's pitch.

"Drop dead!" he called.

"Ted," he heard a familiar female voice say. "It's me."

He muted the television and listened. It couldn't be, could it?

"I need to talk to you," she said.

It *was* her. He hadn't heard that voice in decades, but there was no mistaking it. He ran a hand through his overgrown hair and straightened out his shirt. He wasn't trying to look good, just less pitiful.

Ted opened the door, and there stood Audrey. She looked small and frail. Still pretty, but older, with a deep crease in her brow. And those eyes were the same—intense, worried, unforgiving. As sick as he was, her daintiness still made him feel bulky and potent.

"Oh my God," she said, "you look—"

"Like shit. I know." He stood straighter in the doorway.

"I didn't mean that. They told me you were sick."

"They were right."

She eyed him up and down. "Your clothes," she said. "It looks like you slept in that shirt."

He glanced down. There were sharp creases everywhere. "I did."

Audrey squinted, like she was trying to think of something to say. She smoothed her hair, and he understood that she felt self-conscious and unattractive. "I got old."

"You look fine, Audrey."

She glanced away for a second and then stared back at him, a hint of hurt and accusation in the tension around her eyes. He knew exactly what she was thinking, and it was the word *fine* that had done it. Ted had always held back, never giving her the compliments she craved. Why did he do that? Why couldn't he tell her she looked pretty, or even *good*? But no, he had said she looked *fine*, a weak and noncommittal word, devoid of flattery.

And he knew she wasn't just insulted, she was disgusted that he hadn't changed. She shook her head slightly, and there was communication in that, too. She was letting it go.

Audrey adjusted the shoulder strap on her bag—a big red satchel—and he saw that there was a small puppy inside.

"What's that?" he said.

She pulled out the tiny dog, which was about half the size of a meatball hero. "He's a Cavalier King Charles spaniel," she said, kissing it on the head.

"I thought you hated dogs."

"People change."

"No they don't."

She ignored the remark. "You want to pet him?"

He didn't, but he reached out and ran his rough thumb over the dog's small, silky head.

"I got a lead on a story," she said.

"I heard."

"That's why I'm here. You're my star witness." She gently put the dog back in her purse. He licked her hand and she smiled. She looked up at Ted and her expression turned serious. "I know why they gave me the story—as a favor to you."

"More of a bribe than a favor, but what difference does it make?"

She shrugged. "I need the work. I wasn't in a position to turn it down."

"It's a big story," he said. "You'll be a star."

"I don't know. Once the truth about *Settlers Ridge* comes out I'll be the most hated woman in America."

He knew she was right, but he was still trying to figure out a way to mitigate the damage. "I'll take all the blame," he said. "I'll go on that damned TV show. I'll tell them I drove you to it."

"You think martyring yourself is going to make it better? Face it, Ted, I'm ruined." Her eyes filled with tears. She took the puppy out of her purse again and handed it to Ted. "Hold him for a second," she said, rummaging through the various compartments. Finally, she pulled out a linty tissue and wiped her nose. "It wasn't my fault."

He nodded. They both understood what she meant. He had been crueler and crueler to her, and nothing she did could touch him. When he got drunk and insulted her, she stopped talking to him for a week and he acted as if he were happy about it. When he flirted with a young writer at a party and she begged him to never do it again, he laughed. After he cheated on her for the first time and she threatened to leave him, he promised he would change. But then he finished writing *Settlers Ridge*, and after she typed the entire manuscript for him, proofread it, photocopied every page, and sent it off to Litton, he went on a bender for three days, and the only time she heard from him was when he drunk-dialed her from another woman's bedroom.

Of *course* she took revenge. She had been hanging by a loose thread to begin with, and he frayed it bit by bit until she finally snapped. So they both knew it wasn't her fault, but the world would have a hard time believing it.

"You married a real son of a bitch," he said, handing the dog back to her. It was as close as he could come to an apology.

She nodded. "I know."

"You should have cashed those checks I sent you."

"You didn't owe me anything."

"I wish they hadn't found those manuscripts," he said.

She cuddled the dog for comfort. "It's Aviva's fault. She kept them all these years."

"Aviva had no idea," he said.

She put the dog back in her purse and let out a long breath. "You're right. I just . . . I don't know what I'm going to do." Her eyes filled with tears and Ted remembered how he felt when he met her. She was such a fragile, needy thing. She was his chance at redemption. He had been such a prick to Marlena. With Audrey, he was going to make up for all that. Then he destroyed her.

She dabbed at her nose with the disintegrating tissue and it was more than he could take. "Do you want to come in?" he asked.

"Why?"

He rubbed the stubble on his face. "Because we need to talk about getting rid of those manuscripts."

25

Didi gave Norah a massive hug. "I knew I did good when I hired you," she said.

Norah returned the embrace and almost didn't want to let go. She wished she was as confident as Didi that Ted would come through. God knows she wanted it with every charged ion of her being, but a nagging doubt swelled in Norah's throat. Would he honor his word?

She stepped back to examine the papers her boss had just handed her. They were copies of the guest contract Ted Shriver would need to sign before appearing on *Simon Janey Live*.

"Let's not celebrate until the ink is dry," Norah said. They were in her hotel room at the Algonquin. If all went according to plan, she would be checking out that night and wouldn't have to worry about the show picking up the tab.

"If you say so, sugar," Didi said. "But I know he's going to sign them; I can feel it."

"Clairvoyance or wishful thinking?" Norah asked.

"Bit of both, I reckon."

"He might still put up a fight," Norah said.

"The trick is," Didi said, "don't *ask*. Just hand him the pen, and act like you're in a hurry."

Norah nodded, trying to imagine Ted's reaction to such a performance.

"You sure you don't need me to go with you?" Didi asked.

"It'll be better if I see him alone," Norah said. "I think he'll feel ambushed if we show up together."

"I trust you, bubbeleh," Didi said. "You are saving our hides, as sure as gold is precious and honey sweet." Then she gave Norah one last hug and left.

A few minutes later, Norah was alone at Ted Shriver's door, contracts in hand. This time, she didn't have to beg and plead for him to open the door. As soon as she knocked, there he was—freshly showered and shaved, wearing a clean shirt that was only slightly wrinkled.

"You look . . ." She paused, trying to find the right words. In truth, he didn't look better, just neater. If anything, he looked even sicklier, his gray pallor and sunken cheeks incongruous against the smell of Old Spice and Irish Spring.

"Dashing," he offered. "I could almost pass for human."

Even the room itself smelled fresher, and Norah noticed that the window was wide open. He had been airing out the place.

"You must be feeling better," she said.

"Not a bit. I've just decided to fake it until I'm dead."

This was positive. He seemed to be in a good mood. "I brought the contracts," she said. "I visited Audrey—she's taking the assignment." Norah didn't want there to be any doubt that she did what she had promised.

"So I heard."

"You already spoke to her?"

"She came by," he said, and Norah understood why Ted had cleaned himself up. It was astounding. This cranky, belligerent, dying man was trying to impress his ex-wife. If Norah had any doubts that he was still in love with Audrey, they were officially dismissed.

"Did she interview you about the guest book?"

"A bit. If I'm still alive, I'll be seeing her again tomorrow."

A *date*, Norah thought. *No wonder he looks less miserable.* "That's . . . terrific. I guess you have no reservations about signing the contract then," she said, handing him the pen.

"None at all. I just need to ask for one thing."

"What's that?" she said.

He put the pen down. "Let's grab a bite and talk about it."

"A bite?"

"I'm starving."

Norah took a step back, confused. "You want to have dinner with me?"

"You eat, don't you?"

It was like her dream—having dinner with Ted Shriver. Clearly, seeing Audrey had melted away his belligerence. She knew she should press him to sign the papers first, but how could she risk this chance to connect with him? They would find a quaint outdoor café on a quiet street downtown. At last, she would get to open up and they would talk—*really* talk. It would be the conversation she had always wanted to have, and by the time they were done he would consider her a friend. In fact, she would be the last friend he would make before he died. It was almost too much to bear. She turned away, muttered something about allergies, and ran a finger under her eye to prevent her mascara from running.

"Where are we going?" she asked, hoping he had a European-style outdoor café in mind.

"Downstairs. That's the benefit of staying in a hotel with its own restaurant."

She suppressed her disappointment. So what if it wasn't a perfect match with her dream scenario? They could still connect. And anyway, it wasn't like they were eating at McDonald's. This was the Algonquin—a hotel rich in literary history. Norah decided that it was perfect—better than her fantasy.

He took the contracts from her and laid them on his dresser.

"Why don't we take those with us?" she said. If a perfect moment to get his signature arose, she wanted to be ready.

"I just want to talk," he said. "I'll sign them later."

He wants to *talk*, Norah thought, her heart rate rising. She looked at his bloodshot eyes and could see nothing but the dream she had held so close since the day she and her mother had that conversation at the kitchen table.

"Okay," she said, and they rode down in the elevator to the Algonquin's famous restaurant in the hotel lobby.

The maître d' led them to the back of the long room, where they sat in golden-yellow upholstered chairs flanking a small round table. Ted immediately ordered two martinis.

"With a twist," he added.

"I'm not in the mood for a martini," Norah said, surprised by the mix of chivalry and chauvinism.

"They're both for me," he said. "You can order what you want."

She laughed. "You never disappoint, do you?" She turned to the waiter and ordered a glass of cabernet.

Norah waited until the drinks were served before she steered the conversation in the direction she had always imagined.

"Do you get sick of people asking you about *Dobson's Night?*" she said.

He sighed. "It's one of the things that makes death seem appealing."

She looked into her wineglass, suddenly tongue-tied. Where was the witty repartee she had imagined? Where were the delightful bons mots that were supposed to roll from her lips so charmingly? All these years she had told herself she would be able to impress him, and here she was, approaching him just like any other stupid, gushing fan. She could sense a wave of depression rising in the distance and hoped she could protect herself.

"But go ahead," he said. "It's been a long time since I've even looked a reader in the eye. Maybe I'm ready to answer a question like a fucking human being."

Norah let out a long breath. It was just the encouragement she needed. She took a sip of wine to fortify herself and choked on it. "Excuse me," she said, coughing into a napkin.

He pushed a glass of water toward her and she took a sip.

"Sorry," she said, catching her breath. "Sometimes I choke for no reason."

"I suspect there's a reason."

She took a deep breath, testing her airway. "You're not going to psychoanalyze me, are you?"

"That's more boring than talking about my book."

Norah folded her napkin. "Am I that uninteresting to you?" she said, and immediately regretted it. She didn't want him to think she was a frivolous girl who fished for compliments.

"Don't take it personally. I'm a dick, remember? I'm not interested in anyone but myself."

She shook her head. "I don't actually believe that."

"Now you're going to psychoanalyze *me*, right? I'll tell you a secret—I'm really not all that complicated."

"I've read your books."

"So?"

"You have more emotional depth than anyone I know. I think your bluster is a lot of bullshit."

"Maybe the books are a lot of bullshit."

She looked at his hard face. He had no intention of letting her in. This was going to be hard work.

"I was thirteen the first time I read *Dobson's Night*." She paused, wondering how she could say what it meant to her without sounding banal. "I was young, I know, but—"

"Please don't tell me it changed your life."

"Why not? It *did*."

"No it didn't. You woke the next day and you were the same lonely, miserable kid you were the day before. Or maybe you were the same happy little spoiled brat you were the day before. I don't know. The point is, you were a baby. You had never read a real book on your own before. And *Dobson's Night* was simple enough for you to understand, and complex enough for you to know it was a little more relatable than the crap they gave you in school. So you had a moment of recognition. Maybe it taught you that you could enjoy books that dug deeper than the 'first kiss' shit you and your friends were breathless over. And if that's the case, I'm grateful. I'm grateful it taught you something and opened you up to *literature*, whatever the fuck that means. But don't think it changed your life just because you happened to read it at the very moment your pituitary gland was activated and hormones were exploding from your ovaries."

"You think you understand everything about me."

"I understand enough."

She shook her head. "I know a lot of thirteen-year-olds went cult-crazy over *Dobson's Night*, but I grew up with a single mother—"

"Please, don't," he said.

"Listen to me," she said. "I'm trying to tell you something here. The scene where the father and son are walking toward the church—"

"I don't remember," he said, waving his hand as if the scene were washed from his memory.

"Of course you do. Let me explain why it meant so much to me."

"There are a lot of people who would be happy to talk to you about it."

"But you're Ted Shriver."

"And you're Norah . . . What's your last name again?"

"Wolfe."

"Wolfe," he repeated, looking away. "I knew someone named Wolfe." He pulled the olive out of his martini and dropped it on the table. "Why can't they ever remember to bring it with a fucking twist?"

Norah felt her face flush, and she held her wrists against her cool water glass. She needed to change the subject quickly. "I have to ask you something."

He sipped his martini and sat back, a signal that he was ready to hear it.

"After the father leaves Robert at the church," she continued, "he never comes back."

"That's not a question."

"I think you know the question," she said. "It's *why*. Why doesn't he come back?"

"Why do you think?"

"I don't know. That's what I didn't understand. I mean, he loved him so much."

"Of course he did."

"Why, then?"

He leaned forward. "Let me explain something, Norah Wolfe. When I finish with a book, I'm done. There is no more than what I wrote. You know as much about what happens outside those pages as I do."

"It's hard for me to accept that."

He shrugged.

"Isn't there anything you can tell me?" she said.

"Just this—it's important that you're asking that question."

"That sounds like a riddle."

"Just live with it for a while," he said. "And if I'm still alive a week or month from now, we can talk about it again."

"I'd like you to stay alive."

"Yes, of course. You want me to do your TV show."

"It's not just that."

The emotion in her voice had embarrassed her, and the pause that followed was terrible. She had meant to play it cool, to act as if this conversation was important only for the intellectual stimulation. But that quaver gave it away. She felt naked.

He shook his head. "Don't get too attached to me, okay?"

Norah cleared her throat. "Too late for that."

"You seem like a very smart young woman," he said, "and you've seen what I leave in my wake."

"I just want to be your *friend*," she said.

"I'm too old to be your friend."

"I don't know about that. Some days I feel like I'm a hundred and one."

He lowered his head, as if he could only get a good look at her by looking up. "An old soul, eh?"

"I've been on my own a long time."

"Fine, I'll be your friend—your temporary friend. But if you're looking for a father figure—"

"No!" she said too loudly, and again felt herself flush. She gathered herself and lowered her voice. "What did you mean earlier when you said you needed one more thing before signing the contracts?"

"I want to see those manuscripts you found."

"Why?"

"Just humor me."

"You don't believe me?" she asked.

"You can't take everything so personally."

"Just to be clear," she said, "if I show you those manuscripts, you'll sign the contract?"

"I'll sign the contract."

"Right away?"

"Right away."

"You promise?"

"Cross my heart and hope to die."

She studied his expression to be sure he wasn't making a joke. His brow was low and serious.

She held up her wineglass for a toast. "To *Simon Janey Live*, then."

26

After dinner, they rode the elevator together and Norah got out on her floor, telling him she would fetch the manuscripts and bring them right to his room.

"I'll be up in just a couple of minutes," she said.

Norah smiled as she floated down the hallway toward her room. It had really happened—she and Ted Shriver had become friends. In his own obstreperous way, he had been kind to her. And there was a genuine connection there. She could feel it in every cell.

Not only that, but she was only minutes away from having a signed contract. *Simon Janey Live* would stay on the air. And she had done it all on her own!

Norah slipped the key card into her door and opened it. She couldn't wait to tell Dorothy Parker the great news. She even thought there was a good chance she could get him to sign the guest book.

She opened the book and called Dorothy Parker's name. "I need to talk to you," she added. "I just had dinner with Ted Shriver."

She clicked on a table lamp and saw the dust particles settling themselves onto the side chair. Within moments, there she was.

Dorothy Parker looked straight at her. "Did he use a knife and fork, or just put his face into the food?"

"He was a perfect gentleman," Norah said.

"Where's the fun in that?"

"Listen to me. He's going to do the show. He's—"

"You seem tipsy," Mrs. Parker said. "Did he get you drunk?"

"I had three glasses of wine with dinner, so I may be a bit . . . relaxed. But I'm sober enough to know what I'm talking about. My plan worked. Audrey went to see him and things must have gone really well, because he's almost happy."

"I was almost happy once. Then we ran out of gin."

"What about all those times you fell in love?" Norah asked.

"Yet another form of intoxication."

"Well, I guess that's what Audrey does to Ted," Norah said, "because the transformation was dramatic."

"I hardly think so."

"You don't believe he's in love with her?"

"I believe he feels a bewildering sense of obligation."

"Isn't that love?" Norah pulled off her heels and dropped into a chair.

"If it were, we would all be running off with the tax collector."

"In any case," she said, "seeing her buoyed his spirits."

Mrs. Parker studied her nails. "And I suppose she's doing the story about the guest book, now that she saw me?"

"I know you're angry about that, but there was no other way. Can you forgive me?"

"Unlikely."

"What would you have done in my shoes?" Norah asked.

Mrs. Parker picked up her cigarettes from the dresser and lit one. "The same thing, I should think. That doesn't make it right."

"I'll find some way to make it up to you."

"You can give me that darling puppy, for a start."

Norah sucked air. "About that—"

"Oh, my dear. You didn't give him to that horrid woman, did you?"

"I think they'll be good for each other."

Mrs. Parker took a drag of her cigarette and flicked the ashes. "Well, she certainly has it all now, hasn't she?"

"Here's the good news. I think I can get Ted to sign the book. He was very . . . open."

Mrs. Parker's brow tightened. "That doesn't sound like Ted."

"You should have seen him. He showered and shaved." Norah bent over to open the room safe, where the two copies of the *Settlers Ridge* manuscript were stored.

"What are you doing?" Mrs. Parker asked.

"He wants to see these," Norah said. "It's his one condition. Then he'll sign the contract to do the show."

"Why is he so insistent?"

"He needs to see for himself that we have real evidence."

"He doesn't trust you?"

"He's being cautious. I can understand that."

Dorothy Parker looked dubious. "Trustworthy people tend to be trusting. Untrustworthy people—"

"He wouldn't lie about this."

"Why not?"

"Because he knows how important this is to me."

"My dear—"

"I'm not as naive as you think I am. This is real. Ted Shriver and I connected tonight, and he's going to do what he promised." Even as she said it, Norah knew she sounded like a gullible ingenue, but if Dorothy Parker had only been there to see his face and hear his voice.

Mrs. Parker said nothing. She took a long drag on her cigarette and exhaled in Norah's direction.

"That smoke went right in my eyes," Norah said.

Dorothy Parker crushed out her cigarette. "Exactly what I'm afraid of."

Norah held the two heavy manuscripts and the antique guest book as she knocked on the door to Ted's room. She waited a few moments and knocked again. C'mon, she thought, before my arms break.

At last he pulled open the door. "Come in," he said without looking at her. He seemed drowsy and distant—dramatically worse than he had just a short while ago.

"You okay?" she asked.

"Dandy."

"You look—"

"I was lying down. You want to put those on the table?"

As she followed him into the room, Norah noticed that he wouldn't make eye contact now. Did the simple act of going out to dinner exhaust him that much? He lowered himself into the side chair against the wall.

"Thanks again for dinner," she said as she arranged the two stacks side by side on the table in front of him. There was a breeze blowing in from the open window, and she had to move them to one corner to be out of the crosscurrent.

"You sure you're all right?" she asked.

"Never better."

Norah went to the dresser and picked up the contract papers so she could get a quick signature and leave him alone to rest.

"Well, here they are," she said, indicating the manuscripts. "Did you want to take a look before signing the contracts?"

Ted leaned forward. "Move them closer to me."

"There's a breeze," she said.

"Fuck the breeze. They're not going anywhere."

Norah hesitated a moment, but she didn't want to do anything that might set him off, and so she did as he asked and pushed the two piles closer to him. He put a protective hand on each, and she relaxed. He was going to keep his promise.

Ted looked from one manuscript to the other. At last he picked up the photocopied version and put it on his lap. He sat back in the chair and began going through the pages one by one. Every so often he tsked and shook his head, as if he didn't like what he was reading.

She stood on the other side of the table, watching. When was he going to say something? She folded her arms. She unfolded them. At last she broke the silence, just to remind him she was there.

"I always wondered how writers—"

"Quiet," he said. "I'm concentrating."

"Are you looking for something in particular?"

"This!" he said, holding up the page with the plagiarized paragraphs. He straightened his arm until the page was right in front of the open window.

Norah felt herself go ice-cold. He wouldn't, would he?

What happened next seemed to unfold in slow motion. He looked at her, and there was something in his eyes that made her believe he wasn't going to do it. He would simply put the page down and apologize for what he had been contemplating. But then he looked away and she knew it was over. He opened his hand and released the page.

"Ted, no!" she cried, reaching for his arm, but it was too late. The breeze carried the evidence out the twelfth-floor window of the Algonquin Hotel.

Norah couldn't speak. She couldn't do anything but stare, hyperventilating, and it was as if reality had crashed so hard into her hopes and dreams that she was forced from her own body. Everything seemed unreal.

Ted rose slowly from the chair, holding the rest of the thick manuscript in his hands. He turned his back to her and released the pages. They flew up and out, sailing through Manhattan like a flock of white birds on their way home.

Norah still couldn't move as she tried to make sense of what she had just witnessed. She felt a tug, and realized he was pulling the contracts from her hand. He held them in front of her face, ripped them in half, and threw those out the window, too.

"Thanks for stopping by," he said, and lay down on the bed to sleep.

27

Norah sat on the edge of her bed, numb. She replayed the scene in Ted's room over and over, trying to make sense of it, trying to understand where she had gone wrong. And every time she went through it, she got to a point where her thinking hit a dull black wall that led her back to the beginning. As confused as she was, Norah knew that if she could penetrate that blackness, it would all start to make sense.

"Are you going to tell me what happened?" Dorothy Parker asked. "Or are we going to play charades?"

"He wouldn't betray me," Norah said softly.

"What did he do, dear?"

"He wouldn't."

"I presume that he did. Now take a deep breath and tell me what happened."

Norah looked up at her and realized the room was spinning. "I'm dizzy," she said.

"Nonsense," Mrs. Parker said. "You simply need a stiff drink."

Norah lay down on the bed. "I just don't understand."

Dorothy Parker sat down next to her and took her hand. "Let's go through this, shall we? You brought the manuscripts to his room. What happened next?"

"Happened?"

"Yes, dear. You went up there with two manuscripts and came back with one. What happened to the other one?"

"Gone."

"Gone where?"

Norah closed her eyes and saw the white birds flying through the night sky. "Everywhere."

"Concentrate, Norah. Where is the other manuscript?"

"Out the window."

"Ted threw it out the window?"

Oh, God, Norah thought. *He really did it.* "It's gone," she whispered, and realized tears were spilling down her face into the pillow. "The contracts, too."

Dorothy Parker stood and paced the room. "Lousy son of a bitch," she said.

Norah propped herself on her elbows. "How could he do that? We connected. He liked me—it felt so real."

"You knew he was a horse's ass. You can't honestly say you're surprised, can you?"

"We had dinner. We were *friends.*"

"No, my dear. You were never friends. It was all a ploy."

Norah thought back to that day at her mother's funeral, when she had made the decision to be strong. She never regretted it until this moment. Now she wished she could be like Audrey—a delicate flower who drew heroes and rescuers like an open bloom.

"Ted tricked me," Norah said. It was as if she had been sliced by a blade so sharp she didn't even feel it at first. But now she was starting to bleed and there was no way to stop it.

Mrs. Parker sat on the bed again. "I'm afraid so."

Norah looked into the writer's soft, dark eyes. She had never noticed how sad they were.

"I trusted him."

"That's the part I don't quite understand," Dorothy Parker said. "You're an intelligent woman. You know *exactly* what kind of man he is. What made you let your guard down so completely?"

"I *had* to," Norah said. "I just had to believe he wouldn't betray me."

"But why?"

Norah sat up, feeling feverish. Her face burned hot and she reached for the water glass at her bedside. There was almost nothing in it. She spilled the last two drops on her tongue and stared into the empty glass. The dream was gone forever, and suddenly, after all these years, her secret felt hollow.

Norah coughed into her hand and looked up at Dorothy Parker.

"Because he's my father," she said.

28

Y our father?" Dorothy Parker said. "What do you mean?"
"I mean he impregnated my mother and I have half his DNA."

"Are you sure?"

Norah went into the bathroom to splash cold water on her face. She came back into the room, patting herself with a towel. Had she really just revealed the secret she had kept her whole life?

"I'm sure," she said.

"Does he know?"

Norah shook her head. "Of course not."

"Why?"

She finished drying her face and stared at Dorothy Parker. "Because my mother never told him. She never told anyone but me."

Dorothy Parker studied Norah's face and then nodded, as if she were beginning to understand. "I sense there's quite a story behind all this," she said.

"I want to tell you, but . . . it's hard to talk about. I feel like I'm betraying her."

"There's a cure for that."

"I don't understand."

"Of course you do. It comes straight up or on the rocks. Now let's go down to the bar. The change of scenery will do us both some good."

E xiting the elevator on the ground floor, Norah heard music that sounded straight out of the 1940s. It was coming from the Algonquin's famous cabaret, the Oak Room, where a lively sister act from England was belting a spirited boogie tune that could be heard clear across the lobby. With the guest book secured inside the tote bag once again, Norah led Dorothy Parker away from the music and toward the Blue Bar, which was dark and atmospheric enough to evoke an even earlier time. They slid into a quiet booth in the back.

"What can I get for you this evening?" a waiter asked.

"Order me something fashionable," Dorothy Parker said to Norah. "I'd like to taste what people are drinking these days."

Norah had been thinking about ordering something timeless, not trendy. But this was an easier decision. "Two appletinis," she said to the waiter, who nodded and left.

"I hope that's not something healthy," Mrs. Parker said.

"Don't worry. It's vodka and schnapps. You'll be hammered before you know what hit you."

"In my day, we got drunk like that only on special occasions. For instance, Tuesday."

A few moments later the waiter came back with their drinks. Dorothy Parker made him wait while she tasted it. Norah watched as she took one sip and then another, her expression inscrutable.

"Perfectly wretched," Mrs. Parker said, and then added, "Bring two more."

"Now, my dear," she said to Norah, "tell me how your mother met Ted Shriver and became impregnated. I want every lurid detail."

"I don't have lurid details, but I'll tell you what I know. My mother dropped out of college in the sixties and floundered around for a while. But she cleaned herself up and decided to go back to school. She got a job at a clothing store during the day and went to NYU at night, majoring in bio.

"That's when her health problems began. She was having trouble studying because her eyes hurt. She finally went to the doctor and he told her it was probably some kind of virus, and when it didn't go away he put her on antidepressants."

Dorothy Parker shook her head. "As if depression were a disease and not a sane response to this miserable world."

"It actually *is* a disease," Norah said.

"I was depressed my whole life," Dorothy Parker said. "I never knew it was an illness. I thought I just fell in love too easily . . . and always with the wrong men."

"Always?" Norah asked. She seemed to remember reading that there had been a lot of men in Dorothy Parker's life, including a couple of marriages.

"Yes, dear. Every man I ever loved was handsome, ruthless, and stupid. If there had been a pill for that, I would have taken it."

"Instead, you self-medicated."

"I'll drink to that," Dorothy Parker said, lifting her cocktail.

Norah raised her glass, took a sip, and continued with her story. "Anyway, in my mother's case it was a misdiagnosis. Deep down, she knew something was physically wrong. But there was another problem—she wanted desperately to have a baby. She told me that, on some level, she must have known her time was running out, because she became obsessive. Apparently, she had a vivid, emotional dream about lowering a sleeping infant into a bassinet, and it was an image she couldn't get out of her head. She said she felt like she *knew* that baby."

Dorothy Parker glanced away for a moment and Norah thought

she looked like she was about to cry. But she blinked a few times and recovered, then picked up her drink and finished it in one swallow.

"Are you okay?" Norah asked. "You look—"

"I'm fine. But I understand exactly what your mother was feeling."

Norah was surprised. Dorothy Parker didn't seem like the kind of woman who had wanted children.

"I think I underestimated you," Norah said. "You must have had a harder life than I realized."

"Four suicide attempts and two miscarriages. So you see, there wasn't much I was good at."

"I'm so sorry," Norah said.

"On the bright side, I did have a successful abortion. But of course, even that wasn't without ugly complications."

Norah tried to imagine what that must have been like in those days—the shame, the secrecy, the risk. "I hope you had friends to help you through that."

Mrs. Parker lit a cigarette and Norah looked around. "I don't think you can smoke in here," she said.

Dorothy Parker waved away her comment and took a drag. "Unlike your mother," she said, exhaling, "I told the culprit immediately. I thought at the very least he would visit me in the hospital after it was all done, but the son of a bitch sent me a get-well card. Can you imagine? Serves me right for putting all my eggs in one bastard." She took a long drag and flicked the ashes. "Go on with your story—it's far more interesting than mine."

Norah nodded. "Deep down, my mother was terrified that it was something serious. At the same time, her desperation to have a child was growing. She was kind of a trailblazer, and was prepared to do it all on her own. She consulted her gynecologist about having artificial insemination, but the doctor refused because she was a single woman with health issues. He said, 'It wouldn't be ethical, Sherry.'

She looked into adoption, too, but that was even more difficult for a single woman.

"She started to get sicker at that point, and it was a dark time for her. Still, she had some good days and was trying to get on with her life. Then she saw a flyer tacked up at NYU—it said that Ted Shriver was coming to do a reading. It was right after his third book came out, and she was a big fan. She said she went with no expectations. She was just going to hear this wonderful writer.

"At the reading she ran into a friend, who invited her to the after-party, where Ted was the guest of honor. She was thrilled at the prospect of getting to meet him.

"To her surprise, he made a beeline for her at the party. I guess she was just his type. She was completely floored by the attention, especially since she had stopped dating. She had a hand tremor at that point, and it mortified her. People were so much more private about illness back then, and I guess she felt like a freak."

"So they dated?" Mrs. Parker asked.

"For just a couple of months," Norah said. "My mother lied and told him she was on the pill."

"I see. She tricked him into impregnating her."

"She felt guilty about it, but at the same time she knew it was her only chance. And she couldn't believe her luck, meeting a handsome and brilliant man."

"Did he know she was sick?"

Norah shook her head. "She kept it a secret from him. Anyway, by the time she found out she was pregnant, the romance was all but over."

"What happened? Did he lose interest? Did he cheat?"

"I don't know. She wouldn't go into detail on that part of the story. I was only thirteen when she told me all this, so if he acted like a shit, she probably would have shielded me from that."

"Even if he'd been horrid," Dorothy Parker said, "she could have called and told him she was pregnant."

"I think she was deeply ashamed that she had duped him. And to make matters worse, she got the diagnosis of multiple sclerosis when she was about four months pregnant and didn't want anyone to know. Of course, she had to tell her parents the truth—about the pregnancy and the MS. And they were furious. Her father was a doctor and just went ballistic that she had been irresponsible enough to get pregnant when she knew her health was in jeopardy. They eventually came around and supported her—emotionally and financially—but at the time, they drove home the shame, and she withdrew from the world."

"And she never changed her mind, in all the years that followed? She never wanted to tell him he had a child?"

"Maybe she did. I don't know. Bottom line is that the shame never really went away, especially since she got sicker and sicker. She didn't want him to see her in a wheelchair—she wanted him to re-member the pretty young woman he approached at that party. I think it also helped her hold on to that image of herself."

"And she was able to care for you?"

Norah remembered the night she found out her best friend was moving away. How old could she have been? Six? Seven? She had thought the world was coming to an end. Dawn lived next door and they had been inseparable since they were babies. Norah fell asleep crying, with her mother sitting next to her, trying to offer comfort. When she awoke during the night, Norah was lying on her side, and had a moment of panic at the thought of being alone. Then she noticed something silvery by the side of her bed reflecting the moon-light. She blinked a few times until her eyes adjusted to the darkness and she realized what it was—her mother's crutches. She had never left.

"She did the best she could," Norah said.

"And when she told you all this, did she expressly forbid you from telling him?"

"Not in so many words. But she didn't want him to know, and that's enough for me."

"Oh, my dear, you must tell him."

Norah looked at Dorothy Parker. Had she lost her mind? "Absolutely not."

"He has a right to know he has a child."

Norah stared at her. How could she consider Ted's "rights" when she was talking about her mother's trust? "That makes no sense. He was an unwitting sperm donor. That doesn't give him any rights."

"But he's your father."

"I don't think of him that way."

"Of course you do. You've been thinking about him all these years. Surely part of you wanted him to know. Perhaps you even thought he might take one look at you and intuit the truth."

"So what if I did? So what if I hoped we had some connection that transcended our shared DNA? The fact is, he's a liar and a cheat—a despicable man with a foul, dark soul. If I wasn't going to tell him the truth before, I'm certainly not going to now."

"In my experience, people never stop yearning for a connection with their parents, no matter how awful they are. If you don't tell him, you could live to regret it."

"I won't. My mother never wanted him to know and I've been at peace with that for a long time. Besides, now that I've seen the real Ted Shriver, I'd rather live with the regret than give him a daughter. I'm sorry I ever spoke to him in the first place."

"I wish you would reconsider."

"And I thought you were blowing smoke when you said you weren't a cynic."

"My dear, people often mistake idealists for cynics. We're just so terribly afraid of disappointment, you see? And I believe that's what's keeping you from telling him. You're afraid he might reject you."

"No, I'm *certain* he would reject me. I mean, think about it. Is there even a one percent chance he would welcome the news? Could you picture that?"

"He might surprise you."

"Please. Mrs. Parker, that's a conversation that couldn't possibly end well."

"And here I thought you were a woman of extraordinary courage."

"Sorry to disappoint you."

"What are you going to do now?"

Norah shrugged. She was truly at the end of the line. "I guess I'll check out in the morning, go home, and update my résumé. What else can I do?"

Mrs. Parker didn't look pleased. "I need to ask one final favor," she said.

"And what's that?"

"Bring the guest book to Teddy's room. I need to have a chat with him."

"Why? So you can tell him my secret? I'll do no such thing."

"I wouldn't betray you, my dear. But, fine, if you don't trust me, at least return it here to the Blue Bar, where it belongs. If I'm going to spend the rest of eternity locked in loneliness, I'd like to be able to get a drink once in a while."

Norah hesitated. Saying good-bye to her friend—the only person who knew her secret—felt like yet another loss.

"Right now?" she said.

"We can take our time saying good-bye," Mrs. Parker said. "But since you're checking out—"

"I'll return it tonight," Norah said, and ordered another drink.

Groucho

1977

When a cloud of coal-black dust particles emerged from the Algonquin guest book and shot from one end of the bar to the other—dragging with it the distinct smell of cigar smoke—Dorothy Parker had a pretty good idea who was about to emerge.

The particles pulled together quickly, and there he was, sporting an authentic mustache where his greasepaint used to be.

"Where am I? How did I get here? What's the meaning of this? And where are the girls?"

"Groucho Marx," said Dorothy Parker. "It's good to see you, my dear. But I'm afraid to tell you you're dead."

"Dead? Why, that's an outrage! I paid for my room at Cedars-Sinai through the end of the week. How dare they! Where's my lawyer? Busy shedding his skin, that's where. And he has the nerve to send me the bill? The snake! Of course, it adders up, even if he works for scale. And why would he work for scale anyway? Has he no backbone? Well, I won't pay it, I tell you."

"I was just about to have a drink," Dorothy Parker said. "Will you join me?"

"Why, are you coming apart?"

"Sit down, Groucho."

"Don't mind if I do. You're paying, right? Say, how did I get here, anyway?"

"You remember that guest book you signed for Percy Coates?"

"Are you saying I traveled all the way from Beverly Hills by signature? Have the Wright Brothers heard about this? And do you know that two wrongs don't make a right, but two Wrights make an airplane? That's an old joke. Speaking of old jokes, what are you doing here, Dorothy Parker? Shouldn't you be trading quips with Beelzebub in the fiery pits of hell? That's just south of Fourteenth Street, in case you didn't know."

"Somehow even the worst of us gets a pardon," she said.

"That's the most ridiculous thing I ever heard."

"Sir, what can I get for you?" asked the bartender.

Groucho looked up, surprised. "Where did he come from? He doesn't look dead."

"He's not dead, he's the bartender."

"A likely story. Where was he when Lincoln was shot? No alibi, eh? Well, no matter. Alibi anything you got that's on sale."

"Just make two gin and tonics, Lawrence," Dorothy Parker said, and then looked at Groucho. "Now, dearest, I hope you're planning on staying awhile."

"It depends."

"On what?"

"On how long it takes him to make those drinks. Once I'm done, it's sayonara."

"Lawrence," she said, "take your time with those drinks."

"You don't really want me to hang around, do you? I'm no more fun than a stick in the mud. If you don't have any sticks, send in the stones. If you don't have any stones, send in the cavalry. If you don't have any cavalry, what kind of army is this?"

"I really do wish you would stay," she said. "I haven't been entertained like this in a very long time."

The bartender served the two drinks and Groucho picked up his glass. "Well, cheers," he said, and polished off the contents in three quick gulps.

"And now, my sweet," he said, taking her hands, "I'm sorry, but I must be going."

"You're not serious."

"For once, I am." Groucho looked up overhead. "I'm coming, boys!" he said, and then he was gone.

29

Angel Ruiz carried the guest book back to the Blue Bar, grateful that the pretty young woman had returned it at last. Now he could stop avoiding the hotel's night manager, Mr. Beeman. All week he had been ducking into corners, desperately afraid he would be questioned about the book's disappearance. He could not afford to lose this job.

After she apologized for taking it, saying, "It couldn't be helped," the young woman made him promise to put it right back where it belonged.

She needn't have worried. Angel didn't like being near the thing one second longer than was absolutely necessary.

He entered the bar just as Walter the busboy was finishing up with the glasses. There was no one else around.

"Are you leaving now?" Angel asked. Once the book was opened, he didn't want to be alone in the bar.

"Pretty soon," Walter said.

"Okay," Angel said. "I'll walk out with you."

Angel approached the display case, which had been left open. He blew inside to clean out the dust, wiped it with his sleeve, and gently lay down the book. He opened it to a random page and decided it looked just as it had when he first set eyes on it. He closed the display lid, grateful that he would never have to worry about it again.

"Okay," he said, turning around. "Ready to go?" The bar was empty. "Walter?" he called, looking from corner to corner.

"He's gone," said a woman's voice. It seemed to come from the pitch-blackness at the end of the long, narrow space.

Angel stopped and stared as a form emerged from the shadows. It was the same lady phantom who had terrified him earlier.

"You!" he said. "*Dios mio.*"

"You disappoint me, Angel. I thought we were friends."

"What do you want from me?"

She walked to the bar and took a seat. "Make me a drink, dear. I'm positively parched."

"No, miss. I cannot help you."

"Don't be silly. Of course you can."

"I . . . I think Walter is coming back."

She smoothed her skirt. "The more the merrier."

"Please," he said, "go back in the book. I've never hurt you. I've never hurt no one."

"*Anyone,*" she said.

"Miss?"

"You never hurt *anyone*. If you never hurt *no one*, it means you did hurt someone."

"No! Not me. I swear. I'm a good man. I work hard."

"Yes, dear, of course you do. And I'm quite certain you like this job and don't wish to lose it."

"Yes, miss. It's a good job."

"Very well then, make me a drink and no one ever has to know you were the one who removed the book and delivered it to Mr. Shriver's room."

"I . . . I can't do that."

"Of course you can."

"The liquor is locked up. I don't have a key."

"It so happens," Dorothy Parker said, "that Walter accidentally dropped this." She opened her hand and there it was. "Now be a dear. I'd like an appletini, if you don't mind."

"Appletini?"

"Vodka and schnapps, I believe. You'll have to figure out the rest on your own."

"Find another man," he said. "Please."

"If I could find another man," she said, "I might not need a drink in the first place. In the meantime, here." She put the key on the bar.

He looked down at it. "I have to leave, miss."

"Understand, my dear, that while it's true I can't exit this room on my own, I can still use that house phone behind the bar. Now do as I say. I don't wish to get you in trouble."

Angel swallowed hard. He didn't want to make a drink for the phantom, but he was terrified she would call his boss. What choice did he have?

"Just one," he said. "Then I'm leaving."

He went behind the bar and found the booklet of cocktail recipes. Then he unlocked the liquor cabinet and made the drink she requested.

"Now I go," he said, pushing it toward her.

"Just one more thing," she said.

"No more things, please."

"I'll never make another request of you again, but once I finish this, you must bring the guest book up to Mr. Shriver's room again."

"Ay, no! I can't!"

"Dearest, no one even knows the book was returned, so no one will suspect you have taken it."

"Walter knows. He just saw me."

"Let me worry about Walter," she said.

"I must go. Good luck, miss."

"Very well, I'll just have to make that call to the manager and tell him you were the one who removed the book in the first place."

"You want me to lose this job?"

"I *don't* want you to lose your job, Angel, that's the whole point. Now be a lamb and wait for me to finish my drink."

"But, miss—"

"My dear man," she said, raising her voice, "have you ever seen what happens when you anger a spirit?"

Angel felt a terrible chill. What did she mean by that? What would the angry visitor do to him?

"Well, have you?" she repeated.

He swallowed hard. "No, miss."

"Good," she said, picking up her drink.

Shaking, he stood by and waited while she finished it.

"Okay," she finally said. "Let's go."

Resigned, Angel approached the display case and picked up the book. "Can I close it?"

"No, dear. Carry it open."

He placed the open book on the palms of his hands as if he were carrying a wedding cake.

"I'll be right here next to you," the phantom said, and then she disappeared from view. He could feel her hovering nearby.

When he got to the door, Angel glanced into the lobby to be sure Mr. Beeman was not in sight. There were just a few guests, engrossed in conversation, and a woman sound asleep in a big armchair. The problem was Maria at the front desk. Angel waited until she turned to look at the computer, then he tiptoed quickly across the lobby. He got to the elevator without being noticed, and sighed, relieved.

As he pressed the button for the elevator, Angel heard authoritative footsteps marching across the lobby. He pressed the button again.

The footsteps closed in on him just as the elevator arrived, and Angel positioned himself right in front so he could slip in quickly. The doors opened and Angel stepped in, nearly crashing into a tall, suited figure who was stepping out.

"Mr. Beeman!" Angel said, looking up. He thought his heart might stop.

"Where are you going with that book, Angel? It belongs in the bar."

"Please, don't fire me. She made me do it. I didn't want to. She insisted. What could I say to her?"

"Slow down. Who made you?"

"That woman. The phantom. She took the key from Walter and asked for a drink. I didn't want to give it to her, Mr. Beeman. Then she said she would haunt me if I don't bring the book to Mr. Shriver on the twelfth floor. I told her no, but she wouldn't listen."

Mr. Beeman shook his head.

"I'm telling the truth," Angel said.

The manager put a hand on his shoulder. "Relax, Angel. I know you're telling the truth." He looked around. "Mrs. Parker, are you threatening my employees again?"

The phantom appeared beside Angel. "You're looking well, Barry," she said.

He tsked. "What's going on here, Mrs. Parker?"

"I need to see Ted Shriver," she said. "It's urgent."

"You know I can't have you bothering the guests."

"Teddy and I go way back," she said.

Mr. Beeman turned to his employee. "Let me have the guest book," he said, gently taking it from Angel's hands.

"You are not going to close that book, young man," she said. "Or you'll be very, very sorry."

"Please don't get her angry," Angel said.

"Trust me," said Mr. Beeman, "her bark is worse than her bite." At that, he closed the book and the phantom disappeared. "Now," he said to Angel, "let's put this back where it belongs, and first thing tomorrow morning I'll have someone from maintenance nail down the lid to the display case. It won't go missing again anytime soon."

30

E die Coates was determined. She simply had to get her hands on that Algonquin guest book again. Only, this time she wouldn't rip out a page and run away. She needed to bring the whole book home. When she peered into the Blue Bar and saw two hotel employees, she decided to wait it out. She took a comfortable chair in the lobby and watched. It didn't take long before one of the men came out, but the other was taking his sweet time.

At last she saw him peek his head out of the room and glance furtively around the lobby. Damn. He must have been warned to be on the lookout for her. Edie turned her face away and pretended to doze, hoping he wouldn't notice her. When she heard footsteps she opened her eyes a crack, and realized he had just walked right by her with the book. She had to stop him.

She rushed across the lobby, trying to reach him before he got onto the elevator. When the doors opened, she thought she'd lose him, but he was waylaid by an important-looking man in a suit. Edie backed into the shadows and then there it was—the ghost! She had to cover her mouth to keep from screaming. But why weren't these men terrified? Didn't they understand? Nothing was more dangerous than a spirit who refused to cross into the light!

Still, she couldn't warn them. No one could know she was here.

She leaned against the wall and watched, realizing the dark-haired man looked alarmed. She hoped that meant he understood. But the other man was as calm as could be. Edie wished she could shake some sense into him. Her heart pounded a quick, hard beat, and she knew her blood pressure was soaring.

She saw the suited man take the book and slam it shut. The ghost disappeared instantly. So that was how it worked—the spirit could only emerge when the book was open.

A trickle of sweat dripped down the side of Edie's face. She took a deep breath to steady her nerves and stayed quiet.

The men walked right past her, across the lobby, and into the Blue Bar. When they came out, they no longer had the book.

Thank God, she thought. *The book is there and no one is watching it.*

It was time. Edie wiped her damp palms on her slacks and walked quietly into the deserted bar, repeating the same prayer over and over: "Please let the book be closed. Please let the book be closed."

From a distance, it was impossible to tell if it was or wasn't. Slowly and carefully, she inched closer to get a glimpse.

"Please let the book be closed. Please let the book be closed."

The light above the display case was on, creating a glare that bounced off the glass. She hesitated, trying to work up the courage to get close enough to discover the truth.

Suddenly, someone behind her cleared their throat and Edie jumped. She whirled around and there it was, staring straight at her! The ghost looked exactly as she had that day by the elevator—as real as a flesh-and-blood human, just like Gavin.

"Please don't hurt me!" Edie said. "I come in peace." She squeezed her legs together to keep from wetting herself.

"Nonsense," said the spirit. "You're here to steal the book."

"No! I'm not. I promise. Please understand, I didn't know that book was possessed when . . . when . . ."

"My dear, you've been trying to claim ownership of the book since you read that article."

"That was before . . . before I knew about you. I'll drop the law-suit. I don't want the book anymore. Honest!"

"And I suppose you just strolled in here to get a closer look. Is that it?"

"No! Yes! I can't answer you! Please don't ask me anything else."

"You know you're going to have to pay the price for this," the spirit said.

Edie curled herself up in a ball on the floor. "I never meant to hurt you!"

"Get up, you imbecile."

Edie rose. "What do you want? I'll do anything. Please don't hurt me."

"I have a task for you. If you fail, there will be terrible consequences."

Oh, God. This was exactly what she had feared. "What do you want me to do?"

"I want you to open that case, take out the book, and bring it up-stairs to room 1207. You must deliver it into the hands of the man in that room. Is that clear?"

"What are you going to do to him?"

"That's not your concern."

"No, no, of course not."

"Now do as I say and don't ask any more questions."

Edie nodded, terrified. She needed to do whatever it took to pre-vent the ghost from unleashing her fury. With more courage than she had ever been able to summon, Edie approached the display case and carefully removed the book.

"Room 1207," the ghost repeated.

Edie nodded. She carried the book on her hands just as the man had done. When she reached the door between the bar and the lobby, she hesitated. A group of German tourists had just entered the hotel and were at the front desk, talking and laughing, as if they were still enjoying a raucous night out. Edie couldn't risk passing them; there was just too great a chance she would get stopped before completing the ghost's mission.

"What are you waiting for?" the spirit asked.

"There's a big crowd checking in. I'll cross the lobby as soon as they leave."

The ghost tsked. "Very well. You haven't got a cigarette, have you?"

"A cigarette?"

"Why does everyone act as if I'm asking for uranium? Yes, a cigarette."

"Hardly anyone smokes anymore," Edie said.

"Fools."

"We're just . . . trying to live longer."

"Like I said."

After the tourists got into the elevator, Edie waited a few more minutes to make sure the coast was clear, and then crossed the lobby. The ghost disappeared from view, and didn't even reappear when Edie got into an empty elevator. She rode up to the twelfth floor in silence, and when she found the room number, she spoke aloud.

"Am I supposed to knock? It's the middle of the night."

"Trust me, he's not sleeping," the ghost said as she reappeared.

Edie knocked on the door of room 1207. "Hello?"

"Go away!" a man shouted.

"Teddy, dear," said the spirit, "I have a vital message for you."

"Not interested."

"Tell him you have something for him," the spirit whispered to Edie.

"I have something for you!" Edie called.

"Who the hell is that?" the man said.

"Tell him you brought a bottle of gin," said the ghost.

"My name is Edie Coates, sir. I brought a bottle of gin."

She heard some movement inside the room and then the door opened. "Where's my gin?" he said.

"Hold this and I'll get it," Edie said, then she put the book in his hands, pushed him into the room with all her might, and slammed the door.

31

T ed fell backward, landing on his bottom. "Goddamn it," he said. "Who *was* that?"

"My apologies, Teddy. I needed to see you right away, and I couldn't be terribly picky about the arrangements."

"Shit, that hurts."

"Don't be a child. Get up."

He crawled to the chair and pulled himself into it. "You're going to kill me, you know that?"

"I think you're doing a fine job on your own."

"You came to chastise me for not taking better care of myself?"

"Perish the thought. I have a vested interest in your demise, remember?"

Ted shifted his weight, trying to get comfortable. He had landed right on his coccyx and knew it was the kind of injury that should be iced, but he couldn't work up the stamina to care. "Maybe I should fall on my ass more often," he said, reaching for his Vicodin. "For a second I almost forgot about the pain in my head."

"You look dreadful," she said.

"Don't get excited. I still have no intention of signing that damned book."

She gave him a piercing look and he wondered if she sensed that he had considered—for at least a fleeting moment—what it would be like to live after death.

"I would love for you to sign it, my dear," she said, "but I'm here for a different reason."

"To be an even bigger pain in my ass?"

"Don't be churlish," she said. "Now, where have you hidden your cigarettes? I think we could both use a smoke."

"Gave them up, remember?"

"Then why do I smell stale smoke?"

"Pete brought me a whole box of excellent Nicaraguan cigars."

"That will do."

Ted stared at her. "Seriously? You want a cigar?"

"Why not?"

"And I suppose you'd like a cognac, too?"

"Thank you. I'd be delighted."

Ted exhaled. The offer hadn't been serious, but what the hell. Having a cigar and a cognac seemed like an acceptable way to pass another hour in his life. He pulled himself out of the chair with great effort and poured them each a drink. Then he handed Dorothy Parker a cigar and a lighter.

"You're going to have to light it yourself."

"Barbarian," she said as she flicked the lighter. She puffed on the cigar until the tip ignited, then handed the lighter to Ted.

They spent the next several minutes drinking and smoking in silence.

"You were absolutely beastly to that girl."

"What else is new?"

"That was despicable even by your standards."

"I guess you're talking about what I did with those pages. If it makes you feel any better, I very nearly changed my mind at the last second. But I couldn't let a moment of conscience get in the way."

"Did you think about *her*?"

"Audrey?"

"No, Norah."

"The TV producer?" he said. "Why should I?"

Dorothy Parker looked exasperated as she rested her cigar on the ashtray, and he wondered why she was so invested in this girl.

"The 'TV producer' thought you liked her," she said.

"I don't like *anyone*."

"Yes, dear, but don't you think she has a lot to offer?"

He shrugged, remembering her face at dinner. She was so earnest it made him ache. But he didn't want to have remorse. Not over this. "She's nothing to me," he said.

"You didn't answer the question."

He shrugged. "She's okay, I suppose."

"High praise."

"Why do you care so much about this girl? I thought she was just a co-conspirator."

Dorothy Parker picked up her cigar again and went silent for several minutes. Ted had the feeling she was thinking hard about what to say next, and he wasn't sure he wanted to hear it.

"Did Norah talk to you about her past at all?" she finally said.

"I don't think so. If she did, I wasn't listening."

"She had no father, and lost her mother at a young age."

"What am I supposed to do—befriend every orphan in New York?"

She stared at her cigar, and then stamped it out in the ashtray. "This is actually quite vile."

"Guess that's why I like it."

She sipped her drink again. "Ted, did you ever want to have a child?"

"People like you and me aren't meant to have kids."

She stared into her drink for a long time. "I suspect you're right," she said, looking remarkably sad. "Do you think you would have been a good father?"

"Unlikely," he said, though in truth he had always wondered what would have happened if his first wife, Marlena, hadn't miscarried. Would a child have changed him?

"Teddy, I have to tell you something rather extraordinary."

Extraordinary? He couldn't even muster fake enthusiasm for whatever she thought was so earth-shattering.

"Are you listening?" she said.

"Hanging on your every word."

She put down her drink, stood, and walked over to him. "Norah is your daughter."

He laughed. "That's preposterous."

"Her mother's name was Sherry. She might have had a hand tremor when you met her."

Ted went cold, trying to figure out how Dorothy Parker could possibly know about Sherry Wolfe. This had to be some kind of a trick.

"Norah was born in 1978, so it was probably 1977."

The pain behind his eye turned sickening. She had the right year. Where on earth had she gotten all this information?

"She was studying biology at NYU."

"Enough," he said. Ted put down his drink and lowered his head. The room was spinning. "What's your game? Where did you learn all this?"

"There is no game," she said.

"Why should I believe you?"

"You looked straight into her face. Surely you saw it—that distinctive high forehead, flat as a chalkboard. And those eyes—they're yours, Ted."

He bent over at the waist and stared at the carpet. Then he closed his eyelids and saw her face as it looked in the restaurant. He envisioned her looking down and then slowly raising her head to peer at him. And there they were—his own eyes looking back at him. They were clearer, younger, prettier, but there was no mistaking it. His stomach lurched, and he sat back to give his organs more room. It took several minutes for the nausea to subside so that he could speak without getting sick.

"I have a daughter," he said.

"Yes, you do."

Ted remembered the conversation in his neurologist's office when he refused the surgery. At first, the doctor was condescending, explaining the necessity in simpler terms. Eventually, he turned grim and pushed his business card across the table, telling Ted to think about it. But he had made up his mind, and it felt like a relief. He would let himself die. It was so simple.

Ted looked at Dorothy Parker's cigar, snuffed out and bent in the ashtray, and understood that nothing felt simple anymore.

He glanced back at her. "This changes everything," he said.

32

It was amazing how much dust an empty apartment could accumulate. Norah pushed her Swiffer around the hardwood floor and knew it was all there—months of her life still settling to earth: the pollen that she and Eric had brought in on the bottoms of their sneakers after going for a run, the dryer lint from his socks and underwear, the burnt toast crumbs from the day he left, the hotel carpet fibers she dragged in on the wheels of her suitcase. She pulled the filthy, static sheet out of its plastic grips and stuffed it into the garbage, telling herself she was going to get through this.

Norah washed her hands and opened a bottle of water to drown the dryness in her throat. She had suffered losses before and found the strength to go on. She tried to convince herself this time would be no different.

But of course it was, and she knew why. It was more than losing her job and not having Eric to lean on. It was because the dream about her father had vaporized. That one elusive prize—the thing she believed would complete her—was gone forever.

Norah sat down in front of her laptop and reread her résumé. Didi had given her some tips and she wanted to make a few changes before heading out for brunch with Pamela Daniels, a friend she had met at a press event several years ago. Pamela worked at MSNBC and wanted to talk to Norah about a new show that was in the works. She seemed pretty sure she could get Norah in on the ground floor, if she was interested.

Norah started to retype her objective but found it hard to concentrate. What was it she had wanted to say about her goals?

The loud buzz of the intercom jolted her. She wasn't expecting anyone on a Saturday morning.

"Who is it?" she said, holding the *Talk* button.

She heard an unintelligible half syllable in a woman's voice.

"Repeat that," Norah said.

"I said *Audrey*. Audrey Hudson."

Norah stepped back, surprised. The buzzer sounded again.

"What are you doing here?" Norah asked.

"Can I come up?"

Norah sighed and buzzed her in, hoping Audrey would state her business quickly and leave. She looked at her watch. She had to leave pretty soon if she wanted to get to her brunch appointment on time.

Norah stood by the door to her apartment until she heard Audrey's sharp footsteps in the hallway. She stared out the peephole and saw her, looking harmless in a Columbia University sweatshirt and jeans, like a teenager with a woman's face. She carried a big red purse.

"How did you find me?" Norah said as she opened the door. "There must be thirty N. Wolfes in New York."

"I'm a reporter, that's my job. Besides, it's really not that hard to find someone. Can I come in?"

Norah stood aside. "I have about ten minutes," she said.

"Nice place," Audrey said, stepping inside. "Lots of sunlight."

Norah realized how bright her Brooklyn brownstone apartment looked compared to Audrey's East Side crypt, with its tiny blocked windows. She hoped she would get to keep it. But of course, that would mean finding a new job soon.

"Thanks," she said. "Why are you here?"

"I need your help."

Great, Norah thought. *The broken little bird lands in my nest looking for another free crumb.*

"I'm not sure there's anything I can do for you," she said.

Audrey's narrow shoulders bunched up around her ears as she took in the rest of the apartment. It was if she were afraid the room would swallow her whole. Norah folded her arms. She was not going to rush to this woman's rescue.

Audrey cleared her throat. "I spoke to Ted," she finally said. "I know what happened."

"Good for you. I suppose you're back in love. Did the conspiracy to screw me over throw you back together? Are you having your gorgeously tragic happy ending just before he dies?"

"If it makes you feel any better," Audrey said, "I could never forgive him. So, no, we're not reconciled, but I did call a truce. Mind if I sit down?"

"Actually, I do."

"Please," Audrey said. "It'll only take a few minutes."

Norah shrugged, and led her to the uncomfortable wooden side chair no one ever sat in.

"I'm having trouble with the story," Audrey said as she lowered herself onto the hard seat. She held her purse on her lap. "I have an editor at a national magazine interested, but she wants to see Dorothy Parker with her own eyes—"

"What a shame."

"Norah—"

"Like I said, can't help you."

Audrey put her handbag on the floor and leaned forward. "I have a proposition."

"Not interested."

"Listen to me," Audrey said. "I already spoke to Ted about this. If you help me, he'll do your TV show."

Norah laughed. "I've been down this road, Audrey. It leads nowhere."

"He promised."

"Thank you for stopping by."

"This story is my only hope," Audrey said. "Please."

Norah shook her head. The helpless-victim act was simply not going to work on her. She went to the door and opened it.

"What am I going to do?" Audrey said.

"Don't know."

"Come on. You must have some ideas. Can you at least show me the book again?"

"Nope," Norah said, hoping Audrey would take the cue and leave.

"Why not?"

"I don't have it. It's back at the Algonquin, where it belongs."

"If I went there, would I be able to conjure her?"

Norah laughed at the word *conjure*.

"He really will do your show," Audrey said. "He'll do it for me."

"Good-bye," Norah said. "Take good care of Jim Beam."

Audrey gave her one last long look and walked out the door. Norah watched as she disappeared down the hallway. It was the last chance for both of them.

Norah leaned against her door and wondered why Audrey thought she had even the slightest chance of persuading her to trust Ted again. Talk about a fool's errand. Of course, she might have done the very same thing herself. God knows she had a hard time giving up. Only, she would have found a way to make her argument more compelling . . . especially when approaching someone who had just been so royally screwed over. Was it possible Audrey hadn't thought of that?

"Wait a second!" Norah called down the hallway, even though she knew it was a long shot.

Audrey walked back into her field of view. "What is it?"

"I have a counterproposal. You tell Ted that if he does the show I'll get Dorothy Parker to appear for your editor." Norah folded her arms. This was the moment of truth. If Audrey had been serious about getting Ted to appear on *Simon Janey Live*, she would say yes to this. If she said no, it meant that the two of them had once again planned to screw her over.

Audrey's eyes darted from side to side as she thought about it. "How do you know she'll do it?"

Norah shrugged. "That's the deal," she said. "Take it or leave it."

Audrey's tight face relaxed into a smile. "I'll take it!" she said.

B y the time she shut the door, Norah was in a frenzy, carried away by her own exhilaration. This time, it could actually work. It *would* actually work. Ted would agree to do the show to save Audrey. After all, that was the only thing he truly wanted. She picked up her cell phone and called Didi to tell her the great news. When she got voice mail, she left an excited message to call her back.

Then she tried to call Pamela Daniels to cancel their brunch, as she didn't want to follow a job lead when the show was so close to being saved. It would be bad karma. But that went to voice mail, too. Norah decided she would just head over to the restaurant and tell Pamela in person. It was only about five blocks away, and it would be good to see her friend, even if she didn't think the timing was right for the interview.

A short time later, Norah walked into the restaurant and found Pamela already seated at a small table by the window, a Bloody Mary in front of her.

"Sorry I'm late," Norah said. "It's been a crazy morning."

Pamela, a divorced forty-year-old, tucked her neat blond hair behind her ear and smiled. "You look like you're in a good mood."

"We're not getting canceled," Norah said. "At least I don't think we are. There's been a tremendous development."

"Seriously? What happened?"

"I haven't even told anyone, but I got us a guest that will make history."

Pamela smiled, excited. "Who?"

"I really shouldn't say."

"Come on. I tell you *everything*."

It was true. Pamela was always completely forthright with her. Norah exhaled and leaned in. "Okay, but you have to swear—"

"On Toni's life," she said, referring to her teenage daughter.

Norah leaned back and smiled. "It's Ted Shriver," she said, knowing the impact it would have.

Pamela's eyes went wide. "How did you manage that?"

"Long story, but the upshot is that I don't feel right interviewing for the MSNBC job, not when there's such a strong chance *SJL* will make it."

"Listen, Norah," Pamela said. "I think it's tremendous that you landed such an astounding guest. And I hope *Simon Janey* stays on the air for the next twenty years. But as your friend, I need to tell you that you should still interview for this job. It's an amazing opportunity—an edgy news and opinion show with a woman anchor who's just starting to make a name for herself. She's brilliant, and I think it's going to be huge. With my recommendation—"

"I understand, and I appreciate it. But it's just not the right timing. I have to put everything into saving *SJL*."

"I already told the host about you and she's dying to meet you."

"I hope this doesn't put you in a bad position."

"It's not that," Pamela said. "I just think you're being rash. Opportunities like this don't come along very often. Beth Barbieri got wind of it and has been begging me to get her in. I've been blowing her off because I think you're better for it."

"Beth is great," Norah said. She didn't know the woman that well but had heard she was very smart and very hyper.

"You're better."

"I don't know about that."

"Don't be modest. I'm talking about a job you could sink your teeth into."

"Can you just give me a week or so? By then I'll know if *SJL* is going to make it."

Pamela sighed. "I can try, but I can't make any guarantees they won't offer the job to someone else while you're dragging your feet."

"I understand." Norah reached out and grabbed her friend's arm. "And truly, I'm so grateful."

Pamela picked up a menu and handed it to Norah. "I hope you're not making a mistake."

On her way home from the restaurant, Norah was about to take out her cell phone to try Didi again when she got distracted by a cute guy walking by with an even cuter dog. She wasn't entirely sure the man was straight, but it was probably better if he wasn't. Flirting with someone when she was this hyper would only get her into trouble.

The dog, however, was irresistible. It was a little white-coated terrier that looked like a stuffed animal, with black eyes and a black button nose.

"What breed is this?" she said as she bent to give it a pat.

"She's a West Highland," he said. "A real diva. We call her Celine Dion."

Norah smiled, grateful for the gentle but clear heads-up about his sexual orientation. "I love that she has a first and last name. I had a Cavalier King Charles I called Jim Beam."

"Cute," he said. "You must have adored him."

"I miss him."

"I hope he didn't suffer."

"Oh, he didn't pass on. I had to give him away."

"That's rough, too," the guy said, giving the leash a gentle tug to keep the dog from wandering into the street. "But I'm sure you gave him to someone you trust."

Trust Audrey? Norah opened her mouth to respond and couldn't think of a thing to say. She gave the guy a tight smile and walked away.

As she headed back home, Norah's euphoria dissipated like vapor, and she was aware of a creeping anxiety taking its place. Had she done the right thing in giving Jim Beam to Audrey? Yes, she told herself. Audrey was tightly wrapped, but she would dote on the pup.

Still, the nervousness wouldn't lift, and Norah had to face the source. It was Audrey's volatility. Would she really come through on her promise?

Norah took out her cell phone to see if Didi had called her back. No messages. Before trying her again, she wanted to capture her earlier enthusiasm. But no matter how much she tried to tell herself that everything was fine, she knew she had to double-check. She called Audrey's number.

"I just wanted to make sure you spoke to Ted and got everything all lined up," Norah said.

"Working on it," Audrey said.

"What does that mean?"

"He said he would think about it."

"What does he need to think about? He appears on the show and then I help you with your article. It's a pretty simple equation."

"Nothing is ever simple with Ted."

Norah's face burned hot. This had to come through. It *had* to. "When will he let you know for sure?" she asked.

"Hard to say. We had a short conversation and he said he needed to rest."

Norah paused, contemplating her next move. She would put the pressure on. "The offer is only good for today," she said.

"You never said that."

"Well, I'm saying it now. So you call him back and tell him he has to make up his mind. He has until midnight tonight and then the door is slammed shut. Is that clear?"

"What if he needs more time?" Audrey said.

"Then you're both out of luck," Norah said, and hung up.

N orah's phone didn't ring until the next morning.

"Did I wake you?" Didi asked.

It was just past eight a.m., and Norah had had a restless night. She had stayed up late, waiting for a call from Audrey that never came. When she finally dozed off, her anxiety was too acute to let her get any restful sleep. She kept waking up, wondering if there was any chance Ted would agree to her proposal. At last she came to the realization that it was a ridiculous notion to entertain. He simply was not going to do it. The sun was still hidden when she gave up on sleep and made herself a cup of coffee.

"I've been up since five," Norah said.

"Me, too," said Didi. She took a deep, noisy breath, and Norah could swear she heard a smile.

"What's going on?"

"Don't make plans for Monday, sugar. We are unpacking boxes and making history."

"What are you talking about?" Norah asked.

"Man named Pete Salzberg called me last night," Didi said. "He seemed to think we had met. But it makes no never mind. Ted

Shriver is appearing on the show *tomorrow*. Simon canceled his Sunday golf game and is already locked in his office with the writers, preparing questions. We are shooting thirty-second promos. Kent is eating crow. And everyone is ready to kiss your sweet ass."

"Seriously? I thought it was all over. I was so sure—"

"Don't sell yourself short, bubbeleh. You pulled off a miracle."

"I'll come in right away."

"No, you get some rest. You deserve it. Just be sure you get your tukhus here by seven tomorrow. It's going to be a hell of a day."

Norah got off the phone and walked three laps around her living room, trying to collect her thoughts. Ted had actually agreed to do the show. And it was happening so fast.

Still, the live broadcast was over twenty-four hours away, which meant that anything could happen. Ted could change his mind for no reason at all. And of course, his health could take a turn for the worse any second. This dream could so easily turn into a nightmare.

Norah couldn't imagine how she would manage a single deep breath before airtime tomorrow. The only solution was to keep busy. She would go crazy if she stayed in this apartment, watching the dust fall. She decided she would get dressed as quickly as possible and head into Manhattan so she could tell Dorothy Parker what had happened.

Norah was just stepping out of the shower when her cell phone rang. She toweled her hair and answered it.

"He's doing it!" Audrey said, excited. "He's doing the *Simon Janey* show. He'll be on tomorrow."

"So I heard."

"I just wanted to make sure you were still okay with it."

"Of course," Norah said. "I'm better than okay with it."

"I mean, I want to be one hundred percent sure you're going to bring the signature book to my editor's office. I told her you would come on Tuesday."

"That's fine," Norah said. "Tuesday is fine."

"And you'll be able to get the book from the hotel?"

"That shouldn't be a problem."

"And you'll be able to make her show herself?"

"Absolutely," Norah lied. She wasn't going to risk Ted's appearance on the show by telling Audrey there was every reason to believe Dorothy Parker would refuse to show herself. Besides, after the way Ted and Audrey had deceived her, she owed them nothing.

Audrey gave Norah details about the office address and then asked, "So how do you do it? How do you conjure her? Do you have magic words?"

Norah laughed. "You mean like 'Abracadabra, toil and trouble, Dorothy Parker, appear on the double'? I'm afraid not."

"So you just call her? And she always comes?"

"Always."

"What do you say, exactly?"

Norah hesitated. "Why do you want to know?"

"It's my job to know."

Norah was tempted to ask if Audrey was thinking about sidestepping her, but she kept herself in check. No sense in giving the unpredictable woman any ideas. Besides, it was likely a perfectly innocent question.

"You'll find out on Tuesday," Norah said.

There was a long, uncomfortable pause, and Norah sensed that Audrey was deciding whether to push the question further. At last she said, "Okay, I'll see you Tuesday," and Norah sighed, relieved.

"That's right. I'll see you Tuesday."

About an hour later, Norah was at the Algonquin, nodding hello to the same doorman she had said good-bye to only the day before. She went straight to the Blue Bar, because she knew the guest book was now back where it belonged, safely ensconced in its display case on the shelf.

When she reached the doorway to the bar, Norah saw a stooped man was pushing a vacuum cleaner back and forth. "Not open yet, miss," he called over the noise.

"I . . . I think I left my cell phone in here yesterday," Norah lied. "Can I just take a look?"

"Place has been cleaned out. We didn't find anything—sorry."

Norah asked him when the bar would be open, and he gave her a pitiful look, as if she were someone who could barely wait until eleven thirty in the morning for a drink. She offered him a meek smile, and went back into the lobby to while away the twenty minutes. She positioned herself in a chair facing the entrance so that she could be the first person in the bar. The emptier it was, the greater the chance she had of summoning Mrs. Parker to appear.

She took out her cell phone and scrolled through her e-mail. There was one from Pamela Daniels, saying she went ahead and promised Beth Barbieri a recommendation. Norah was only halfway through the e-mail when something brushed against her leg and made her jump. For a moment, she expected to see Dorothy Parker, but Norah looked down and realized the culprit wasn't a ghostly presence but Matilda, the Algonquin's famous cat in residence. The enormous feline knocked against her, begging for a pat.

"Hey, you," she said, gently stroking the cat's long fur. She wondered how the cat would react to being picked up. Before she could give it a try, though, Matilda lost interest and wandered away. Norah leaned back, drowsy. Her restless night was catching up with her and it was hard to keep her eyes open. Norah fought the urge to drift off, but the chair was so soft and deliciously comfortable that she ultimately lost the battle and fell into a deep, dreamless sleep.

By the time she awoke she could hear voices from within the bar. Damn. She had missed her opportunity to beat the crowd.

Norah stood and shook off the sleep, then went inside. There was a couple at one of the tables, and several people at the bar. Norah went to the table closest to the guest book, and took a seat with her back to it. She hoped Mrs. Parker would have the gumption to materialize in the seat opposite her, though she knew it was a long shot with so many people around.

Norah glanced toward the bar and saw an older man in aviator glasses trying to catch her eye. She took out her cell phone and pretended she didn't notice.

"Mrs. Parker," she whispered into the phone, "if you can hear me, please make yourself known. I need to talk to you. It's urgent."

She waited several moments and nothing happened.

"It's about Ted," she continued. "Please, Mrs. Parker, we need to talk. Are you here?"

Norah scanned the room for floating dust particles. She stared at the seat opposite her and squinted, trying to determine if there were stray specks visible. She thought she saw something starting to swirl, but couldn't tell if it was merely wishful thinking.

After a few more minutes, the bartender approached with a drink on a tray and put it in front of her. It was a frothy white concoction with a slice of pineapple wedged onto the glass, and two small orange straws set at a jaunty angle.

"I didn't order anything," Norah said.

"It's from that gentleman at the bar."

Norah looked over and saw the man with the aviator glasses smiling at her. He was missing an incisor.

"Please take it back," she said. "I don't want it." Norah knew the man at the bar might be insulted, but she needed to send a strong message that she wasn't interested.

"I understand," the waiter said, putting it back on his tray. "Can I get you something else?"

She didn't want anything, but felt compelled to order something since she was sitting in the bar. "I'll just have a Diet Coke," she said.

When the waiter left, she pretended to talk into her cell phone again.

"Mrs. Parker, if you're hovering, please give me a sign."

Nothing.

"I need to talk to you about Audrey and about the guest book. Are you there?" She waited a few more minutes and tried again. "Ted agreed to do the show. I know that must surprise you."

She tilted her head right and left, staring hard at the space where she thought she saw something earlier. The waiter arrived with her soda.

"The gentleman at the bar insisted on paying," he said.

"Please tell him I can't accept and I'm not interested."

The waiter gave her an apologetic smile and said that he would relay the message.

Norah spoke into her cell phone again. "He's gone. You can come out now. Please!"

She leaned forward to see if the air was changing. She still couldn't tell, but she saw some dust and held her breath.

"Is that you?" she said.

Norah became aware of a presence nearby, but it wasn't Dorothy Parker. It was the big dolt in the glasses. He slid into the booth opposite her.

"I'm Russell," he said. "You look lonely."

"I don't mean to be rude, Russell, but I'm not lonely. Not at all."

"Why don't we just talk for a moment?" he said. "No harm in that, is there?"

"Listen," she said, "I'm expecting a very important . . . client.

Could you do me a huge favor and leave right this minute? I'm sorry to ask, but it's urgent. I'm sure you understand."

"Why don't you give me your number, then?"

"I can't, Russell. I'm sorry."

"What a bitch," he said.

"Okay, fine. It was lovely chatting with you."

"And you're not that good-looking anyway."

"Well, my whole feeling of self-worth hangs on what you think of my appearance, so thank you for setting the record straight."

At last, he got up to leave, but not without whispering a word under his breath that Norah hoped no woman would ever be called again. She watched as he approached the bar and said something to his friend that made them both laugh. The men paid their tab and left, but not before giving Norah the finger.

She was glad to be rid of him, but disappointed that she had come so close to summoning Dorothy Parker and failed. Now she doubted the spirit would risk trying to materialize in public again. There was another possibility, however. She could try to sneak the book out of the bar.

Norah stood and walked casually toward the display case as if she had just noticed it. The waiter had just gone into the back, and if the bartender looked down for even a moment, she would grab the book and saunter out as casually as she could.

When she got close, however, Norah noticed something that stopped her cold. The display case was empty.

The waiter came back into the room and she waylaid him. "What happened to the book?" she asked.

"The book?"

"There was a book of signatures in this case."

"It's not there?" He approached and looked inside. "I'll be damned. It was missing for days, and yesterday we finally got it back."

So those dust particles weren't her friend after all. "When did you last see it?" she asked.

"It was here last night."

"Do you have any idea who might have it?"

"Beats me," he said. "Sometimes I think this place is haunted. Can I get you another drink?"

She declined, and left the bar to ask the people at the front desk if they had seen the guest book. No one even realized it had disappeared again. She asked the maître d' at the Lounge and a few other staff members, but no one knew anything about it.

Dizzy, Norah let herself sink into the soft armchair again as she considered who might have taken the book. She wanted to believe it was that terrible Edie Coates, but as she replayed her last conversation with Audrey, she understood the truth. Audrey *had* been pumping her for information. In fact, she had probably meant to steal the book all along.

Norah put her head in her hands. If Audrey could manage to get Dorothy Parker to reveal herself before tomorrow's interview, there was nothing she would need from Norah, and Ted would back out of the interview.

She headed for the exit but stopped to talk to the doorman. "I'm wondering if you've seen my friend," she said, and proceeded to describe Audrey.

"Lady with a big red purse," he said. "I remember her—she seemed very nervous."

"Thank you," Norah said, and knew what she had to do. She had to steal the book back from Audrey.

34

Norah walked toward Audrey's apartment, growing angrier with every step. It was all so clear now. The woman had played her like a ukulele, extracting information about the guest book in order to figure out if it was worth stealing. Norah guessed that, after Ted had agreed to do the live show, the two of them conspired to find a way out, and came to the conclusion that if they had deceived her once, they could do it again.

Her fury continued to mount. She was angry with Ted. She was angry with Audrey. Most of all, she was angry with herself for trusting that woman. How could she have been so foolish? A person who would set up her husband for plagiarism was capable of anything.

Norah reached Audrey's building and announced herself through the intercom. Audrey sounded confused, but buzzed her in.

"I wasn't expecting you," Audrey said when she opened the door to her apartment.

I'll bet, Norah thought, but she hid her anger under a broad smile. If she was going to find that book, she had to pretend she didn't know Audrey had it. Her ruse was the dog.

"Why are you here?"

Norah smiled again. "I hate to intrude," she said, bringing her hand to her chest to illustrate the depth of her sincerity, "and I know I seem like an overzealous social worker, but I wanted to check on the puppy. I'm sure you understand. I still feel responsible for him." That part, at least, was true.

"He's fine," Audrey said. "Really. I'm doing a good job."

"Can I see him?"

"You're not going to take him away, are you?"

"I just want to see him," Norah said. "May I come in?"

Audrey hesitated. "I'm sorry, of course." She opened the door and led Norah inside.

Right away, Norah could see that Audrey had made quite a few puppy-related purchases. There was now a gate at the entrance to the kitchen and a towel-lined crate in the living room. Plastic chew toys were everywhere. The apartment smelled like a not-quite-housebroken puppy.

Audrey leaned over the gate and picked up the little dog. "I'm training him to go on pads," she said. "I don't keep him locked up in the kitchen all the time."

"I can see that," Norah said. "It looks like he has the run of the place. Can I hold him?"

Audrey placed this puppy in Norah's arms, and she could tell that his little belly was rounder. She patted his head, and already felt her anger dissipating. Norah understood why Dorothy Parker felt so lost without her beloved poodle. These creatures had a way of making a home in the tenderest part of your heart.

"You can take him in the living room," Audrey said. "I'm just going to clean up the mess he made."

Perfect, Norah thought, refocusing. She carried the puppy into the living room and held him while she searched for the Algonquin guest book. She looked under throw pillows and newspapers. She scanned every surface, trying to imagine where Audrey might have quickly stashed it before letting her in. Norah opened the cabinet doors on the bottom of the large bookcase, and it held nothing but CDs, DVDs, and a stack of paperback romance novels.

Norah looked around and thought she saw something under the big blue easy chair. Still holding Jim Beam, she got on her hands and knees and peered beneath it. There was definitely something there, but she couldn't tell what it was.

She heard Audrey come back into the room and turned around. "I think one of his toys rolled under the chair," Norah said, standing.

Audrey folded her arms. "Tell me the truth," she said.

"Excuse me?"

"You didn't really come to make sure I'm taking good care of the dog."

Norah went cold. "Of course I did," she said. "Why else would I be here?"

"Norah, you can admit it. Believe me, I understand."

"I don't follow you . . ."

"You missed him. You missed Jim Beam. I can't say I blame you."

She let out a breath. "It's true," she said, giving the pup's head a kiss. "The little guy really works his way into your heart."

Audrey reached out and squeezed Norah's arm. "You can come visit him anytime—you don't even need an excuse. Who knows? Maybe we'll even become friends."

God, she's good, Norah thought. "That would be nice," she said, and sat in the blue chair with the puppy in her lap. She pretended to cough—a ruse to get Audrey out of the room again. "I've had such a scratchy throat today," she said.

"Can I get you a glass of water?" Audrey asked.

"I hate to trouble you, but do you have tea?"

Audrey nodded. "I'll be right back," she said, and went into the kitchen.

Norah waited a beat and then went back to looking under the

chair. She reached in, grabbed the mysterious object and slid it out. It was a wooden serving tray. Norah shook her head and put it back. Manhattanites with tiny apartments found the strangest places to store things.

Norah pulled a chair over to the bookcase so she could look on top of it. There was a jewelry box, two toner cartridges, a pile of file folders, and no guest book.

"How do you take your tea?" Audrey called.

Norah climbed off the chair. "Strong, if you don't mind!"

She tiptoed into Audrey's bedroom, carrying the puppy with her, and began looking through drawers as quickly as she could. She heard noise in the kitchen and realized there was simply no way she would be able to search the entire apartment. She would have to use another tactic.

"Mrs. Parker," she whispered, "if you're here, please make yourself known."

She held still to wait for a reply and heard Audrey call her name. She hurried out of the bedroom and sat in the blue chair, holding Jim Beam on her lap.

"Did you want milk?" Audrey called.

"No thanks," Norah said.

Audrey came back in holding two cups of tea on saucers. "For the life of me," Audrey said, "I can't remember where I put my serving tray." She handed Norah her tea.

"Thank you," she said. "You're very kind."

Audrey took the puppy from her. "I have to put him back in the kitchen now. He might need to . . . you know."

When she came back into the living, Audrey sat opposite Norah and picked up her tea.

"So what have you been up to?" Norah asked. "Just a relaxing Sunday?"

"I took Jim Beam for a long walk, but he got tired and I had to carry him home."

"Do anything else? I mean, since we spoke this morning."

"Nope."

"You haven't been out at all?"

"I've been close to home the whole day."

I've got her! Norah thought, and leaned forward. "Why are you lying to me?" she asked.

"I'm *not* lying."

Norah stood. "Where is it?" she asked.

"Where is *what?*"

"You're not going to be able to conjure her, anyway," Norah said. "So you may as well give me back the guest book."

"The guest book?"

"I know you have it."

"I do *not* have it. Why would you think that?"

"Because it's missing. And because you lied to me about going to the Algonquin. I checked with the doorman. He saw you."

"That was *yesterday.*"

"Yesterday?"

"I stopped in after I visited you," she said. "I interviewed hotel staff about seeing a phantom at the Algonquin. For the article." She went to the bookcase and grabbed a steno pad. "Here are my notes. You can see for yourself."

Norah stared down at the pad. She didn't need to read what it said. Audrey was telling the truth—that much was clear. She handed the pad back and put her hand to her forehead, feeling almost dizzy from the quick change in direction.

"I . . . it's okay," Norah said. "I believe you."

"The Algonquin guest book is missing?" Audrey said.

"I . . . um . . ."

"That means you won't be able to show proof to my editor," Audrey said, her voice rising.

"I'll find it," Norah said.

"If you can't . . ." Audrey said, and Norah understood the rest. No guest book, no interview with Ted.

"Don't worry," Norah said. "If you didn't take it, I know who did."

35

Dorothy Parker knew at once that there was another spirit in this strange, dark, cluttered house. And though she sensed this had been where Percy Coates lived, she knew it wasn't him. Percy had been a gentleman, with a generous soul and a hearty laugh. The specter who lingered here was weak and angry. She would stay out of sight and watch.

She recognized the woman hunched over the writing desk. It was that insufferable Edie Coates, who had been suing the Algonquin Hotel for the guest book. Apparently, she'd decided to take matters into her own hands and abscond with it. This was very bad news. If someone didn't come looking for the book, Dorothy Parker could be stuck in this horrid place forever.

She swirled unseen throughout the room. There were knick-knacks and bric-a-brac on every surface, but she was looking for one thing in particular, and at last she found it on the top shelf of a tall curio cabinet. There it was—a volume that looked very much like the Algonquin guest book, only smaller and darker. It was held open on a book stand and looked insignificant between a thick antique dictionary and a signed first edition of *Shouts and Murmurs*. There were so many thousands of collected pieces in this room that it would be hard for most people to even notice. Besides, it was on a high shelf, above the eye level of all but the tallest visitors.

Edie remained at the desk, busy with something that involved pulling pieces of clear tape from a dispenser and applying them to the Algonquin guest book. What on earth was she doing?

The other spirit appeared at the doorway. He was an unattractive man with deep-set eyes and almost no chin. He wore a silk kimono over his clothes.

"What are you doing?" he said to Edie. His voice was angry, but Dorothy Parker detected that it was mostly bluster. He meant to intimidate this woman.

She looked up, her eyes wide. "I didn't see you there," she said.

"Obviously."

"I got the book," she said. "See?" She seemed eager to calm him.

"You managed to do something right. Did anyone see you leave with it?"

"I hid it under my jacket."

"I should have known. You stole a house. Stealing a book is small potatoes."

"I believe it's very valuable," she said.

"If you think I'm going to let you sell it, you're an even bigger idiot than I thought."

"But, Gavin. I need the cash so badly. I don't know how much longer—"

"It stays in the house. Now close it."

"Why can't I sell it? It wasn't part of the original possessions."

"You want me to unleash more spirits?" he asked.

"Gavin, please!"

"Don't argue, Chubs. Now listen to me and shut the book."

She pulled a tissue from a box on the desk and blew her nose.

"Stop crying and do what I said," he seethed.

Edie finished her business with the tissue and dropped it into a wastebasket, then she pulled out another piece of tape. "I'm almost finished fixing it," she said.

"To hell with fixing it! What do you think that's going to do, anyway?"

"The spirit—" she began, but was interrupted by the sound of the doorbell.

"Who are you expecting?" he said.

"No one."

"Send them away. But shut that book first."

Edie stood. "I'll close it when I'm done," she said as she left the room.

"Imbecile!" he shouted after her.

With Edie gone, Gavin tentatively approached the Algonquin guest book to get a closer look. Dorothy Parker materialized in a blood red leather arm chair directly behind him.

"How do you do?" she said, startling him.

He whirled around and looked at her. "You!" he said. "I knew there was another spirit here. I *knew* it. Get out and never show yourself again. You don't belong here."

"That makes two of us, doesn't it?"

"This is *my* house."

"I think not. Besides, why did you have her bring the book here if you're so frightened of me?"

"Frightened? Ha! I'm not scared of you. I'm going to have my sister close the book and then you'll be gone forever."

"Don't be rude, dear. Fix me a drink and we'll have a little chat."

"I'd sooner pour a drink on your head."

"Charming."

"She's going to walk back in here any second," he whispered.

"And then she'll shut the book and you'll be gone forever. I'll have her wrap the book in sheets and put it in the attic, where no one will ever find it."

"Yes, that's a distinct possibility. Of course, I could convince her to close the book *you* signed and then all her problems will be over, won't they?"

"I didn't sign any book! It's the kimono that brought me here." He held his arms wide to show the full splendor of the garment.

She laughed. "My dear, you may have succeeded in convincing Edie of that fiction, but I know the truth."

"It's the kimono!" he said. "It has special powers."

"It's no use, precious," she said. "I saw the book. Your sister will be learning about it the moment she returns."

He folded his arms. "What do you want?"

"I see. You think you have something of value to me."

"I'll make you a deal," he said. "You keep your mouth shut about the book, and I'll let you have the downstairs."

"The downstairs?"

"That's right. You have this floor and I'll take the upstairs. You just have to keep your mouth shut about the book."

"I understand. You want me to let Edie go on thinking it's the kimono that brought you here, so she never suspects that all she has to do is shut that book and you'll be gone from her life forever. Why would I ever go along with such a plan?"

"Because she's more scared of you than she is of me. She'll shut both books and lock them away forever."

"Gavin, dear, I hardly think—"

Before Dorothy Parker could finish her sentence, Edie walked back into the room and headed straight for the desk. It was clear from her purposeful stride that she intended to close the book. Gavin sensed it, too, and smirked.

That son of a bitch, Dorothy Parker thought. But she had been around far longer than he, and knew a difficult trick he had probably never mastered. She rushed the particles of her matter through the air, heading straight for Edie. If she was fast enough, she could merge with the woman's being and try to stop her from closing the book. But Edie picked up the volume, and before Dorothy Parker could get close enough, it was shut tight, and she disappeared into the dark void.

36

Norah rushed back to the Algonquin and checked with the doorman, who confirmed that Audrey had been there yesterday, not today. She thanked him and went straight to the office on the second floor to see if she could talk someone into giving her an address for the one other person likely to have stolen the Algonquin guest book: Edie Coates.

The woman in the office, a cheerful redhead named Debbie, told her that the only individual who might have Edie Coates's home address was their attorney, and Norah knew that she would never be able to pry that information from someone who makes their living keeping secrets.

"Would a Manhattan phone book help?" Debbie asked, pulling a large volume out of her overhead cabinet.

Norah thanked her and quickly thumbed through the tissuey leaves until she reached the right page. She ran her finger down the column of people named Coates, picturing them spread throughout the city, their apartment windows lit up like stars in the night sky. There was no "Edie" in the constellation, but there was a "Coates, E."

Norah wanted to find out if it was the right person before embarking on her surprise visit, and so she called the number and asked for Edie.

"Who?" said a man with a gravelly voice. Norah was pretty sure she had woken him up.

"Is this the residence of Edie Coates?"

"*Ezra* Coates," he said.

"Any relation—"

"Wrong number," he said, and hung up.

Norah sighed and handed the phone book back to Debbie. "I hate to ask," Norah said, "but could I use your computer for a minute?"

"I wish I could, but I'm not allowed," Debbie said. "You want to check the other boroughs? I have every phone book."

"That would be great," Norah said. "Thanks."

Debbie opened the cabinet again and grabbed the thick volumes one by one, dropping them heavily onto her desk. Norah picked up the Brooklyn book and began to look through it as Debbie went back to work, typing furiously at her computer.

"Is that *Coates* with an *e* on the end?" Debbie asked, as she stared at her computer screen.

"Yes, why?"

"You didn't hear it from me," she said, "but try Queens."

The subway ride to Forest Hills, Queens, was shorter than Norah had expected. She exited the station and walked past the commercial part of the neighborhood into a quiet residential area filled with tall trees and substantial brick houses with red tile roofs.

She located the address she had found in the phone book, and it was a pretty house, though not as grand as some of the others. It looked like a storybook colonial, and Norah guessed it was well over a hundred years old. She knew that a lot of these historic New York residences stayed in the same families for generations, and she wondered if this place had ever been home to Percy Coates.

The front door, framed in white-painted molding that contrasted dramatically with the dark red brick, gave the home a stately character. Norah walked up four stone steps to reach it and pressed the bell. A few moments later she heard Edie's voice scream "Who's there!" in a way that sounded accusatory.

"My name is Norah Wolfe. We met at the Algonquin."

Edie Coates pulled open the door. Her hair was wild and unbrushed, and she was dressed in a colorful floor-length dashiki. *This woman,* Norah thought, *has the most unusual wardrobe I've ever seen.*

"What do you want?" she demanded.

"Can I come in?"

"No!"

"Edie, I'm not here to make trouble, but I think you have something that belongs to the hotel."

"What's it to you? You don't work there."

That took the wind out of Norah. Edie Coates had been doing her homework. She struggled to find something to say.

"That's right!" Edie continued. "I asked around and found out you were just a *guest.* And a thief, too! Now you have the nerve to come to my door? I should call the police."

"I'm not a thief," Norah said. "I . . ." She remembered how terrified Edie had been when Dorothy Parker had appeared, and quickly decided she would play the fear card, pretending she had some potent and mystical connection too mysterious to speak of. "I'm just someone who knows the *power* of that book."

"Power?" Edie asked.

"It's not something you want to keep in your home," Norah said. "It could be very dangerous for you."

Edie went pale. "I know that! You think I don't know that?"

"But you . . . have it," Norah said.

"I didn't *want* to take it," Edie said. She looked over her shoulder as if someone might overhear her. "I had no choice," she whispered.

Norah took a deep breath. "It's vitally important that I get it back," she said.

"Why? So you can sell it? Make a pile of money?"

"No, nothing like that. There's a reporter who's doing a story about it and . . . a lot is riding on this."

"That book is very valuable," Edie said.

Norah waited for her to finish making her point, but Edie just stood there and stared. At last she understood. "Are you offering to sell it to me?"

"Maybe."

"I'm pretty broke," Norah said.

"How much do you have?"

"On me?"

Edie nodded. "In cash," she said.

"Maybe sixty bucks?"

"Okay."

"Okay what?"

"Okay, you can have it for sixty bucks. But you have to give me the money right now."

Norah looked at Edie's wild, desperate eyes. Was this woman for real? Was she really selling Norah back the book for only sixty dollars? Or was she going to take the money and slam the door in her face?

"I think it's a pretty fair deal," Edie said.

With no other ideas on the horizon, Norah decided to risk it. She opened her purse, took out her wallet, and extracted all her cash—fifty-seven dollars. She handed it to Edie, who counted it, then folded the bills in thirds and stuffed it into her bra.

"Can I come in?" Norah asked.

Edie shook her head. "I'll be right back," she said, and slammed the door. Norah heard her footsteps and about thirty seconds later the door opened again.

"Okay, you can come in," Edie said. "Just don't touch anything. And go along with anything I say. Got it?"

Norah nodded and followed the woman into the house, wondering how dangerous it was to be alone with someone who was so clearly paranoid and delusional.

When they reached the living room, Norah saw that her hunch about the house had been right—it had been in the family for generations. The decor was an accident of years, faded old wallpaper and a crazy conglomeration of mismatched furniture, from dark and cumbersome antiques to midcentury kitsch. And right in the middle of it all was a cheap contemporary couch that looked like the result of a weekend excursion to Ikea.

"Wait here," Edie said.

Alone, Norah studied the knickknacks that graced every shelf and surface. There were sleek Lladró sculptures and grotesque Toby mugs depicting the faces of weathered seamen in shiny ceramic. One shelf held an assortment of empty wine bottles coated in oily dust. There were seashells and rocks, trophies and souvenirs. Some resident of the home had clearly been an Empire State Building aficionado, as there was an entire case of miniature replicas. The china closet contained dishes from at least three different sets, one of which was heavily rimmed in gold. Incongruously, the bottom shelf held an assortment of Barbie dolls from the 1960s and '70s, propped up on stands. The smell of mold was oppressive.

"You didn't touch anything, did you?" Edie said.

"Of course not."

Edie presented her with the Algonquin guest book. "Thank you for not pressing charges," she said loudly, as if there were an audience present. "I honestly don't know what I was thinking when I walked off with it. I guess you knew it was me because you saw it on the security tapes."

"Uh, yes. That's right," Norah said, opening the book to inspect it.

"Don't open it!" Edie cried, pulling the book from her hands and slamming it shut. She looked around and then whispered, "I don't like ghosts."

"I understand," Norah said, prying the book from Edie's tight grip. "I promise I won't open it."

"Please tell your employers at the Algonquin that I'm very sorry, and that I'm dropping my suit. I have no interest in owning this thing." This, again, was loud.

"No problem at all," Norah said. "We're glad to have it back."

"I'll walk you out," Edie said. She went out to the front stoop with Norah and closed the door behind them. "I fixed the book," she said in her normal voice.

"Fixed it?"

"The page with the paw print," Edie said. "I taped it back in."

"You're the one who ripped it out?"

"When I first read about the book in the *New Yorker*, I almost *died*. I mean, here I was desperate for money, and the answer to all my problems was just a subway ride away. It was perfect—a family artifact that my brother didn't even know about."

"Your brother?" Norah said.

"Never mind," Edie said. "The point is, I figured it was rightly mine, and that I could easily sell it without . . . well, let's just say that no one had to know. I'm totally broke, you see, and I have no prospects."

"I understand," Norah said, though she didn't. If this woman was so desperate for money, why didn't she just sell her house, or one of the millions of collectibles inside?

"At first, I wasn't going to sue. I went up to the office and very politely explained to them that I was Percy Coates's great-niece, and that I was the rightful heir. But they were so rude! They didn't even believe I was who I said I was. I was so furious I marched right down-stairs and ripped out the last page of the book. I know I shouldn't have done it, but, oh . . . I was in a state!"

"Why did you want to put it back?" Norah asked.

"Are you kidding? When I found out it was a book of ghosts, I *had* to put it back. No way I wanted that hanging over my head."

"You did the right thing," Norah said.

Edie leaned in. "You don't think the ghosts are still angry with me, do you?"

"I'll put in a good word for you," Norah said, holding the book tight against her chest.

"Hey, would you like something to eat?" Edie asked. "A cup of mushroom soup, maybe?"

"I'm fine, thanks," Norah said, pretending it was an entirely normal question, and left as quickly as she could.

Norah hurried toward the subway station, grateful she still had her MetroCard so that she could get all the way home without stopping at an ATM for cash. She was eager to reach her apartment so she could open the book and have a chat with Dorothy Parker. Then she would return the book to the Algonquin Hotel once and for all.

Norah was also curious about the page Edie had taped back in. Was it possible the book's magic would continue to work, and that Dorothy Parker would get her beloved poodle back for all eternity?

Still clutching the book to her chest, she descended into the dark maw of the subway station, realizing it was nothing but wishful thinking. Dorothy Parker was no more likely to get her dog back than Norah was to recapture her dream of having a meaningful con-nection with Ted Shriver.

She got a seat on the train and opened the book to inspect it. The pages looked unharmed. She turned to the back to see how Edie had mended the torn leaf, and discovered that she had done a fairly careful job of matching up the ragged edges and covering them with transparent tape.

As she studied it, Norah became aware of something in her periphery. She looked to her right and saw a swarm of floating dust particles. This time, it wasn't her imagination—the specks were arranging themselves into the shape of a woman. She stared, surprised that Dorothy Parker would materialize right there on the F train.

Norah glanced around, wondering if she should slam the book shut. In typical New Yorker fashion, everyone looked away before she could make eye contact. And when the dust particles settled themselves into a human form, no one reacted, except to go back to their books and newspapers, pretending they hadn't seen it. *This town*, she thought, *is shocked by nothing.*

Dorothy Parker looked up, her hands neatly folded in her lap. "Well," she said, "this is a pleasant surprise. I didn't expect to be rescued quite so soon."

"You're a surprise for me, too," Norah said. "I didn't think you would materialize in a crowded public place."

"I knew no one would notice," Mrs. Parker said. "New York straphangers are an unflappable lot."

"Straphangers," Norah repeated, smiling. The term wasn't exactly archaic, but it wasn't something she heard very often.

Dorothy Parker looked up. "Dear me, they've done away with the straps, haven't they?"

Norah glanced around, trying to imagine how it all looked to Dorothy Parker. This had to be her first time on the subway since the 1960s, when most men wore suits and hats and women didn't dare wear pants to work. And certainly, the seats weren't made of orange plastic back then. "I guess all the charm is gone," she said.

A large man in an olive-green jacket walked down the car and stopped, grabbing the overhead bar in front of them.

"The subway never had *charm*, my dear," Dorothy Parker said. "It was dreadful then and it's dreadful now." The subway car lurched and the man's open jacket swung into her face. She batted it away. "Speaking of which, I would be remiss if I didn't thank you for rescuing me from that ghastly house."

"It was like something from one of your short stories," Norah said.

"How did you know I would be there?"

"An educated guess. I was in a panic when I discovered that the book had disappeared. At first I thought Audrey had taken it. Then I realized it had to be Edie Coates. I wound up finding her in the phone book, listed under her full name. A lucky break."

"I'm surprised you even knew the book was missing. I thought you left the hotel."

"Did. But I came back to talk to you. Mrs. Parker, something extraordinary happened. Ted agreed to do the show. He's being interviewed tomorrow."

"Well, that's happy news for you. Congratulations, my dear."

"I thought it was all over," Norah said. "The show was shut down and we were all let go. Then Audrey showed up at my apartment. She said the editor who's interested in her story about the guest book insisted on seeing you before giving her the green light. She wanted to strike a deal—if I could get you to appear, Ted would do the show. I refused, but made a counterproposal. I said that Ted had to do the show first. I honestly didn't think he would bite, but it looks like it's actually happening."

As the subway rounded a curve, the man's green jacket swung toward Mrs. Parker's face again. "Do you mind?" she said to him, and Norah froze. The man was at least three hundred pounds, and looked like a suspect in a police lineup.

He stared down at Dorothy Parker, and Norah broke out in a sweat, certain they were in trouble. But the man shrugged sheepishly and apologized, as if overpowered.

Norah looked back at Mrs. Parker, who was smoothing her skirt, oblivious. Norah made a mental note about commanding respect. The trick, it seemed, was assuming you would get it.

"Listen," said Norah, who really did have respect for Dorothy Parker. "You don't have to do it. We don't owe them anything. I can tell Audrey I tried my best and you refused. Actually, it would serve them right for how they treated me."

Mrs. Parker got very still for a moment as she considered it. "I shan't give an answer right now," she finally said. "Let's wait until to-morrow and see what happens with the show."

"I'm surprised you would even consider it."

"My dear, I don't want Ted angry with you."

"Why not?"

Dorothy Parker gave her a loaded look.

"You're not still stuck on the idea that I should tell Ted he's my father?" Norah said.

"It's imperative."

"Mrs. Parker—"

"Norah, dear, you will not get another chance."

"So what? He doesn't deserve any consideration."

"What about yourself?"

"Don't worry about me," Norah said. "I'll be fine."

"I beg to differ. If you don't tell that man he is your father, you will regret it . . . perhaps on the very day he takes his last breath."

"That's a chance I'm willing to take," Norah said.

Dorothy Parker sat quietly for a moment. "You said he's doing the show tomorrow?"

"That's right."

"And you'll be there?"

"I'm always in the studio during the broadcast. Why?"

"No reason, really. Be sure to send Teddy my best."

37

Peter Salzberg made sure to arrive at the Algonquin at least an hour early, hoping he had left enough time to deal with whatever mess Ted might be in. He knew that anything was possible. Ted could be drunk or stoned on painkillers. He might be in a fury that needed an outlet. Or he could just be too dirty and disheveled to appear in public. At Aviva's suggestion, Pete had brought along a sports coat and tie in case Ted didn't have anything clean and pressed to wear for his big television appearance.

He knocked on the door to Ted's room and when it opened, he stepped back, astonished. Ted was clean-shaven and neat, dressed in a halfway-decent dark suit, a tie draped around his neck. He even smelled good.

Pete recognized the aftershave—it was the same one Ted had worn the first time they met back in 1968. Pete had finished reading *Dobson's Night* and asked Ted to come to his office. After the introductions, they went out to lunch—on Litton's dime—and spent an hour talking about the book. Then Pete got ready to launch into his pitch to convince this young author to sign with them. He was well prepped with a list of reasons, from the company's reputation to their marketing plans for the book. He was even prepared to discuss money. But Ted cut him off.

"I don't want to hear it," he had said. "Just shut up and give me the contract."

"Why?"

"Because I trust you."

And that was it. They had been friends ever since.

Now Pete wondered what force of nature had convinced his stubborn friend to shave and primp and join the living.

"You look good," Pete said. "What happened?"

"I haven't forgotten how to shower and dress. Not yet, anyway. Come in."

"You feeling okay?" Pete said as he looked around the room.

"Hell, no. But unfortunately, I'll probably live through the interview."

"Nervous?"

"I'm actually looking forward to it."

"You're looking forward to being on TV?" Pete asked.

"No, I'm looking forward to dying."

Pete walked to the window and looked down toward the street. "Dying is easy," he said. "TV is hard. We should talk about what you can expect."

"I think I can handle myself."

"What's this?" Pete said, pointing to a room service cart. "You ordered coffee?"

"Courtesy of your publicity department. And the TV people sent a fruit basket. It's a conspiracy."

"Well, I'm having a cup," Pete said as he poured. "You want one?"

"I don't need sobering up."

"I just asked if you wanted a cup of coffee. Don't turn paranoid right before a live interview."

"I'll take it black."

Pete poured the coffee and handed it to him. "They're going to press very hard on the plagiarism."

"And all this time I thought we'd talk about baseball."

"I mean it might get . . . heated."

Ted laughed. "And you think I can't handle that?"

"I was just wondering if you planned to tell the truth."

"You'll see."

"Ted—"

"You have to trust me, Pete. I'm going to keep things interesting."

He sighed. "That's what I'm afraid of."

"I promise I'll give the publicists plenty to work with. You'll sell lots of books."

Pete put his hand on his friend's shoulder. "I know this was a tough decision. For what it's worth, I think you're doing the right thing."

"That would be a first." Ted walked to the mirror and threaded his tie beneath his collar. "There's something I need to tell you."

Pete walked behind him and looked at Ted in the mirror. "I'm listening."

Ted raised his chin and looped the wide end of the tie around the top. "I've decided to go ahead with the surgery."

"What?"

"I'm scheduled to go in tomorrow."

Pete stared at his friend's face to see if he could detect a trace of sarcasm. He was serious. "You're having brain surgery? What changed your mind?"

"Does it matter?"

Pete shook his head. It *didn't* matter. His friend was going to live. He took a moment to compose himself. "Ted, this is great news!"

"Is it? I'll probably die on the table."

"Don't say that."

"The tumor's grown, Pete. I don't know what my chances are."

"I'm sure you'll be in good hands. I'm just . . . I don't know what to say." Pete felt his eyes sting and turned away.

"If you start to cry, I'll punch you in the throat," Ted said.

"No crying," Pete said, and turned around to embrace his friend.

Ted glared. "And if you hug me I'll break both your arms."

"Fuck you," Pete said. He gave his cantankerous friend a backslap version of a hug and pulled away.

He assumed the dramatic reversal had something to do with Audrey, but he didn't want to press it and risk derailing this change of heart. "Who's taking you to the hospital?" he said.

"Whoever's driving the cab."

"Absolutely not," Pete said. "I'm taking you."

"You have a job."

"Screw the job," he said, quite sure that the reason Ted even told him about the surgery was because he wanted someone there with him. "I'll cancel everything for tomorrow."

"Suit yourself."

There was, Pete knew, a lot of bluster in Ted's attitude. But if his friend didn't feel at least a little positive about the surgery, he wouldn't be going through with it. If nothing else, it showed that there was a will to survive.

"Who else have you told?" Pete asked, eager to figure out the reason for the change of heart.

"No one."

"Not even Audrey?"

"Audrey has nothing to do with this."

"You just changed your mind?"

"I didn't say that."

Pete waited a beat but Ted didn't elaborate. "You're not going to tell me what happened?"

"It's not your business. It's not anyone's business." Ted opened his bottle of Vicodin and poured two into his hand.

"Should you be taking painkillers now, before the show?"

"It's either that or kill myself this minute."

"The pain's that bad?"

"Worse," he said, and slipped the medicine bottle into his pocket. "Let's go."

They left the hotel and got into the back of the Town Car Pete had hired. Ted closed his eyes, leaned his head against the window, and rode in silence. Pete imagined he was counting the minutes until the surgery.

They were stopped at a red light when Ted mumbled something Pete couldn't quite make out.

"What did you say?" Pete asked.

"Never mind."

"No, tell me."

Ted closed his eyes for so long that Pete thought he had fallen asleep. "You all right?" he asked.

Ted didn't open his eyes. "I have a daughter," he said.

"What do you mean you have a daughter?"

"I mean, there is a woman on this earth who carries my DNA."

"I don't understand. You never told me this."

"I never knew."

Pete watched out the window as a woman pushed a stroller across the street. "So this is why you're having the surgery?"

Ted shrugged.

"Did she just call you out of the blue?" Pete said, worried that some fraud had emerged. News about the manuscripts was starting to leak, and that kind of information was bound to shake vermin out of the woodwork.

"She doesn't even know I know."

"The mother called you?"

"The mother's dead."

"Who was she?" Pete said, trying to recall past girlfriends Ted had mentioned.

"You never met her. Though you might know a bit about her if you read *Genuine Lies*. I based a character on her."

"It's sitting on my desk," Pete said. "I'm almost finished with it." The book was about a mother and an adult daughter who both get mixed up with the wrong men. The mother just keeps trying to replace her ex-husband with someone she can fix. The daughter has a palsied hand and is too embarrassed by it to let anyone she really values get close to her.

"April?" Pete said, guessing it was the younger woman.

"It's not a true story," Ted said. "But someone I knew a long time ago inspired that character. I haven't seen her in all these years. I didn't even know she died."

"So how did you find out?"

"Not important."

"But you're sure? I mean one hundred percent?"

Ted winced in pain. He held up his hand to indicate he needed a minute to regroup. "She has my eyes," he said, and Pete noticed his friend's face was pale and sweaty.

"You okay?" Pete asked.

Ted dropped his head. "Never better," he said, looking like he might pass out.

"Did you eat anything today?"

"I don't know."

"Are you supposed to take those painkillers with food?"

"What are you—the interviewer? How the fuck should I know?"

"Let's get you something to eat," Pete said. "There's a hot-pretzel cart on the next corner." He leaned forward. "Driver, pull over."

38

Norah sat in her small office with the door closed, a worm of
panic working its way through her system. What if Ted didn't
show up? There were dozens of coworkers counting on this, not to
mention millions of TV viewers. If it all blew up at the last minute,
Norah would take the heat. She would have to—otherwise, everyone
would blame Didi, and she simply couldn't let that happen.

Aviva and the Litton publicist had arrived almost an hour ago,
buzzing with the energy of anticipation about the event. Norah had
met them at the elevator and led them to the green room, where they
continued their lively chatter, unconcerned about Ted's whereabouts.
Aviva had assured her that Pete had gone to pick him up, and that
they would arrive any minute.

At first, Norah was buoyed by her confidence. But after twenty
minutes ticked by, she became anxious. At thirty minutes she was on
edge. And now she was starting to hyperventilate.

Didi's assistant, Marco, knocked lightly on Norah's door and she
looked up.

"Someone named Audrey Hudson arrived," he said.

"Where is she?" Norah asked, realizing she should have left instructions to keep her away from Aviva.

"I took her to the green room."

"Shit."

"There a problem?"

"Never mind," she said. "I'll take care of it."

She dismissed Marco, and felt so overheated by stress she was starting to sweat. She pulled her blouse from her body to let in some air, but it did little to help. She headed to the green room.

"Any word?" she said, poking her head in the doorway. To her surprise, the atmosphere seemed convivial. There was no discernible strain between Aviva and the friend who had pulled a gun on her. Either all was forgiven or simply repressed. Perhaps the publicist had suggested a detente and set a cheerful tone. They seemed to have a genius for that.

"I heard from Pete," Aviva said. "They stopped to eat."

That didn't do much for Norah's nerves—time was too tight for a side trip. "Don't they know there's a whole spread here?" she asked.

"Apparently Ted was queasy. Pete wanted to grab a pretzel on the street, but Ted insisted on popping into a Chinese restaurant."

"For egg foo yong?" Norah said.

"How did you know?"

Norah shrugged. She wasn't going to get into it. "They'd better get here soon or he won't have time to get into makeup."

Norah looked up and saw Simon Janey down the hall, chatting with Kent, the network CEO. Simon was wearing his dark blue pinstriped suit—the one he usually saved for heads of state. His tie was red with a subtle white pattern that made it look pink on camera. It worked on him, but then, everything did.

Simon walked toward her with his usual long, heavy strides. He could be brusque, especially just before airtime, but Norah knew that was focus and intensity, not rudeness.

"He's on his way, Simon," she said, anticipating his question.

"It's getting late."

She swallowed hard. Despite Aviva's assurance, she wouldn't be able to relax until he actually arrived. "We still have time."

"Not much."

Didi rounded the corner. "He's here!" she called. "They're on their way up."

Relief. Norah's eyes watered spontaneously as the reality of her accomplishment threatened to overwhelm her. She coughed to cover the lapse.

"I'll greet," she said, because meeting guests at the elevator was one of her usual duties.

"Wait up," Didi said. "Simon, you need anything?"

He held up his question cards to show that he had it all under control, and Didi and Norah headed for the elevator banks. This was always the moment when the adrenaline started pumping and everything came into hyperfocus. But today it was heightened, like a crazy fever. The clock was ticking. The public was waiting. They would be going live very soon. This interview would save their jobs, and it would make history.

The twenty seconds it took for the elevator to arrive felt like precious time wasted. At last the soft ding heralded its arrival. But when the doors opened, Norah's blood seemed to stop flowing. Ted was bent over and leaning on Pete, who supported him.

"Lord have mercy," Didi said.

"Is he drunk?" Norah asked.

"He's just feeling a little under the weather," Pete said. "He'll be fine. Let's get him some water and a seat."

They brought Ted into the makeup room and gave him a bottle of water with a straw.

"I'll be fine," he said.

"Can I get you anything else?" Didi asked.

Ted shook his head.

"Sometimes the pain clobbers him hard," Pete explained. "But it passes. It's probably a good thing that it's happening now. He'll be fine by airtime."

"That's less than fifteen minutes from now," said Norah.

"It's okay," Pete said. "He's coming around."

"Is that true, sugar?" Didi asked Ted. "Are you coming 'round?"

Ted lifted his face. His eyes were bloodshot and pained. "Coming around," he said, and sat up straighter.

Kerri, the makeup artist, tucked a tissue into his collar and began applying foundation to his pale skin. She gently pushed his head to the left so she could get his ear, and his eyes rose to meet Norah's. She could tell he hadn't known she was in the room until that second, and his expression changed in a way she couldn't quite pinpoint. He looked sad but also something else. Was he contrite? Norah didn't think the great and belligerent Ted Shriver could actually feel remorse, but it was hard to assign another emotion to that expression. She pictured the way his face had looked the moment he threw the pages out the window, and it was as if this were a different man entirely.

"Norah," he said from a place deep in his throat, and it made her nervous. She simply could not tolerate any tenderness from him after what he had done.

"I'll tell Simon we're almost ready," she said, fleeing the room.

A few minutes later she was in the engineer's booth, watching Simon and Ted get miked, when Marco poked his head in.

"Someone wants to talk to you," he said.

Norah stepped outside the booth to find Peter Salzberg waiting for her.

"What is it?" she said, and he stared at her eyes without saying a word. Ted was already in the studio, so she couldn't imagine what this was about. Surely he wasn't backing out now. "Is everything okay?"

"I'm sorry," he said. "I just . . . I have to ask you a personal question."

Norah sensed that it was something she did not want to hear. "I don't really have time," she said, and started to walk away.

He grabbed her arm. "It's important."

She closed her eyes for a moment to gather strength and to convince herself that it was probably nothing. "Fine, what is it?"

"Did your mother know Ted?"

She fell back against the wall. "Who told you that?"

"It's true, isn't it?"

Norah shook her head. She could not let her secret out. "No. I don't know what you're talking about." She was breathing so hard she could barely speak.

"Was your mother's name April, by any chance?"

She didn't know where he got his information from, but he had traveled down the wrong path and she wasn't about to help him find the right one. "Sorry, no. You must have me confused with someone else," she said, and walked off, but Pete called after her.

"Was it Sherry?" he said.

Norah stopped dead. She turned to face him.

"He dedicated a book to her," Pete said.

"A book?"

"It's called *Genuine Lies*. I think there's a character based on her."

Norah grabbed on to the wall. Her legs felt rubbery. "Does he . . . When did you . . ." She was so overwhelmed she couldn't find the right question to ask first.

"He didn't tell me it was you, Norah. But I saw the way he looked at you in the makeup room. It's true, isn't it? Ted Shriver is your father."

39

Norah didn't know where she was going. She only knew she had to get out of that studio as quickly as she could. She tramped through the streets of Manhattan, trying to sort through explosions of fury so powerful that she felt like she could lift pedestrians off the sidewalk and throw them out of her way. *How dare she! How dare she!* The words matched the cadence of her march as she found herself heading straight for the Algonquin Hotel.

When she entered the Blue Bar, she barely noticed that it was filled with dozens of patrons, enjoying evening cocktails. It didn't matter. Crowd or not, she was going to summon Dorothy Parker.

She was heading for the shelf that held the guest book when someone grabbed her arm. "You again," he said. "If you had a change of heart, you're going to have to prove it to me, baby."

She stared at him for a moment as she got her bearings. It was the man in the aviator glasses who had tried to buy her a drink and then called her that despicable word. He pointed to his cheek, as if he expected her to give him a kiss before he released her arm.

Norah took a careful breath. Her first instinct was to raise her knee so far into his groin it came out his mouth. Instead, she leaned in until she was close enough to lick his ear, then whispered, "Don't fuck with me, Russell, or I will take those stupid glasses off your face and shove them up your—"

Russell released her and teetered back. Norah turned around and understood why. Dorothy Parker had materialized in the middle of the bar.

"What the hell?" Russell said.

"Norah, dear," said Mrs. Parker, ignoring him, "you look like you could use a drink. Let's have a seat, shall we?"

Russell fell back onto his barstool as Norah glared at Dorothy Parker.

"Traitor," she said through closed teeth.

"Come, dear, let's not make a scene in public."

"And why not? After what you did!"

Customers started to turn around and look at them. A waiter rushed over. "Can I get you ladies a table?" he said.

Reluctantly, Norah let him lead them to a dark booth in the back.

"You're a monster," Norah said as she slid into her seat.

"I hardly think so."

"How *could* you!"

"I imagine you spoke to Teddy and that he told you I spilled the beans. Was it a joyous revelation?"

Norah narrowed her eyes. How could she find words in the face of such betrayal? "That wasn't your secret to tell."

"It wasn't yours to keep."

"I see," Norah said, gripping the table as if the booth were too small to contain her fury. "You think he has a *right* to know."

"Doesn't he?"

"His rights are not more important than *mine*."

"Come now. Deep down, you wanted him to know."

"That's not true!"

264

"Then why did you tell me?"

"Because I *trusted* you."

Dorothy Parker let out a small laugh. "Oh, my dear, that simply isn't possible."

Norah didn't want to cry. She wanted to scream or put her fist through something. But she knew there was no one left to hurt but herself. She closed her eyes for a moment, picturing her mother's face, trying to find a way to convey how sorry she was.

She tried to recall the details of the day her mother had told her about Ted as they sat at the kitchen table. So much of it was so indistinct. Her most vivid memory—the one that wouldn't leave—was waking up that August morning after she had the vision of her mother coming to say good-bye. How long had she lain in bed, trying to convince herself that it had been a dream and that she would hear her mother's wheelchair rolling down the hall any minute?

When she rose at last, she had a decision to make—check on her mother first, or just pick up the phone and call her uncle? She stood outside her mother's closed door and knocked.

"Mom?" she had called, feeling foolish, for she knew there would be no answer. "Are you up?" She paused. "Are you dead?" She waited several minutes, and then pushed the door open a crack and saw her mother, blue and stiff, as dead as anything she had ever seen. Norah slammed the door shut, called her uncle, got dressed, and sat at the kitchen table, feeling like she was living in a strange space, on hold from reality.

Later, when her uncle told her, "There was nothing you could have done," Norah nodded. After all, her mother was clearly dead when she found her. But later, when she learned that her mother had choked to death on her own mucus, Norah had a terrifying thought: maybe she *could* have saved her. If only she had been listening that night. If only she had heard her mother coughing. But no. She had watched an episode of *Melrose Place* and gone to sleep.

Norah tried not to blame herself—she was just a kid, after all. But she decided there was something she *could* do—protect her mother's secret. And she had been faithful to that self-made promise all these years. Now even that was over. Norah stared at Dorothy Parker, then let her head fall on her hands as she wept.

The waiter came back and asked if he could get them anything. Norah didn't lift her face.

"Two appletinis would be lovely," Dorothy Parker said.

Norah looked up and knew she was a mess of tears and runny mascara. Dorothy Parker handed her a cocktail napkin from the table and she wiped her face.

"My mother didn't want him to know," she said.

"Because she was ashamed," Dorothy Parker said.

"So what if she was? You and I can agree that she shouldn't have let shame rule her life, but it was *her* decision. If she wanted to keep her illness and me a secret from him, that was her choice to make—not mine . . . and certainly not yours."

"You think Ted didn't know about her illness?"

"He didn't."

"He most certainly did. He didn't know the diagnosis, but he knew there was something wrong. She tried to hide it, but he saw."

"Where are you getting this from?"

Dorothy Parker laid a key card on the table and pushed it toward Norah.

"What's this?" she asked.

"It's the key to Teddy's room," Dorothy Parker said. "He and I had a long talk after I told him about you, and he gave it to me."

"Why?"

"So I could pass it on to you with these instructions: If you look in his closet, you'll find a green suitcase. Inside are copies of the three manuscripts he turned over to Pete. These are the books he's written since *Settlers Ridge*. Read the one called *Genuine Lies*."

"Why should I?"

"Because your mother thought he would have turned against her if he knew she was ill. Please, dear. At least take a look at those pages."

"Did you read it?" Norah asked.

Dorothy Parker shook her head. "No, but we discussed enough. And I have a good guess as to the rest."

Norah pushed the key back. "I have no interest."

"Do you know what he said when I told him he was your father?"

"I can imagine."

"I don't think you can."

Norah folded her arms. "I suppose you're going to tell me."

"He said, 'This changes everything.'"

Lillian Hellman

1984

Anger. Dorothy Parker felt it swirling about her, chilling the air in the dimly lit bar. She didn't need to look up to know whose dust was rising from the Algonquin guest book. It was her old friend and fellow writer Lillian Hellman. Dorothy Parker finished the rest of her drink and signaled for another. The bartender was quick, but not quick enough. She barely had time to fortify herself with one determined gulp when she heard the rustle of someone at her side.

Dorothy looked up and there was her old comrade, regal in her Blackglama mink, and as familiar as always with her teased coif and heavy nose.

"Oh, Dottie," Lillian Hellman said, "isn't it terrible? We didn't make a damn bit of difference after all."

"Hello, Lilly."

"Scotch on the rocks," Lillian said to the bartender as she threw her mink over an empty stool. She took a seat next to Dorothy, helped herself to a cigarette, and lit it. She took a long drag and exhaled heavily, as if there were more troubles inside her than she could be expected to contain. "What a disappointment."

"The cigarette?"

"The world, silly girl."

"What did you expect?" Dorothy said. "People are shits."

"I thought I'd make a difference. I thought we'd make a difference."

"Don't be polite, dear. You never believed anything I did made a difference."

Lillian took another drag and flicked her ashes. "Fine, you were a disappointment, too, scribbling away at your little stories and verse, never bothering to try anything bigger. And then one day you simply died. Pitiful."

"But I did try. That's the sad truth. All I ever wanted was to follow in the exquisite footsteps of Edna St. Vincent Millay, unhappily, in my own horrible sneakers. But I couldn't even manage that."

"Nonsense. You didn't lack talent—you lacked drive." The bartender set Lillian's drink in front of her and she picked it up. "Cheers."

"Cheers," Dorothy said. "Good to see you again."

"Ha."

"I'm always glad to see you, Lilly. You know that."

"Even when I'm awful about your writing?"

"I was surrounded by sycophants all my life and it's been no different in death. The honesty is refreshing."

"I'm always honest," Lilly said.

Dorothy Parker turned slowly toward her friend, trying to read her expression. Did Lilly actually believe what she was saying? For as long as Dorothy had known her, Lillian had indulged in the dangerous habit of substituting fantasy for reality. Her memoirs pushed the truth further still, and even Dottie was surprised by the audacity of her friend's lies. She was already here, in this post-life, when the books were published, but she followed the news with interest, especially when the truth came out and the whole world learned that the memoirs were more fiction than fact. Lillian Hellman had been exposed.

"Of course you are, dear," Dorothy said, letting her sarcasm do the heavy lifting. "Who could ever doubt you?"

Lilly shook her head. "Not you, too."

"I've been hovering around here almost all these years, Lilly. I know about your memoirs. I know about the allegations. I even know that Mary McCarthy said—"

"Allow me," Lillian interrupted. "That bitch told the world that every word I wrote was a lie, including 'and' and 'the.'"

"You must admit you took quite a few . . . liberties."

Lillian waved away her comment. "I'm an artist."

So that was her excuse. Dorothy lit a cigarette. "No regrets?"

"Oh, I have plenty of regrets. But I stand behind what I wrote. In any case, I'm flattered you've kept abreast of me all these years."

Dorothy finished her gin and tonic and signaled for another. It was time to tell Lilly what else she knew. She had been waiting for this moment a long time.

"I've kept abreast of most things, my friend."

Lilly paused, looking into her drink. "That sounds quite pointed."

"I'm giving you the opportunity to apologize."

"Me?" Lillian said. "What do I have to apologize for? You're the one who needs to apologize, Dottie."

"Don't be ridiculous."

Lillian's eyes went cold and she lowered her voice. "You didn't leave me a cent. Not even a token. You made me executor of your estate and left everything to a complete stranger."

"I left everything to Martin Luther King, Jr."

"Like I said."

"Oh please, Lilly. You didn't need my money. Besides, I had almost nothing. The least I could do was make a statement about where I stood on civil rights."

Disgusted, Lillian made a sound in the back of her throat and brought her glass down on the bar. "Saint Dorothy of the Upper East Side," she said.

"Weren't you just complaining that we hadn't made a difference? Well, I died trying. Literally."

"You could have told me." She picked up her drink again and took a sip.

"So you were angry."

"Damn right I was angry," Lilly said.

"Is that why you purposely denied my one final wish?" Dorothy's will had been unequivocal: there were to be no funeral services, formal or informal. Yet Lilly had arranged a lavish affair, inviting friends and acquaintances. She even delivered a long-winded and disingenuous eulogy—exactly what Dorothy wanted to avoid.

"People needed a chance to say good-bye, pay their final respects," Lilly said.

"What about respect for me? I made my wishes quite clear."

"But you were wrong, Dottie dear."

Dorothy exhaled a long trail of smoke. "Lilly, you are insufferable."

"You made me the executor. It was my duty to make things right."

"Please. It was an act of vengeance. You were furious that I didn't leave you the rights to my work."

"If I'm so evil," Lillian said, pointing to a spot over her head, "why have I earned eternal peace? I can feel it right there, calling for me."

"That's a riddle I can't solve. But consider this: Can you sense Dash there waiting for you?" Dashiell Hammett had been Lilly's mate and lover—a hell of a writer, but a brutal son of a bitch.

Lilly glanced up, her expression softening. "He's there, and he's happy."

"So you see," Dorothy said, "you don't need to be a paragon of godliness . . . or even decency."

"I thought you liked Dash."

"I liked his work, dear. As a man, he was monstrous."

"He wasn't too fond of you, either," Lilly said.

"Yes, he made that quite clear. But you're the one who wounded me."

Lillian looked over at her. "All these years you've been holding it against me that I organized a memorial service for you? That's rather small of you, Dot."

"If only that were your worst offense."

"Don't keep me in suspense," Lillian said. "What was my other unpardonable crime?"

"My remains, dear. You never even claimed them."

"You didn't leave instructions."

"I didn't think I had to. Besides, you wouldn't have followed them anyway. I certainly never imagined that my ashes would remain at the crematorium and eventually wind up in the bottom drawer of a filing cabinet in a lawyer's office. On Wall Street, of all places. Really, Lilly. No one deserves that kind of indignity."

"Since when do you care about dignity?"

"Don't be glib. If I thought it was an oversight or some kind of mistake, I could forgive it. But let's be honest for once. You were furious with me over the will, and it was the only way you could get even."

Lillian Hellman finished her Scotch and stamped out her cigarette. "I guess this is my cue to leave."

Dorothy watched as her friend rose and reached for her mink coat. After all these years, it felt good to make Lilly face the ugliness of her behavior.

"Good-bye, Dot," she said.

Dorothy looked up, and as she pictured Lillian disappearing forever into the white light, a familiar depression bore down on her. It could be years before someone else materialized from the guest book, and all that time she would be sitting here, alone. Dorothy lowered her head and realized that, despite everything, she didn't want Lilly to go. Not yet. Surely she could stay for another drink or two. She touched her friend's arm.

"What is it?" Lillian said.

Dorothy tried to speak, but the fear of isolation choked her and she couldn't utter a word. Lilly shook her head, her disgust softened only by pity.

"Well?" Lilly said, and Dorothy could tell by her voice that she was willing to stay for a while. It was an act of mercy.

Accept it, Dorothy told herself. Lilly owes you at least that much. And anyway, what is pride compared to the oppression of loneliness?

Dorothy Parker considered that as she stared at the woman who had betrayed her so heartlessly. Where was her mercy then?

Lilly grew impatient. "No last words?" she said.

Dorothy picked up her cigarette and took a long drag, stalling as she decided what to say. At last she snubbed it hard in the ashtray and spoke.

"Send my regards to Dash."

40

There was no studio audience on the set of *Simon Janey Live*, but there was a small seating area off to the left. Visitors were instructed to remain quiet and to be careful of the cables running across the floor.

Pete sat in the middle, between Aviva and Katie, his Litton publicist. Audrey sat on the other side of his wife. He glanced back into the glass booth to see if Norah had returned, but there was no sign of her. Clearly, his assumption had been right—she was Ted's daughter. But for some reason she had kept it a secret from him. Pete didn't know who finally told Ted the truth, but he was grateful. The knowledge had given his friend the desire to live. If only Norah was willing to face him, it might stick.

A cameraman steered his equipment toward the stage and the lights went on, bathing Ted and Simon in brilliance. Simon smoothed his hair. Ted did nothing.

"Quiet on the set," came a voice through the loudspeaker—presumably from the director inside the engineer's booth. A man kneeling under the camera held up his fingers and counted down out loud, pointing silently when he reached *one*.

Simon looked directly into the camera and spoke. "Ted Shriver is a writer who rose to fame in 1969 with the publication of his first book, *Dobson's Night*, which the *New York Times* called 'a rich exploration of a contemporary male ego unable to cope with the depth of his own love, rendered in luxuriously restrained prose and destined to become a classic.' It sold over one hundred thousand copies in hardcover and was a finalist for the National Book Award. That was followed by two more critically acclaimed novels, *The Worst of Daniel Prince* in 1973, and *Last Game*, which was published in 1977 and went on to receive the prestigious Clampett Award. In 1981 he published his much-anticipated *Settlers Ridge*, a darling of the critics until the *New York Times* discovered that it contained several paragraphs lifted almost verbatim from a memoir of Vietnam veteran Rick Beardsley. Mr. Shriver never addressed the allegations and withdrew from public life. That was over twenty-five years ago. He has never done an interview since. That is, until tonight. He is here with us in the studio to break his long and mysterious silence. Welcome, Mr. Shriver, and thank you for being here."

Pete glanced from the stage to the monitor and saw that Ted's face was on camera, looking somber and terribly old. He nodded in recognition of the welcome but didn't say a word. Pete shifted in his seat. The camera went back to Simon.

"Let's jump right in to the issue of timing. After all these years of cutting yourself off from society and refusing to make any kind of public statement, you have agreed to come on a national television show. Why now?"

Ted cleared his throat. "Just to be accurate," he said, "I didn't 'cut myself off from society.' I wasn't living in a cave in Afghanistan—I was in a house in Connecticut, reading the papers, having drinks at a local pub most Friday nights, sometimes even talking to a neighbor."

"Fair enough. But you certainly shunned the media."

Ted's face filled the monitor again. This time, he opened his mouth to speak and then winced. He rubbed his forehead. Audrey and Aviva leaned forward simultaneously.

"Yes," Ted finally said. "That's true."

"So I'll go back to my question—why now?"

Ted sucked his cheeks and Pete could tell he was in terrible pain. Pete tried willing him to make it through. It seemed to work. Ted took a few breaths and responded, "You left me no choice."

"What does that mean?" Simon asked.

Ted bowed his head in thought and the camera stayed on him. After several moments, Simon spoke again. "Mr. Shriver?"

Ted still didn't lift his head.

"Are you okay?" Simon asked.

The camera stayed on Ted as he sunk lower, bending over at the waist. Audrey rose from her seat, her hand to her throat. Pete stood, too.

"Mr. Shriver?" Simon repeated, but there was no response. The camera went back to his face as he tapped his earpiece. "Apparently, Ted Shriver needs a few minutes to recover and we're going to break for commercial. Please stay with us."

"We're out," someone said.

Simon pulled off his mike and jumped from his chair. He grabbed Ted's shoulders so that he could lift his head and look into his face.

"He's unconscious!" he called, and they were immediately surrounded.

Pete rushed onto the set and knelt in front of his friend. "Ted, can you hear me?" he said.

Someone tried to hand Pete a glass of water, which confused him. Was he supposed to splash it on Ted's face or pour it down his throat? He shook his head and went back to his friend.

"Ted," he said, gently patting his face. "Can you hear me?"

"I'm calling an ambulance," Aviva said, taking out her cell phone.

"We're already on it," came a voice over the speaker.

"Let's lay him down," Pete said, because it seemed like his friend was about to slide off the chair. Two stagehands helped him lift Ted off the seat and lay him gently upon the carpeted set floor.

Ted groaned softly and Pete sighed in relief. "I think he's coming around," he said. "Ted, can you hear me? Do you know where you are?"

Ted mumbled something unintelligible.

"Can you say that again, pal?" Pete asked, putting his ear near Ted's mouth.

"Where's Norah?" he whispered.

"Don't worry, we'll find her. Hang in there." He looked up to see Didi standing over him. "He's asking for Norah."

"I haven't seen her," she said, and then spoke into her headset. "Can someone find Norah?"

"Is he going to be okay?" Audrey asked.

"Of course he's going to be okay," Pete said. He leaned toward his friend. "You're going to be fine. The paramedics are on their way."

"Salz," Ted whispered, then he took a sudden deep breath and his whole body went rigid in some kind of spasm. When it relaxed, he was unconscious.

"Ted!" Pete said. "Ted!" He looked behind him. "Does anyone know CPR?"

41

Norah let herself into Ted's hotel room. It was the first time she had seen the place clean, and she imagined he had finally let housekeeping in to tidy up. The bed was made and the clothes that were usually scattered about had been neatly folded and placed on the dresser.

She opened the closet, which contained a few pairs of slacks, a sports jacket, several shirts, and a knobby cardigan that seemed intentionally ugly. Just as Dorothy Parker had promised, there was a green suitcase on the floor. It was the old hard-shelled type that didn't have wheels. Her grandfather would have called it a *valise*.

Norah pulled it out and carried it over to the table. She popped open the latches and lifted the lid. Sure enough, there were three manuscripts inside, each bound with a red rubber band. She took out one called *Genuine Lies* and rolled off the rubber band. She lifted the title page and stared at the four words on the page beneath it.

```
For Sherry
With Affection
```

The reality of it hit her like a rolling boulder. Their relationship had meant something to Ted. He carried a piece of her around with him. Norah ran her hand over the words as if it would somehow connect her with her mother. *He did this for you*, she thought, and wondered if her mother had ever pictured her name like this—on the dedication page of a manuscript, proof that he had felt something for her once, and that she had been young and healthy and worthy of love.

Norah went into the bathroom to grab a tissue and blow her nose. She brought the whole box out with her just in case. Not that she intended to read the whole book, but she wanted to get enough of an idea of the main character to see if she was truly based on her mother.

She turned to chapter one and began to read:

April's mother burst into her room without knocking.

"I want you to meet Mr. Munson," said Doris, presenting an awkward man with oily hair and narrow shoulders.

Twenty-eight-year-old April Carner, who was back in college to get the degree she had abandoned years ago, quickly hid her twisted left hand under the *Modern Biology* textbook on her desk.

"For God's sake, Mother," she said.

Doris laughed. "Sorry!" she chirped and then turned to the stranger. "I'm terrible—always forgetting to knock."

"I apologize," the man said to April, and his eyes looked so earnest she had to look away.

"Mr. Munson is interested in renting our room," her mother said. "He's a teacher."

"It's Tige," he said. "Please."

"Tige," her mother said. "We can get used to that, can't we, April?"

"I have an exam tomorrow."

"She's such a serious student," her mother said. "I don't know where she gets it from. Well, we won't bother you, dear."

Tige Munson gave her one last look before shutting the door behind them, and April knew he would rent the room. Her mother's painfully obvious plan had paid off. April was being offered as an incentive, and Tige Munson was exactly the kind of man who would be drawn to her.

There were men who didn't notice April—rough men, the kind who laughed too loud and drove too fast. But the other kind—men who were lonely and gentle— picked her out in a crowd, drawn in by her lithe grace and dark curls. And later, when they discovered her tender smile, they ached with gratitude. This lovely girl, they thought, appreciates me.

And they were right. But no matter how kind they were, April turned them away. She had decided long ago that she would never marry.

It was her left hand that made April feel she was too monstrous to be someone's wife. Due to a few minutes of incompetence by the young doctor who had over- seen her birth, April's newborn brain had been de- prived of oxygen just long enough for her cerebrum to suffer damage, causing the muscles in her hand to con- tract in paralysis, leaving her fingers and wrist twisted into an awkward fist. At a young age, she learned to keep this hand hidden behind her back or inside a pocket.

There were moments during her day when she didn't think about the shame of her condition, but even then it was there, an ever-present high-pitched noise, tinnitus of her heart.

Norah sat back in the chair. This was her mother. The facts were changed, of course. She had multiple sclerosis, not cerebral palsy, and her hand had a tremor, not a contortion. Also, it wasn't a birth defect but a condition she developed later in life. Still, this was her. Ted had found the essence of Sherry Wolfe and captured her in April Carner. And how perfect that he had chosen tinnitus as a metaphor. It was a condition her mother later developed, and the high-pitched ringing in her ears plagued her the last years of her life.

She picked up the manuscript and read on, eager to see what kind of fictional life he had created for her. He had changed her grandmother from a cold and withholding type to a giddy narcissist who slept with any rake who paid her a compliment. The tall, homely teacher was clearly Ted. And the more April fell in love with him, the more she pushed him away.

Norah wanted to put the manuscript aside, but she couldn't stop. She had to read on and find out what happened.

It was excruciating. Tige Munson was a bit of a prick, but it was also clear he was right for her. They would have transformed each other. But this woman simply could not get out of her own way.

In the second half, Tige sleeps with April's mother, which is described as "ugly sex, exciting only for its baseness." Once Norah got to that part, she couldn't put the book down, because the idea of April finding out was just too painful a possibility to abide. In the end, of course, she did, and the results were disastrous. Doris suffered, Tige suffered, and any chance April had of ever getting past her disability was forever destroyed.

By the time she finished, Norah was depleted, both physically and emotionally, as if she had spent the entire time running up and down a flight of stairs. She thought back to what Dorothy Parker said Ted had told her: *This changes everything.*

It was exactly how she felt about reading the book.

Norah had always defended her mother's position on keeping the secret from Ted. She had been so vulnerable, and Norah wanted only to protect her. But that vulnerability was tied to a massive mistake, a perception of herself as too damaged to love. If Norah got anything from this book, it's that we're all damaged. The tragedy is letting it define you.

Her mother should have told Ted. Norah had always known that, but it was a truth she kept in a dark place, telling herself it didn't matter. What mattered was what her mother *wanted*. But Norah always knew. It was her own tinnitus, the noise in her head she wanted to ignore.

Maybe Dorothy Parker was right. Maybe deep down inside she knew that the outspoken spirit would go straight to Ted with the truth.

In any case, it didn't matter now. He knew. And Norah wanted to lay her head on his chest and weep for what she had lost. This father she'd never had.

She glanced out the window at the skyline—a pitch-dark night cut by a mosaic of lights, dim and bright, blinking and static. She had read the book quickly and voraciously, but nearly four hours had gone by. Norah had silenced her phone before she even ran out of the studio, as she needed to cut herself off. No doubt Didi and the rest of the crew were now celebrating the show and wondering where the hell she was. But Norah was in no mood for a party.

She picked up the remote control and clicked on the television to see if there was any news coverage about Ted's historic appearance. After going through all the channels twice, she realized there wasn't any information being broadcast. If she didn't want to call someone, she would have to go home and do an Internet search, or wait for the morning newspapers.

Norah sighed and took out her cell phone. She didn't feel like listening to all the calls from Didi asking where the hell she was, so she played back a message from her friend Pamela Daniels.

> *Hey, just wanted to know what the hell happened. I was watching the interview and it looked like Ted passed out, but they didn't give any info. Is he dead or alive? Call me!*

Passed out? What was she talking about?

Norah replayed the message, feeling suddenly cold in the middle of Ted's warm room. She played the first message from Didi.

> *Something's happened. Where the hell are you? Call me.*

The next message was from Peter Salzberg:

> *Norah, I'm so sorry I upset you, but you have to meet us at Lenox Hill Hospital. Ted collapsed and we don't know if he's going to make it. He asked about you, Norah.*

42

Dorothy Parker sat demurely at the bar, waiting. It didn't take long for a man to approach her. He had white hair and the ruddy complexion of a drinker. That was the good news. The bad news was that he wore a brown suit, heaven help her.

"Hi," he said in a voice that was likely a full octave lower than he normally spoke. "I couldn't help noticing you sitting there. You look like the consummate New York lady—sophisticated and confident."

"And you look like a mattress salesman from Idaho."

He laughed heartily. "You're not that far off, darling. I'm from Nevada and I rep a line of commercial bathroom fixtures."

"How enchanting," she said. "You sell toilet bowls."

"That's about the size of it," he said. "I hope you're not disappointed."

"I would say you've met my expectations rather neatly. However, if you tell me I have a porcelain complexion I may not take it kindly."

He looked perplexed, and then straightened his tie, as if it would help him think about what to say next. "Are you interested in politics, by any chance?"

"Only after a few drinks."

"I'd love to buy you one, if you'd let me."

"I thought you'd never ask."

He summoned the bartender and they both ordered drinks. The man introduced himself as Cliff Calder and she said her name was Liz Bathory. She asked pointed questions about his career for as long as it took her to finish her drink, and he ordered her another. She repeated this trick until she'd had four gin and tonics and heard more about toilets than any human should have to endure. As he continued on about state-of-the-art industrial fixtures and sales records and how important it was to "stay one step ahead of the other guy," she thought she would sooner dry out than listen to another word.

And then, just as she was about to grab a bottle of gin from the bar and crack it over her own skull, he invited her up to his room.

"That sounds perfectly lovely," she said.

"It does?"

"I'll tell you what," she said, "you go on up and I'll meet you there in a few minutes."

Excited, Cliff Calder rubbed his hands together, gave her a key to his room, and left. She remained at the bar, nursing her drink and hoping someone less dull would come along.

After a few minutes, a man in glasses sat down heavily on the stool beside hers. She recognized him as the fellow Norah had been ready to exterminate.

"Well, I'll be a son of a bitch," he said. "I must have been pretty sloshed the last time I saw you, because I thought you were a ghost or something, materialized out of nowhere. But here you are—flesh and blood and pretty as a picture." He stuck out his hand. "Russell Hetterich."

"Lucy Borgia," she said. "Charmed."

"Can I get you a drink, Lucy?" he asked.

"What a thoughtful idea. I'll have a gin and tonic."

Russell snapped his fingers at the bartender and ordered them both drinks. He leaned toward her. "Tell me all about yourself, lovely Lucy. What brings you to the Algonquin—business or pleasure?"

"Are those my only choices?"

He laughed and put a meaty hand on her shoulder. "You're a funny one, aren't you?"

"That's my reputation," she said, removing his hand.

"Don't you want to be my friend?" he asked.

"Ask me again after a few drinks."

"That's my kind of girl," he said, slapping her on the back.

The bartender put their cocktails in front of them and she drank hers quickly. This fellow was even worse than the last.

"What do you do for fun, Lucy?" he asked.

"I walk on hot coals," she said.

"Is that fun?"

"By comparison."

"You tease!" he said. "What do you *really* do for fun?"

"I drink."

"Is that all?"

"I'm afraid I've given up most of my hobbies," she said.

"And why's that?"

"I was never very good at them. Falling in love, for instance. I always picked the most loathsome men."

"I could give you some good loving," Russell said, running a finger down her neck.

She batted his hand away. "And then there was suicide. Boy, I was lousy at that. But I'd give it another shot now, if I thought it would do any good."

"Last call!" the bartender announced.

"Buy me another drink, would you, dear?" she said.

"And what do I get for it?" he said, leaning in to kiss her.

She backed away. "Are we negotiating?"

"You seem like a lady who drives a hard bargain."

"I'll tell you what. Buy me that drink and I'll meet you up in your room just as soon as I finish."

"You're not going to disappear on me, are you?"

"I might. It's my last remaining talent."

"Last call!" the bartender repeated.

"What the hell," Russell said, "you're worth the risk. I like a frisky gal." He ordered her another drink and told her his room number. Then he gave her a sloppy kiss and left the bar.

Dorothy Parker nursed her last drink, and by the time she finished, everyone but the bartender had left. At least that's what she thought. But just as she drained the last drop of gin from her glass, she became aware of a familiar presence on her right.

43

A hospital.

In the years since her childhood trauma, Norah had tried twice to get past her fears. At age sixteen, her friend Summer had been hit by a car while crossing a major street, and needed surgery to put the pieces of her shattered leg back together. Norah made it as far as the front entrance before she realized she simply couldn't get inside. She tried again when the first of her friends had a baby. Determined to conquer her phobia, she charged forth to the elevator bank like a warrior. But she didn't have the weapons to control her nervous system, and within seconds she was so overcome with dizziness that a passing stranger had to catch her before she hit the hard floor.

Norah paid the driver and got out of the cab in front of Lenox Hill Hospital. She stood before the entrance, staring up at the austere structure. It's just like any other building, she told herself—bricks and mortar and plaster and steel. There was simply no reason to panic. It was not a death machine. The people inside dedicated themselves to saving lives. She would eventually walk out just as she had walked in.

Besides, Ted was in there. And for all she knew, he could be tak-ing his last breaths. She had to reach him.

But her rational thinking did nothing to stop the impulse her brain sent to her central nervous system, and she was instantly flooded with the primitive survival hormones that had given her ancestors the boost they needed for fight or flight. Only, she couldn't slay a hospital . . . and there was nowhere to run.

She closed her eyes and pictured Ted, weak and barely conscious, on a hospital bed. She saw him turning to her, his eyes looking as they did in the makeup room. Only, this time she would take his hand. And they would connect before it was too late.

Norah charged through the doors into the lobby. *Just keep walk-ing,* she told herself. *Get on the elevator. Go right upstairs to the room number Didi texted you.* Ted had been checked in and scheduled for emergency surgery—with only a fifty percent chance of survival. Norah needed to see him before he went under the knife.

By the time she got into the elevator and pressed the button for the eighth floor, she was woozy. And as the doors closed, she felt tingling pinpricks in her fingers and the kind of dizziness that could overtake her. There was a minor jolt as the old elevator began its as-cent, and a push of nausea sent her to the brink. The room began to go dark and Norah felt so sick that unconsciousness seemed like a welcome relief. But she fought it, bending at the waist to put her head between her legs. She didn't give a damn what the other elevator passenger—a man in blue scrubs—thought of her.

"You okay, miss?" he asked.

"Just your run-of-the-mill panic attack," she said, sounding breathless.

"Sit down," he ordered, and she hesitated. "It's okay," he said, pat-ting the floor.

She did what he said, and he told her to keep her head down. He led her through an exercise of slow, deep breaths. She heard the elevator doors open on another floor. She wanted to tell him she had no time for this, but she knew if she rose too soon she would pass out.

"Ignore that," the man said. "You're doing great. In two-three-four, hold two-three-four, out two-three-four."

He kept at it, even as the elevator reached the top floor and began its descent. Eventually, she realized that the dizziness was gone and she was feeling calmer. But he was insistent that they keep going for several more minutes. At last he stopped and took her pulse.

"Feeling better?" he asked.

"Much," she said, starting to rise.

"Slowly," he warned.

She took his advice and uncurled inch by inch. When at last she straightened, Norah tested her hands by making fists. The tingling was gone. She was okay.

"I don't know how to thank you," she said. "I've always had panic attacks in hospitals. This is the first time I've ever recovered from one without fleeing the building."

"No problem," he said. "If you practice that breathing it'll become second nature. You're going to eight, right?"

He pushed the button for her floor and his. "You must be visiting someone very special to you," he said.

"I am," she said as the doors opened on her floor. "My father."

She got off the elevator and made a right turn, where a set of double doors separated her from the hallway. All she had to do was push through and find Ted's room number. Norah paused for a moment for a long, slow breath, and then advanced.

It was a wide hallway. She could see a nurses' station up ahead on the left. The wall on her right was lined with patients' rooms. She walked past them, looking at the numbers. "Eight eighteen, eight eighteen," she repeated to herself as she continued down the path, looking at the descending numbers.

At last she reached the end of the hall and made a left turn. It was a stark, empty corridor except for two lone figures holding on to each other, crying.

Pete and Aviva.

She knew what this tableau meant, but in an instant it became too much to comprehend and something inside of her shut down. Light bounced off surfaces in a way her brain couldn't process. She couldn't think or move.

"Norah!" Aviva called, still holding tight to her husband.

The couple pulled apart, and Norah could see that Aviva's face was wet and swollen from crying. Pete's eyes were so red the word *bloodshot* formed a new association in her brain. They approached her and she wanted to flee. She couldn't hear what they had to say.

"Norah," Pete said, putting his hand on her shoulder.

"No," she said.

"I'm so sorry," Aviva said, trying to hug her. "It just happened. He's gone."

She pushed Aviva away. *It can't be,* she thought. *It can't.*

"Let's go sit down," Pete said gently, trying to guide her toward a waiting room, but Norah broke free from his grip and ran down the hall. They called after her, but she didn't want to talk to them . . . or anyone. She fled through the double doors, and took the elevator to the lobby. Norah didn't know where she was going or what she was doing—only that she needed to be as far from the hospital as she could get. She went through the exit door and into the street, running. Soon enough, her lungs couldn't keep up, and so she walked. And walked and walked. Norah wasn't even conscious of where she was heading. The urgency was to keep moving, no matter what.

He was dead. Her father.

Why hadn't she told him? Why had she kept that stupid secret for so long? Now it was too late. She couldn't apologize. She couldn't do anything.

Norah heard her phone ringing inside her purse but she ignored it. She went on, step after step after step. The momentum kept her from crying.

At least she thought it did. Norah wasn't conscious of weeping, but her cheeks stung as the cool night breeze blew past her wet face. Then, at a crosswalk, she found that she couldn't catch her breath and had to bend at the waist to get enough air in her lungs. When she looked up, Norah realized she had been heading south and was just a few blocks east of the Algonquin Hotel.

A garbage truck passed, and Norah stood there as the stench of rot hovered, the noxious cloud working its way deep into her sinuses. She was glued to the spot, the awful smell offering a respite from her throbbing chaos.

When it lifted, she was compelled to keep moving. There was no place she wanted to be, but the Algonquin's West 44th Street address played like a song and she wandered toward it as if the music were driving her.

When she reached the hotel, Norah stood outside the glass entryway, not sure she wanted to go in. When someone held the door for her, it felt like an invitation she was meant to accept. Still numb, she crossed the threshold, passed the doorman, and headed straight to the Blue Bar. It was closed for the night, but no one tried to stop her.

She sat on a stool in the darkness. There was comfort in the solitary stillness of this place. Norah placed her hands on the smooth bar, grounding herself. It was real. The news she had heard from Pete and Aviva was not a bad dream. Norah covered her face with her hands and wished she could disappear into the blackness. *It's over*, she said to herself. *Over.* She would never get to speak to Ted as her father.

Norah felt a presence next to her but didn't look up.

"Hello, dear."

She removed her hands from her face and glanced to her right. There was Dorothy Parker, looking as inscrutable as ever.

Norah knew it was up to her to deliver the news. She inhaled slowly, taking the air deep into her lungs so that she would be able to say it, but a coughing fit overtook her. Dorothy Parker said nothing. At last, Norah took a jagged breath and stared down at the bar.

"I should have listened to you," she said. "I should have told him."

She looked up at Dorothy Parker, who had no reaction.

"He's dead," Norah continued. "Ted. My father. He's gone."

Mrs. Parker looked pensive, as if she were weighing her words. "I'm sorry for your loss," she finally said.

"And I'm sorry I got so mad at you. You were right to let him know." She looked into Dorothy Parker's face and saw that her expression had softened. Norah felt the pity right to her bones and it broke her. She laid her head on her arms and cried like a child. She had missed so much.

"I didn't get to have one conversation with him as my father," she said without looking up. "He always thought I was just some ambitious stranger. That's the worst part. I would give anything to have one more talk with him."

"Oh, my dear girl," Mrs. Parker said.

Norah raised her head to read her friend's expression, but she was gone.

"Where are you?" Norah asked, and saw a swarm of dust particles gathering near the guest book. She stared, wondering why the legendary writer chose this moment to turn to dust. But as the particles took shape, she realized it wasn't Dorothy Parker.

Norah slid off the stool.

"It can't be," she said as she watched a male figure appear out of nothing. He stood a step out of the shadows and she saw that she was right. It was Ted Shriver.

44

Norah and Ted were so focused on each other they didn't even notice Dorothy Parker backing into the shadows. Still, she knew they would be freer with each other if they didn't sense they were being watched, and so she made her presence undetectable by letting her molecules scatter.

In the beginning, when she first arrived here after dying, Dorothy Parker felt a small pang of guilt about eavesdropping on personal conversations. But after a time, that dissipated, and now she felt it was her right. Sometimes she even let her molecules mingle with those of a living person to experience what they were feeling. She didn't like to do it with strong individuals like Ted or Norah, though, because it was simply too intense. Besides, the weaker types were more fun, because it was easier to infuse them with her spirit and influence their behavior. These two would be a formidable challenge.

They stood in the middle of the bar, looking at each other, and Dorothy Parker knew it would take Norah a moment to find her voice. Finally, she said simply, "It's you."

"Disappointed?" he asked.

"I . . . I don't understand."

"She got me to sign that damned book after all." He shook his head. "You women always get what you want."

Norah looked down for a moment, and then met his eyes again. "Not always."

He stepped toward her. "Norah," he said, and his voice took on a paternal warmth.

"I'm sorry I didn't tell you," she said.

"Me, too."

"I should have given you a chance," Norah said. "You might have been a good father."

"For minutes at a time, maybe." He pointed to a table. "Let's sit."

"How long will you stay?" she said as she slid into the seat.

He glanced upward for a moment and seemed lost in whatever he was staring at. He looked back at her. "Until you get rid of me."

Thank goodness, Dorothy Parker thought. *Thank goodness he is going to stay around for a while.*

Norah looked up, confused. "Do you see a white light?"

"It follows me," he said to her. "I don't deserve it. If I lived a million years, I wouldn't deserve forgiveness. But there it is."

She put her hand to her chest and began to cry.

"What is it?" he asked.

She shrugged, as if the reason for her tears should be obvious. When he didn't respond she said, "I'm glad, that's all."

He waved away her comment. Clearly, he didn't think the gift of forgiveness was something he was even worthy of acknowledging. "Did you figure out that scene in *Dobson's Night?*" he asked.

She sniffed, and wiped her nose with a cocktail napkin. "I wanted to talk to you about that," she said. "I think I get it. The father thought the boy was better off without him. That's why he didn't come back, right?"

He nodded.

She looked into his sad eyes. "But he was wrong."

"Was he?"

Norah balled the napkin and squeezed tight. "I'm sure of it."

"You deserved a father," he said. "Someone better than me."

"I would have loved you no matter what."

"You might have hated me," he said. "I might have ruined your childhood."

"Maybe." She shook her head. "I don't know."

He took her hand. "I'm sorry about your TV show."

"It doesn't matter."

"It does. And the manuscripts." He closed his eyes tight against the memory and a look of pain returned to his face. "Your father is a shit, Norah. I'm sorry for that. You deserve better. You deserve someone who would have been good to you and to your mother."

She stared down at the table for a long time, like she was trying to figure out what to say. "I forgive you," she said, and looked straight at him.

"No you don't."

Norah nodded and went quiet again, and Dorothy Parker sensed that something was about to change. Alarmed, she swirled closer, in case she needed to intervene.

"Come here," Norah said, taking Ted's hands and pulling him from the booth. They stood facing each other.

"I want you to go," she said.

He looked down. "I understand."

It was exactly as Dorothy Parker had feared, and she couldn't let it happen. She had worked so hard to get Ted to sign the book—she couldn't let him just disappear like the rest of them. She would talk him out of it. She had to. But before she could pull her molecules together into corporeal form, she realized that there was nothing she could say that would convince Ted to stay. If Norah wanted him to go, he would go.

There was only one thing left to do, and with a single turn, Dorothy Parker pushed her molecules right into Norah and merged with her.

Norah shuddered.

"What's the matter?" Ted asked.

"I don't know," she said. "I just got a chill."

"Do you want to sit down?"

"No," she said, shaking it off, and Dorothy Parker could feel her pulling strength from deep inside. "I want to finish what I was saying, because it's important for you to know. Despite what you think, I really do forgive you. Maybe not completely—not yet, anyway—but enough for now. The point is, there's a more important kind of forgiveness waiting for you, and you have to accept it. You've been blaming yourself for so much for so long. It's your time."

He glanced up, and she saw something change in his face. He wanted it.

"What if you need to yell at me?" he said. "What if you need to rant and tell me I've been a fuckup who ruined everything?"

Yes, I need you here! Dorothy Parker thought, and tried to push the idea into Norah's stubborn psyche. *I changed my mind. Don't go!*

"I'll shout at the walls," Norah said.

Damn this girl, Dorothy Parker thought.

"Norah—" Ted said.

"I need to work this out on my own, Ted. It'll be a bear, this complicated grief. But I need to do it. And you need . . . *that.*" She nodded upward.

No, Dorothy Parker thought. *He doesn't. Not yet. It can wait.*

"I didn't think I would want it," he said.

"But you do."

"It's damned strong, that pull."

Norah put her arms around him and he returned the hug. Dorothy Parker felt it all, including the press of his lips on the top of her head. At that moment, she felt Norah weakening. She loved him so much, and being in his arms like this felt so right.

At last she pulled away and looked into Ted's face, and Dorothy Parker understood. Norah loved him too much to keep him here, but the little girl in her—the child who never recovered from losing her mother—wanted him to stay.

It was Dorothy Parker's chance. Norah was weak, and all she had to do was give a little push and she would do it. She would tell Ted not to go.

And then Norah pulled the light of love from a place so deep inside her that Dorothy Parker was overcome with terror. *No, no, no,* she thought, and yanked her molecules from Norah's being to lock herself in the safe fortress of her own hard melancholy.

Norah closed her eyes and opened them. "For a moment there . . ."

"What is it?" Ted asked. "Did you change your mind? Do you want me to stay?"

Norah shook her head. "Take care of my mom," she said.

"Are you sure about this?"

"I'm sure."

He stood, motionless.

"Go," she said.

Ted Shriver nodded, and peered heavenward. For a second he looked as gray as he had in the hospital bed. Then he disappeared.

Gone.

Norah ran her hand through the space where he had been. She swayed, as if she were about to faint, and lowered herself into the booth where they had been sitting. "All alone," she whispered.

"Don't be ridiculous," said Dorothy Parker, materializing in the seat across from her. "I'm right here."

"I guess you heard all that," Norah said.

"Heard enough," Mrs. Parker said.

"Do you think I did the right thing?"

Dorothy Parker still felt the vibration of Norah's love for Ted circling through her. She went quiet for a moment and then said, "I *know* you did."

Norah looked up at the dark ceiling. "Why do you stay?" she asked. "Doesn't it call to you?"

Dorothy Parker stole a quick glance at the terrifying white light and looked back at Norah. One day, perhaps, she would have the courage to face it. But she couldn't imagine that happening for a very long time. "It holds nothing for me," Dorothy said.

"But you're alone," Norah said.

At that moment, Dorothy Parker felt a strange surge of electricity coming from the guest book. She turned to look and saw a small swirl of particles rise and then travel toward the floor. She knew what it was.

"Not anymore," she said as she got out of her seat. She crouched and called out, "Come here, my darling," and the little poodle trotted across the floor into her arms.

"I'll be damned," Norah said. "Is that Cliché?"

"Of course," said Mrs. Parker, petting the dog. "But then, I've always been a sucker for happy endings."

45

A week later, Audrey Hudson received an anonymous note, penned in old-fashioned feminine handwriting.

Dear Audrey,

I regret that you cannot write an article about the true nature of the Algonquin guest book, which now resides in a sealed case at the hotel. However, there is another book with similar powers. It is on the top shelf of a tall curio cabinet in a home in Queens, New York (address below). I urge you to ask the owner, Edie Coates, to allow you access to it.

Do note that Miss Coates may be hesitant to let you take it from her home. However, once the book is closed, she will gladly hand it over. I promise you this.

Audrey had a pretty good idea that Dorothy Parker had written the note. Or maybe it was someone pretending to be Dorothy Parker. In any case, it seemed like some kind of trick, so she crumpled it in a ball and threw it away. Later that day, she thought better of it, removed it from the trash, and smoothed it on her coffee table, where it remained all week while she graded the final papers of her

Columbia students. At least once a day she looked up from her work to ask Jim Beam, "What do you think I should do about this, boy?" He never had much of a response.

After turning in the students' grades, Audrey realized she had no freelance work on the horizon and a whole summer stretching before her. She decided the anonymous lead was worth the risk, and took a subway to the address in Forest Hills.

The woman who answered the door was oddly dressed in a teal bell-bottomed jumpsuit that was much too tight. "Can I help you?" she asked.

"Are you Edie Coates?"

"Who wants to know?"

Audrey introduced herself as a freelance reporter who was researching a story. "I understand you own a book of signatures that might have paranormal powers."

"I gave that back to the other lady. I don't want anything to do with that Algonquin book. I hate ghosts. *Hate* them."

"I understand," Audrey said. "But I'm not here about the Algonquin guest book. I'm here about a second volume—one that's in your house."

"Really?" Edie Coates furrowed her brow. "There's a second book?"

"You haven't seen it?"

"I don't think so, but there's so much stuff in this house it's hard to know what I have."

"Do you mind if I come in and have a look? I promise I won't take long."

Edie hesitated for a second and then shrugged. "Why not," she said. "I'm kind of curious myself."

She led Audrey from the dark entryway into a strange living room that was packed with oddities. Audrey glanced around until she spotted a large piece of furniture that could be described as a tall curio cabinet.

She approached it and stood on her toes. "Do you know what's on the top shelf?" she asked.

Edie stepped back to see if she could get a look. "Hang on," she said, and scraped over a rickety, cane-bottom chair.

"You're not going to stand on that, are you?" Audrey asked.

"It'll be fine," Edie said, and Audrey wasn't so sure. She held the chair in place as Edie climbed up on it.

"Careful," she warned as the dry old caning creaked under the stress.

"I'll be a son of a gun," Edie said. She pulled a book from the shelf and the seat gave out at the same time. Her foot went right through it, and the chair tumbled over, taking Edie and Audrey along with it. They both landed on their bottoms.

"Are you okay?" Audrey asked.

"I think so," said Edie. Her foot was still in the broken chair and she pulled it out. "How about you?"

Audrey wondered if she should tell Edie that the seat of her jumpsuit had ripped wide open, but something else caught her eye—the book had landed right next to her. Audrey picked it up and flipped through the scant pages, which bore only one signature.

"Who's Gavin Coates?" she asked.

Edie looked terrified. "My brother. Why?"

Remembering the specific instructions in the letter, she slammed the book closed. At that moment, a colorful silk kimono seemed to appear out of nowhere, hovering overhead. They watched as the satin floated gracefully toward the floor. When it landed, Edie gasped and got to her feet. She lifted the kimono and looked under it.

"He's gone!" she said. Then she laughed and laughed. She helped Audrey up and hugged her.

"What did I do?" Audrey asked.

Edie smiled, crying. "You saved me."

46

Norah missed him. She even missed *the idea* of him. And that made the grief confusing. What was she really mourning—Ted Shriver or the dream she'd had for so long? All she knew was that her life had been hollowed out and she had nothing to fill the void.

She often thought about going back to the Algonquin's Blue Bar to talk to Dorothy Parker, but she put it off, as she doubted the melancholy wit would have anything to say that might cheer her up. Besides, the memory of Ted was so tied to the place that she simply couldn't face it. She needed to be in a much better state of mind before she could walk in there again.

Then she suffered another loss. *Simon Janey Live.* Two weeks after Ted collapsed on the air, the network president announced that the show was canceled. That night, any fans tuning in to see a hard-hitting interview were surprised to find themselves watching *What Happened to Your Face?*, a reality show about plastic surgery mistakes.

The cancellation came as a surprise to no one, of course, but it was still a crushing disappointment. Norah was determined to find a way to cope in the midst of her grief.

"Give yourself a break," Didi said. "Take some time off. You can afford it now."

It was true. Due to Ted's quick action after finding out Norah was his daughter, she had inherited his estate and no longer needed to worry about making her rent. But she knew that taking a break from her career would give her far too much time to dwell on the pain, and that was something she just couldn't do. She needed to ride it out without examining it too closely, for the grief seemed to have a terrible dark spot—like a stain on a stain—that made her feel sick and scared. She wanted to leave it alone.

So Norah went right back to sending out résumés. She hoped to quickly find something that would fill up her life.

A few weeks later, she got a call from her friend Pamela Daniels, who said that the folks at MSNBC didn't hire Beth Barbieri after all, because the show's host found her a little too testy.

"I can still get you an interview, if you're interested," Pamela said.

Norah was indeed interested, and a week later she sat across from Rose Salinas, the director of human resources, who screened every potential employee before sending them on. Pamela had told Norah they were looking for someone upbeat, so she put on her best game face, giving the right answers to all the typical interview questions: *What have you been doing since your last job? Where do you see yourself five years from now? What are your strengths and weaknesses?*

Then Rose asked Norah a question she didn't expect. "What was the last book you read?"

Norah answered honestly. "I just finished *The Portable Dorothy Parker*," she said, expecting the woman to nod and scribble it down in her notes.

But Rose Salinas smiled. "Rachel's going to adore you. She's a huge Dorothy Parker fan."

The next interview went even better, and two weeks later Norah started her new job. It took a few months for her to get her footing, as there was a lot to learn and she ached for her old friends at *Simon Janey Live*. But eventually she made it her home, and got to channel her drive toward helping the show succeed.

Didi was the one who wound up taking some time off. With funding from Norah, she was finally able to finish her documentary, which took almost a year. The screening was on a warm July night, and Norah was delighted when Aviva and Pete said they could make it.

Aviva kissed Norah hello and handed her a thick envelope. "I brought you something," she said. "It's my newest acquisition."

Norah reached into the package and pulled out a bound manuscript. The title page said:

HELL HATH NO FURY
Why I Framed Ted Shriver
by Audrey Hudson

"Is this for real?" Norah said. "Audrey wrote a tell-all?"

"It's going to be huge," Aviva said. "She did a hell of a job."

Norah noted the heft of the manuscript. Clearly, Audrey had a lot to say. "But she devoted her whole life to keeping this secret."

"I convinced her to do it. The news was coming out anyway. I thought if she owned it, at least she could play a role in the conversation."

"Won't people despise her forever?"

"Some will and some won't," Aviva said, "but they'll all buy the damned book."

"It'll probably sell more than *Bad Husband*," Pete added.

Norah stared at the title page and understood what this meant for Ted's reputation. Audrey was setting the record straight. There would be a fair amount of controversy, as many would find Ted's behavior as a husband inexcusable. But everyone would know he wasn't a plagiarist.

This lifted Norah more than anything that had happened since she lost him. In fact, she felt like the dark spot on her heart had finally dislodged. She teared up and turned away, embarrassed.

"Did you ever get that dog?" Aviva asked.

The last time they spoke, Norah had told Aviva about a schnauzer mix she had picked out from a shelter. Ultimately, she thought the timing wasn't right and let the opportunity pass. She visited the shelter three more times after that, and always got cold feet. Somehow, Norah didn't trust herself to take care of a pet.

"I didn't feel ready for a dog," Norah said.

"Why not?" Aviva said. "You're the most responsible person I know."

Responsible? Something about the word related directly to the pain that had just lifted. And late that night, as she read Audrey's colorful book, she finally understood why. Norah had always felt responsible for her mother, even in death. And when Ted died, that feeling compounded, because she had not been able to repair his reputation.

But now his legacy was safe. Not only that but he had found peace. Even Audrey Hudson had discovered a path to self-forgiveness.

It was time for Norah to take herself off the hook, too.

She put down the manuscript, shut off the light, and had a long, dreamless slumber. The next morning, Norah went back to the animal shelter, where she found a two-year-old cocker spaniel mix with long ears, sad eyes, and a crooked white stripe down the middle of his face. He had to be coaxed out of his crate, and trembled when she went to scoop him up. The dog issued one halfhearted growl, and then relaxed in Norah's arms, his muscles loose and liquidy. He gave her hand a drowsy lick and fell asleep, nuzzling against her as if he wanted to burrow right into her heart.

He did. Norah took him home that very afternoon, and named him Dobson. And while she knew that there would still be moments when she mourned for all she had lost, Norah's heart now beat with such brightness that at last she felt filled with the stupidity of hope. She couldn't wait to tell Dorothy Parker.

ACKNOWLEDGMENTS

First, I wish to thank Dorothy Parker for being the most audacious, talented, complicated, and inspiring muse a novelist could wish for. I also want to thank my editor, Meaghan Wagner, for her unwavering support, keen insights, and knowledgeable guidance. I couldn't ask for a better partner in this journey.

Thanks, too, to the rest of the wonderful team at Putnam, including Ivan Held, Jessica Butler, Katie Grinch, Lydia Hirt, Kate Stark, and Shannon Jamieson Vazquez.

My beta-readers, Myfanwy Collins and Saralee Rosenberg, are not only brilliant writers but generous friends, and their feedback was invaluable. Additional thanks to the supportive lit pals who were always there with advice and encouragement, including Mary Akers, Don Capone, Katrina Denza, Mark Ebner, Pamela Erens, Kathy Fish, Kelly Flanigan, Andrew Gross, Susan Henderson, Carol Hoenig, Debbi Honorof, Tony Iovino, Brenda Janowitz, Elinor Lipman, Debra Markowitz, Marion Meade, Ellen Parker, Patricia Parkinson, Jordan Rosenfeld, Robin Slick, Maryanne Stahl, Alix Strauss, Andrew Tibbetts, and David Toussaint.

A very special shout-out to the professionals who answered my research questions with patience and intelligence, including Pamela Lopez, my guru on all things television-related, Alice de Almeida of the Algonquin Hotel, and Terrence Palmer of Rallye BMW. To Spirit Airlines flight attendant Tonya Rabuck, who was kind enough to find me a roomy place to work as I struggled to meet my deadline on a crowded flight, thank you.

Navigating the unpredictable seas of a writing career can be scary, so having the world's greatest advocates steering my ship is a tremendous asset. Huge thanks to my agents, Annelise Robey and Andrea Cirillo, as well as the rest of the gang at the Jane Rotrosen Agency. A special thanks to Joel Gotler, too.

To my parents, Marilyn and Gerard Meister, thank you for always believing in me. And to Mike, Max, Ethan, and Emma, thank you for making it all worthwhile.

And finally, a special nod to Dorothy Parker fans.

If you spend a lot of time on social media, where angry trolls abound, it's easy to lose faith in humanity. But I've learned that there is a vast community of intelligent, educated, witty, and wonderful people out there. Over one hundred thousand of them follow my Dorothy Parker Facebook page (facebook.com/DorothyParkerQuotes), and they inspire me every day. I'd like to thank every single one, and am delighted to specifically acknowledge the following folks, who provided their names to be included in this heartfelt expression of gratitude:

April Aandal, Russell Aaronson, Erin Abbamondi, Sharifa Abdul-Wahid, Eshaam Abdurahman, Joan Adamo, Denise Adams, Jill Adams, Britt Adams, Natalie Adams, Patti Adams, Reade Adams, Kathleen Adams, Marlene Adelle, Magdalena Aders, Adam R. Adkins, Jeffrey Agnitsch, Carlos Aguirre, Carol Aka, Carol Albers, Brigitte Albert, Edwin Albetski, Michele Alcock, Leslie Alden, Pat Alder, Cliff Aldridge, Lane Aldridge, Emily Alexander, Rona Allan, Suzanne Allen, Jennifer Allen, Theresa Allen, Joyce Allen, Sara Allison, Jaye Allison, Sara Allkins, John Allred, Celia Aloia, Jordi Alonso, Anne Alonzo, Jodi Altenhofen, Robin Andersen, Tiare Anderson, Barbara Anderson, Tonda Anderson, Kirk Anderson, Lawson Anderson, Carolyn Anderson, Sayward Anderson, Holly Anderson, Harriette Andrews Harra, Martha Andrews-Schmidt, Veronica Andris, Ilene Angel, Nazli Anwari, Rocelle Aragon, Christian Ares, Faith Arkel, Jeffrey Arkin, Geraldine J. Arko, Bev Armstrong, Holly Armstrong, Eric Carl Artherhults, Pam Arthur, Subramanian Arunachalam, A. J. Ash, Kathleen Ashe, Jerry Ashley, Janice Ashmore, John Ashton, Denise Ashworth, Marilyn Avila, Paula Ayers, Ron Ayers, Josh Aylor, Sonia Azzi, Loura B., Clare B., Lorraine Babb, Dean Babcock, Nicole Bach, Samuel C. Badger, Jeffrey Baer, Luke Bailey, Christine Bain, Joette Baity, Sharyn Baker, Mark Baker, Jodi Baker, Ellie Baker, Kelley Baker-Ewert, Ananth Balasubramanian, Lisa Balatbat, Bruce Baldwin, Shelly Baldwin, Sue Bale, Ann Ballard, Joshua Balog, Sherianne Bangham, Jonathan Banks, Tammie Banks, Paula Barber, Ericka Barber, Betsy Barber Bivin, Holly Barbour Wales, Paige Barcus, Kevin Barger, Ferne Barishman, H. V. Barnard, Joseph Barrett, James Barry, Melissa Bartell, Elle Barton, Ruth Barton, Patricia Barton, Leanne Baskett, Mazie Baskin, Tami Bates, Lori Bates, Chandra Batra, Art Battiste, F. Kay Baumann, Gene Baumwoll, Sally Be, Bonnie Beagel-Rhodes, Anita Beall, Heidi Jo Bean, Rosa Beason, Theodore

Beattie, Melanie Becerra, Suzi Bechtold, Tally Beck, Adele Beck, Ed Beck, Ken Beck, Bill Becker, Cynthia Beckes-O'Connor, Marie Bednar, Su Bee, Gina Beeley, Valeri Beers, Emily Behrmann, Jennifer Beikes, Theresa Belanger, Thomas Bell, Laura Belluzzi, Genevieve Beltran, Andrew Bemis, Gretchen Bender, Lynnette Bender, Luis Benkard, Liza Bennett, Shelli Bennett, Christine Bennett, Anita Bensabat, Janet Benton Gaillard, Martha Bergh, Kathy Bergold, Janet Berkman, Mara Berman, Patricia Bern, Cheryl Bernini, Gary Bernstein, Janet Berry, Carrie Berry, Julie Bestry, Barrie Betts, Payel Bhattacharyya, Nancy Biagini, Jenny Bick, Joseph Bifulk, Michael Billow, Dara Bilow, Xander Bilyk, Elizabeth Bindas, Richard Binder, Linda Binder, Eileen Bird, Paul Birkby, Scott Bishop, David Bishop, Lucy Bishop, Liz Bishop, Leslie Bissell, Nina Bjornsson, Kerry Black, Tracy Blackburn, Jo Ann Blackburn, Trevor Blackwell, Pamela Blackwell-Nwonye, Grainne Blair, Sophie Blakemore, Sarah Bland, Zero Blank, Amelia Blanton, Jarrod Blasius, Jo-Anne Bliss, Suzy Blu, Edith Bluhm, Kelly Bo-Belly, Neil Bobrick, Melissa Bock, April Bodendorfer, Pamela Bogle, Ambre Boissevain, Mackenzie Bolin, Armand Bolling, Helen Bollman, Victoria Bolotaeva, Candace Bolt, Kenton Bolte, Linda Bolton, Kristine Bonstrom Vial, LisaJo Borchers, Lori Boren, Allyson Borkgren, Michele Borys, B. D. Bossidy, Scott Bostick, Brian Bostron, Deborah Bouchard, Barbara Boucher, Noureddine Boughanmi, Bridget Bounds, Heather Bourassa, Doreen Bourke, Leslie Bousquet, Veronica Bowe-Murphy, Fay Bowen, Theresa Bowen, Linda Bowen, Sunny Bower, Claire Bowes, Kathy Bowl, Noel Bowles, Scott Bowling, Margaret Bowser, John Bracewell, James Easter Bradford, Larry Bradley, Dona Bradley, William Bradshaw, Greg Branch, Erik Branch, Emily Brandenberger, Barbara Brandt, Victor Brandt, Rose Brandt, Henry Brann, Maria Brannigan, Cheryl Branscum, Philip Branton, Maura Brattested, Lyn Braun, Cristiane Breining, Sandra Brennan, Sean Brennan, Kathe Brenner Deane, Melissa Briggs, Laura Brink, Andrea Brisson, Pauline Brock, Lynne Bronstein, Tony Brooks, Barbara Brooks, Dorothy Brophy, Karen Browder, Ann Brown, Nicole Brown, Dusty Brown, Beverly Brown, Dortha Kay Brown, Donald Bruce, Julie Brumlik, Judy Brunswick, Cass Bruton, Patricia Bryant, Paula Bryder, Kathleen Buchanan, Esther Buck, Michael Buckley, Diane Buglewicz Foote, Jeff Burlew, Betty Bullard, Gary Bullock, Mitchell Bullock, James Bunnelle, Kendra Bunyon, Edward Burch, Denise Burchard, Jacky Burdett, Meaghan Burford, Justin Burgess, Peter Burgess, Elvis Burgos, Niki Burke, Barbara Burkett, Laurie Burnard, Linda Burnham, Dirk Burns, Gary Burns, Liela Burns, Darlene Burns, Janice Burns, Elaine Burns,

Christine Burns Lehrfeld, Margaret Burns Reyes, Wanita Burrell Boyar, Susan Burrows, John Allen Burtner, Linda Burtt, Buzz Burza, Deanna Busdieker, Jonathan Bush, Susan Bush, Kelly Butler, Kim Buxton, Brian Byers, Elizabeth Byers, Shana Byrd, Kathleen Byrne, Connie Byrnes, Ed Bzomowski, Mona Cabel, Delia Cabrera, John Cahill, Erika Cailao, Erin Cain, Victoria Cairl, Ruth Calia Stives, Suzy Q Calkins, Marcy Camano, Sharon Cameron Lawn, Margaret Campanella, Malcolm Campbell, Paddy Campbell, Rosalie Campbell, Geri Campbell, Erin Campos, Amy Canaday, Karen Candee, Shana Cannavaro, Fran Capezio, James Cappio, Mary Capps, Liz Cardenas, Ann Marie Cardin, Andrea Cardwell, Theresa Carey, Stephen Carleston, Windy Carleton, Mike Carlin, Catherine Carlisle, Denise Carlon, Tim Carmain, Timm Carney, David Olof Carney, Lorraine Carolan, Lily Carousel, Laura Carr, Jackie Carr, Nicole Carrero, Leslie Carroll, Wesley Carscaddon, Sela Carsen, Diane Carson, Julie Carter, Karen Carter, Lisa Carter, Mary Caruso, Natalie Casetti, Vanessa Cass, Carol Cassell, Rafael Castillo, Jesse V. Castillo, Hilton Caston, Sarah Catlin, Suzanne Catterick, Heidi Vega Cavanaugh, Norma Cavazos, Amy Cavender, Kristen Cesconetto, Bonnie Chakravorty, Marilyn Anne Challis, Lorraine Chamberlain, Andrea Chambers, Valerie Chambers, Joanne Chando, Mekisha Chansler, Marsha Chapman, David Chase, Cheryl Chatzis, Jeremy Chestler, Nancy Chorpenning, Vince Chura, Rebecca Church, Robin Church, Lisa Churinskas-Hulit, Catherine Chute, Suzette Ciancio, Laura Ciarrocca, Edana Cichanowicz, Louis Cigliano, Ann Cihon, Marie Ciriello, Pamela Clark, Aubrey-Aaron Clark, Colin Clark, Leigh Clark, Dimitra Clark, Rick Clark, Kelly Clark, Maggie Cleveland, Julian Clift, Valerie Cline, the Reading Cline Family, Russell Clower, Ronda Cluff, Bob Coard, Linda Coats, Sam Cobb, Van Cockcroft, Michael Cockerel, Charles Coffman, Katy Coker-James, Terry Cole, Craig Coleman, Kenneth Colgin, Kathy Collier, Emily Collins, Marie Collins, Amy Collinsworth, Lorraine Combs, Amie Conant, Marissa Concepcion, Rúairí Conneely, Margaret Connell, Susan Connolly, Sharron Connor, Regina Connors, Myriam Contiguglia, Deborah Conway, Danielle Cook, B. C. Coolen, Marguerite Cooney, Tosha Cooper, Alison Cope, Clare Copeland, Kristine Copeland, Deb Copeland, Joe Copeland, Richard Cordoni, Rick Cornell, Jerry Cornwell, Cathy Corral, Suzanne Corrigan, Steve Corso, Carrie Corson, Natalie Corzine Moore, Carole Cosentino, Alicia Cosgrove, Melissa Costa, Michael Costa, William Costlow, Emilia Cotiga, John Cotter, Susan Cotton, Lisa Cottrell, Bob Counihan, Jeff Courtade, Forrest Courtney, Darlene Cousins, Diane Coussan, Suzanne Coutanceau, Inara Couto, Gina Covarrubias, Mo

Cowan, Richard Cowen, Jessica Cox, Bethany Cox, Katrina Cox, Mauna Faye Crabtree, Taylor Craig, Debbie Craig, Kim Craigmile, David Crane, Catherine Craven, Josephine Crawford, Susan Cregan, Susan Crippin, Jim Cripps, Beverly Crockett, Deborah Cron, Bill Cronauer, Douglas Cronk, Boyce Crowell, Erin Crowley, Cathleen Crowley, Jonathan Crowley, Karen Crump, Peter Cruz, Irene Cruz, Catherine Cryan, Lillian Csernica, Kathleen Cullen, Monica Cumming, Michael Cuneo, Destiny Curran, Liam Curry, Tere Curtis, Jody Cvetas, Melissa Cynova, Leon Czikowsky, David Dacus, Barbara Dale, Camilla Dalerci, Malcolm Dalkoff, Tom Daly, Babette d'Amours, Barbara Danahy, Mayme Daniell, Lisa Danielson Twomey, Ann Marie D'Antona, Mary D'Arcy, Jill Darville, Olivia Das, Carol Datt Mattar, Charles Davidson, Laura Davis, Shay Davis, Nathan Davis, Janey Davis, Debra Davis, Janice Davison, Courtney Davison, Don Davison, Jenaya Dawe, Athena Daytona, Nannick De Coster, Jan-Hein de Nobel, Gail de Vos, Jill Dealey, Cate Dean, Wendy DeAngelis, Angeline Deaton, Kerfegar Deboo, Grace Anne DeCandido, Tim Dedinsky, Thierry Defize, Maryann DeGregorio, Randal K. Delaney-Mars, Grant D. DeLanoy, Andrea DeMar, Alicia Demarco, Agnes Dembowski, Stephen Demény, Emily Dempster, Philippa Denney, Sheila Derrwaldt, Pia Desselle, Jennifer DeVenuti, Roseanne DeVincenzo, Christina Devlin, Derek DeVries, John DeWilde, Constance DeWitt, Lisa Di Giannantonio, Elina Di Leo, Michael Diaz, Joe DiBattista, David Dickason, Laura Dickinson-Turner, Karen Didorek, Jennifer DiGaetano, Angelo DiGiacomo, Bonkuwari Dilip, Mary Dils, Joanne DiMare, Fox DiMera, Misty Dishman, Dave Dix, James Dixon, Lorin Dixon, Joseph Dobrian, Cary Dockery McGregor, Paul E. Dodaro, Kristie Lee Dodd, Susan Dodge, Laura Doering-Strite, Kathleen Dolan, Diane Dolan, Keith Dolder, June Dollar, Arlene Domkowski, Sandra Donahue, Dede Donahue, Siobhan Donald, Catherine Donato, Michelle Donk, Thomas Donley, Heather Donnelly, Joy Donovan Brandon, Joni Donze, Jennifer Doorenbos, Jane Dornsife, Patricia Dorwin, Patty Doscher, Vic Doucette, Alanna Dougherty, Jann Dougherty, Sherry Dour, Michael Dowd, Tricia Dower, Melissa Dowling LaRoe, Michael Downend, Helen Downing, Angela Downs, Delores Doyle, Jennifer Drabble, Joe Drago, Betty Dravis, Christopher Drayson, Terri Drennan, Grace Dressler, Frank Drew, Kathleen Drohan, Alan Drucker, Kristen DuBois, Sandra Duchon Byrne, Nel Ducomb, Duke Duczer, Roz Dudley, Wren Dugan, Ellen Dugas, Vincent Duggan, Becky d'Ugo, Mary Davis Dulany, Liz Duncan, Lisa Duncan, Christine Dunham, Marlene Dunkin, Paul Dunlap, Christopher Dunworth, Theresa Duplessis, Anusha Duray, David L. Durkin, Suzanne

Dusch, Audra DuVall, Bonnie Dykes, Olivia J. Eagan Rowell, Michael Eakins, Erin Earley, Tonya East, Jude East, Shanda Easterday Ph.D., Priscilla Ebright, Jordan Eckerling, Todd Eckert, Victoria Eckholm, James Edgar, Shirley Edwards, Margie Edwards, Jessica Edwin, Fred Eggers, Sara Egolf, Lynn Eickhoff, Jessica Eik, Lisa Eisele, Kathy Ekberg, Linda Eldridge, Betty Eliason, John Elliott, Barbara Elovic, Sterling Ely, Susan Ely, Patricia Elzie, Miles Emanuel, Michelle Encomienda, Adrienne Eng, Garry Epstein, Heather Ercse-Spence, Pamela Erens, Susan Erichsen, Tina Erickson, Carol Erlingheuser, Bonnie Ermalinski, Catherine Erney, Callie Eros, Alison Errington, Naomi Estrada, Carrie Ethridge, Linda Ettinger Lieberman, Lindsey Evans, Richard Evans, Bonni Evans, Rona Evartt, Chris Evenden, Irene Evory, Kathryn Exner, Cynthia Eyres-Lutz, Elly Faden, Jay Fahey, Fran Fahey, Paul Fahey, Judith Falcigno, Bartolo Falcone, Barbara Fama, Alicia Fansmith, Constance Fantora, Wynna Faye Fargo Smith, Cherilyn Farley, Anne Farma, Ashley Katherine Farmer, Jes Farnum, Noeleen Farrell, Lori Farris, Christie Featherstone, Ianthe Feeney, Howard Feinberg, Rachel Feinerman, Barbara Fellencer, Jeri Fendler, Annie Ferguson, Stacy Ferguson-Sandstedt, Marci Fermier, Laurie Ferns, Laura Ferrante, Robert Ferrante, Sharon Fetter, Gretchen Fields, Heidi Filipowic, Stephanie Finder, Randall Fine, Jessica Finkelberg Silver, Lisa Finkelstein, Terry Finn, Jennifer Finney, Cynthia Fiore, Cat Fisher, Greg Fisher, Amy Fisher, Tracy Fisher, Sandra Fitzgerald, Geri Fletcher, Susanne Flø, Susan Floss, Barb Flynn, Shirley Flynn Johnon, Toby Folwick, Melanie Fonville, Tara Lee Ford, Beverly Ford, Mary Forester, Lennon Forever, Elena Forni, Lyn Forrest, Ian Forsyth, Heather Fortney, Louis Forward-Henry, Lisa Fosnaugh, Sherri Foster, Anthony Foster, Thomas Foulke, Julie Fournier, Angelique Foust, Damon Lee Fowler, Andrea Fox, Ron Fox, Robert Fox, Roisin Foy, Ana Maria Fraijo, Dori Fram, Patty Franchi, Lisa Francia, Gillian Francis, Margie Freedle, Jamie Freeman, Robert Freidin, Christy French, Raejean French, Leslie Friedman, Lisa Frisch, Rebecca Fritz, Christine Fronczak, Annie Frost, Michelle Frost, Heidi Frost, Phil Fryberger, Bronwyn Fryer, Joan Fuglewicz, Laurie Fuhr, Scott Fullmer, Lori Fulton, Martha Futterman-Gonzalez, Gregory Gabbard, Brad Gabriel, Barry Gabriel, Kitty Gagen, Meaghan Gagnon, Danielle Gaines, John Gale, Gia Galeano, Ana Maria Gallegos-Maxwell, Mike Galos, Nicole Gamez, Manisha Ganguly, Kathleen Garcia-Horlor, Sharon Garfield, Larry Garland, Jean Garner, Rosemary Garofolo, Patricia Garretson, Mary Garrett, Jan Garver, John Garza, Sylvia Gates, Anna Ruth Gatlin, Carolyn Gattegno, Christine M. Gatto, Sheila Gaudet, Robert Gaudio, Christina Gay, Phyllis Gay, John Gaylord,

Victoria Gear, Kathryn Gearheard, Cathy Gellis, Paul Gengler, Sandrine Genier, Anna Gerard, Patricia Geritz, Carla Germany, Meredith Gertz, Diane Getson Olive, Holly Getz Holdren, Jackie Gibson, Ann Giese, Sharon Giesfeldt, Van Ruiswyk, Carolyn Giles, Diane Gillespie Cook, Beth Gilman, Andrés Giménez Rodríguez, Bruce Ginsberg, Laurie Ginsburg, Eileen Gizienski, Bathsheva Gladstone, Sonia Glenn, Teresa Glenn-Harrell, Jack Globenfelt, Michelle Gloss, Vicky Go, Susan Gobeo-Vansickle, Helen Goddard, Jelena Godrijan, Glenn Godsey, John Godwin, Gregory Gold, Larry Goldberg, Stephen Goldberg, Steve Goldfield, Jane Gole Lieurance, Victoria Gonzalez, Moxie Goodsell, Paul Goodwin, Helen Goody, Maggie Gordon, Mary Jo Gordon, Avery Gordon, Marcus Gorman, Jan Gourley, L. J. Gouveia, Share Grace, Michelle Grace, Catherine Graham, Kristina Graham, Eric Graham, Patrice Graham, Stefan Gramenz, Maria Gramieri, Sayo Granich-Lee, Lisa Grant, Karen Gratch, Wendy Gray, Libby Gray, Patricia Green, Elizabeth Green, Delone Green, Joseph Green, Heyward Green, Joe Green, Natalie Greene, Elaine Greer Baldwin, Karla Griffin, Christopher Griffin, Gail Grimes, Buckey Grimm, Jyssica Grohowski, Bill Groom, Lois Gross, Ron and Robin Grotjan, Kimberly Groupé, Amelia Grovenor, Lorien Gruchalla, Kristina Guckenberger, Dani Guerard, Lisa Guillory, Jim Gulledge, Vivian Gulyassy, Sahag Gureghian, Januki Gurung, Margie Gustafson, Mary Gwaltney, Lindsy Gwozdz, Jan Gyn, Jan Haag, Jeff Hadfield, Denise Hadley, Francesca Hagadus, Karin Hagemeister, Marissa Hagen, Joan Hager, Zane Hagy, Tamiz Haiderali, Susan Haigh, Resa Haile, Benjamin Hain, Nicole Halcoop, Kathi Hale, Sara Hall, Jamie Hall, Sissy Hall, Hal Hall, Faye Hall, Velmer Hall, Beretta Hall, Leslie Hall, Shannon Hall, Richard Hamel, Head Hamel, Katie Hamill, Ginger Hamilton, David Hamilton, Martha Hammerquist, Alicia Handa, Tracie Handley, Joan Haney, David Hankerson, John Hanley, Wendy Hanna, A. J. Hanratty Baumay, Erika Hansen, Andrea Hansen, Paul Hanson, Martin Harbour, Teresa Hardister, Michael Harkin, Lynn Harler, Kyle Harney, Marietta Harouse, Natasha Harrington, Karolyn Harrington, James Harris, Brad Harris, Joy Harris, Michael Harris, Lorin Harris, Morgan Harris, Kirsten Harris, Debbie Harris, Melanie Harris, Autumn Harrison, Hilary Harry, Lori Hart, Melissa Hartley, Laura Hartman, Jeffrey Hartmann, Mark Harty, Mary Jane Hartzell, Lola Hatmil, Jennie Hausler, Madeline Havrilla, Christine Hawkins, Sharon Hawkins, Kathy Hawthorn, Heather Hay, Herb Hays, Chris Hayslett, Linda Head, Carole Healey, Rhona Healey, Jamie Heasman, Carol Heckman, Jarrett Hedborg, Ula Hedwig, Randy Heinz, Laura Long Helbig, Sara Heller, Jesse Hellman,

ACKNOWLEDGMENTS

Stephanie Hellmann, Normandy Helmer, Lori Helper, Tiffeney Henderson, Dorothy Henderson, Bill Henderson, Frances Hendron, Clair Hendry, Laurie Hennessey, E. B. Henningsen, Diane Henson, Danielle Her Many Horses, Penelope Hernandez, Karen Herold, Misty Herr, Shannon Herrick, Christy Hertel, Helene Hertzlinger, Tom Heugele, Susan Hewitt, Christopher James Heyworth, Louise Hibner, Heather Hickok Ferguson, Shannan Hicks, Odessa Higdon, Sharron Higgins, Chris Higham, Lindsey Hileman Bowshier, Jennifer Hilvitz, Mary-Lucille Hindmarch, Stacy Hinojos, Mary Hinze-Joyce, Deana Hipke, Carroll Hippeard, Mary Hirsch, Karen Hirst, Heidi HitsIt, Pamela Hnyla, Beth Ho, Stephanie Hodge, Kathy Hodges, Russell and Linus Hoffman, Ellen Hoffman, Betty Hoffmann, Dene Hofheinz Anton, Lisa Hofman, John Hogan, Lisa Hogan, Jerry Holderman, Mary Holland, Tiff Holland, Mary Margaret Holland, Joshua Holley, Penny Holliday, Annabel Hollins-Cliff, Jennie Hollister, Sharon Holloman, John Holly, Sheila Elaine Holman, Darren Holmquist, Ron Holmstrom, Melissa Holston, Robin Holtmann, Annie Honjo, Janet Hood, Celia Hooper, Kim Hopewell, Bernice Hopkins, George Hopkins, Amy Hopper, Gillian Horgan, Jason Horne, Jonathan Horne, Christopher Horrocks, Sheri Horton, Jessica Horton, Brian Horton, Mickey Houlahan, Christine Houseworth, R. L. Pete Housman, Sophie Houston, Mike Houston, Jacqueline Houston, Andy Howarth, Jo Howarth, George Howerton, Roberta Hoyt, Renee Hudon, Tracy Hudson, Jill Hudson, Charles Huepers, Cecilia Huerta, Vicki Hughes, Ginger Hughes, Melia Hughes, Joe Huis, Georgiana Huizenga, Scott Hunter, Tod Hunter, Jessica Hurlburt, Laura Hurley, Stephanie Huthmacher, Daniel Hyman, Toshinaro Imchen, M. Heidi Imhof, Danielle Indovino Cawley, Kat Ingalls, Blass Ingame, Sherri Ingrey, Jordan Inman, Tony Iovino, Renee Irvin, Sheryl Irwin, Sheri Israel, Jo Ann Jaacks, Heather Jaber, Cheri Jackson, Melanie Jackson, Lorraine Jackson, Tom Jackson, Tracy Jacobs, Linda Jacobs, Jennifer Jacobs, Deborah Jacobs Cole, Laura Jacoby, Teri-Ann James, Roy James, Margaret Jankauskis, Becky Jansch, Karen Janssens, Jeanne Jenny Jared, Ellin Jarmel, Steve Jarrett, Ayyla Jarvela, Samiya Javed, Savvy Jay, Jackie Jean, Deborah Jeans, Geoffrey Jeavons Klein, Kristi Jefferson, Eggs Jenedict, Maureen Anne Jennings, Mary Jensen, Tom Jensen, Christa Jensen, Mikki Jerdet, Devin Jessup, Kristen Jett, Lisa Jimenez, Juliet Jimenez, The Jodester, Mary Johannsen, Gale Johansen, Bodil Johansson, Jennifer John, Jill John, Christine Johns, Keith Johnson, Isabel Johnson, Kristi Johnson, Jessica Johnson, Bob Johnson, Janice Johnson, Maz Johnson, Christina Johnson, Winter Johnson, Shelia Johnson, Claire Johnston,

316

Paula Johnston, Nancy Johnston, deLinda Jones, Lynda Jones, Cynthia Jones, Kate Jones, Michael Douglas Jones, Dan Jones, Harris Jones, Gordon Jones, Akiko Jones, Jennifer Jones, Kay Jones, Harris Jones, Mike Jones, Tara Joy, Meighan Joyce, Gregg Juhlin, Jenny Jung, Val Jupe, Harry Kachline, C. C. Kahn, Doug Kaiser, Mark Kalan, Todd Kalinski, Murray Kane, Priyanka Kapoor, Jim Karabin, Amy Karatz, Joanne Karmik, Jeri Lynn Karr, Preeti Kasbekar, Kerri Kat, Erin Katalinic, Rebecca Kauffman, Sandra Kay, Eddie Kaylor, Kristen Kean, Michael Kear, Jennifer Keck, Scott Keen, Karen Keeney, Denise Keliuotis, Ellen Kellam, Susan Keller, Rik Kellerman, Peg Kelley, Steve Kelley, Linda Kelley, Richard Kelley, Teresa Kellmer, Mark Kellner, Jacqueline Kello, Pam Kelly, Thomas Kelly, Nancy Kelly, Cory Kemp, Vida Kenk, Neil Kennedy, Joan Kenton, Lark Kephart, Sophia Kercher, Mike Kerins, Cindy Kerr, Janine Kershaw, Judith Keselowski, Jennifer Ketterer, Stephanie Keyes, Dave Keyte, Gurukarm Khalsa, Hina Khan, Roseanne Kibler, Gregory Kiefer, Josh Kiem, Steve Kightlinger, Julia Kilcoyne, James "Kiley Jr.," Julie Killeen, Madonna Kilpatrick, Jenny Kim, Kit Kimberly, Coretta Kimble, Marcy Kimbrough, Phil Kimmins, Susan King, Michelle King, Thèrése King, A. Garry King, Margie King, Mickie King, Catherine King, Lolita King, Therese King, Kimberly King-Woodbury, Karen Kinsel, Penn Kinsey, Anne Kircher, Kelly Kirkpatrick, Robert S. Kissel, Alexia Klayman, Michele Kline, Leslie Klingner, Lauren Kloos, Valerie Knapp, Olja Knezevic, Tiffany Knoell, Lily Knol, Jana Knudson, Melissa Kobin, Cheryl Kohan, Mary Lou Kohne, Ben Kohrman, Katherine Kollef, Ron Kolman, Vera Korcok, Margarita Korol, Evangelia Koulizaki, Kirsten Kowalewski, Maureen Kowalski, Michael Kraft, Victor Krall, Bobbie Kramer, Murray Kramer, Donna Kramer, Leslie Kranz, Kelly Krei, Sasha Kreinik, Minna Kronberg, Kate Kruley, Lisa Krupa, Zeb Kunst, Michelle Kunz, Karla Kuzmic-Mueggenborg, Dean La Douceur, Jennifer Labach, Ryan Labay, Valerie LaClair, Tara LaDore, Tammy Lahrmer, Alison Laing, Kate Laity, Paul Lally, Richard Lamma, Cynthia Lammel, Samantha Lancaster, Jill Landis, Linda Landowski, Ray Lane, Steven Langhorst, Sharon Langlois, Pam Langworthy, Lance Lankford, Kelly Laramore, Deborah Large, John Larkin, Heather Larsen, Rebecca Larson, Marci Lash, Joe Laszlo, Karen Laufenberg, Bethany Lauterbach, Rosalie Lavery, Meredith Lawrence, Marcia Lawrence, Amy Lawson, Gerry Laytin, Sheri Lazare, Charlotte Le Moignan, Michael Leach, Beth Learn, Gunilla Leavitt, Suzanne LeBel, Maddy Lederman, F. S. J. Ledgister, Helen Lee, Fern Lee, Kelly Lefever, Bgelita Legarda, Toni Leggio, Kristin Lehigh, Debra Lehl, Allison Lehman, James Lehr, Cary Leibowitz, Sandra Leigh,

ACKNOWLEDGMENTS

Yasmin Leischer, Jonathan Leiter, Patty Lemoine, Derek Leo, Kirsten Leo, Catherine Leonis, Gayle Leslie, Hugh Lester, K. Letter, Suzanne LeVieux-Hall, Michelle Levine, Sammy Levitt, Virginia Levy, Laura Lou Levy, Lanis Levy, Eliza Lewis, Shannon Lewis, Nick Lewis, Rachel Lewis, Susan Lewis, Judy Libby, Jean Sue Johnson Libkind, Sue Lievers, Stefani Light, Jacob "Lile MPA," Robert Liljebäck, Enna Lill, Ruth Lindeman, Susan Lindsay, Cindy Linville, Rick Allen Lippert, Ann Liston, Susan Littman-Loukedis, Natasa Ljubisavljevic, Bryan Loar, Robin Lobb, Dennis Locke, Carmen Lomellin, Richard Long, Sandra Long, Frank Longoria, Karen Lopez, Medea Lopez, Caitlin M. Lord, Tiffany Loria, Barbara Lotsberg, Dianne Lott, William D. Love, Sharol Lovett, Deborah Low, Sandy Lowe, Tessa Lowe, David Loxham, Jeff Loxterkamp, Lisa Lubchansky, Peggy Lucas, Anita Lucas, Ken Lumberg, Jamie Lumm, Raven Lunatic, Ravel Lutz, Bill Lutz, Ericka Lutz, Carol Lyman, John Lynd, Katherine Lynn, Lisa Lynott-Carroll, Sheila MacVeigh, Carol MacDonald, Sheila Machado, George Machen, Ann MacLaughlin-Berres, Suzanne MacNeil, Barbara MacRae, Neahle Madden, Martha Maddy, John Maeder, Scott Magee, Christine Maggard, Linda Maguire, Jay Mahone, Pamela Mains, Michele Maiorano, Corinna Makris, Lisa Males Courtney, Gregory Maley, Mark Malinowski, Kate Mallow, Ellyne Jo Manask, Joan Manchester, Rowan Mangan, Grace E. Mangum, Fran Mann, Noelle Manna, Elizabeth Mannion Gibba, Caroline Manown, Tricia Marden, Jules Margraf, Bianca Marin, Joe Marin, Audrey Markey, Pamela Markley-Trexler, Gilly Marks, Bunny Marks, Josh Marowitz, Laura Marran, Helen Marshall, Kent Martin, Albina Martin, Heather Martin, Martha Martin, Jon Martin, Sonja Martineau, Agustin Martínez, Manuel Martinez-Maldonado, Lisa Martinis, Sheri Marvin, Sal Marz, Sharon Masters, Susie D. Matias, Allison Matney, Donald Matrow, Jeniene Matthews, Melissa Matthews, Sue Mattison, Eric Mattison, Lisa Mauk, Jacqueline May, Ashley Mayer, Heather Mayhugh, Lou Mazzucchelli, Susan McAfee, Colin McAndrew, Christy McBrayer, Jo-Anne Carol McBride, Marilyn McCain, Martha McCann, Mickie McCarter, Joan Marie McCarthy, Cathleen McCarthy, Eileen McCarthy, Catherine McClarin, Julee McClelland, Maureen McCormick, Teresa McCoy, Pamela McCoy Boyer, Maryann McCurdy, Leslie McDade, John McDermott, Timothy McDermott, Linda McDonald, James McDonald, Brendan McDougall, Laura McDowell, Sarah McElhiney, Cynthia McGarvie, Mickie McGee, Doreen McGettigan, Martha McGill, Janene McGilvrey, Kathleen McGinley, Elicia McGinn, Susan McGlennan, Susan McGrath-Smith, Deborah McGraw, Jeffery McGraw, Kevin McGuire, Janet McKay, Alistair

318

McKinlay, Sheena McKinney, Paige McKinstry, Lazarus McKintosh, Chloe McKnight, Debbie McKnight, Allen McLain, Phil McLaughlin, Mary Moore McLaughlin, Crystal McLaughlin, Triston McLaughlin, Glenn Mclean, Denise McLemore, Alison McLin, Brian McMillen, Narn McMoo, Michael McNally, Jane McNally, Eileen McNamara, Margaret McNeely, Marsha McNeese, Terrie McNulty, Jan McNutt, Elise McPherson, Dennis McQuaid, Kim McShane, Ed McShane, Elaine McSherry, Patti Meagher, Patti Meagher, Caolifhionne Mears, Bill Mecklenburg, Amy Medel, Kate Meehan, Kim M. Meehan, Andrea Meehan, Jan Meehan, Erin Megin, Lisa Meiner, Tanja Meißner, Marilyn Meister, Sean Melton, Ed Mendez, Patty Mendys, Kate A. Mercier, Byron Meredith, Adam Meredith, Nancy Merehouyias, Doug Merenda, Jennifer Merlis, Doreen Merriman, Georgina Merry, Earl Messer, Laurie Ann Meyer, Clifford Meyer, Christine Meyer, Tim Meyer, Kendra Michael, Sharon Middleton, Kay Milford, Sarah Miller, Sue Miller, Butch Miller, Glenn Miller, Monica Miller, Timothy Miller, Cindy Suzette Miller, Lempi Miller, Candice Miller, Cynthia Miller, Julia Milligan-King, Stephen Millner, Candi Milo, Jac Milsom-Payne, Kate Miner, Gina Mink, Patrick Minor, Stephanee Mirachi, Sofia Misenheimer, Jennifer Mitchell, Henry Miyamoto, Angela Mizell, Donj Moj, Sue Ann Molinell, Jim Moll, John Molley, Katrina Monroe, Phyllis Montana-LeBlanc, Lori Montcalm, Perilous Moo, Alyssa Mooney, Dana Moore, Lauren Moore, Maureen Moore, Paula Moore, Dianne Moorefield, Lorraine Morabito, Jessica Moreno, Marianne Morey, Stacy Morgan, Mary Morgan, David Morgan, Amanda Morken, Ken Morlan, Jessica Morris, Kay Morris, Maryjane Morris, Louisa Morrisette, Heather Morrison, Althea Morrison, Tami Morrissey, Deb Morrone, Arba Morrow, Patricia Morrow, Wanda Morrow Clevenger, Mike Mortimer, Will Moschke, Diane Moseley, Scott Moss, Sean Moynihan, Melissa Muckart, Wadell Muhammad, Madeline Muir, Pattie Mulderig, Donna Mulgrew, Sarah Mullan, Joyce Mullis, Laura Mumma, Francisco Munhoz, Monica Munn-Schreml, Jill Munson, Lynn Mary Munson, Rachel Murawski, Simonne Murphy, Murphy Murphy, Jennifer Murray, Dorothy Murtagh, Bonnie Musselman, Rosamond Myers, Steven Myers, Joanne Myrah, Valeriya Nakshun, Marni Nancekivell, NripsIngh Napalchyal, Kim Naphegyi, Susan Naple, Greg Nardi, Orysia Nasar, Joan Nash, Sarmija Nathan, Jody Nathan, Gina Nations, Veronica Naylon, Gerard Nedich, Theron Neel, Larry Nehring, Karen Neko, Karen Nelson, Robert Nelson, Vivian Nelson, Kristin Ness, Tom Nessinger, Wendy Neumann, Hubert Neuner, Pamela Newberry, Hannah Hull Newman, Lori Nicholes, Emma Nicholls, Stephanie Nichols,

Lilly Nichols, Maria Niculete, Valerie Nielsen, Lorraine Niemczyk, Paula Nieminen, Brenan Nierman, Niki !, Michael Norce, Vivian Noriega, Pamela Norman, Dana Norman, Malcolm (Noddy) Norman, Paul Normandin, Kimberle Northcutt, Jennifer Novacek-Toft, Linda Novak, Susan Novales, Kathleen Nutter, Anne O'Neill, Debbe Oberhausen, Susan Obral, Anne P. O'Brian, Gin O'Brien, Ellie O'Connell, Darcy O'Dell, Tara O'Donnell, Barbara O'Donnell, Terri O'Donnell, Helen O'Donoghue, Audrey Ogilvie, Mary O'Hare, Margaret O'Hora, Victoria Oiso, Susan O'Keeffe, Paddy O'Keeffe, Terry Oldes, Mel O'Leary, Krysta Oliszewski, Nancy Oliveri, Joan Oliveto, Anita Olp, Gwyneth Olson, Anne Margaret O'Malley, Beth Omansky, Keane Onath, Daniel O'Neil, Lynne O'Neil, Michael O'Neill, Patricia O'Reilly, Maureen O'Reilly, Erik O'Riley, Jeffrey Orth, Alyce Osborne, Kevin Osborne, Lynn O'Shea, Joan Osterberg, Amy Ostrem, Maureen Ott, Kathy Otto, Diane Overcash, Tushar Oza, John Pack, Gail Pacurai, Deb Snarky Paige, Chad Painter, Cass Paley, Kate Palley, Barbara Palliser, Karen Palmer, Elaine Panneton, Dana Pantazopoulos, Eric Pape, Roger Paquette, Jessica Paris, Kelly Parker, Suzy Parker, Richard J. Parker, Jim Parker, Sheila Parker, Rachel Parks, Peggy J. Parks, Sherry Parman, Patricia Parra, Susan Parsons, J. B. Parsont, Anthony Pasaye, Ali Paskun, Su Paterson, Penny Pattison, Christopher Patton, Conrad W. Paul, Janna Pawlak, Carmen Paxton, Brian Payne, Matt Payne, Cynthia Payne, Dana Payne, Lauren Pazik, Tim Peacock, LouAnn Peacock, Tamara Pearce, David Pearmain, Jenn Peaslee, Cory Peeke, Pamela Peitzman, Aaron Pelcomb, Brian Pelton, Alisa Pelz, Mary Penley, Rozália Péntek, Marjo Peppelaar, Nancy "Perchitti, R.N.," Janice Ann Perez, Charles Perkins, Toni Perrin, Kevin Perry, Patricia Perry, Doug Perry, Virginia Perry, Linda Pessis, Paul Peterson, Carol Peterson, Holly Peterson, Meredith Petran, Ljupcho Petreski, William Pettengill, Olivia Pettijohn, Roy Pettis, Krys Pettit, Deborah Pettry, Patrick Petty, Denise Pfleger, Marge Pfleiderer, Ginny Phares, Jessica Phillips, Joy Phillips, Frank Phillips, John Phillips, Gary Phillips, Velissa Phillips, Emily Philp, Raye Lynn Phoebus, Lisa Photakis, Arrow Picasso, Suzy Pickett, Louise Pierce, Sara Pietrzak, Natalie A. Pinto, R. J. Pisko, Edie Pistolesi, Vicki Pitluk, Ryan Pitt, Julie Pittilla, Eldon Pittman, Penny Piva, Chandra Placer, Susan Plake, Linda Plancich, Susan Plant, Lorelei Plasko, Laura Pleasants, Dave Plomin, Kevin Plumb, Barbara Pollock, Susan Polston, James Pomeroy, Carliss Pond, Emma Pope, Mara Popoff, Josie Poppy, Mary Portele, Therese Porter, Ian Post-Green, Tricia Potts, Alan Povey, Cathy Power, Paula Pratt, Stacey Preble, Jenn Presutto, Ellen Prewitt, Susan Price, Judi Price, Bob Price, Lawrence Prichard,

ACKNOWLEDGMENTS

Cynthia Pring, Scott Pringle, Amy Pritchard, John Proe, James Province, Jimmy Pruitt, Lenore Pryor, Ann Pryor, Carla Paola Pulido, Billy Pullen, Laura Purcell, Debbie Pure, Douglas Qualls, Dave Quillen, Victor Quillen, Kelli Quinn, Petra Radel, Paul Rader, Diane Radford, Thomas Raher, Aron Rainwater, Meg Raminiak, Steven Ramos, Jenny Ramos, Juliette Ramphrey, Kat Ranalli, Penny Rand, Guy Raphaely, Robin Rapoport, Sophie Rapp, Andrea Ravenwood, Janet Ravka, B. A. Ray, Michelle Ray, Carole Ray, Thomas Raymond, David Read, Sydney Reade, Lisa Recker, Miki Reed, Amanda Reen, Thomas Rees, Dawn Reese, John Reesman, Chris Reid, John Reiner, Foxxy Rella, Debbie Remonte, George Renan, Joel Rendle, Jennifer Rengger, Maria Renna, Debbie Rensen, Laurie Reuben, Bob Reveley, Barbara Rew, Amabilia Reyes, Meredyth Reynolds, Nikki Reynolds, Shelly Rhodes, David Rhodes, Shannon Rhodes, Janice Richards, Patric Richardson, Bonnie Richardson, Laura Richardson-Gentry, Colin Ricketts, Francesca Ricondo, Rebecca Riechers, Sue Rimkus, Carol Ristine, Arabella Rittenhouse, Shelley Ritter-Geesey, Lauri Rizio, Catherine Rizzetto, Russ Roberts, Noni Roberts, Jon Roberts, Gwyn Roberts, Huw Roberts, Chekesha Phoenix Roberts Katsiris, Mary Ruth Robinson, Sally Rose Robinson, Cat Robson, Cynthia Roby, Patricia Rocha, Patina Rodgers, Angel Rodrigues, Patricia Rodriguez, Ida Rodriguez, Mary Rodriguez, Caroline Roel, Carol Rogai, Elizabeth Rogers, Donna Rogers, Darcy Rogers, Amy Rogers, Jane Roland, Beth Romanik, Jacky Romanik, Janie Romer, Marinda Romesser, Judith Ronci, Kathy Root, Julie Ropelewski, Mary Roque, Cris Rosales, Karen Rose, Tami Rose, Katherine Rosen, Wendy Rosen, Sari Rosenheck, Richard Rosevear, Rennae Ross, Minette Ross, Alicia Ross, Cydney Ross, W. C. Rossberg, Mart Ross-Sila, Richard Roth, Jamie Rothschild Curtis, Frances Rove, Robin Rowe, Scotty Ruane, Caroline Rudisill, Virginia Rudloff, Laurie Rudnick, Ella Rue, Joan Ruland Donnelly, Erin Rumsey, Frances Runcie, Donald Rupp, Rosie Russell, Rosemary Russell, Danna Rutherford, Cyndi Rutledge, Heather-Rose Ryan, Marty Ryan, Melissa Rybb, Caroline Ryder, Eamon Ryw, Tuuli Saarikoski, Steven Saenz, Arlene Sahraie, Teresa Salgado, Jacqueline Sallow, Joan Sampieri, Meg Sampson, Charles Sanchez, Trish Sand, Michael Sande, Joe Sanders, Lynne Sanders-Braithwaite, Peter Sanderson, Linda Santackas Degnan, Quannah Santiago, Ginny Sargent, Joseph A Sasenick, Andrea Saturno-Sanjana, Carrie Savage-Zimmerman, Theresa Sawyer, Carolyn Saxon-Ruccio, Misty Sayre, Julie Sayres, David Scalzo, Janis Scaramucci, Kerry Scherer, Valerie Schiafone, David Schildkret, Renate Schlehhuber, Lysa Schloesser, Lisa Schlossberg, Corinna Schueftner, Peter

Schuyler, Nancy Schwalen, Debora Schwartz, Tommy Scognamiglio, Annette Scott, Kay Scott, Cynthia Scott, L. J. Scott, Catherine Scott-Dunkes, Jack Scruggs, Sally Scuderi, N. M. Scuri, Dean Seabrook, Cynthia Seagren, Linda Sealey, E. C. Seaman, Sheila Sears, Cecilia Seay, Clare Seche, Ana Marija Sedmak, Celeste Seibold, Tamara Seidman, Machele Seiver, Marcela Selvaggio, Meredith Seppanen, Karen Serunian, Pamela Serure, Marilyn Seymour, Nikki Sgro, Tonya Shaffer, Dennis Shaffner, Laurel Shamray, Gigi Shapiro, Stacey Sharp, Patrick Sharp, Walker Shaw, Kathleen Shea-Barber, Shiela Shedd, Sandi Sheehan, Helen Shepard, Robbie Shepard, Trey Sheppard, Beth Sherring, Jaysie Sherrod, T. L. Sherwood, Michael Sherwood, Lisa Shillingburg, Veronica Shine, Kim Shipala, Wendy Shipps Bush, Ginger Shirley, William D. Shoff, Samantha Shokin, Belita Kay Short, Lori Shriner, Tara Shrodes, Elizabeth Shultz, Lee Shum, Maria Siciliano, Emily Sickenger, Rachel Sidorowicz Sellers, Rebecca Siefert, Sylvia Sievers, Mark Sievert, Joy Sigle, Sari Signorelli, Barbara Sihombing, Tim Sika, Denise Simms, Willonee Simone, Lorraine Simpson, Amy Simpson, Jeanne Simpson, Lori Simpson, Jane Simpson, Erica Sims, Ursula Sindlinger, Diana Sioria, Melody Siracusa, David Sisson, Jo Skehan, Melinda Skelton, Rebecca Skinner, Daisy Skinner, Sarah Skoniecki, Beata Skrzypczyk, Ellen Slater, Laurie Slattengren, Collene Slininger, Adrienne Sloane, Anne Sluhan, Vicky Smart, John Smart, Tina Smeby, Coleman Smith, Dale Smith, Doug Smith, Diane Smith, Gail Smith, Florence Lee Smith, Stella Smith, Candi Smith, Diana Smith, Kathleen Smith, J. D. Smith, Sara Smith, Karen Lee Smith, Amy Smith, Susan Smith-Goddard, Elizabeth Smolinski, Janice Snellgrove, D. H. Sobel, Mike Soden, Allysin Sokol, Steve Sola, Robin Solano, Mike Soliman, David Solis, Errol Tony Soma, Amy Sommer, Susan Sonnen, Ellie Sorce, Wendy Sorrell, L. J. Sosa, Amanda Bowling Souders, Wendy Spall, Leah Spangenberg, Danny Sparks, Alan Sparrow, Dan Speake, Robert Specht, Linda Spector, Raine Spencer, Martin Spencer, Debbie Speregen, James Spielberg, Sharlene Spingler, Gabriele Sposito, Toni Spring, Dorothy Spruzen, M. Lynne Squires, Vickie Stahl, Kathie Stamps, Elisa Staneff, Tomas Stanger, Sue Stanisiach, John Starr, Diane Staudt, Bonnie Stebbins, Gini Steele, Richard Steele, Amy Steier, Vicki Stein, Faith Stencel, Jan Stephan, Kevin Stephens, Jim Stephens, Julie Stephenson, Craig Stevens, Erik Stevens, Carter Stevens, Marjorie Stewart, Erica Stewart, Tommy Stewart, Amy Hamilton Stewart, Meredeth Stieglitz, Brooke Stillwell, Diane M. Stillwood, Alexander Stinson, Laura Stipancich, Bruce Stirling, Brenda Stockton-Hiss, Freddy Stockwell, Peter Stoffers, Sandy Stolberg, Bethany Stollar, Jon Stone, Suzi Stone,

Donald Storey, Tabitha Stoudenmire, Heather Strang, Nellie Strange, Nicola Stratford, Sophia Stravoravdis, Moses Street, Donna Streetenberger, Tonya Stremlau, Julie Stricker, Emily Strickland, Stacey Stringer, Heather Stringfellow, Cory Strode, Robin Strong, Mary Stroud, Dale Strough, Matthew Stuart, Kari Stuhmer, Keith Stump, Patti Sullivan, John P. Sullivan, Blaine Sullivan, Linda Sunderland, Sue Sunderland, Mark Sunderland, James T. Surtees, Margaret Flint Suter, Dave Sutherland, Marylee Svezia, Cara Swann, Mary Swanson, Sara Swanson, Janie Swartz, Mary-Marg Swift, Charles Swift, Angela Switzer, Christina Szabo, Heather Szymanski-Crews, Connie T. Empress, Itapatricia Taaffe, Susan Taggart, Mary Jane Tala, Rawaa Talass, Katherine Tancre, Carole Tanzer Miller, Linda Tarantal, Bill Tasker, Karissa Tatman, Harry Taylor, Ellen Taylor, Teresa Taylor, Ashley Taylor, Eleana Tee, Joan Temple, Shannon Templeton, Adela Terrell, Dorothy Terry, Uddhipan Thakur, Reagen Thalacker, Jennifer Tharp, Susan Thatcher, Jean Thaw, Craig Thom, Bob Thomas, Gwennan Thomas, Pamela Thomas, Rebecca Thomas, Sherry Thomas, Stan Thomas, Stephanie Thomas, Ryan Thomason, Beth Thomerson, Deborah Thomison, Kathryn Thompson, Patty Thompson, Jane Thompson, Ana Thomson, Marcus Thomson, Eric Thoresen, James Thorn, Andrew Thornton, Martha Thorp, Peggy Thorpe, Beverly Threadgill-Robey, Liz Throop, Sara Tick, Tara Tieso, James Tiffany, Glennda Tingle, Tom Tipton, Kate Tipul, Amy Tish, Gregory Tittle, Stephen Titus, Ruby Toledo Swaim, Ginger Tolman, Andrews Tolman, Elizabeth Tomboulian, Hans Tonjes, Nancy Tonkins, Josiah Tooley, Cassie Tooley-Cordero, Leslie Torkelson, Dawn Toth, Alison Totten, Nooneh Tovmassian, Helen Towill, John Towle, Kathi Townsend, Donna Trammell, Lisa Traubitz, Don Traverso, Jaime Travezan, Christine Traxler, Cedric Trespeux, Frances Trexler, Amber Tribe, Ford Trojanowski, Patricia Trotta, Gwen Truax, John Trudell, Debra Tuccillo-Kenney, Lora René Tucker, Aimee Tullos, Scott Turner, Mimi Turque-Marre, Allen Tweddle, Anne Marie Tyler, Sharon Tyler-Hicks, Susan Tyson, Julie Uhl, Hailey Ukelele, Robert Ulsrud, Anne Unangst, Greggory Underwood, Linda Underwood, Jeri Ursetti, Paula Uruburu, Anita Vacation, Jillian Vagnini Frati, Mario Valencianp, Carla Jean Valluzzi, Yurgen-Jericho van de Velde, Lisa Van Deman, Hilde Van den Bulck, Paul Van Deusen, Suki van Dijk, Patricia Van Oss, Alex Van Schuylen, Kathleen Van Assche, William Vandegrift, Angela Vangelisto, Nancy Van Kirk, Dan Van Landingham, Ralph Van Loton, Mark Varner, Susan Vasi, Mavvy Vasquez, Christopher Vassiliades, Astrid Vegas, Tom Veitch, Caryl Velisek, Colette Verdun, Blair Verner Coe Schweiger, Jared Viar,

Francisci Vicens-Miranda, Jerry Victory, Judy Viers, Christine Vigil, Jessica Villa, Larry Vincent, Dottie Vining, Mart Vinson, Ceci Virtue, Catherine Vitale, Steven Vlasak, Cindy Vnook, Bill Vock, Cheryl Voeller, Marlies Volckaert, Olaf von Appen, Sheila Von Beckeman, Aaron Vowels, Lissa Vrtjak, Paula Wade, Steve Wahl, Steven Wainick, Sherrie Waite, Edith Wajswasser, Paige Waldron, Angie Walker, Nan Walker, Dominique Wall, Liz Wallace, Debbie Wallace, Kathy Wallace, Phillippa Jane Walmsley, Melanie Walsh, Lilian Walsh, Tom Walsh, Darwin Wandersee, Sandra Ward, Jacqueline Ward, Mary Ward-Eaton, Kate Warren, Lee Warren, Elayne Warren, Patricia Warren, David Wasserman, Karen Waters, Jennifer Waterston, Linda Watkins, Anna Watkins, Maria Watkins, Valerie Watts, Katie Watts, Ken Waxlax, Gail Weatherill, Marsha Webb, Elizabeth Webb, Shileen Weber, Andrea Webster, Martin Webster, Megan Webster, Linda Weg, Susan Wehrle, Alice Weidner, Lisa Noelle Weigand, Manda Weintraub, Stephanie Weisend, Kate Weiskopf, Melanie Weiss, Jenny Weitner, Martin Welborn, Leah Welch, Bill Welch, Liz Welker, Liesel Weller, Tara Wells, Susan Wells, Frank Wendeln, Angela Wennemar, Karen Werthmann, Wilma West, Marlette West, Emily West, Mason West, Helene Weston, Angela Wetherill, Cathy Whaley, Mary Bess Whidden, Trac Whitaker, Robert Arleigh White, Jason R. White, Gordon White, Lowell Mick White, Charlotte Whitehead, Nikki Whiteley, Judy Whitford, Alexandra Whitney-Edwards, Jennifer Whittlesey, Judy Whitt-Mason, Teri Wichman, Kevin Wickart, David Wickers, Scott Wickman, Bethany Widick, Chantalle Wigley, Hadiya Wilborn, Jude Wild, Genean Wildeisen, Staci Wilkes, Patricia Williams, Helena Williams, Heather Williams, Helen Williams, Veronika Williams, Cindy Williams, Crystal Williams, Barbara Williams, Kim Williams, Dale Williams, Dawn Williamson, Jennifer Williams-Wilson, Lorna Willis, Cara Wilson, B. J. Wilson, Roy Wilson, Tina Wilson, Zelmer Wilson, Amanda Wilson, Ticla Wilson, Martin Wilson, Ginny Wilson-Gordon, Elaine Wimberly, Alison Windmill, Pia Windrider, Valera Windsor, Cecily Wingsong, Ken Winker, Susan Winnie, Laura Winston, Margaret Winter, Steve Wintermute, Paul Winters, Tiara Winter-Schorr, Lily Witham, Laura Witherington, Keri Witman, Susan Witt, Mary Witter, Jennifer Wobser, Christopher Wolfe, Donna Wolff, Victoria Wolfson, Dar Wolnik, Bernard Wolsieffer, Kathrin Wolters, Amanda Wood, Charles Wood, Anne Wood, Xandrea Wood, Julie Dorothy Wood, Erin Woodell, Lorna Woodhams, Jack Woodruff, Terry Woods, Michelle Woodward, Amy Wooley, Mariah Wooster-Lehman, Lori Worley, Tara Linda Wortman, Albert Wratten, Angela Wright, Georgiana Wright, Gil

Wright, Aleksandra Wroblewski, Michael Wroblewski, Barbara Wurtzel, Agnès Wyler, Virginia Wyngarden, Anthony Wynn, Gail Yates, Nancy Yates Mekelburg, Cynthia Gwynne Yaudes, Dorothy Yeatman, Tyler Yoder, William York, Kevin Young, Rhona Young, Anne Young, Sabra Young, Melanie Young, Frank Zaccone, Samantha Zahringer, Pamela Zaiko, Patricia Zalewski, Miriam Herrera Zalles, Lida Zannier, Cory Zatek, Jane Zelazny-Belz, Diana Zelman, Andrea Zimmerman-Rogers, Leah Zisserson, Christina Zuniga, and Valerie Zwald.